HOME SWEET HOME. AT LAST.

It stretched out before him, a sea of lights, all of it tucked comfortably, all that twinkling surface innocence beneath a velvet sky, the countless stars, and a quarter-moon. It was just as he remembered it, only larger, more sprawling, more populated with choice victims. It all looked so grand, he thought, this paradise they had built, clung to, were terrified of losing.

Upon further inspection of this massive suburban mecca, the hot light of the power turned into a cold swirl inside. He despised these people, what they were, what they had.

What they had done to him. Over ten years later, how many would even remember?

He would find out, soon enough.

SILENT SCREAM

DAN SCHMIDT

LEISURE BOOKS   NEW YORK CITY

For my Wife, Mandi.
Her love has been a gift and an inspiration.

A LEISURE BOOK®

January 1998

Published by

Dorchester Publishing Co., Inc.
276 Fifth Avenue
New York, NY 10001

ISBN 0-8439-4342-4

The name "Leisure Books" and the stylized "L" with design are trademarks of Dorchester Publishing Co., Inc.

Printed in the United States of America.

SILENT SCREAM

Chapter One

The letter ressurrected ghosts from a graveyard of angry and bitter memories. Even worse, a silent but raging voice in pen brought demons shrieking back at him from the distant past. Fear churning in his gut, John Wilkins stared at the words before him.

Having just read his brother's letter for the third time that morning, he was still trying to make sense of it, grab any shred of insight into the bile and poison that spewed at him. Through words that sounded almost demonic in their fury, he could clearly hear his younger brother's voice raging at everything, it seemed, living and dead, under the sun.

It had been, what, two hours since the letter had arrived in his office mailbox? Reading then rereading it. Frozen by the past, remembering, but wanting to forget. Numb with disbelief, staring, blank and afraid, at nothing. Locked up, it seemed, by an eternity of anguish.

A thousand questions with no answers boiled into his mind, over and over, maddening in their repetition.

Perhaps the letter was some twisted and dark path that would somehow wind its way toward him? Was

7

that what he feared the most? A collision of the present with the past? Or was he being overly paranoid? Was he more concerned about his own peace of mind, the future welfare of his family? Maybe suffering from guilty knowledge of some crime, real or imagined, he had inflicted on his own blood?

John Wilkins stepped out of the air-conditioned chill of the *Glendale Morning News* office and felt the stab of the early summer's heat as soon as he began angling for his red Saturn. Everything around him seemed to glare and burn. Squinting as harsh sunlight beat on the stark white office building where he resided as editor in chief, he walked slowly across the lot. He felt wooden, drained, wanting desperately to deny the mounting fear he felt. Total denial became impossible.

He was all too aware of the rippling, meshing forces rolling out from the core of his being, seizing, then burning every nerve ending in his body. All the anxiety and fear, guilt and paranoia, fighting to struggle free from a crushing weight of compassion came flashing to the surface. Sweat coursed down the back of his neck, soaking into his white sports shirt, spreading a slow stain. Maybe it was shame he truly felt? Perhaps he simply lacked the courage to confront, face-to-face, what had happened between him and his brother? Did he now want reconciliation with his brother? To forgive and forget? To live in peace?

The hot air seemed to sting his face with fiery needles, and John Wilkins felt as if he had just walked blindly into a furnace. He swiped at his brow, felt the sweat burn into his eyes. Forecasters predicted the hottest summer on record, but the sudden flowing stream of sweat was from fear.

He kept willing his limbs to move. Tormented, he had felt a desperate urge to get out of the office, digest this rush of buried yesteryears that had come out of nowhere to strike a terrible blow to his heart. There was no return address on the envelope, but it was postmarked Philadelphia. Even from across a distance of three states, a spirit of raw anger, of contempt and hate, of resentment and envy, contaminated every word. It was so long ago, but it seemed like only yesterday since his brother's angry and shameful departure from Glendale. Indeed, it had been more than a decade since he'd last laid eyes on his younger brother, but he could feel Mike's presence as if he'd just seen him.

He couldn't help himself, and so he read the letter again. Make sure it's really real, he told himself. He had to make sure what he read was actually there, that it was the right voice. Not some joke perpetrated on him by a lunatic. And to keep his own voice from asking the same questions, over and over: Why now? Why had his brother chosen now to contact him by letter? Like this, defiant and unrepentant?

Dearest Brother,

If you've gotten this far, it means for once in your small and narrow life of spinelessness and sniveling and ingratiating yourself before the hand that feeds you, you showed some courage and actually read beyond my warm greeting to my only living blood—blood that disowned me, blood that spurned me, burned me like fire falling from the sky to eat the flesh off my bones. Surprised by this kind of talk? Yes, I've been thinking about you, for lately I've thought of no one else. The years of suffering have piled up, but I am here to tell you my pain is my armor and pain has made me far stronger than I once was, instead of wearing me down to some shriveled skeletal shell of a man, instead of transforming me into some worm that has to crawl and slither through the refuse, the breathing, walking feces which is ninety percent of inhumankind. Yes, I'm still alive, doing what I do best, which is surviving in an empty, loveless, desperate world of liars and cheats, beggars and addicts, thieves and murderers, existing hand-to-mouth among the shunned and the forgotten. Be so kind as to allow me the dignity of kicking you in the balls a little. Read on, if you have the courage.

Despite the best and the most deceitful efforts of worms and maggots who have the gall to keep on breathing the air around you, walking vomit in human skin who drove me from your tidy little suburban enclave in shame and disgrace, shrouded as I was by false testimony and lies, I'm still running on anger, to be damn sure, but living in the truth of righteous knowledge. Knowledge that for more than ten years has haunted me. Am I so close maybe, you can almost hear me breathing the fire of the truth on your neck? No, I'm not in town, not even close, not even headed that way. I'm sure that's what you're worried about the most. This shame of the baggage of your own blood showing up unannounced before your wife and brood, worried about me perhaps casting a lustful eye on your pretty vaginal counterpart, anxious perhaps that I may lead your offspring astray into a rebellious life of godless hedonism. And no, to ease any other anxieties, I don't need your soiled money either, that sweet chunk of change Mommy and Daddy left you. You do remember them, don't you, you do acknowledge your gratitude to them, even though they may or may not be in a much better place? For all we know, they could be burning in hell or they could be basking in the glory of your God. My, how the universe saw fit to take their miserable lives when all saw their golden years weren't going to be so golden. Simple fact of life, dearest brother. Death comes for all us. Another fact. None of us knows where we go, when we go. Maybe that's why you cling to your God, to your church, to your Catholicism. Fear of death. Fear of eternal damnation. You seek only to save yourselves, you ask for forgiveness, you confess your sin but carry on in the same way as before.

What hypocrisy! All of you are nothing but blood-dripping, engorged assholes; you are like a whore with her legs wide open, no shame, no conscience, no soul. Thank your God for me that I carry no such baggage. You see, I'm perfectly content to scavenge the cities for the scraps of the self-righteous, to hunt or be hunted by my fellow wretches, to keep on being a man in a gutless world, much like Glendale, where the spineless dwell and spin their webs of deceit while they cloak themselves in the appearance of righteousness. After all, that's what a man is meant for, isn't he? To hunt? To stand on his own pair? To seek his way on his own terms— seek and ye shall find. But, of course, I couldn't expect you to understand anything about balls. And speaking of no balls, how's your world out there, Johnny? Still clean and tidy and orderly? Sweet job, loving and obedient family. Go to church every Sunday, make the show, say and do all the right things. Got Mommy and Daddy's money all tucked in the bank, and conformist and conventional investments to make your clean world a little more secure, sweeten the pie, future as bright as the summer's midday sunshine. Uh-huh, sure always looked to me like you had it all. What a farce you perpetrate on yourself, creating some tragicomedy you dare to call a life. Fact is, you've got nothing, but that is the inevitable downfall of all men who give the appearance of strength and righteousness, who believe they are beyond the reach of wickedness, who think they are clean in the eyes of the world.

Well, you made the show, congratulations, you were invited to the big party of life, but I always knew you would make it, the favored son. Careful, Johnny, before you cast your criticism and condemnation upon me, lash out at me from your heart at a distance with more poison than a thousand adders. After all, we both are Catholic, we both know the Bible. Where is your heart these days? Where is your spirit of forgiveness and understanding, all this compassion for your fellow man? Wrapped up and all neatly cloaked in matters of the world? Or is your heart quiet and still and ready to receive justice for and toward all?

Let me tell you something. Even though I'm the fallen one, I am strong and courageous in my filthy, rotting flesh—strong because I, unlike you, have nothing to lose, not even my sanity, and certainly not even my soul. You know what they say about a man who believes he has the world by the tail, so to speak. Here today, gone tomorrow, the breath of the Grim Reaper sowing his justice, taking it all from a man when he least expects it. The proverbial thief in the night.

Do I sound bitter? Angry? Jealous? Maybe a little, but not that much. You think? And, no, these are not the demented ravings brought on by a runaway binge of alcohol and drugs. By the way, I always meant to thank you for putting me through two treatment centers. Worked wonders, dearest brother. Now I've learned how to control it and not let it control me. That's what it's all about, isn't it, life, I mean? Control? Power? Who has the control and the power. Who can be the haves, thus blind themselves to the plight and the suffering of the have-nots, the unfortunate wretches of the world your Lord surely seems to have forsaken. And we surely do live in a world where the innocent suffer and the guilty go free to fatten their pots of gold and live lives of sweet luxury, spitting in the face of truth and justice. Makes me wonder about your God. This all-loving being who sits there in glory and ultimate power and control, throwing the big party for all his angels and his chosen, while death and misery eat most of the human race alive, every day the maggots eating a little more flesh off our bones.

Thing you don't understand, never have, is that those who don't want power have it the most; those who don't seek control over others have the most control. But, hey, I'm an artist, remember, the drawer of strange pictures, painter of fornication, the oddball kid you were all so embarrassed by. Shunned, humiliated, stabbed in the back, taking everyone's steady stream of urine right in the face, forced to choke it down, take my shame like a man, carry my cross, feel the nails driven through the palms of my hands, my feet. Crying in the dark, alone, cast aside, so much human garbage to be blown in the wind, burned up by the fires of everyone's contempt. Forget understanding; all that matters is the truth. All I seek is knowledge. And truth for all.

Truth, Johnny, that's what it's all about. But you wouldn't know the truth about a goddamned thing even if it had teeth and bit you on your sac. You live in a world of lies and liars, Johnny, surrounded by silent evil, behind every face a heart seething with impurity and selfish desires and ambitions. Can't see it? Or don't want to? It's what I always saw when I grew up in your haven of silent evil. Keep on living your lie, Johnny. Could be the death of you someday. Thy neighbor could steal your wife, and she could turn on you, spit in your face, all but emasculate you as she takes a younger, more virile lover. Some young punk may take advantage of your sweet young daughter, get her pregnant and walk on, laughing in your face, sneering at your family values. It all comes to death anyway. Even when we're alive we can be dead. Speaking of death, you ever notice something? You've got what, two sons and a daughter? Remember our sister, dead now when a drunk, such as myself, catapulted her through the windshield, our dearest and most fair Mary, her body so mutilated, her face so disfigured from that tragedy it was a closed-casket affair. Of course, I disgraced the family then, too, showed up full of booze, fighting back real tears none of you had the courage to shed for her. What I'm saying is, do you see some pattern, déjà vu, perhaps. We were three, you are three. I've read where three is a mystic number. Think about it. Everything comes full cycle, Johnny, and there is justice in this world.

I know you remember the past. I know you know everything from which and by which I speak. Does this mean you'll be seeing me again? Maybe. Maybe not. I care but I don't. I hunger for justice, but at times I decide it's not that important for a mere nobody, a nothing such as myself to feel worthy enough to stand in the light of retribution. But I've been doing a lot of thinking. There are a lot of wrongs that need to be righted, a slew of lies that need the light of truth. Maybe someday, Johnny. Maybe not. Maybe I'll be dead by tonight and you'll never have to worry about me coming back. Not that I would. Or would I? Who knows? Who cares?

It was signed, "Out there."

For what felt like an hour, John Wilkins stood, his hand trembling, his whole body shaking as he felt his clothes plastered, slick and cold, to his flesh. He discovered he was standing by his car. He suddenly found himself staring at his reflection in the glass. It took another eternal moment for John Wilkins to recognize himself, to see that he was alive and whole and not some grotesque caricature of a human being. Then a shadow rolled over his face. The whites of his eyes stared back at him, eyes that were wide with fear, anguish, all the dark and terrible emotions the letter had resurrected. He felt paralyzed by the haunted mask that stared back at him. Or was he seeing the face of the future? As the clouds hid the sun, the stark white of his face came flashing into his eyes, it seemed. He was a forty-year-old man, but he looked twenty, thirty years older at that moment.

Don't think about the letter, he told himself. He knew his brother, what his brother had endured. Or did he know his own blood at all? After all these years, all the pain and suffering that his brother had—what? Gone through, or put himself through? Now this letter. What did Mike want? Vengeance or forgiveness? Blood or reconciliation? Was Mike coming back to Glendale? John didn't think so. Too much shame and suspicion had hounded his brother out of the community. Then again, John simply didn't want to think about his brother . . . coming home.

It was all too much to think about. He was overwhelmed. He felt the urge to go see his wife. He needed some reassurance that all was still right in his world, his quiet family life together, under control. Why did he feel so threatened? Why did he have to reaffirm that his world was safe, unsoiled, untainted? Did he have no faith? Was this a test of his courage?

He wasn't sure why, but he decided to keep the letter. Maybe it was all he would ever have to remind himself that he still had a brother, "out there" somewhere, still suffering, still in need . . . but in need of what?

He couldn't deny what he really felt for Mike. A part of him feared his brother and feared for him. Another part of him longed to take Mike in his arms, comfort him, let him know just how damn sorry he was, that if he was the cause of any of his brother's suffering he, too, needed forgiveness. Yes, he wanted to make things right between them, he wanted to see Mike pull himself together, let the past go, like so much broom sweepings hurled into the wind. It would be the Christian thing to do. Then again, he had his family to consider. They were his life now, his whole world.

He knew he couldn't let Paula be even remotely aware his brother had written him, with hints of his coming back to Glendale. He knew how his wife felt about Mike, how she would react. There would be a scene, anger followed by dread, then dire warnings, with Paula laying down the law if Mike's cryptic insinuations of his return to Glendale came true.

He was putting the letter in his pocket, opening the Saturn's door, when a voice struck him. A cold voice, rife with aggression.

"Mr. Wilkins, do you have a minute you can spare me? I think it's important we talk."

Wilkins jumped, felt his heart skip a beat. He turned a little too quickly, a haunted look on his face, a sharp set to his features, and saw his top reporter and staff writer. It was Sam Watterson, but it took a few moments for Wilkins to register the face, much less the reason why the man seemed poised for confrontation. For a second, Watterson looked taken aback by the sudden reaction on the face of Glendale's editor in chief. But Wilkins knew what the man wanted, and Watterson got right to business. Forget the fact that it looked as if Wilkins had just come face-to-face with a demon; Watterson was concerned only with what he wanted, and he had made it an ongoing point of contention between them. Wilkins knew the man had been clamoring around the office for weeks for his own editorial column. Twenty-eight, Watterson was tall, blond, trim, and solid in the shoulders. Single, he was the focal point of a lot of gossip around the office, rumored to be something of a sexual wolf around Glendale. Off the job, Watterson chased a good time. On the job he chased himself and let everyone who would listen for even a few seconds know just what a great columnist he could be—if only Wilkins would give him the chance.

"I got your memo that you wanted to speak to me about the idea I've had for starting up an editorial column of my own," Watterson said, his tone just aggressive enough to shake Wilkins out of his grim reflection. "I saw you leaving. Well, I thought it might be a good chance for us to talk alone, you know, away from the others."

Wilkins sighed. Head bowed, he ran the back of his hand over his face to wipe off the sweat. That Wilkins was in obvious distress, sweating profusely, didn't seem to concern Watterson. The man's chiseled, handsome face was a relentless mask, his blue eyes hard with determination.

"I'd like very much for you to seriously consider letting me have that column, sir. What I mean is, I don't feel you've really heard or understood my point of view. The least of which is that this paper needs something to bolster its rep, give it new strength, if you will, that can define the times we live in. I know we have discussed it before—"

Wilkins held up a hand. It was clear to him that there was no reasoning with Watterson. They had danced through this argument before. Glendale's was a small paper, catering to the needs of a small, essentially tight middle- to upper-middle-class community. There was no crime in Glendale, no drugs, had never even been a murder in the paper's twelve years of existence. None of the ills that afflicted the cities had struck Glendale. Stick to the news, he had told Watterson repeatedly, most of which came out of Chicago. Watterson wanted to taint the paper, in Wilkins's view, with the sensational, even the outrageous. Gloom and doom, pull up the drawbridge, the savages are coming. Every argument he pursued with his editor in chief ended up sounding as if the man wanted to turn their paper into the *Enquirer*.

"Can we take this up later, Sam? Please. I really don't feel up to an argument right now."

"I don't want to argue, sir. I'd just like for you to hear me out."

"Please, Sam. Not now. If you'll kindly excuse me."

Watterson frowned, but before he could pursue an argument that might lead to a bitter quarrel, Wilkins settled into his car. As he fired up the engine, he felt Watterson's angry stare boring into the side of his face. The matter wasn't settled, and Wilkins knew he would have to deal with Watterson's anger and arrogance later.

As he drove away, he heard his brother's voice echoing through his mind. A voice from the past, disembodied, floating around him, coming at him from every direction.

I know you know everything from which and by which I speak.

The voice rang through his mind, again and again, the words feeling alive in their anger, strong and relentless in their torment. It felt like the cold steel of a sharply honed knife's edge was carving, cutting, slashing through his brain. He was unable to clear those words out of his head. The words in that letter felt as if they lived inside of him, trapping him in the past. Indeed, John Wilkins knew the truth. That was the problem. The letter would haunt him the rest of the day, and beyond.

He could feel his brother out there, somewhere. It was why he suddenly dreaded the future.

Anger and fear were his only friends. Today was the same as yesterday, and the only thing he could be sure of was that tomorrow it would be worse.

Anger and fear. Fear of not having, anger at not getting, and the union of both over not "being." After all, Mike Wilkins surely lived in a world where he had no power, no control, no status, no influence, no voice. And he most certainly had no one and nothing—except a brother, and a past bursting with bad memories.

It was yesterday, though, that spurred him on to live for tomorrow—only he wasn't sure what he was living for, nor what he was looking forward to.

It had been so long, Mike Wilkins couldn't even recall how many years it had been since he fled Glendale, lived on the run. The years blurred into more of the same angry nonexistence, the same foamy-mouthed animal survival.

The obsession over his plight seized him, that endless drama he ran through his mind, over and over, just to remind himself he was alive. There he was, scuttling from city to city, spending a night in jail here and there for vagrancy, or drying out in the drunk tank, recycled to do the same thing again and again. Perhaps finding food and warmth in men's shelters, taking comfort in the awareness that there were many others suffering like himself. Shadowy days and dark nights of panhandling. Begging. Scavenging. Maybe stealing to meet a momentary need—as he had done in the men's shelter up on Osage, three days ago. Lifting that pen, paper, and a book of stamps from the office when no one was looking, just so he could write his brother. Only now he was left wondering why he had done that.

Out of nowhere the years flashed through his mind, jumbled and distorted images from which he couldn't grasp any memory that stood out, that could give any single day even a shadowy semblance of sanity. A flood of places where he scrounged and groveled through the endless days. New York. Boston. Baltimore. Cleveland. Pittsburgh.

Now Philadelphia. Another city where brotherly love was as nonexistent as it was anyplace else. It was pitiless as it consumed, devoured his life, trampled whatever his needs were—forget his wants; it was enough just to have a cigarette, a beer, find shelter from the elements. Indeed, it felt as if life were nothing but an unseen razor, cutting his soul up a little more each day.

Everywhere he turned he saw the same merciless faces, silently spitting on him, full of contempt. All the clean and the well-to-do shunning him, this breathing virus to be avoided at all costs. More of the same faceless throng who didn't have a clue as to what kind of man he really was, much less could be. After all, he told himself, he was a man of talent, of potential greatness, robbed of a future, now forced to hide from his past shame.

What was he going to do, he asked himself.

Mike Wilkins knew what he wanted to do, but he didn't know how to go about planning a triumphant return to the birthplace of his humiliation.

So he made his way east from the Schuylkill River, where he had slept last night in a drainage ditch beneath an underpass, somewhere along I-76. He was just in time to catch the midday crush of humanity, or "inhumanity," as he saw them. They were the enemy, after all, every last one of them. He was surrounded.

He shuffled down Walnut Street toward Rittenhouse Square, oblivious to the city's countless historic monuments, cypress-ringed parks, and mammoth old-style colonial buildings mingled with the newer and more fashionable apartments and condos, everything shining and pure under the scathing glare of the early afternoon sun. He was searching for a pigeon, businessman, or tourist, it didn't matter. He would take whatever they gave him. Even a handful of loose change could see him through the day, since he'd killed the last of his quart of malt liquor an hour ago. Soon the alcohol would wear off, leave his body screaming with thirst, trembling. Even if he were to bum only a few cigarettes, he decided that would pass as something of a victory.

Then he began seeing their faces with a sharp tunnel vision of pure and mounting rage. Saw the fear in their eyes as his wretched form, hunched over in tattered and torn wool and denim, soaked with sweat and stained from vomit and urine, trudged into their midst. He read the defiance in their eyes—if they even bothered to acknowledge his existence. Or they swept past him at a safe distance.

Rage. It was so intense a burning inside, he imagined some small carnivorous creature was struggling to break free of its chains in his belly. Teeth were flashing through his intestines, curled and razor-sharp talons tearing at the walls of his already

queasy stomach, this creature of fury warring to rip
through his belly or battle its way lower, ripping
through the bile, until it came roaring out to take on
the whole world in one last suicidal explosion of sensible violence. Oh, but it was maddening to hold
back all this rage, to live with such a beast inside.
Suddenly he wanted to scream at all of them, "How
dare you look at me like that! I am a man! I am somebody! Who are you to see me as trash? Show me your
life if you think you're so much better!"

All he found staring back at him was contempt.

Just another day. So he held out his paper cup. He
wandered through the park, searching for the least
bit of kindness, a spark of hope in someone's eyes, a
soft mark so he could prey upon their fleeting sym-
pathy. But they bowed their heads, didn't meet his
eyes. Someone snarled for him to "Get a job, damned
bum."

His mind kept screaming. The beast inside kept
raging. A part of him wanted to believe he was still
lucid enough to understand their fear. He knew he
was a ferocious sight, after all. Long black hair,
swept back from a gaunt face, sharp as an ax. Eyes,
red and bulging, flashing with anger. Scraggly beard.
Fierce yet wretched. Proud and defiant but seared by
shame.

He wandered out of the park. His mind kept racing. His brother. Glendale. The past. It had all con-
spired to reduce him to this. *Why?* his mind
screamed, or was he now talking to himself? *How
have I come to this? How has this happened to me?
I'm nobody, I'm less than nothing. I've never been any
good to anyone. Maybe I am just some animal.*

His gaze then fixed on a beautiful blond girl, probably a student in the city. One terrified glance at him,

and she nearly ran as he approached her, his cup out.

His heart sank as he watched her scurry off. How long had it been since he'd been with a woman, other than paying for a twenty-dollar blowjob on the street? Those fleeting moments of pleasure when he could clean himself up long enough to get a job somewhere washing dishes, or maybe clinging to a bartending stint for a few weeks. Those dollars in his pocket, always destined merely to feed the beast, keep it subdued with booze or drugs.

He couldn't stand it any longer. His heart seemed to implode, the fiery tears damming up behind his eyes. His body collapsed. He found himself on his knees, his face in his hands, weeping. He wanted to go home. He thought about the letter. Still, even when he'd written his brother he knew he couldn't, wouldn't go back. Not like this. Not as this homeless, penniless creature who would be viewed as a monster, maybe to be caged up, locked away, forgotten.

So he had mixed truth with lies. He had told his brother he had power and control, when he had neither. He desperately craved something, anything that would lend him some appearance of triumph, something to help wash away this stain, this stink of utter nonexistence.

The prayer, he thought. Yes. He had been promised a way, but only if he believed. Stand up, be a man, take charge, keep seeking.

He took the small black book from his pocket. He stared at the pentagram on the cover, fascinated by the symbol, as if it held the key to all his problems. He had gotten it somewhere in the city in some obscure bookstore, maybe stolen it during a dreamy alcohol haze. It didn't matter. The book was his property, the source of his only hope. He stood up, still gazing at the cover. The book was written by someone called Shanda. The forward of the untitled work stated she was a priestess, a prophetess. Her basic philosophy declared there was no good or evil, that these were concepts man had created out of his own selfish motives, that they enslaved all humankind to fear. All that mattered was personal pleasure, the sating of the instincts for food and sex. Further, she said, the key to getting what one wanted in the world was simply to find, then believe in one's own ability, that each of us is blessed with a talent that can be channeled to fulfill the individual's life. She also said it was critical to acknowledge that the real world around us, what we see, coexists with the other world, the unseen. Thus the seen and the unseen work in harmony, if we allow them to, guiding us to full potential, to live productive and happy lives, but only if certain forces were called upon, sought after, prayed to. She called them forces of power, of control, of money, of love, among a dozen other so-called forces that drove, controlled, and seemed to obsess all people. One was to choose a force one desired, then cut the tip of the right forefinger, place it on the symbol of that particular force, all of which were included in the book. Then recite a short prayer to that force, three times.

Yesterday, Mike Wilkins had decided to do that, summoning up the courage after rereading the entire work, knowing he had been in search of something, some answer, some miracle that would deliver him from his wretchedness, for years. So with the jagged edge of a broken bottle he had carefully cut his right forefinger, dabbed his blood on the symbol for the force of power. After smearing the symbol of the lone human eye of power, he had prayed.

He considered reciting the prayer again. Power. Getting it, keeping it, had become an obsession, especially since he had begun thinking about his brother and Glendale, the thought of going back.

He was walking down the street, head bowed, opening the book, when he slammed into what seemed like a brick wall. The book dropped from his hands. He felt the anger twist his lips as he looked up, heard a man growl, "Hey, why don't you watch where you're—"

Wilkins locked stares with brown eyes that were boring into him. The sudden impulse to punch that face turned to something else as he was struck by a distant memory. His mind screamed at him that he should recognize the handsome face. That aquiline nose, nostrils flared, the dark brown hair short and neatly trimmed, the square jaw and solid, the lean body of an athlete. No. It couldn't be. Here in Philadelphia, hundreds of miles from that place?

Wilkins squinted as the sunlight danced off the man's jewelry, dazzled off the gold Rolex. A narrowed gaze as the stranger's own anger turned to a dark awareness. When the man's lips quivered and his eyes widened, Wilkins was almost sure of it. He had an urge to know, to say a name he hadn't thought about in years.

"You," he said. "I know you. Tom . . . Tom Bartkowski."

Fear in those brown eyes, the man shook his head, backed up. "No, I don't know you. I'm afraid you're mistaken."

The voice matched the memory. Now Wilkins was certain.

"Yes, you do," Wilkins insisted, ignoring the

strange looks of the passersby blurring past them. "It's me, Mike Wilkins."

"I told you, I don't know you. Get away from me," he said. Then the man with the gold blended into the sidewalk crowd, brushing past men and women, picking up his pace within seconds, looking as if he might burst into an all-out sprint. Scooping up the book, Wilkins followed him.

"Tom! Tom? It's me, Mike Wilkins."

Tormented yesterdays boiled into his mind as he recalled how they were once friends, high school buddies who had drifted apart as kids who become adults often do, moving on to the next phase of life.

"You know me! Stop! I just want to talk!" Wilkins shouted, bowling past someone, as the man he was sure he knew stepped off the sidewalk. When that handsome face he so vividly recalled turned on him with a look of dread and shame, Wilkins knew it was hopeless to pursue him. "I know you know me!" he stated in cold anger. Wilkins stood there, watching, as the man turned and surged across the street. Horns blared, cars jerked to a stop as the man darted through the traffic. Suddenly doubt crept through Wilkins. The man kept looking over his shoulder, afraid he might be followed. No, the more the man looked back at him, the more Wilkins was certain it was the only person he had ever called a friend in his former Glendale life. "You know me, Tom!" he shouted as the man angled toward the front doors of one of he city's finest hotels. "Are you ashamed of me, Tom, is that it? Are you afraid of me? Are you too good for me, Tom?"

The man threw one final look across the street, hesitated, then walked on quickly, as if he couldn't reach the safety of his hotel soon enough. Mike Wilkins stood, trembling with rage, and shouted a curse across the street.

He felt shame, a terrible urge to flee, to hide from the truth. But he couldn't deny reality. It was incredible, frightening. Who was more ashamed? he wondered.

Tom Bartkowski told himself that after all the years that had passed since they had been friends, maybe Mike Wilkins would believe he was mistaken. Bartkowski hoped so, for his own sake.

Well, they hadn't exactly been friends, he told himself. More like acquaintances. He had hung around Mike some, way back in high school, feeling something like pity for the guy who didn't have any friends, who was a loner, an oddball. Maybe trying to strike up something like a friendship with Wilkins to make himself a little different or unique or better in the eyes of his classmates. But that same peer pressure had forced him to disassociate himself from the loner, even ignore him. The farce of friendship couldn't go on, not if he had wanted to keep his image, his real friends. Then there had been a couple of those incidents involving girls and allegations of sexual assault by Mike Wilkins that had swept through Glendale, which back then had been called Millston. The rumors made it easier for Bartkowski to distance himself altogether from Wilkins. As if the guy had never existed. Then, and certainly now.

Bartkowski shoved the past out of his mind as he reached the foyer of his hotel. He hoped the guy didn't follow him. One last look over his shoulder and he found him standing across the street, railing at him. What had happened to the guy to reduce him to something like that? The man was a pitiful, disturbing sight. What decent individual would even bother to acknowledge such a thing?

Bartkowski wished the cops would come, pick him up for vagrancy, disturbing the peace, whatever. Hell, he was in Philly for a two-day R and R. Get away from Glendale, supposedly on business. There to meet a buddy in the same line of work. Selling sporting goods allowed him to travel, get away from the wife and kids, all the dull routine of middle-class suburbia. Thank God he was tuned up on three double vodkas, grateful for the booze now, his jittery nerves calming some as he rolled into the lobby, putting behind the wretched thing he once almost considered a friend.

He decided it would be best to call his mistress and have her come to his suite. No way was he going back out on the street, chance another scene with that creature who had caused him such embarrassment.

Chapter Two

John Wilkins sat in his personal booth in the far corner of one of Glendale's busiest restaurants. He picked at his roast beef and cheese with heavy trimmings, forced down a mouthful, but was unable to go on eating. Food hit his churning stomach like a large stone. He pushed the plate aside, told himself to relax, worried that his wife might notice how distracted and anxious he felt.

Then he looked around the restaurant, honing his ears to the pop music that filtered from the speakers. He failed to fall into the casual mood he so desperately wanted.

Silently he prayed. *God, help me to stop thinking about the letter. Should I throw it away? Is it wrong for me to wish he won't come back? Was I wrong somehow? Is it wrong for me to think only about my wife and my children?*

He rubbed his face, sighed. There was no answer to his turmoil.

It was best to focus on the present. If it was God's will that his brother should return to Glendale, then so be it. He could deal with it.

He saw but strangely didn't see the faces of the countless diners. Life felt warped, out of proportion, dreamlike. Gradually, he groped himself into the present. He was no stranger here; in fact, he co-owned this place with his wife. The regulars knew him. Friends and neighbors might see he was in distress, maybe come at him with the usual "What's wrong?" if he didn't pull himself together.

Their restaurant was called the P and J, and it did plenty of business, seven days a week. The joint man-wife venture had been bought with part of the small fortune his parents had left him in their will. The locals considered the restaurant one of the best in town, the in place to go and unwind, the food some of the best and most varied to be found in or beyond Glendale, with everything from sandwiches to filet mignon and prime rib to seafood. And the bar was always lined with locals who had plenty of money in their pockets and the time to burn it up. He could have devoted himself, full-time, to helping his wife run the restaurant, but he had always wanted to be a newspaperman, a journalist, first and last. The paper was his life, away from home, of course. It provided him with a good salary, personal recognition, perhaps direction. Add in the good fortune of the restaurant and there was all the hope for a continued good tomorrow for Paula and their children.

He had a lot to be grateful for, but he suddenly questioned the motives behind his gratitude. After all, the *Glendale Morning News* owed its launch to the real-estate developers who had turned a once sprawling farm community into a suburb that was fast expanding in both money and population. It was then that he realized he wasn't the creation of his own rugged individualism, some lone stand-up act, taking on the odds and coming out on top, a warrior. He soured at the thought that a lot of what he had

had been given to him. That proverbial charmed life. There was more truth in his brother's letter than he cared to admit.

His somber mood held firm, the past clinging to him like a stained and heavy coat.

His brother's angry words were certainly keeping him locked in this brooding reflection. He even imagined his brother standing there in the restaurant, condemning those who had condemned him, sneering at their creature comforts, railing, "Look at yourselves! Full of your own lives and all you think you have. Living in your fat comfort while people go on suffering and dying around you. What have you become? Are you all so blind?"

Indeed, my brother. What have we become? John Wilkins thought.

Wilkins sought out his wife. He found her talking and laughing with the Milligans, who owned a small chain of hair-styling shops in and around Glendale. Nineteen years of marriage, and Wilkins still marveled at how beautiful his wife was, his tall, buxom redhead with green eyes that still sparkled. It was good to be there, with his wife, among the living. He needed his life. He clung to it. Everything controlled, in order, having its proper, comfortable place. Yes, they were the fortunate, the lucky. Was that a crime? A sin? So they were enjoying the day, the lunch crowd in full swing, the place packed with locals, businessmen, shopowners. Once a small town, now a fashionable suburb for the potentially wealthy and the privileged, that ambitious white-collar working man with dreams of his own better tomorrow.

On the map Glendale might have been just a speck ninety miles southwest of Chicago, but Wilkins knew the population was forty thousand and growing all the time. They moved down from Chicago and settled into this prosperous enclave, removing themselves from all the chaos and danger of living or working in the Windy City. Many of the faces he knew, but newer additions were always being added to the ever-burgeoning populace.

Wilkins pulled a pack of cigarettes out of his pocket. It had been two years since he'd quit smoking, but just like that he had the urge. Worse, he wanted a whiskey, but decided it was too early in the day. A stiff drink would most certainly tip his wife off that something was troubling him. He was lighting his smoke when a familiar voice came out of nowhere.

"Hey, Johnny, how they hanging? I was over at the bar, well, thought you looked like you needed a little company. Even bad company."

Wilkins found short, beefy Mickey Tomlin standing over his shoulder, a drink in his hand. The grin seemed to split Tomlin's sagging jowls, his eyes glassy from booze but full of the laughter of the self-indulgent. Wilkins had known Tomlin for years, and he knew the man was already half in the bag. Without being invited Tomlin plopped down in the booth, across from Wilkins, and took one of Wilkins's cigarettes.

"Help yourself, Mickey," Wilkins said. "I was just thinking about quitting again."

The sarcasm escaped Tomlin as he smiled at Wilkins. "Yeah, I thought you gave up the deathsticks, Johnny. What happened? Problems at the paper? Sam still after you about getting that editorial page?" He laughed. "Some guys, huh, they don't know when they have a good thing until one day they wake up and it's gone. Price of greed, right?"

Wilkins tried to ignore Tomlin but knew the man was relentless for companionship after a couple of drinks. Tomlin was something of the town drunk, but kept himself just enough under control to keep it from becoming a problem. Several years ago, Tomlin's parents had left him a chunk of land that he had sold to the same real-estate moguls who had put Glendale on the map. He was also one of Sam Watterson's drinking cronies, and Wilkins already knew what Tomlin wanted.

"All right, all right," Tomlin said, grinning as he fired up the smoke. "I'll skip the small talk, get to business. This isn't about Sam. Hell, I know he's been hounding you, can't even have a drink with the guy anymore without him burning my ears how he could be the next Dan Rather or whatever. I know, I know, we've talked about this before. Hey, but we live in hope, you know. My hope is you're not gonna tell me no again, Johnny, send me packing back to my stool. What I'm saying, I got talent I'm not using. It's killing me. Guy like me, I need something to do. Direction."

"Enough already with the sales pitch, Mickey," Wilkins said, then drew deep on his cigarette, hoping the smoke he pulled into his lungs would subdue his irritation. "I've already told you, I'm not hiring."

"I know that, we both know that. What did I tell you last time? Remember? My suggestion was for you to let me do some freelance work. Way I read you, I thought you were gonna give me a shot, really thought I had you hooked. Hell, John, I got some great ideas, I mean, you know I can write; I've been published before."

A wry grin danced over Wilkins's lips. "You'll have

to forgive my skepticism. But I'm not sure porn novels qualify as artistic genius, Mickey."

"Come on, John, what would it kill you, huh? Just give it some thought. I'm not looking to conquer the world—like Sam. I've told you, you don't even have to pay me until I prove to you I can do it. I mean, let's look at some facts here. Here we are, living in this upper-middle-class fortress. A slice of heaven, grant you, but I've told you before not everything in Glendale is as it seems. There's got to be some big story here, and I've told you what that story could be. You with me so far?"

Wilkins listened with one ear. He knew the spiel Tomlin would launch into. He'd heard it before. That Lansing Development enterprise was shady. That the same real-estate moguls who had created Glendale might be tied to organized crime. No proof, of course, but Tomlin had friends in the real-estate business in Chicago and he'd heard rumblings—over a few drinks, naturally—that Lansing Development bought up property, made cash deals, but no one seemed to know where all the cash went, much less where it came from.

"I'm telling you, you want to be big, grab the brass ring. I mean, put your paper up there with the *Tribune*; this could be the single greatest conspiracy since the bootleg days of Capone," Tomlin said, leaning in, eyes lit with excitement. "You run with me on this, picture the possibilities. Briberies, graft, corruption, guys who look squeaky clean, the money men, pushing their dirt to some dark corner of the room where they think nobody can see it. Happens all the time. What's to say Glendale's any different? Think about it, John. These guys came out of nowhere, nobody'd ever heard of them, but they start throwing money around to a bunch of farmers going broke and staring down grim-faced bankers ready to snatch it all up, and here we are, more than ten years later, with Lansing setting up shop right in the middle of town. Guys with thousand-dollar suits, diamond-studded Rolexes, icy eyes, and grim attitudes that tell me they aren't in real estate—'less they're buying up the bottom of Lake Michigan to deposit a few of the skeletons in their closet."

Tomlin was talking crazy, full of booze. But in some way he made some sense. Some of what Tomlin said might or might not look true on the surface. Then again, something odd, maybe a little dangerous, had always struck Wilkins about the men who had come to this farm country and turned it into the suburban mecca it now was. Still, Wilkins would stick to his principals, not turn his paper into a gossip rag. There was no point in creating trouble where there was no bonafide indication there was any.

Wilkins caught his wife's eye. Paula waved, threw him a big smile, then excused herself from the Milligans. Wilkins made an impulsive decision, if for nothing else than to get Tomlin off his back.

As Paula weaved her way toward him, Wilkins said, "Find another story. Anything, I don't care. Write an article about the Boy's Summer League. But forget Lansing."

Dejected, Tomlin killed his drink. "Forget Lansing. But that's my whole point. I'm telling you, John, I could—"

"You want to do this or not? You want the ground rules or not?"

"Okay, I'm listening."

"As I was saying, let me see you can write something, maybe I can you assign you some outside work. Maybe."

Tomlin smiled, then glanced at his empty glass. "You telling me what I think you are?"

"Don't celebrate the day away, Mickey. Find a legitimate story, write it; then come talk to me. Sober."

"Fair enough, John. Hey, and thanks; I won't let you down."

"It isn't me you have to concern yourself with, Mickey. Now, if you'll kindly excuse me, I see my wife coming this way."

A quick hello to Mrs. Wilkins; then Tomlin made a beeline for the bar.

Paula Wilkins looked from Tomlin to her husband. "I haven't seen Mickey so excited about something since his wife divorced him. What was that about?"

"An act of charity."

"A what?"

"Never mind."

Paula sat beside her husband. She frowned as she watched him smoke. "When did you start those again?"

"Two minutes ago."

"Okay, John, what's wrong?"

"Just a minor disturbance at work."

"It's Sam, isn't it?"

"It's Sam. I'll deal with it." He paused, smoking, searching the restaurant. "I don't see Jenny here. I thought she was supposed to come in for her lunch shift."

Paula smiled, but Wilkins wasn't sure how to read his wife's expression. "Our daughter has discovered boys, I'm afraid."

"What? She's only fifteen. When did this start? Who is it?"

"Calm down, honey," Paula said. "It's just Paul Stallings. They're friends, that's all."

"Friends? I suppose next you're going to tell me it's nothing serious."

Wilkins saw the concern that hardened his wife's face.

"John, yes, you are overreacting. They're in the same summer class, they study together, with parental supervision, not alone in the bedroom. Maybe they take walks in the park, or go to a movie. It's what teenagers in Glendale do, remember? They maybe see each other all of three times a week. Most of the time Jenny's here, with me, waiting tables. I thought you knew they've been seeing each other."

Wilkins worked on his cigarette. "I didn't think it was anything more than . . . Okay. I'll take it for what it is. You're right; it's what kids do. Teenagers growing up." He softened his voice.

"Timmy and Robert have a ball game tonight?"

"At six. We can have an early dinner here, then go straight to the park."

He looked away from his wife, but felt her peering at him. "That'll be fine. I was going to take the rest of the day off anyway. I've been wanting to catch up on some reading at home."

His wife fell silent, and he still felt her searching his face. They had been married long enough for each other to know when something was wrong, but they respected each other enough to know when not to push. He knew his wife would be there, waiting for him to get out of himself and talk to her when he was ready.

Impulsively, Wilkins took his wife's hand, squeezed it, kissed her on the cheek. "I love you, Paula. Everything's all right. I'm sorry if I'm letting something make me a little short-tempered."

Smiling, she stroked the back of her husband's head, mussing up his hair. "How about paranoid?"

He forced a chuckle, but it felt cold, empty. "I seem that way?"

"Honey, relax, do what you want with the rest of the day. It might be good for you to stay out of the office. Cool off, think things through. The paper will still be there tomorrow."

Wilkins lapsed into his somber mood again. *Tomorrow,* he thought. *It will still be there.* "Life's been so easy, so uncomplicated for us for so long. . . . I don't know. Kids grow up, my daughter grows up. Everything has a way of changing. I just want what's good for all of us."

He looked into his wife's eyes, wishing he could stir confidence in his heart. She looked puzzled, even worried. Suddenly he regretted coming to his wife like this, anxious, tight. He wanted to tell her the truth but he couldn't. He ground out his cigarette, kissed his wife, and said, "I'll see you here in a couple of hours."

As he left, Wilkins felt his wife following him with her worried stare.

Thirty minutes later, John Wilkins found himself in a bar on the outskirts of Glendale. He was perched on a stool at the far end of the place, near the pool table, working on his second whiskey and Coke, when his solitude was interrupted.

"John? John Wilkins? Is that you?"

Wilkins jumped at the soft but familiar voice. Turning, he saw the past roll right out of the gloom. It stared him right in the face, smiling as if he were some long-lost friend.

Cassandra Dooley. She was one of the two women who had helped create the shame that apparently had haunted his brother to this day.

"Cassandra?" He felt compelled to say her name, wondering if it was really her. Why was she there? Why was she looking at him like that? All smiles, eyes flashing. Suddenly he couldn't trust reality. The booze had kicked in, loosening him up. Against his will, his gaze flickered over her. Her smile turned to something else, but what he wasn't sure.

She stood there in tight black spandex pants that hugged long shapely legs. He glanced at her large, firm breasts, jutting against the sheer fabric of some frilly silk tank top. How could he, or any man, not notice her, her body? It was only natural. She was so close he could smell the fragrance of the perfume on her creamy, tanned skin. His senses tingled; he felt a pang of shame. Finally he pried his stare away from that long mane of golden blond hair, those full lips, ripe, a little moist. What was he thinking? That she looked good? What was this sudden flash of lust? It was her, not him, looking at him that way. Or was it the booze? Or the letter?

"Surprised to see me here?" she said in a satin voice he imagined had lured his brother in.

She slid onto the stool next to him, ordered a gin martini. Wilkins turned to his drink. "Glendale's not that big."

"Small world, like that? Too small, sometimes."

They sat in an awkward silence before Wilkins fired up a cigarette, cleared his throat, said, "How come I get a feeling this is no chance encounter?"

She laughed, put a slyness in her voice. That was the thing that had struck Wilkins so long ago. He could never tell when the woman was acting.

"All right, Mr. Wilkins, I was following you," she said sarcastically. "Yes, I've been watching you for weeks, wondering when you and the Mrs. might invite me over for cocktails. We're practically neighbors. Or haven't you noticed? Like Sam, I know I'm something of the talk of the town. But the good people of Glendale need people like Sam and me. We sort of breathe life into your humdrum little existence."

"What's your point?"

"No point. My second husband left me a nice chunk of change, so I bought a little house, one block over from where you live, I believe. Maybe you've seen me. I jog every morning."

Wilkins had seen her, all right, but he said nothing. He believed he knew what kind of woman she was, but he didn't see the sense in dredging up the past, dragging them all through the mud again. He wished she would leave. But she wanted something.

With each lingering moment, he became more uncomfortable. She sat there, like a queen on a throne, her look and demeanor betraying her, just as her words had. The world should bow before her.

He tried to pretend she wasn't there, smelling sweet, all tight curves, blue eyes laughing at the world. He could see the dangerous effect this recently divorced woman could have on a man. Twice divorced, he recalled. If nothing else, she was right that gossip was alive and well in Glendale. What web did this spider now seek to weave?

Wilkins looked around. Two men he'd never seen before were shooting pool. Some couples sat scattered around in booths. Someone played the jukebox. Wilkins was grateful for the music.

"Don't worry, John. I come here because no one

knows me. If they don't know me, they don't know you. Unless you drink here every day. Do you?"

"What do you want, Cassandra?"

That smile again. It infuriated Wilkins. Was she toying with him?

"I told you. Didn't I?"

Wilkins killed his drink, ground out his cigarette. "Have a nice life, Cassandra."

He rose, but she put her hand on his arm. "Wait."

He stared into her eyes, felt mesmerized by her sudden strange, imploring look, the warmth of her touch. Just like that, she changed. One moment acting as if she might want to seduce him into adultery, then in an eyeblink sincere, the little child, pure and innocent.

"Maybe this is no coincidence. You believe in karma, John?"

"I've never given it much thought."

"What I'm saying . . . what I want to say . . . I'm sorry. I'm sorry about what happened."

Wilkins clenched his jaw. "It was a long time ago."

"I hurt you, John, very badly. And your brother."

"My father gave you three thousand dollars. He quieted your outrage act. You got what you wanted. You always do."

"It was no act, John. Please. Let me explain; you never gave me the chance. That's what I wanted. A chance. I wanted you, I've always wanted you. But you never even paid me the least bit of attention. I always wondered why. It made me crazy. Maybe it made me do what I did. I cared for your brother, or I thought I did. He was a little weird, but he was an artist. I wanted to understand him. I don't know, maybe I felt sorry for him. Look, we weren't much more than kids, barely eighteen. We were in his car,

I let him kiss me. It got out of hand. I told him to stop."

"And he did. Something you always neglected to mention to a lot of people around here. He told me he stopped. And you told me he never raped you. You remember that, don't you? When I confronted you about it? My regret is that I never went to him and told him I knew the truth."

"John, please. All these years, don't you think that hasn't hurt me? I just wanted to tell you how sorry I am. If nothing else, can you tell me you forgive me?"

He thought about it, found the words wanting to come out. But he couldn't do it.

"Good-bye, Cassandra," he said, pulling himself free of her grasp.

"John?"

He turned, looked back at her. Something hard, pitiless, flashed through her eyes. Once again, he was disturbed by the strange effect she was having on him.

"Tell me something. Does your wife know?"

No, Paula didn't know about Cassandra, but she knew about the other trouble his brother had been in. Wilkins decided not to give this woman whatever answer she wanted.

She looked remorseful again, a sudden chameleon change that baffled Wilkins, made him believe he should be afraid of this woman. Was she fighting back tears? he wondered. Or was she on the verge of laughter? What did she want? Was life just a game to her, using people as she saw fit to serve her whims, indulge her wants? He was repulsed by her spirit, but at the same time . . .

"Never mind," she said softly. "If you should sometime . . . Well, I want nothing more than to hear you say you forgive me."

He broke her stare. He wasn't aware how fast he was walking until he barreled out the door and the harsh sunlight stabbed into his eyes.

Chapter Three

Silently Mike Wilkins seethed. *Something, anything, anywhere, save me—save me from myself. I'd rather be dead.*

He stumbled on through the city, enveloped by darkness, feeling as if his heart were on fire.

He was subdued a little, though, for the moment. That fistful of loose change earlier had secured a pint of bourbon. Ah, it was the fleeting moment of salvation he needed, but it had been several hours since he'd killed the bottle. With the alcohol wearing off, he focused, again and again, on the prayer to the force of power. Keep trying, he told himself. *Ask and ye shall receive.* Wasn't that what he had always heard?

To go on like this, a prisoner of the past, invisible in the present, was unbearable. He had to believe that out of desperation, from the poisoned depths of his misery, his prayers would be answered. He wanted only to be free of what he was.

Which was nothing. Which was something in human skin, but less than an animal. How can one come to detest his very existence? he wondered.

He prayed for deliverance. Shanda, the wise, she could help. She was his last resort.

Dan Schmidt

Grant me what I seek, O Divine One. Grant me the power to make me strong and whole in the eyes of my fellow men. Hear the suffering in my heart. Uplift me and grant me something that will fulfill my life.

Then he stopped and searched his surroundings, unsure whether or not he was praying aloud. He put Shanda's book back in his shirt pocket. The fear came back. Faces were searching him out.

Nightfall had dropped over the city. The workforce had fled to their suburban fortresses. With darkness the predators roamed every corner, alley, and park between the Delaware and Schuylkill rivers. Shadows flitted everywhere. If they were contemptuous and pitiless by day, then by night they could be outright merciless, even murderous. Dealers and junkies, hookers and pimps, the homosexuals, transsexuals, and transvestites, crooning and begging, bartering and luring, all the swirling and angry voices of an army surrounding him as they had in every other American city. Even when they were silent their presence was an obscenity, blighting the night, that breathed and walked and could kill. So Wilkins stayed alert for the human carnivores who might hurt him just so they would have something to do. Still, the animals of the night would more or less ignore him, he knew.

He was scuttling past Logan Circle, unaware he was staring at three shadows ahead until one of them growled, " 'Scuse you! What you lookin' at, hobo?"

Three punks in gangbanger getup hugged the shadows of the park. Wilkins ignored them but stayed poised to fight if they moved on him. Or should he run instead? he wondered. Shame and fear boiled in his belly. There were three of them, most likely armed with knives or guns, hearts pumping with the same rage he felt, but they were experienced in violence, blooded in savagery and cruelty. What could he possibly do to defend himself, much less strike back? The biggest of the trio, the one with a Phillies baseball cap on backward, cursed him as Wilkins moved past them.

"Worthless wino." He heard Baseball Cap laugh. "Oughta mess him up jist for the hell of it. Maybe I will, drunken bag a' shit. Yeah, keep walkin'."

Wilkins felt the cold anger stiffen his shoulders. He wanted to go back, just start whaling on them for as long as he could until they eventually stomped him to a bloody pulp. He wasn't sure he even had enough strength to begin such a hopeless fight. They kept cursing him, laughing at him even as he put distance between himself and the bangers.

He was powerless, utterly adrift in a world that swirled around him in at least some semblance of the controlled insanity of the wicked and the heartless. He hated this feeling of powerlessness, of abysmal helplessness, more than anything. Even in an explosion of rage he wasn't sure how much damage he could inflict on another human being. Could he kill? Even if his life were threatened, could he find the courage, the strength, whatever it took to take another life? He even questioned if he had the guts to take his own life.

He wandered on in a haze of churning anger and fear. The night was a blur of sight and sound. Shadows skirted around him. Mutterings. Vicious oaths. A sound like the crack of a pistol from somewhere. Let them come, let his unknown enemies take his life. Living no longer mattered. Tomorrow would only bring more of the same.

His belly grumbled. He needed food, so he slipped

into the first alley he found. Often he could rummage through the litter, usually a Dumpster, to find a half-eaten burger, a scattering of French fries. If he walked these streets long enough, he might even strike it rich. Sometimes the narcs would descend on a street corner where the bangers and the dealers gathered. During the police raid, the dealers would throw their stash to the gutter or a yard and run. In the chaos and confusion he could scoop a rock or two of crack cocaine, fade into the night. If that happened, he would smoke it, since it took too much effort to seek out a safe buyer for cash.

The alley seemed to swallow him into its dark bowels. A lone lightbulb hung from the side of a large brick building. He wasn't even sure where in the city he was, how long it had been since he roamed from Logan Circle. He fixed his gaze on the large Dumpster, its lid bulging with overflowing garbage. He would find something in there to eat.

Midway down the alley, he tripped over something. Nearly stumbling on his face, he cursed. Impulsively he lashed out, kicked whatever it was that had blocked his path. There was a wet thud, a soft object giving way to his blow. Something wet spattered his lips, something that tasted salty. He touched his lips, looked at his fingers, saw the blood. He looked down.

And froze.

The first thing he saw were the whites of the eyes, bulging in horror and agony from their sockets, seeking him out in lifeless accusation. Then he saw the blood, nothing but blood, a river of dark crimson, still flowing from the gaping yawn in the neck.

Bile slithered into his throat. Mike Wilkins staggered back, choking down the greasy vomit, the acid taste of liquor squirting up his chest. He wanted to run but his legs wouldn't move. The sight of the dead man mesmerized him with his own terror. He looked in both directions down the alley. Nothing but trash, another Dumpster. The killer or killers had surely already fled. Or had they? In the distance he heard the blare of a car horn, and jumped. A siren wailed but faded into the night.

He moved toward the murdered man. His jacket appeared to be made of silk, but it was hard to tell with all that blood. Bending, he could see that the man's throat had been cut so deeply, with such vicious force, that vertebrae were exposed, white, dully gleaming bone in the naked light. Whoever had done this had nearly severed the man's head off his shoulders. Further inspection showed that the shirt had been ripped off, his jacket and its pockets shredded, whether by hand or by the murder weapon he didn't know. The shoes were made of soft leather. A discarded wallet was open just enough to show Wilkins it was empty. A man of means.

And he had been murdered for money. But what had he been doing in this alley, in this part of town at this time of night? Drugs? Buying sex? What had lured him here?

It was a ghoulish thing to do, but life, he reasoned, had long since stripped him of any dignity. Wilkins searched the strewn garbage around the body for anything the killer or killers might have left behind. Perhaps a watch, maybe some money had fallen from the dead man during his struggle, overlooked by the killers in the heat of their violence.

His grimy hands tore through the debris, scattering papers and bottles and broken glass. It was an act of wild desperation, a futile search for something valuable that might see him through the night. His heart raced. Sweat poured down his face. He could feel the dead man's eyes on him. The murderer could come back. The police could roar into the alley anytime. His search became frantic. There was something here, he knew it. Something he could take from this deathbed. Had to be. It was meant to be.

Something glittered, scuffed the asphalt. There it was. The object sparkled as it flew from his rifling fingers, vanishing beneath some rubbish. He dug through the scattered trash, then found the thing he thought had glittered, even in the poor light.

It looked like a gold star on a gold chain. Gold! He laughed, a nervous, strained sound that made him scour the alley. He was still alone. And in the presence of some gold object. He was sure it was gold. It had to be.

Almost as if he couldn't believe his eyes, he reached down, touched it. It was small, fit perfectly in the palm of his hand as he picked it up, stared at it, felt hypnotized by its shape. There was a small black object in the center of the star, with curved gold bands above what the creator of this object had perhaps intended to be an eye. An eye? The eye of power? The one he had seen drawn in the book of Shanda? What was this thing? An amulet? What did it symbolize? He stood, slipped it over his head.

Did it belong to the dead man?

It didn't matter. It belonged to Mike Wilkins now.

He put the gold star inside his shirt, against his chest, and hustled out of the alley.

Something as valuable as gold had to be kept hidden from the predators. Tomorrow he would take it to a pawn shop, determine if it even *was* gold, establish its dollar value. Tonight he would savor this find as nothing but his hope for a better tomorrow.

He started to smile, skirting the sidewalk in front of the Cathedral of Saints Peter and Paul, when something happened. It came without warning.

At first Mike Wilkins thought he was having a heart attack. There was a heat, an incredible heat on his chest, then something that felt like a knife plunging through his heart, ripping, tearing, twisting with blazing hot steel. He couldn't cry out, scream, even move. He was paralyzed. Then he realized the incredible heat came from the gold star. It felt like a branding iron on his chest, but the fire was going inside, burning deep. Finally he managed to claw at his shirt, open it, even though it felt as if his arms were tugging themselves free from unseen ropes. He grasped the gold star in trembling hands. It was hot, scalding his hands, but there was no sign of his flesh burning, not even a singe, not even a faint odor of burning flesh.

Then, again without warning, the world erupted in his eyes, a blinding supernova of brilliant light. The feeling that his chest was being ripped open ended, but then he couldn't see. There was nothing but a sheet of pure white light in his eyes. Oh, God, he heard his mind scream, I'm blind!

There was a roar in his ears as the light slowly, ever so slowly faded and the skyscrapers of downtown loomed, and shadows of people darted past him. The roar was maddening. Every sound he could imagine came shrieking at him from all directions. What was happening to him? Car horns and sirens, music of all kinds and something that sounded like the soughing of wind, a maelstrom of countless voices, some laughing, some screaming, some crying and cursing, muffled grunts and cries of sexual release swirled through his mind, still coming from unseen directions, on and on, roaring and rushing through his brain, filling his whole body with a heated explosion of every known human emotion and desire.

Suddenly his body eased from hot to a warm glow. From somewhere deep inside, from some point in the center of his belly, another wave of blinding light erupted. Eternal seconds later he felt a tingling sensation, as if electricity were shooting through every nerve ending. He believed he knew now what was happening. Some voice he couldn't be sure was his own told him to be still, to stay calm, to feel it and let it be. Yes, his mind seemed to be absorbing all the noise of the city, his energy bonding with that of every human being in Philadelphia.

A sensation of pure strength began flowing through his arms and legs. He could feel it, a living force, purifying him, wiping away all the torture, the physical exhaustion, deprivation, hunger, and thirst. It was both terrifying and euphoric, a hundred, no, a thousand times more gratifying, uplifting, exhilarating than narcotics.

Still, the din of a shrieking, crying, bellowing city kept rushing through his mind. He heard what he thought was the crackle of a police radio, a female dispatcher's voice telling a patrolman of a domestic disturbance on Osage. He heard the angry voices of a couple in a bitter argument. The noise faded; then there was utter silence, a blissfully calm sensation that filled him. Then, for another frightening moment, he saw but didn't see the world. It was as if his eyes had rolled around in their sockets to stare into his own soul.

The light vanished, and the world came back.

But the world had changed somehow. It felt different; everything seemed slower, more controlled. Some primal instinct told him he was different, but he didn't know how he was different.

He spotted the shadow of a man in a shirt and tie walking his way. Mike Wilkins read the fear in the man's eyes as he approached him, clutching his briefcase tight to his body. Mike Wilkins heard a voice in his head, a voice that wasn't his as he stared at the man.

Oh, no, here we go. Why don't the cops do something about these damned vagrants? Damned bums, all of them begging for my money.

The man slid a few steps farther across the sidewalk to put distance between them.

Something urged Wilkins to speak to the man. Something in his mind told him the other voice he heard belonged to the stranger.

Mike Wilkins stared the stranger in the eye, and in a calm voice said, "The police have better things to do, sir, than waste their time with us 'damned vagrants,' as you so unkindly put it. And I don't need your money."

The man balked, his lips quivering, his eyes widening in fear.

Wilkins heard the other voice. This time it was stronger, louder, clearer. He could feel the man's fear, a living thing he was pulling into his body.

Crazy drunk bastard. What the hell? Must have been talking out loud.

"No, sir," Wilkins said, stopping in the middle of the sidewalk, blocking the stranger's path. "Your lips never moved; you never spoke." Wilkins had to be sure. He went on, "You were thinking it, *thinking* I'm a crazy drunk bastard. I'm no crazy drunk. And my mother and father were married, which doesn't put me in the bastard category."

"Get out of my way," the stranger cried aloud.

There. It *was* the stranger's voice he had heard in his head. Wilkins could read thoughts.

A vision flashed through Wilkins's mind. It was a jumbled image, but he saw the briefcase arcing for his face, slamming him in the side of his skull. Another flash and Wilkins saw himself lying facedown on the sidewalk, the stranger running away.

"You won't need to do that, sir."

Fear became terror in the man's eyes. "Do what?"

"You were thinking about hitting me in the head with your briefcase. You were, weren't you? You want to lay me out on the sidewalk." Wilkins peered at the stranger, unsure why he had said that. Even he was suddenly afraid of what he was seeing, of what he believed was going on.

The stranger was frozen in fear and utter confusion. He started trembling, his mouth open, his eyes bulging. Suddenly he whirled and ran from Mike Wilkins.

Mike Wilkins laughed. He felt good. He felt alive.

They could wear their masks over their lies and deceit and secret motives, but they could no longer hide from him. At first, his fear of other people intensified as Mike Wilkins walked the streets with his power. Now that he could hear their thoughts, invade and probe the ultimate privacy a human being had, he became terrified of what he discovered, but the voice inside told him there was nothing to be afraid of. Rich or poor, man or woman, black or white or whatever, most people, he discovered, seemed to be products of the world around them, in both thought and desire. Wherever he walked, their thoughts seethed with anger or envy, or were clouded by fear or doubt or anxiety. They wanted to take, possess, they hungered and they connived, they worried about themselves, their money, their status, their image, or they brooded over their lack of importance. Every man and woman he looked at was consumed, no, obsessed with themselves. Desire raged around him. Violence lurked in their hearts. It was disturbing but at the same time enlightening. For the first time in his life, he felt in control. And superior.

He heard greed boiling in the mind of a well-dressed man leaving a restaurant near Rittenhouse Square. *I need this deal. I've got to have this nailed down or I'm screwed. Fuck those guys, they can pick up the check. They had my problems . . . Damn it, how can I get McGuire to sign that contract? All right, think up an angle, play the old stingy bastard. I'll get that money, I earned it, I deserve it.*

Wilkins looked at and touched the gold star. He didn't understand what had happened, much less what this power was, but the voice in his head told him to use it, not to question it. Accept what you now are, the voice told him. But use what? What was the purpose of knowing the thoughts of other people? What good did that do him, other than maybe giving him some edge over them, keeping him one step ahead? There must be something he was overlooking. His voice told him to wait, be patient. But was it his voice?

As if to quiet his fears, the warm glow sent calm reassurance through him. He felt strong, alive, clean, without fear. Even his physical appearance had changed. His hands were no longer dirt grimed, scabbed. Now the skin was so clean it was almost shining, he thought. He caught his reflection in the tinted window of a Cadillac. A streetlight reflected itself in the image. His eyes showed a confidence he never imagined he could possess. But there was something else staring back at him. The fierce intensity was gone, but now his eyes seemed to burn, penetrate. Or was it simply the light striking the glass?

Searching the street, Wilkins began walking again. He saw a hooker glance at him with contempt. He heard her thinking, clear and angry. *Look at this loser. Come over here, honey, try some bullshit with me. . . .*

Another flash, and Wilkins stopped suddenly in midstride. The image was stronger now than it had been with the stranger near the cathedral, more alive in his mind—in her mind, from her mind—as the image locked in his head. She was thinking about the switchblade in her purse; he saw her pulling it out and sticking it in his gut. The voice again, telling him to keep moving, she wasn't worth it. He looked at her again. Another image in his mind. He saw her, stretched out in a pool of blood, her throat cut open. What was he seeing now? Her future? Her murder? It had happened so fast, he couldn't be sure if what he had seen was real.

Wilkins kept walking, looked at the sparse traffic, stared at a man sitting behind the wheel of a BMW, stuck at a light. The voice nearly leaped at Wilkins, full of impatience, fury. *Come on, come on.* The driver glared at Wilkins, who smiled back and focused the light inside him on the man's eyes, probing, invading, taking the stranger's thoughts into his own mind. *What's your problem, asshole? Miss your bus?*

The BMW screeched off. Wilkins caught the faint echo of the driver's thoughts, rife with more cursing of him. Then there was silence. Distance seemed to save others from his invasion into their secrets. Then he heard the voice say, *No, that isn't so. Be patient. Trust me.*

A young couple strolled out of a restaurant as Wilkins walked on. The man was laughing, talking about a great bar he knew a few blocks north, why didn't they go there for an after-dinner cocktail? The woman didn't look all that pleased to be with her date, seemed annoyed. Wilkins stared into the man's eyes. It seemed that was all he had to do to invade someone's thoughts. Look, focus, and listen, let the warm light spread, take charge. He concentrated on the man, relaxed himself to let this strange energy flow, this electricity he felt in his head. It was getting easier. He drew the man's thoughts to him. *Couple more drinks in this one. All the money I've spent on this little slut, least she can do is go down on me. Dinner cost me a mint. It's the least she owes me. She's doable.* Then Wilkins looked the woman in the eye as they passed him.

Another limp noodle in a suit, just what you needed, Barb. Talking about himself, his money, his job, like that's going to get him somewhere with me. Oh, please, just take me home. Please shut up. I'm not impressed. I hope he doesn't put his arm around me. Why did I go out with this self-obsessed, egotistical jerkoff? Oh, well, dinner wasn't bad, except that waiter kept looking at my tits. Like I'm supposed to slip some peon waiter my phone number. Maybe I'll get a few drinks out of this joker. Why not? By then I can figure some excuse to ditch him.

For an hour straight, Mike Wilkins walked countless blocks, probing the minds of the denizens of the night. Soon, he wondered if anyone, anywhere in the city, had a kind or decent thought or purely selfless motive. The faces could look innocent enough, bland enough, but when he looked into their eyes he heard lust and anger, he latched onto fleeting thoughts of violence, heard their hunger for money and the drive of ambition. They thought they deserved something simply because they wanted it. They thought about how they could steal other men's women, how they could pad expense accounts, lie to their wives, steal a drug stash, lie to the court. No matter who they were, their thoughts were raw, venomous, poisoned with hate and jealousy, fear of losing what they had, fear of not getting what they wanted. After a while Wilkins lost his fear of people. All this hate, all this hostility and animosity, want and self-seeking. All was silent madness. Soon he wasn't even shocked by what he heard in their minds. The whole world was every bit as insane as he had always believed himself to be.

But what good was this power if he couldn't use it?

Trust me, the voice told him. *You will be shown the way, and the rest will be up to you. Take heart.*

Suddenly Wilkins heard a vicious curse, the sound of flesh smacking flesh, and the yelp of a woman. A large man with light brown skin, an expensive silk suit molded to his muscular frame, was slapping and screaming obscenities at a skinny redhead. They were more or less standing in the mouth of an alley. One look at the silver Mercedes Benz, the high heels and the short miniskirt on the redhead, one earful of the one-sided conversation and Wilkins knew he had stumbled across a pimp teaching one of his girls a lesson in street economics. Wilkins searched the street. Shadows were on the move, but staying well clear of the beating.

"I told you, I ain't got the money. I'll get it to you by the end of the night, I swear, H. K., I will."

"Don't lie to me, bitch; you holdin' out so you can go smoke up my money. Fuckin' crack slut."

She screamed, tried to cover her face, but the pimp struck at her face, again and again. First, with the heel of his palm, then the back of his hand, striking, cracking, sending her reeling, crying in fear. Blood flew from her nose.

Wilkins heard his voice tell him, *Be strong. Do it. Go on. Do what you have always wanted to do to a man like this. Have courage and trust me. This is your moment of truth.*

Wilkins walked toward the pimp. Strangely enough, he felt no fear. He trusted the voice, let it guide him.

The pimp whirled on Wilkins, bared his teeth. "What the . . . What? You want some of this? I'm gonna blink my eyes, asshole, one time, and you better be runnin'."

The pimp blinked, opened his eyes.

Wilkins took another step toward the pimp and smiled.

Chapter Four

Mike Wilkins felt himself changing, evolving, becoming stronger. To read minds was now almost as natural as breathing.

He invaded the pimp, searching for images of his past, seeking to know exactly what kind of man confronted him. The power came to Wilkins, took control with no effort, no thought. Wilkins felt and saw a screen of light burn through his mind. Images rolled together, a runaway train of visions, telling, warning him about the pimp. His own energy seemed to draw the life force of all the man's pride and rage and hatred into his own soul but without clouding his judgment or distorting his emotions.

Wilkins could clearly see the man beating women to bloody pulps, counting money, using and peddling drugs, strong-arming those he kept in his debt. Finally he caught a fleeting glimpse of the man holding a gun, riddling a rival's chest with bullets. He knew without knowing then that this vicious predator was called H. K.

Thought for Mike Wilkins was quickly turning into—what? Pure energy? Whatever was now happening to him, instinctively he knew what to do, no longer needing his other voice. Still the voice guided, but now it whispered he could take action through thought alone.

He could control someone else through sheer force of will.

The pimp was walking up to Wilkins, cursing, rearing his arm back.

Wilkins held his ground, let his energy erupt from the source of burning light within, reaching out to envelop the pimp with an invisible wall. The instinct for self-preservation seized Wilkins, and his mind growled *Stop.*

Suddenly the pimp staggered, his arm locking as if it were instantly paralyzed. Confusion bulged the predator's eyes. The hooker, wiping the blood off her face, cried the pimp's name, baffled by what she saw.

This pimp would have beaten him half to death, Wilkins knew. A feeling of utter coldness hardened Mike Wilkins. He had never committed a single act of violence in his life. Up to now he had been afraid of others, himself, perhaps what he might do to another human being if all his anger exploded. Before now he had known that shedding someone else's blood would only leave him feeling guilty and ashamed afterward, feeding that image of himself as something less than human.

Now it was different. Indeed, he was something now more than human. The voice whispered, *Take heart, take action.*

So right, so just. Now that he had this power to control, he suddenly decided that after what he had heard in the minds of others, what he had seen this man do, there were clear and definable wrongs, there was evil all around him that demanded immediate and appropriate justice. *Use your gift; don't question it. You are a god.*

Mike Wilkins believed it. The pure energy of his thoughts bored his will into the pimp. Mike Wilkins wasn't about to let this man off easy. He was to squirm, to feel and taste the fear he had made others know.

You can't breathe.

Just like that, it happened. The pimp clutched his throat, gagging, sucking for air that wouldn't come. His eyes nearly popped from their sockets, his knees shaking.

Wilkins felt the man's pure fear, an electrical charge that emanated from the pimp's whole body.

"I can't . . . breathe," the pimp gasped. "What did you . . . do to me?"

Silence. I control you. You will do exactly what I tell you to do.

From the corner of his eye, Wilkins saw the hooker slumped against the wall of the alley, staring at him in terror. The pimp's lips moved but he had no voice.

Hearing the voices of confusion and terror in their minds, Wilkins ordered the hooker to back into the alley. *Don't run. Don't be afraid. I won't hurt you.*

She stepped back, and Wilkins commanded the pimp to do the same. He did. It was incredible. The power kept speaking to him without speaking.

And he drove them deeper into the alley, away from any watching eyes. Wilkins probed the hooker's mind, demanding her memory. It was easy to dig into her past, since he found it was something she always dwelled on. He discovered she was eighteen years old, a runaway from Syracuse. She hated this man who beat her, forced himself on her, had practically kidnapped her as soon as she got off the bus in the city, a frightened child, no clue as to what she wanted in life, much less what she needed. He saw a stepfather who raped her, the drinking, the drug abuse, heard voices screaming in rage at the girl, others coming at her with an energy of pure lust and a desire to control and dominate her. He sensed she believed she was trapped in this hopeless downward spiral of drug addiction, the degradation of men taking her however they pleased, humiliating her. He knew she hated herself, that she wanted freedom but didn't know how to take charge of her life.

Mike Wilkins took charge for her. Then he heard the pimp thinking about the 9mm Glock in the waistband of his pants. Some concentration, demanding the man's memory, putting his thoughts into his mind; then Wilkins told the pimp out loud, "You got that gun from a dirty cop, a little gift from a . . . Sgt. Rawlins, I think. I see it, I see this cop taking your money. I can see him, a fat, naked slug of a man, with your hookers. I hear both of you, laughing at everyone you use, at the ones he deceives. You . . . both of you . . . you worship violence, you want to hurt."

"What the . . . Who are you?" the pimp cried.

"Take out the gun, H. K. Put it in your mouth. Put it in deep, feel the cold metal against the back of your throat."

"Kiss my ass, freak!"

Wilkins turned his will into a force of pure anger, watched as the pimp slowly dug the gun out. The pimp didn't want to do it. Too bad. He would.

You have a terrible pain in your stomach, like a knife ripping through your bowels. Feel it. You scream but you have no voice. No, don't lose your bowels. Not yet. What a shame that would be, such nice clothes. Oh, yes, you're terrified. How does it feel?

The pimp nearly collapsed, wanted to grab his

stomach but Wilkins wouldn't let him, wanting him to know pure agony, fear, shame. The pimp's mouth widened to scream but there was no sound, just a silent wail of agony that only Wilkins heard in the man's head, an endless dark tunnel of screaming and cursing. *Put the gun in your mouth.* The pimp's hand trembled, his eyes widening even more. Slowly the gun went into his mouth, the pimp's silent shrieking of curses locked in the screen of light filling Wilkins's head, the tunnel of darkness within the pimp stretching for infinity.

Wilkins felt the light fill his eyes. He told the pimp, "That's right, H. K., in your mouth. I believe you did that to someone before. You should know the feeling."

Wilkins felt the resistance, but it was getting easier to control the pimp's body, the power of his will turning hotter inside him, growing stronger, angrier, turning his eyes into orbs of fire, or so it felt—only there was no pain. He could feel the man's terror, a living force, could even feel the pimp's bowels rumble, this predator on the verge of soiling himself.

"I could kill you," Wilkins said as the pimp put the gun deep in his mouth, gagged. "It would be so easy. No, too easy. I want you to live. I want you to remember. Now, give me the gun."

The pimp handed Wilkins the gun.

"Give me your money."

Wilkins kept feeling the tugging, churning energy of the pimp's defiance, hatred. Teeth gritted, H. K. dug a wad of hundreds and fifties from his pocket. Wilkins took the money, handed it to the hooker. He stared her in the eyes, put the thought into her mind: *Leave this city; don't come back. Nod if you understand.*

She gave a shaky nod, her eyes still wide with fear.

Stay where you are, and you'll die. Move on, leave everything behind, and you may have a chance. The choice is yours.

He couldn't get a fix on her intent, but heard her mind cry, *Who are you?*

This never happened; you never saw me. He conjured up an image of someone else, just in case she talked about this encounter. He put a picture of a short, stocky, dark-haired man in a coat and tie in her mind. One last thing for her to do. Out loud, Wilkins commanded the hooker, "Kick him where it will hurt the most."

A soft probe and he discovered it was exactly what she had always wanted to do. *Go on. He can't hurt you.*

The pimp knew what was coming. Wilkins took the pimp's voice from him at the last instant before the hooker buried her toe in his sac, putting all the force she could into the blow, with Wilkins lending her energy from his own will. The pimp's mouth seemed wide enough to stuff a basketball in it, as he doubled over, fell to his knees. No scream ripped from his mouth. Again, Wilkins heard the man's scream of agony in both their minds, a long wail that lingered in the union of their thoughts.

Go! Wilkins commanded the hooker, who then seemed to stagger from the alley. She didn't look back.

Then Wilkins ordered the pimp to stand up, face the wall. Again he heard the pimp viciously curse him in his thoughts, vow to find him and kill him. Wilkins searched the man's mind, found an image of Sgt. Rawlins. When he left the alley, Wilkins had no doubt H. K. would believe Sgt. Rawlins was the one responsible for all this misery.

Smash your face into the wall until you collapse. Smash your nose, then your mouth, then the sides of your eyes until your face is ruined.

It worked, and Wilkins heard the pimp's mind screaming curses at Sgt. Rawlins. The first time was difficult, since H. K. fought to keep from banging his face against the brick wall. *I told you, smash your face into the wall!*

There was a squelch of bone, blood spraying the air. Then the pimp hammered his face, again and again, into the wall. Slick crimson poured down the pimp's face. Screams of pain and confusion, of rage, tore the pimp's mind. Wilkins saw the stars explode through the pimp's mind with each blow to his face. He could hear the cries of agony, see the man delivering this self-beating, heard in his head the crunching force of soft flesh and bone yielding to an unyielding object, saw the onrush of unconsciousness, but at the same time disconnected himself from all that pain of tearing flesh and crushing bone.

Finally the pimp crumpled in a heap on the alley floor. With his mind, Wilkins found the man's heartbeat as the pimp twitched in a growing pool of blood. With a darting image Wilkins found the pimp would live. Beyond that, Wilkins couldn't find any visions of the man's future. Strange, he thought, there was nothing.

Suddenly Mike Wilkins had an urge to flee what he had done. As he moved down the alley, swift and silent, melting into the deep shadows, he tossed the gun into a Dumpster. He had just wondered what his next move should be when he suddenly found he was fighting back vomit. He had used this power, this gift, to inflict violence, and wondered if it was a good thing. Wasn't it right, he asked himself, to stop someone's pain and suffering, even if it meant using brutal force against a vicious and remorseless attacker?

Then his other voice came back, whispering he would be all right, that he had just done a good thing, taken the only possible course of action. He was told—or was he telling himself?—that his will now worked in the interests of all that was good and just.

Stay strong. You have been given that which you so desperately sought. Behold. I will show you the way. And the world, and all that is in it, can belong to you, but only if you trust me.

Why was he suddenly so very afraid?

John Wilkins was nursing his third beer, fighting the urge to light a cigarette. He was watching the eleven o'clock news, alone in the living room. Paula was upstairs, reading a book, maybe waiting for him. He'd seen the way his wife had glanced at him during the evening. That funny, slightly suspicious eye, first at the restaurant, then at their sons' baseball game. She was never one to make a scene, demand to know what was wrong. She was ever the patient wife, but she had a way of biding her time, measuring him when she sensed trouble, her silence making him feel guilty even when there was nothing to feel guilty about. He toyed with the idea of telling her about the letter. He hated keeping anything from her. He knew she'd smelled the liquor on his breath, but she hadn't said anything. How much longer could he sit, though, stewing in isolation?

He looked at the grandfather clock, one of the many pieces of antique furniture his parents had left him, and wondered why his daughter wasn't home.

Sitting in his easy chair, in the shadows of the soft lamplight, he heard the refrigerator open in the kitchen.

"Timmy? Bobby, is that you?"

"It's me, Dad. Just getting a sandwich."

Timmy, the middle child. His sixteen-year-old son sounded sullen. It was the game. Timmy had struck out in the final inning with the bases loaded, and missed a chance to win the game.

"Do you know where your sister is?"

No answer; then Timmy came into the living room, munching on a fat ham-and-cheese sandwich. He spilled some crumbs on the carpet, made a half-hearted attempt to pick them up, mumbled, "Sorry."

He could tell his son's pride was stung by his failure to drive in the winning run. Robert, the oldest, was the athlete of the family, the one who came home with all the grades, the awards, the trophies, had all the friends, seemed to say and do all the right things. Timmy was the shy one, a little skinny, wore glasses, since he was a little farsighted.

"Did you say something, Dad?"

"Your sister. Is she home?"

Timmy shrugged. "How should I know? Maybe she decided to close the restaurant. Sometimes her friends come in right before she closes. I think Mom asked her to close tonight."

Wilkins sipped his beer, hid his concern. Which friends? he wondered. The boyfriend? The Stallings boy seemed like a good kid, but he knew he was two years older than Jenny. Then he remembered how she was coming home late these days. He even thought he had smelled beer on her last week after another one of those late evenings. All he had to do was remember how he felt about Paula back in those days, the raging hormones. It was a little more than kid stuff, and he decided he'd better take some kind of stand before it was too late.

"Are you okay, son? The game, is that what's bothering you?"

Timmy worked on his sandwich in brooding silence, then said, "I screwed up. I had a chance to win the game, and I let everyone down. I could have been . . . I don't know . . . a hero."

"It happens, Timmy. You'll get 'em next time. Hey, forget about it."

"Yeah. Easy for you to say."

John Wilkins chose his next words carefully. Just then it struck him, out of nowhere, just how similar his family situation was to the one in which he, a brother, and a sister had grown up in. It hit him that Timmy was a lot, maybe too much, like Mike. Timmy thought he could hide it, but there was a lot of quiet seething inside of him. He wanted to be the best, wanted to succeed, excel at something, anything, but found himself falling short. More and more lately, Timmy seemed to be withdrawing into his own isolated world of books and music.

"Would you mind a little fatherly advice?"

His son thought about it, then said, "Sure. Why not?"

"Everyone is afraid to make mistakes, to fall short, to fail. But every one of us strikes out at some time, with the bases loaded. Thing is, it's going to happen. No one can be that hero all the time, even when they think they should be. You fall down, best thing to do is get up and try again. I make mistakes all the time, son, but I don't dwell on them. When you don't succeed when you really think you should, look at it, think about what happened, sure; then decide what you can do differently next time. No one's embarrassed by what happened tonight. You didn't let anybody down. You went to the plate, you stood there, and you took your cuts. There will be a next time. Just keep trying. Any one of us stops trying, *then* we fail. Best thing to do, go to bed; tomorrow evening we'll go down to the batting cage and work on it. You up for that?"

There was a flicker of hope in Timmy's eyes, but John Wilkins wondered if he had reached his son.

"I guess so."

"You want to sit here and watch some TV?"

"Nah, I'm tired. I wanna go to bed."

They said good night. When he was alone again, John Wilkins found his own brooding thoughts creeping back. He focused on the news, but all he heard was the usual bad news. A drug-addicted mother on the south side, abandoning her bady in a Dumpster. A cop in court on charges of corruption and brutality. Sex scandals. A triple homicide-suicide, a father going berserk somewhere in the state. Racism. Shouts and demands for rights from all the various howling mobs. A church vandalized with hate graffiti. A black church in the South fire-bombed. It was the usual insanity, but for some reason he was suddenly hearing it, thinking about it.

What was happening out there?

The front door opened. Wilkins looked up, saw his daughter slowly appear from the foyer.

"Hi, Dad. Sorry I'm late getting home."

"Where have you been?"

"Well, I was at the restaurant with some friends; Kim and Judy came in, they hung around and helped me clean up. I just lost track of time. Besides, I had to take inventory, and it was so busy tonight I didn't get a chance until after I got rid of the last table. You know all this responsibility Mom's given me, I wanted to show her I can do it."

The explanation sounded rehearsed. He looked at his daughter, felt a stab of anger followed by a pang of loss. Fifteen, strawberry blond hair. He had the prettiest daughter in Glendale. But . . . she was growing up. In this day and age, he couldn't help but worry about her. Something didn't feel right with his daughter. Or was it more paranoia about Mike? What was he thinking? That his daughter was in some kind of danger?

"Glad you're home, Jen." He let it go at that, didn't insist on a good-night kiss, even fought down the temptation to tell her he hoped everything was all right, and to ask if there was something she might want to talk about. If he did smell beer on her . . . let it go, he told himself. Children grow up. His fatherly instinct was to protect her from the world, demand the impossible. He recalled that he hadn't seen her at the restaurant when they'd had dinner before the game. Was she lying to him?

"Missed you at the game, hon."

"Maybe next time. You know how summer is around here."

"Busy, right."

"Were you and Mom still planning to have our annual summer party this weekend?"

"It's sort of become a family tradition, how we Wilkinses help kick off every summer. We'll all be out by the pool, old Dad sweating over the barbecue pit. Some girlfriends you wanted to ask over?"

"I . . . well, yeah, but I was wondering if I could invite Paul? I mean, not just have their whole family just show up, maybe ask Paul . . . myself."

"Sure, Jen," he told his daughter, knowing it would be a good chance to see for himself just how serious his daughter might be about this potential first boyfriend. "I'm sure your brothers will be inviting some of their friends, too."

Her blue eyes seemed to shine as she said, "Great, and thanks. Good night, Dad. Love you."

"I love you, too, Jen." He watched his daughter go upstairs, suddenly wondered why he found himself unable to communicate with his children, why he felt some gap widening between them.

He believed he knew why. He made a decision. He would show the letter to Paula. But when?

Mike Wilkins felt them, in the night. They were following him. In fact, they had gone looking for him after they believed this worthless wino had "dissed" them. Then again, a part of Mike Wilkins had seemed to be outside himself, urging his body on, searching them out. The power demanded their respect and homage.

Wilkins turned, saw the three shadows hastening their strides. He wasn't that far from Logan Circle, veering away from the cluster of apartment buildings and museums and hotels that lined the wide Ben Franklin Parkway.

"Yo! Bum! Hold up!"

They closed the distance. Wilkins felt his heart race. His other voice came alive, strong, filling him with silent laughter. His fear of them vanished. He knew he was on the verge of crossing some point of no return, but felt unable to stop whatever was going to happen. The pimp had merely been a small step on a ladder that ascended to something, but what the something was, he didn't know.

Even at a distance, he could feel the force of their hate and anger seeking him out.

He couldn't help but question what he was becoming even as his other voice eased his fears, then retreated, silent altogether.

He found an alley, long and narrow and dark. He moved into a shadowy area that looked like an alcove. He didn't have to wait too long for them to appear.

They fanned out. Baseball Cap was in the middle, grinning.

"What do you want?" Wilkins said, even though he already knew.

One with a purple headrag laughed, reached inside his jacket. Wilkins knew it was a switchblade even before Purple Headrag pulled it out and flicked open the blade.

"An apology's what we want, bum."

Mike Wilkins felt the light in his eyes turn to fire.

Chapter Five

You can't move, you're paralyzed from head to toe. Stop!

They blanched, balked for a fleeting moment, a flicker of confusion in their eyes, but then the trio of gangbangers started forward again. Two drew pistols, Purple Headrag holding the switchblade low by his side. Their eyes gleamed with an animal hunger. Mike Wilkins started to worry, fear worming through him with a slithering icy chill. It wasn't working. Why?

Stop! I command you to stop!

Focus. There are three of them, keep them in sight, put your will into them. The voice seeped out, the light sending a new and fiery wave of energy through his limbs. His other voice told Wilkins without telling him to use his sudden surge of utter desperation to try to find the source of the power, concentrate to harness it. *Concentrate! Turn your fear into action!*

The three of you can't move! his mind shouted in fear and anger, his silent voice bellowing in his head as they took one more threatening step toward him. A vision leaped through his mind. He knew they weren't going to kill him outright, but they were going to bust him up. Another image showed him on the alley floor, the knife carving him up while one of them urinated on him. His fear became righteous fury.

All three of you are paralyzed!

It worked, coming back full-force, putting him in control once again. They froze, living, breathing human statues, mouths just beginning to open, white eyes starting to bulge. Now Wilkins could hear their thoughts, a distorted union of fear. He took it in, slowly at first, then growing, raging.

The light inside him felt renewed, with more strength, more heat, and more anger. He probed their minds. He found nothing, merely a strange and very cold emptiness inside them. He felt their hearts beat inside his light, but beyond their fear and the rage that was cooling ever so slowly in their racing blood, there was nothing—no thought, no emotion.

Instinctively Wilkins began to understand why his power had not worked at first. He was faced with young sociopaths. There was not even a shred of humanity in their minds. A deeper probe, seeking reason, found only unreason, every thought of theirs irrational, everything distorted and misshapen by desire. The power warned Wilkins they didn't care about anything or anyone, not even themselves. Wilkins felt himself inside of them, but the void inside them was an icy dark pit and he was left groping at nothing. They couldn't feel; therefore he had been unable to reach them. It was something of an education, but he had seen armies of their type in every city, and it was really not a startling revelation. They murdered without guilt. They preyed upon the weaker, without conscience. And he knew without knowing that they would never change.

There. He caught it. A flicker of an image. It was

Purple Headrag. He saw something, a blaze of gunfire, the banger chasing what appeared to be another kid, no more than twelve or thirteen, down a street, pumping a bullet into the back of his head. Purple Headrag laughing, standing over the body, firing another bullet into his victim. What was he seeing? Wilkins wondered. The past? Or tomorrow?

He stared into Baseball Cap's eyes. A vision of iron bars slammed shut on a face twisted in anger, arrogance. Another vision darted through his mind, but Wilkins caught enough to see Baseball Cap strapped into an electric chair, all the rage and arrogance still in those eyes even as they sizzled, and his skin smoldered and smoked as electricity boiled his insides to fire.

The voice told him he had the power to change the future, to save lives. *Do it! You have the power to be someone's savior. Take their lives. You must. It doesn't matter what their crimes will be; it is enough that you know there will be future suffering inflicted by these animals.*

Wilkins heard the laughter roll in his head, put the laughter in their minds. They wanted to curse, cry out, but he took their voices. They were surrounded in darkness, utter silence. Wilkins reached out into the night, the power telling him the four of them were alone.

Out of nowhere, he heard, *I am your Lord, your God, and you will tremble before me.*

He heard a simultaneous cry of terror, mingled with their vile thoughts.

Wilkins arranged the table for their executions with his imagination. Was it their emptiness and coldness he began to draw into his soul, or was he changing again? Whatever was happening, he found himself wanting to kill them, save their potential future victims, or avenge their past crimes. He hungered inside to purge, cleanse, save others from misery, wipe these three from existence, cast them into oblivion. Plunge them, shrieking and thrashing, into a cold dark world where they belonged for all eternity. For he found no hope inside them. They needed death to feel alive. So be it. *Give them what they seek.*

And he had the power to change the future! Or did he? What was happening to him? What was he seeing? Becoming?

Don't question me. Yes! I am your lord, your god! All will tremble before me! All must be punished for their crimes! They know nothing good and right! They worship nothing but their sin! You three are but animals who glorify your money and your violence, worship your drugs and your sexual perversion! Come to me now! I call you into my eternal fire!

The energy of pure thought bored into them. It happened without Wilkins giving it any thought, any effort. They moved, slowly, woodenly, without sound, with nothing but confusion and terror pumping in their hearts. A trace of tears came to Purple Headrag's eyes.

Wilkins heard them beg for their lives, their thoughts ripped and jumping.

They knew they were going to die. If nothing else, Wilkins decided—and told them through thought—he had at least brought life to them where there had been no life. *Enjoy an emotion, a feeling of being alive before I kill you.*

His other voice rolled with proud laughter, telling them, *See how the dogs grovel. I will make you choke on your own vomit.*

He branded the image of what he was going to do to them in their minds. He felt them squirm inside, recoiling in terror.

Their minds kept screaming, cursing, begging as the power forced Purple Headrag to his knees. Rage burned in the eyes of Baseball Cap, his lips contorted to a snarl as he staggered up to the one with the green bandanna, who knelt, then opened his mouth, accepted the barrel of his homeboy's gun in his mouth.

Wilkins put laughter in their minds, drowning out the seething terror he heard. *See how he sucks it! He always thought he was a man but now he's a woman! Squeeze the trigger! Do it, now!*

A muffled crack. The back of the banger's head erupted in a tuft of wet meat. He toppled in front of Purple Headrag, his blood spraying his friend's face.

Kill yourself! Put the gun in your mouth!

He felt Baseball Cap fight it, but the banger slid the gun into his mouth.

Good-bye, Wilkins said in his mind.

The banger blew his brains out, abruptly silencing the raging curses in his mind.

Now the second body crunched, twitched. Twin pools of dark scarlet spread around the knees of Purple Headrag.

Wilkins loomed over the last banger, smiled.

That knife you would have used on me, I want you to place it against the side of your neck.

He heard the cursing, felt the defiance, the wall of hatred.

Wilkins made him place the edge of the blade against his jugular, against the sweating and pulsing flesh.

Cut your throat from ear to ear, deep and hard, with

every bit of strength you possess. Don't fight it. Make it clean and quick for yourself or I can make it worse, far worse.

Somehow the banger managed to cry out, but the scream ended abruptly as Wilkins forced him to slice his neck open. The blade cut deep, hard, tearing open a spurting gouge, the banger's eyes screaming in silent rage and terror. Thick fingers of crimson jetted from that gaping second mouth. Wilkins stepped back as blood flew through the air. He heard the banger screaming in their entwined thoughts, in a swirling vacuum of vanishing rage and hate; then the voice slowly faded. Then there was no voice, and even the cold darkness inside the banger vanished as he toppled facedown in the river of his own blood.

For a long moment, Mike Wilkins stood over them, seeing but not seeing the blood, the vacant, bulging whites of their eyes. For some reason, the night looked darker than ever, left him feeling shrouded in an icy cold rush of wind. He trembled, realizing what he had done, a man coming to from the murky haze of a bad dream. But it was no dream.

At least now he didn't feel the urge to vomit as he had with the pimp. He sucked in a deep breath to steady himself, searched for the light inside, but couldn't find it. Instead, his face suddenly felt hot, his brain simmering with heat. Feverish, he tasted the sweat on his lips, his mouth dry but sticky. Then, slowly, the heat faded from his head, leaving a blessed coolness that washed over him. He wondered about the fire in his brain, the sudden rush of fever, but it had cooled as quickly as it had come burning through him. Strange. He didn't think about it anymore.

Then he felt the warm spread of the light through

his limbs. It was still there. The power. Good.

He felt stronger than before, a surge of new heat in his blood.

Without another look at the carnage, he walked past the bodies, stepping around the pooling blood. There was something else he needed to do right away.

For at least a full hour after his "cleansing of the city," Mike Wilkins toyed with several images of what he was going to do, what he must do. No matter what he decided, it would only mark a beginning.

Either way he was going home.

First, he decided to send a message back to Glendale, a mere warning. It would have to be subtle enough to sound silent alarms, but nothing that would have them circle the wagons, leaping at every shadow. Oh, what to do? Why not have a little fun? After all, he was in control, the world was his. Souls to save. Wrongs to right.

He came to the door of the suite, summoned the power, and worked the locks. A click, a tumble, the soft rattle of a chain.

It had been easy to get this far into the four-star hotel. The bellhop and the desk clerk had been probed and their memory of him erased. From the desk clerk he had gotten what he wanted. Any strangers he encountered in the lobby or on the elevator he likewise wiped even a memory of his being there from their minds.

He hesitated in the doorway for a moment. Again, something was happening to him, inside the light. He felt hunger, but it wasn't a physical craving for food. He was thirsty, but it wasn't for drink, and even—no, especially—the churning compulsion for alcohol was no longer there. No, it was something else, something in his soul that demanded filling. But what? What did he hear in the back of his mind? There. It was a voice, soft and beckoning. It was saying, *Feed me. Use me or lose me. We need one another. We can never exist apart, ever again.*

Yes. He believed that. He had been given a profound gift, blessed by divine intervention. He was superhuman.

Better yet, he had found that which he had sought all of his life. Power. Control.

Time to take charge. He felt their energy beyond the marbled walls and floor of the foyer. In fact, he could see them, the two of them in his mind, the whole layout of the suite. Everything was swank, posh, glistening and clean. Only the best for Tom Bartkowski.

They were in the living room, tooting up, passing between them a tightly rolled hundred-dollar bill. He was in a silk robe, a glass of red wine at his fingertips, a pair of blue bikini briefs, appearing all relaxed, in charge, but his energy was twitching, jumping around. There. Anxiety. Thinking he should slow down, worried about getting an erection. Mike Wilkins couldn't suppress a smile. This was going to be very interesting. The only question unanswered, he knew, was how to go about exacting sweet revenge.

"Did you hear something?"

The woman. Paranoia, induced by the cocaine, sensations razor sharp, but her own energy distorted with twisted motives and perverse desire to even be there with a man she knew was married. Oh, my, she looked sweet. All blond, young and curvy, nubile and creamy in a white, skimpy one-piece, a bare breast sticking out, laughing at the world. A woman who always got what she wanted when she wanted. Even then scheming how much she could take, could do. Money and drugs, her only reasons for being alive.

"Somebody there?"

He rolled around the corner, stood before them, found them exactly as he had seen them in his mind. He smiled at Tom Bartkowski. "Yes, old fair-weather friend of mine, there is someone here to see you."

Mike Wilkins heard the laughter in his head, put his laughter in their minds. Then the shock, the guilt, the fear on their faces made him laugh out loud.

Bartkowski's lips quivered as he struggled to find his voice. "What . . . how did you get in? What do you want?"

"Who's that?" the woman cried.

Quiet.

They couldn't speak, grabbed at their throats. He heard, then sensed, the energy of their pure fear.

"It's been a lot of years, Tom. I hope you don't mind if I join the party. I do believe we've got an awful lot of catching up to do."

Chapter Six

He made them silent and frozen prisoners. Again, Mike Wilkins sensed the wall of fear around them, a living force of sizzling heat and crackling electricity, felt but not seen. He clearly heard the trapped and suffocated screaming from the voices in their heads. Felt their dark and convulsing energy reaching out to him. Glimpsed inside them what appeared to be a vision of frothy tentacles with sharp teeth, leaping from them and through his mind—then gone.

Desire. Want. Self. These were the only things he found in their souls. Once again, Wilkins instinctively knew—or was it just a part of some new sense?—what he had experienced. This sudden churning light, this lightning flash of sensation he was drawing to him, in a melding but soundless thrash, was the core, the crux, the sum total of each of their essential characters, that from which all desire, emotion, thought, and thus action sprang.

Ease off a little, then bore back into them, slow, easy.

Oh, but how they raged inside. He took them into his life force, pushed his own force of will into their beings. It was the pure energy of a spiritual intercourse, a whirlwind rushing through Wilkins, back and forth, this dark light swirling between the three of them. Wilkins sensed these two were alive but dead. There was nothing inside them—other than the fury of their needs, the perverse cravings that seethed without end in their hearts, even when they were faced with this unknown, terrifying force. From the swirl he heard the usual battery of questions, on and on, demanding answers, found their voices begging for freedom from this sudden nightmare of paralysis. This time he blocked it out after another fleeting probe.

Enough. He wanted peace from their thoughts, their relentless craving—if only for a few moments—before he went to work. He looked at their faces, avoiding their frozen stares of silent begging. Except for the quiet rasp of air through their flaring nostrils, Bartkowski and his mistress looked dead, like pale and waxen mannequins. The voice inside—was it his voice?—told him to proceed, to do as he pleased with them. Do what? So much he could do to them, these helpless, pathetic liars, cheats, these two adulterers, shameless thieves of all decency and morality. So much shame and humiliation, physical, mental, and sexual, he could heap on their souls, burn into their memories for the rest of their lives. So much, oh, so much here he could work with—and use. But to teach them a much-deserved lesson? Or for his own pleasure, to slake his thirst for vengeance?

Once again, a part of Wilkins questioned the power, demanding to know what was right and what was wrong, perhaps to draw it out in visually clear terms, but perhaps only to salve his nagging conscience. In the shadowy depths, beyond the light inside, he heard, *You have long since been ready to receive him; your soul has hungered all of your life for the knowledge, the wisdom and the light of his way.*

Now he has appeared, to you, for you, to aid in your struggle against all those who have wronged you. Take courage! The path will not be easy nor without pain. The truth—what is right is what is in your heart, my son, for you will never again have to be alone and without him.

He? Who was he? And why did some remote part of him—buried deeper each time he used the power—whisper in warning that he was acting against his own will?

No! Your will is your own.

The power—his power—needed action, had to be used, he sensed, in order to stay strong. A worm of fear had left behind a shadow of dread in Wilkins. Where would it all end? How strong would he become?

Feed me! I am here, I need you!

Mike Wilkins rubbed his face, forced away the lingering wave of mental anguish. He pulled a wing-back chair from the corner of the room, sat in front of the coffee table. What to do? Punishment was certain. Justice was his to mete out. Punishment, though, must fit the crime of the criminal, the sin of the sinner.

He glanced at the bottle of wine, the pile of white powder. He figured there was at least a half ounce of coke on the mirror, knew without knowing that Bartkowski had more stashed in the suite—in his suitcase, in fact.

Strange, how Wilkins found he had no craving for alcohol or drugs. In fact, he felt content just to leave it there, untouched, a relief that it meant nothing to him, nothing more than candy. Before, he knew he would have dived right into that mound, then sucked greedily from the bottle like there was no tomorrow.

No longer. Not even a twinge of the compulsion. Another miracle, another gift? Whatever it was, he was free from the maddening obsession to poison his body, mind, and soul with chemicals. If he could be free of that madness, then perhaps he had the power to heal, to set free others who suffered from that insanity? Certainly he could use the power inside to do good. He even toyed with the thought that he could become rich, a healer, an angel who could restore the insane, the addicted, the afflicted. Or what? That he could waltz right into the White House and declare himself president? What power on earth could stop him?

No. Absolutely not. Pursue his own course of justice, seek his own destiny, he was the one and the only in his eyes, in his mind. He was larger than the world, better than mere human desire. The world, with all its perversion and lust and greed and avarice and violence, with all of its stubborn, relentless pride and selfishness, he decided, did not deserve him, was unworthy of what he had, what he was and would be. It was enough to know he could take whatever he wanted, whenever he wanted. Right now, he had a personal and much more righteous mission. Some strength of his original grim resolve returned. He would make his own world. He was God.

And now he had killed. There was blood, though it was the guilty blood of evil men on his hands. Was it murder or was it divine retribution? With those three in the alley, he had felt all-powerful, justified in his actions, knowing what they intended to do to him. Or was he just trying to convince himself that what he had done was right? Still, shedding blood was something he had never even dared dream himself capable of doing before tonight, before finding the gold star. Yes, he had taken life willingly, even if it was wicked life with no hope of becoming good. Still . . . was it he who had killed, or was it the power? And, even if it was the power, why question it?

Right then, he couldn't be sure.

What he knew was that there was no turning back. The hardness, the coldness, was becoming stronger and stronger inside. Even if he wanted to—which he didn't—he would never take off the gold star with its black eye. It belonged to him forever.

He looked Bartkowski in the eye. He heard Bartkowski's mind, boiling with fear-edged questions. *What the hell's happening to me? Why can't I move? The coke, it's gotta be the coke, the little slut put something in it, the drink, she knows this asshole, they're going to rob me blind, they want money. I got the picture, you fucks, I cough it up or they run to the wife. Good God, to think I felt sorry for this guy. Shit, look at his eyes. He doesn't even look human, he's not human!*

The eyes? Wilkins glanced down at the glass-topped coffee table. Yes, the eyes. Staring back at him, white orbs, pupils obsidian, but they appeared to shine, to glow with the vague hint of a fiery light. Wilkins became a little afraid of what he saw, but his other voice told him it was all right, he would be fine, his eyes would return to normal soon.

Reassured, Wilkins smiled at Bartkowski. He had a sudden urge to torment this man. Laughter rolled inside his head, and he put his thoughts into Bartkowksi. *I assure you, I'm quite human, Tom, perhaps more human than ever. Please. The slut, as you called her, has nothing to do with anything. Don't ask questions that can't be answered, Tom. Not even I under-*

stand what I've become. What I have is power, the power of life and death. Watch what you think of me. You see, I can hear your thoughts. I can, well, I don't know how I can, but I can see your soul, and, Tom, I've gotta tell you, it's pretty damn ugly in there. Okay. Here we are. What I want from you is very simple. Right now, we're just a couple of guys, old high school chums. Give me your memory. It's important I know. There was too much, Tom, something happened so long ago, I can't explain it, but I know I was wronged somehow. I'm haunted, Tom, and you have to help me know.

Resistance. *Okay, Tom, I can hear some cursing in your mind. What was that? I'm a bastard? Okay, that's how it's going to be? Well, well . . . I wanted this to be fairly easy, but now you've gone and made me angry, Tom.* Wilkins put an image of a knife in Bartkowski's mind, brought it to visual life in the union of their thoughts. *That blade, it fills your mind, it's alive, it's very real to you. It cuts through your head, carving apart the inside of your brain, right down the middle of your skull. Feel it cut you. Feel it!*

It worked. The blade sliced along a dark tunnel of red and gray dripping tissue, convulsing folds of pulsing meat now suddenly running with pools of crimson. He heard Tom shriek in the silent walls of confined agony, the cursing, the roaring of unanswerable questions, all the ripped energy coming together, then dispersing just as suddenly. Pain, white-hot pain, more and more pain, so intense, Wilkins saw the flashes in Bartkowski's mind, flashes of lightning. It was so beautiful, this excruciating agony he inflicted on this man, this betrayer, this malicious backstabber. And Bartkowksi could only sit there, paralyzed, looking out at the world from behind those lightning flashes, as razor-sharp steel dug through his brain, grinding, cutting, surgery without blood, a lobotomy without physical consequence, body and mind to remain intact, unharmed, but changed forever. All was light and pain, all was beautiful in Bartkowski's exquisite misery.

Relax, Tommy. You don't mind if I call you Tommy?

Fuck you, Mike. I don't know what this is—

Wilkins sent the knife carving down the inside of Bartkowski's throat, and the man's thoughts abruptly turned to another bone-chilling scream. He heard Bartkowski whimper, silently, feverishly begging him to stop the pain, that he would give him anything, he could take the coke, do what he wanted with Toni.

Toni?

Yes, Toni!

Sweet name. And she does look pretty sweet. You know, I could take her right in front of you, and you couldn't do a thing to stop me. I could have her do things to you. The coldness rolled over Wilkins, telling him what he must do, that they needed a display of his power, that the power—his power—demanded their homage, their humiliation. He had a brief urge to fight it, but something was forcing him to give in to a sudden perverse desire. *Okay, Tommy, I'll show you just what I'm capable of. I hear the doubt in her mind; she thinks we set her up. Unbelievable, I mean, there's this complete lack of trust between the two of you lovebirds. Hey, relax, the night is young. Don't look so unhappy; this is supposed to be a party. Lighten up. Let the good times roll.*

Wilkins made her stand up. He found her mind was raging with all the whining, simpering anger of the self-indulgent. *I'll kill you creeps, you fucking bas-*

*tards, you put something in my drink, they used that
drug they're talking about on TV, slipping those pills—
whatever they're called—into some woman's drink.
You'll pay for this. I don't know what you've done to
me. Oh, please, oh, God, oh, my God—*

*Calm down, Toni. I know you can hear me. Please
don't ask questions. I'm in control here. Do as I want,
please, my dirty little thing. Don't fight it; you have no
choice. Now. You are my toy. Take off that little thing.
I want you naked. Oh, yes, that's right, dollbaby, slow.*

Did he say that to her in his thoughts? Was that
his voice? Did it matter?

She couldn't believe what was happening. She resisted, but Wilkins made her take off the skimpy one-
piece, one shaking arm at a time. Wilkins almost
found it comic somehow, the way someone moved
under his power. They didn't move smoothly or naturally. Instead they trembled, or twitched, or suc-
cumbed with shaky or darting motions. Maybe in
time the power would become strong enough to
make them move naturally.

I want you to watch this, Tommy. He forced Bartkowski to turn his head as she stood naked before
them. Then the same cold perversions he found in
them seemed to take control of Wilkins as he forced
Bartkowski to his knees. What voice was he using?
*Since you always believed me a sick pervert, Tommy,
I guess I'll show you just how sick I am.*

She fought him, but Wilkins forced a living image
in her mind of her using her mouth on him. There.
It came naturally next, another revelation, a new
power, new insight into his gift. Suddenly he found
he could put the same image of what she saw into
Bartkowski's head, make it live. Felt the man squirm
inside, curse the image, Wilkins. Laughter, some

willing, some of it rolling from some other part of him inside, and Wilkins felt the shame and outrage in her, shifted it into Bartkowksi, then felt the man's fury—and envy. Interesting. He could now put someone's thoughts into another's mind, bounce them back and forth. There. Something darting through Tom—what was that? *Come back. Caught it. Okay.*

Wilkins chuckled, sensing another revelation through his electric sense of Tom. Sensed, what, doubt in there, self-doubt? There it was, a feeling that he knew more and more about Bartkowski, even—especially—against the man's will. Then he knew all the guy's angst and anxiety.

The rage from Bartkowski came to Wilkins, rife with a hot deliciousness. *You sick little bastard. I always knew you were sick, Mike. They were right.*

They were wrong, Tommy. I'm only giving you what you want. I feel it, you foolish, selfish man, I know what makes you tick. Can't hide it, Tom. I can feel it as easily as I could feel your heart beat. So, you like to use, to shame women; you prey on weak women. You use money and drugs because you have no character, nothing of value to offer. It helps you feel superior when, in fact, you know you're a loser. You know what I see in your soul? I see nothing but a bully, a coward, a liar, a manipulator. This one here, she's nothing but another coke slut to you. Yeah. You can't stand the sight of her actually. You end up feeling dirty every time you sleep with her.

Toni's outrage struck Wilkins. *You asshole, is that what you think of me? Oh, believe me, I'll show you, the both of you! Oh, God, this isn't happening, I'm having a seizure, that's it!*

Silence! Wilkins used anger to drown out her silent rage, to stay focused and inside them. *Yes, Tom, I hear it in you, I hear you lying to her all the time, how you're going to leave your wife, how this one here's the only woman you want to spend the rest of your life with. The usual lies. My wife doesn't understand me, she doesn't give me enough love, attention, sex. Okay, people. It's showtime. I have to tell you, the both of you deserve something especially vile. Hey, it's only your nature. Accept it. Now. Let's enjoy.*

Concentrating on her natural lust, his hot anger building and building, Wilkins forced her body to heat up, made her go moist between the legs, felt her heart race, blood hot, like fire in her veins, within moments. But he wanted her shame, he craved her disgrace, his will assuring him it was the only way to cleanse this wicked creature of her impurities.

See what you and the others have made me, Tommy? How can I be to blame?

What am I doing? Toni's mind cried. *Why is this happening to me? I can't . . . I don't want to do this!*

Yes, but you do! matter of fact, tell us both how much you want to do this.

On a whim, Wilkins gave the woman back her voice. *This is no dream, people! This is real, this is your life!*

Moans, mixed with curses, tore from her mouth. Her knees trembled, her eyes glazed with desire. He made her turn around, forced her to smile down at Bartkowski, even with hatred burning in her eyes, then made her shake her ass. She fought it, but slowly gave in to the overwhelming power, felt her own will collapse in on itself. Wilkins forced her to play with herself, then felt her quickly, oh, too quickly reach orgasm. He kept the strong and living vision of the two of them locked, naked in grunting sexual union, in her mind, in Bartkowski's mind.

Wilkins toyed with several images, different positions, clearly saw him in her mind, taking her, branded the same visions in Bartkowski's mind. He forced the words out of her mouth, words he demanded from her. Her lips, wet with saliva, quivered as she sputtered, "Yes . . . oh, God, yes, yes. . . . M-m-mike . . . do it, deeper, I love . . . you . . . love you . . . so much. . . . Oh, you . . . bastard, don't . . . do this to me!"

Still another sensation, power feeding on more power, growing to bursting, feeling her body scream for orgasm.

She's coming, Tommy, she's coming with me. She's thinking only about me. See us there, together, naked, fucking away like that! She's coming, I can feel her, she'll never want to be with you again, Tommy. Hear her scream! She loves me! Listen, she even said she loves me!

Wilkins felt light-headed, intoxicated by what he was doing, unable to stop himself, to rein in the power, wanting but not wanting to stop it. Oh, he could feel her tingling down there, all hot and pulsing and . . . exploding. She cried out, a long, erratic wail of release, her insides seeming to implode. She shuddered against her will, on and on, crying out, climaxed again, cursing them in her mind. He was losing her. She wanted to collapse on the couch, and Wilkins felt the fire of her tears of shame welling up in her eyes. He forced her to stay standing. He blocked out her voice of fury and disgrace, her vile stream of vowed revenge.

He smiled. "Sorry about that, Tommy. I just wanted you to see just how far I can go, just what I'm capable of. See, thing is," he said, showing them his hands, palms out, "I don't need someone's leftovers today, I don't need to soil these hands with your used garbage. Hell, that was better than the real thing. Not only that, she couldn't fake it. You saw it, you felt it, I know you did."

What do you want?

Bartkowski, he sensed, wanted to fight, show defiance to save face. Wilkins bored his will into the man, found he had to fight, to focus intensely to bore past Bartkowski's burning wall of hatred. *Your pain and your suffering, the kind you caused me. It's real simple, but it's only the beginning, my friend. Relax, Tommy, be a man. What I did with the knife, it's only an imaginary knife, Tommy, it wasn't real. But I can cause you great pain. That's the point. Your will, your life, belong to me to do what I want with them. Are we clear on that much, old buddy? Oh, come on, Tommy, stop cursing me like that. Okay. Let me do something here again. How about down there in what you worship the most, what you're worried won't work on your slut because of all the coke in you.* He heard the scream intensify as he sent the blade carving through Bartkowski's groin, ripping, twisting from the inside out, feeling the man about to explode from mindless agony.

Wilkins pulled the pain back, let the knife vanish from Bartkowski's mind. The man sat, breathing hard, Wilkins feeling his heart beating out of control, throbbing dynamite in his chest.

Wilkins pierced his mind with a forced but soft wave of calm. *There. Relax, relax. No pain now. You're all right, Tommy. . . . Let's go back. Let's think about us as kids. I want to know, Tommy, I have to know the truth. Don't fight it, please.* It started to boil up, memories, images, flashing at first, then bonding, tight and alive. The inside of both their minds blazed with light, thoughts locked in those lightning flashes. Only now it came with no effort, no words of thought, just a flow of pure energy.

Young Tom with kids Wilkins knew by name, so alive in their minds he believed he could reach out and touch their faces. "Why do you hang around that goofball, Tom?" "I don't know, I guess . . . maybe I feel sorry for him." "You mean you don't like him?" "Well, yeah, I guess so, not really. How can I? He's a fruit." "Yeah, the Fruit, good name for him." They were laughing at him, as he sat in the cafeteria, eating by himself, every day. Older kids, friends of Tom's, bullying him as he wandered alone. The taunting, the name-calling, far beyond the natural cruelty children could display toward one another.

"So, you felt sorry for me, Tommy?" Wilkins said out loud. "No, hold on, I'm getting something else. What was that? Contempt? Oh, you . . . contempt, huh?"

We were just kids, stupid kids.

Keep going back, you're doing fine, Tommy. Think!

He drew forth more memory, and with it came the thoughts and emotions Bartkowski had experienced with each recollection.

There. Coming alive, boiling out of the mist. Stan Thompson. "You hear what your buddy, that little pervert, did to Christine?" "He's not my buddy, let's get that straight." "Whatever. Well, the Fruit molested her, she slapped him, Tom, or the guy might've raped her. She told me herself, hell, I thought she's been acting kinda weird lately."

That isn't what happened, Tommy, Wilkins injected into his thoughts. *We dated, one time. We sat alone, we talked, just a couple of shy kids, scared of even the thought of touching each other. Well, I asked for a kiss;*

I thought she wanted me to. I really liked her, I really wanted her to like me. She never slapped me, but she became afraid of something. She asked me not to kiss her. Obviously she sensed how much I wanted to. That was Christine, quiet, sensitive, something about her I felt drawn to. All right, I kissed her impulsively, I'll admit. But then I saw she became . . . terrified of something, someone else maybe, I was hoping not me, and she even told me it had nothing to do with me. I always knew she was troubled, but I didn't know why. She always seemed . . . lonely, but so . . . innocent. After that night, she said she just couldn't see me anymore. I never understood, but I left her alone. My heart was broken, Tommy, you know anything about how that feels? Hey, excuse me for being lonely. I don't know why Christine said that, but I sense in you a lie, that you knew your boy Stan was lying about that. He never talked to her. You know, don't you? I feel it, I feel the truth in there, Tommy. He was angry she would even think about breathing the same air I was. But . . . there's more you want to tell me, isn't there, Tommy? Come on. Don't fight it.

He searched again and saw Bartkowski denying the two of them were friends, even went along with the beating that Wilkins had suffered, agreeing with the others that maybe the little perv needed to be taught a lesson, but that Tom didn't want to be a part of it, not outright anyway. There he was, young Mike, going across the baseball field, alone, head down, another day of isolation, shuffling through the torment. There was mist shrouding the memory. Someone was watching him from a distance. Bartkowski. Then they came at him, a pack of wild animals, surrounding him. Soundless fists flying into his face, then the thud, thud, crack, crack, echoing over the field. He went down beneath their blows, shielding his face. They kept punching, kicking, cursing him.

Enough. Let it fade.

It was only one of many incidents, though, that demanded retribution. Oh, yes, he was going home. That senseless beating was something he had forced himself to forget—with good reason. For the worst part was after, Wilkins remembered, going home, bloody and ashamed, lying to his parents about the reason for the fight. He faced down hard silence from the family, his brother, as if he deserved what he got. Okay. It was making more sense to him. Bartkowski had washed his hands of the injustice. Doing nothing. Many back there were guilty, regardless. Sometimes the sin of omission was far worse. . . .

The power demanded more truth. Wilkins felt his anger boil, hotter and hotter. Bartkowski's mind screamed as Wilkins saw the fire racing through the man's mind. So, his anger could become fire, Wilkins thought, his emotions alone could cause suffering, even without conscious attack.

There. Some resistance. Something shadowy in the light. Bartkowski kept struggling to hide something; he could feel the man shifting thoughts, memories, as if a hand were attempting to lift a heavy stone inside his head.

Give it to me, Tommy. What is it you don't want me to see? You can't hide. He sent three knives now, tearing through him, brain to toe. More screaming; then Wilkins saw, heard more. "It looks like the little shit got what he deserved." "Good to know we got your blessing, Tom." Laughter, cruel and cold. But what was Bartkowski still hiding?

More memories started jumping around, one after another. Bartkowski's pretty blond wife, back in—

Glendale? Yes. She looked happy, content, smiling as she fed her two small children. Why was Bart kowski fighting to think about his wife and children? It made no sense, or did it? Wilkins already suspected how the man really felt about his sedate suburban life. "Daddy will be home soon." He felt the anger in Bartkowski, a restlessness, sensed his boredom with what Bartkowski saw as a dull, empty suburban routine, grinding drudgery of the same bills same responsibility, same sex with the same woman Saw another mistress going down on him, the man smiling in ecstasy. Sensed this man, full of nothing but selfish desire, burning with discontent with his loving, faithful wife, taking for granted that she would always be there, everything could stay just as it was. He was the man, the big breadwinner; without him they weren't shit. He fled Glendale every chance he could, using business as an excuse to cheat on his wife, had several drug connections in different cities, his party buddies.

"Why, Tom?" It was something Wilkins couldn't help but ask. Now it was his turn to feel pure but righteous contempt, and give it voice. "You have it all, you have a life I . . . I could only dream about You have a good woman who waits for you, who loves—God, who has nothing but love in her heart whose only interest, only desire, is to love her husband and her children." Contempt burned up into pure loathing for this man.

The flash again. This time Wilkins found something churning up from the darkness. He searched the dark recesses of Bartkowski's memory. A girl Running through some woods. Wilkins could feel the girl's terror, even through Bartkowski's memory.

"Wait. Stop running!" Tom. Angry. Enraged. The girl turned.

Wilkins felt his heart skip a beat. The flashes followed, one after another. The girl stumbling. Tom descending on her, demanding to know what was wrong. She fought, resisted, but he slapped her, then laughed as she pleaded with him to stop, but Tom was like a wild animal, cursing her. He pulled her pants down, forcefully but careful not to tear her clothes.

Wilkins felt an anger, a hate so intense that strange fire boiled up in his brain. He had to stop searching this nightmare, heeded some instinctive warning inside the voice. He broke Tom's stare, the man's eyes wide with terror, shame, guilt.

Wilkins felt his face, hot and sweaty. Suddenly tears broke from his eyes, his eyes feeling like two glowing coals in his heated skull. He wasn't sure if he was crying or his body was simply reacting naturally to the power, releasing all the pent-up fire of his emotions, trying to cool the invisible flames searing his face.

Wilkins croaked, "You raped her . . . you raped Christine. And you got away with it."

Chapter Seven

Roughly thirty minutes later, Mike Wilkins slumped beneath the icy spray from the shower nozzle, while the raging fever gradually cooled in his head. The revelation of Christine's rape and the energy he expended to torture that truth out of Bartkowksi had left him numb, exhausted.

And growing more sickened by—and of—human life.

Wilkins was tired, so damn tired, drained, as if some maelstrom, once raging inside, had sucked his life down a vortex, leaving behind a hollowed-out shell of vacant, cold darkness.

At that point he wasn't even sure he was capable of using his power for anything more than holding the man and his mistress at bay and in silence while he composed and cleansed himself. The power seemed to have retreated deep inside, beyond the now dim, flickering light he could see inside his head. Was it resting? Recharging? Waiting for him to summon it? If nothing else, he was reassured that the light was still inside him. Better still, he found he no longer had to see it to know it was there; rather he could feel that vague but slightly pulsing heat, around the sockets, behind his eyes, the rolling warmth spreading through his brain, the tingling of snapping electrical charges just beneath his skull like a buffer between bone and brain.

Shivering, he stepped out of the shower. They were both still kneeling on the white marble floor. Before forcing them into the large bathroom, afraid that he had been losing them as the fever had seared his brain, Wilkins had discovered something of the nature of the relationship between Bartkowski and his brother. But he decided that discussing that with Bartkowski could wait until the two of them were alone. And he had also probed the woman's mind again, found her burning with a fire for revenge. She could pose a problem. But the fury and shame inside her seemed to be cooling into something else, her thoughts slowing, then darting into other dark areas. Wilkins sensed she was seeking to manipulate the situation to some new advantage for herself. But that was just her nature. She was a skilled and crafty liar, an actress who could play any role to suit her whim.

Toweling himself off, he looked into her eyes, concentrated. He wasn't certain what he saw in her eyes as she looked him up and down. He wrapped the towel around him. Her gaze then wandered over the gold star.

Give me your tomorrow, Toni. I want to see what it is you intend to do once we leave here. He caught a flicker of something in her mind, a glimpse of her on a phone, but he couldn't hear her voice at first. Focus. In the mist, she was livid, screaming, threatening someone, her face flushed, spittle flying. Then he heard a faint voice from inside her mind snarl, *Your husband, let me tell you, honey, just what kind of man he is. . . . No, I'm sorry, man is the wrong word, what he is is a—*

Her voice vanished abruptly. The fever started to boil up in his brain again, the sudden fire cutting off the rest of the vision. He looked away from her. He needed to rest. Again, he began to fear the fever. It grew stronger with renewed fire each time he used the power. Why? What could he do? Maybe, if he searched for some way to control the fire, he could master it? There. *Come to me. Tell me something.*

It did. A distant whisper from the light told him he could do exactly that—control it—but it would take time and struggle and the willingness to endure pain.

He sought out, then heard his other voice. It whispered, *No gain, no good is achieved, my son, without personal sacrifice. No pleasure secured without its own pain. No reward without its price.*

Stop thinking, stop doubting, stop worrying, he told himself. It was time to get busy with the future.

Quickly he used the small scissors he'd found in Toni's purse. It took some time, but he finally cut enough of the beard off to use Bartkowski's razor on the scraggly remains. The whole time he avoided looking directly into his own eyes. Indeed, his eyes frightened him, and he now understood the fear they caused in Bartkowski. He brushed his long hair back used the man's cologne and deodorant, taking his time, enjoying the feel of clean skin, the masculine scent, the aroma of power.

Still, he couldn't look at his eyes, but felt compelled to know the new Mike Wilkins, his new appearance, the change, standing before him. Slowly he looked up into the mirror. His image was a stark contrast to the wretch in rags he had been, and his heart skipped a beat as he forced himself to look into his eyes. Oh, but what had he become? Why had the eyes changed to something . . . what? Nonhuman? Inhuman?

The eyes still had a dull white gleam to them, a faint radiance glowing forth from the iris. At least the pupils were back to normal, but that was all. When first stepping into the bathroom, he had recoiled at the sight of his eyes, had seen nothing but two black orbs, smoldering coals, they had seemed, or the black orbs of a reptile, or the lifeless but ever-searching black eyes of a white shark. It had been all he could do to choke down a cry of terror. Then the fever had cooled a little, and some of the iris began to return. Still, the eyes would attract attention to him. He was grateful for the dark sunglasses he had found in Bartkowski's suitcase. Without the shades, his eyes would make him look like a new species of animal, he knew, walking around in public, some man-creature, viewed as if it should be in a cage. Barred. Feeding time at the zoo. Look at the new animal, kids. Where did it come from? What is it?

He felt her then, heard her mind. He listened.

He almost looks handsome now, cleaned up and shaved—oh, God, be careful. He can hear you, Toni, damn you. But . . . it's those eyes of his. What's wrong . . . stop it, stop thinking. . . . But I can't help . . . that star on his chest. Stop it. But it's gold . . . I know gold when I see it. Is that where he . . . is that what gives him . . . Stop . . . stop thinking. I don't mean it, oh, please, forgive me, if you can hear me. . . .

Wilkins turned his head, smiled down at Toni. He told her, *Go on. I'm listening.*

Okay, I'm sorry . . . I didn't mean it, I'm just scared. But, look, hey, he can't hear me, and I wouldn't give a damn even if he could. I'm tired of his bullshit. The guy's not even that much in the sack, even though he sure makes you think he is all that. Okay, I say we ditch him, you and me, just us, we could be a team, we could have it all. I can make you happy, I'll do anything you want. I mean anything!

All of that stunning beauty, and he found her so repulsive he could have thrown up. She was one of the ugliest women he had ever met. *Really?* Wilkins glanced at Bartkowski, who didn't have a clue what was being passed between them, but the smoldering anger in his eyes told Wilkins the man suspected the worst. "Yup, Tommy, if you only knew. I think she's falling in love with me."

Screw him! Mike, is it Mike?

"Yes, Toni, the name is Mike."

Oh, please, don't talk out loud. What do you say? You and me, just split. I'll make you happy.

You want to know my power.

Of course, but that's only a part of it. I mean, I don't know what it is you have or how you can do it, but it's like a gift from . . . I don't where. God, maybe.

Is that what you think? If only you knew what I've heard in the minds of others, seen in their hearts, knew what I've done and what I'm capable of doing, knew the darkness in my own heart . . . you wouldn't be so quick to assume what I have is from God. The answer is no. Even a fleeting search of your soul has shown me that for us to be a team would be my poison. This is not about money, nor is it about getting the world.

He felt her anger boil up. *Okay. Have it your way. What are you going to do to me now? You can't leave me like this.*

Please. Quiet yourself. He and I are leaving. You'll be on your own. I'll restore your body. Take what you want out there, since it's what you came here for anyway. I doubt that you'll ever see him again.

Oh, bullshit, fella. Let me tell you—

Quiet! I already know what you're going to do.

Oh, do you now? I don't think you know what I'm going to do. . . . Okay, look, I'm sorry, it's not you I'm angry at, not really. But I've invested way too much time in this jerk just to walk away and get nothing out of it. You don't know me as well as you think you do. I'm gonna get what's coming to me, and I mean either his money or his ass, and maybe both.

"I told you, I already know that," he said, and glimpsed Bartkowski's curiosity turn to a hard mask of anger. "You do what you feel is necessary. I'm through with you." He sized up Bartkowski, figured they were about the same height, though he was considerably leaner than Bartkowski. "Okay, Tom, I'm going to find something of yours to wear. Then you quietly check out of this place. I'll return her voice and her body to her before we leave. I warn the both of you not to cause a problem for me. I think you understand just how serious this can get." Before Bartkowksi could even finish the question in his thoughts, Wilkins smiled and told him, "Why, we're going home."

Mike Wilkins sat in the backseat of the Taurus rental, on the passenger side. Bartkowksi drove, chain-smoking, staring ahead. Wilkins was content to stare at the blackness beyond them, already knowing what he was going to do, but wanting Bartkowski to sweat it out a while longer. It was dark, so very dark out there, Wilkins thought. The gently rolling pitch-black hills of the Amish countryside flanked the Pennsylvania Turnpike, looming sentinels, brooding and silent but intrusive somehow on the tight silence between him and his pawn. There was very little traffic at this hour as they headed for the Ohio border. They were in their own world, moving on into the night, toward destiny.

And justice.

They put the hotel behind them without a problem, left Toni in the suite. Bartkowski and his mistress didn't say a word to each other in parting, but Wilkins heard the hate, the angry thoughts, the loathing they felt for each other in their minds. Wilkins was tired, glad to be rid of the woman, a creature of pure greed, wicked to the point where there was nothing remotely feminine left in her soul. She was unimportant, he sensed, in his destiny, but she had proved a critical impetus.

Bartkowski's mind, however, was churning with anxiety, paranoia, and he *was* important to Wilkins. Wilkins needed to keep feeding on the man's fear to launch his justice. Since leaving the hotel Wilkins had listened to the man's thoughts, but found very little that surprised him.

Bartkowski was worried about what the woman was going to do, snubbed and abandoned after her shame, what was going to happen to him, to his world. Where they were going, what the plan was, how he was going to deal with his wife. What Toni and Wilkins had said to each other in their thoughts, damn them. They were talking about him, he was sure, figured Toni was ridiculing him, promising Wilkins a lifetime of sexual ecstasy if he would take her with him, show him the secret of his power. And then he was thinking about confessing his sins to his wife, but hoping after a furious scene she would be so humiliated and shamed over his betrayal that she would grant him a divorce. She could keep the kids, the house, she would get a nice settlement. Guy had it all figured out. Amazing, Wilkins thought, hearing clearly this whole sordid line of thinking, over and over, the man's self-obsession both maddening and revolting.

Wilkins felt his anger boil, the power tuning him up, back, alive but still demanding rest, calling to him that he desperately needed sleep.

He met Bartkowski's gaze in the rearview mirror, knowing without knowing that the man had been watching him for exactly one mile and three hundred and thirty-three feet, stealing glances at him every quarter mile, then down to every four hundred and sixteen feet. . . . Now what was this? Why were these numbers tumbling through his head? Instinctively he knew why, groping through the pulsing sensation coming awake inside, bringing to him the first faint wave of knowledge. Distance was being gauged by the power down to the foot, the inch. Why? Was it finding its range, seeking to increase its power? Would he soon be able to control others from a safe distance?

In time, in time. I have nothing but time. Be patient.

"Listen to me very carefully, Tom; this is what you're going to do. At some point, you'll pull over and drop me off. You will loan me two, no, let's say three hundred dollars, just to be on the safe side. I know, I know, I could see my way out of any expenses, but I don't want any more attention drawn to me than necessary. Thanks for the clothes, by the way. Nice black sports shirt. Like the white albatross emblem. These slacks feel like they're made of silk, the underwear, too. And these shoes? Only the best for you, Tom. A little tight, but the leather's so baby soft—"

"Cut the crap, Wilkins, get on with it."

Wilkins showed the man a patronizing smile. "All

right, if you insist. Here we are. You'll go back to Glendale. First order of business, you go and see my brother. You tell him you've seen me. You tell him whatever you want, I don't care. What you say to him really isn't that important. But after our experience he'll see in your eyes something to fear. Perhaps you'll even attempt to warn him of my power. Naturally he'll think you're crazy, or scamming him, something along those lines."

Bartkowski's gaze narrowed in the glass. "Since you've picked my mind and my memory apart, you should know your brother and I were never what I'd call friends."

"I know that. You played all the sports together, big heroes, sort of competitive rivals, a little chilly toward each other, but you guys were all caught up in that macho routine of teenage boys. You were the better athlete and I sense my brother sort of resented that, but he looked up to you. Maybe he was even afraid of you. He certainly never rushed to my defense even when his younger brother got the crap kicked out of him. . . . Anyway, we were never friends either, Tom, but that's the whole point of your charade. You patronized me back then. You lie, you deceive, you get what you want; then you move on. What was I to you? Some freak, some oddball? Some trophy of your compassion to hold up to your friends, test their friendship? Were you looking to show everyone what a great guy you were? I'm curious. I saw a lot of ugly things in your soul, but that doesn't mean I have all the answers."

"I'm not going to snivel for you, Wilkins."

"I wasn't asking you to, Tom."

"Okay. I never liked you. Yeah, I felt sorry for you. Okay, maybe I was curious about what made you tick. I thought you were different, smarter than the rest of us, maybe too different, too smart. But I never intended to befriend some guy who spent all his time alone in his own little world. People always talked about you, Wilkins. Freak. Fruit. Pervert. Weirdo. A lot of rumors about you. That you stole money at the bar where you used to work in Glendale, that you drank too much, stole money to support a drug habit. People always saw you, head up your ass, talking to yourself. What a lot of people were afraid of was that maybe you were a walking time bomb, set to blow. You know, a psycho like you see on the news, the guy who walks into a McDonald's with an automatic one day, goes nuts, kills a few dozen people. People whispered about you: you never had a girlfriend, never even dated. There was even a rumor that you attacked Cassandra Dooley and your family paid her family to keep it quiet."

Wilkins chuckled. "I remember, Tom. Just another score to settle."

"Is that what this is about? Revenge? For people you made nervous? That's what loners do, Wilkins, oddballs like you. It's not natural the way you were."

"And I suppose cheating on your wife and running around all over the country with a nose full of coke is?"

"What you did to Toni was sick. What you did ruined what her and I had. Don't you dare sit there and judge me, pal. What you don't know is a lot."

"I know enough. And what I did was set the both of you free of each other."

"Gee, thanks. Now I've gotta be looking over my shoulder, waiting for the doorbell to ring with Toni showing up, ready to do battle. Do you have any idea what could happen to me if she wants to make trouble for me?"

"You know, Tom, it's interesting. Usually anger makes just about anyone sincere, since they're venting what they really feel and think. Not you. You're still blind, even in anger. You're still thinking only about some way to save yourself. The whole time we've been riding here, you're all you've thought about. And even after what I know you did to Christine. Uh-huh. Let me tell you what I found. I found you raped her before I ever went out with her. What you did to her destroyed the chance of anything good and real and decent I might have found with her. I found that I was beaten by your buddies for something you did. You. It was you she was terrified of."

Bartkowski lapsed into a sullen silence. *Shit, why did he have to know that, why? I hadn't thought about it in years. Damn it all. She looked so good, all ripe and wet like a little piece of fruit, all itching to be picked and eaten. It wasn't my fault. Things got out of hand, it was her fault, she was a little—*

Bartkowski froze, his stare turning from the road, riveted on the rearview mirror. Fear was back in his eyes.

"She was a little what, Tom? Forget it. I can finish it for you. Does Christine still live in Glendale?"

"Yeah."

Wilkins nodded. "Okay, Tom, here's what you do. I'm giving you a choice, a chance you never gave me, and certainly never gave Christine. Two more items. Soon, very soon, your whole life's going to start to unravel. Your Toni is going to start making trouble for you. There are going to be phone calls, there'll be real ugliness under your roof, the kind you fear the most, the kind you never dreamed could ever happen. Again, don't ask me how I know, I just know. I can see the future, or enough of it to be able to prepare myself. Earlier you were thinking about the gold star on my chest, you were thinking that's the source of my power, that if you could somehow get it off me, I'd be powerless and you could stomp me into a bloody pulp. Am I right? Don't lie to me, Tom. Remember the knives?"

Bartkowski bared his teeth. "Can you actually blame me? My whole life's on the line, everything I've worked for, all that I've gotten in life, it's all about to be taken away from me."

"Who's to blame for that? Come on, Tom, you played. At least own up to your sins. At least do that much. You've done enough groveling for one day, don't you think?"

Bartkowski fired up a cigarette, took several deep drags, filling the interior with thick clouds. "What do you want from me?"

"Confession. Tell your wife about Toni, come clean with her. It's tough, I know, but it's the only way to cleanse yourself. She'll go berserk, we both know that, but that's only natural. At least give her the choice to stay or go."

Suspicious, Bartkowski asked, "And that's it? That's all?"

"No. You'll phone Christine, you won't go see her, not even go near her. Tell me—is she married?"

Bartkowski stared at Wilkins with renewed fear. "Yes."

"That's even better. Okay, here it is. Tell her you want to make restitution for what you did to her, that you're willing even to go to the police and pay for the rape."

Terror darkened Bartkowski's face, his shock so

sudden he nearly bit his cigarette in half. "No way, that would ruin me. No. I can't do that, I'll never do that!"

Calmly, Wilkins stared at Bartkowski's reflection in the murky shadows. "Like I said. I was giving you a choice, a way out, a way to make it right before it's too late. We all need redemption, Tom. The only way to get that is by taking action. Man commits a wrong against someone else, he puts his fate in that someone's hands. There's either forgiveness or there's vengeance. Right now, I'm hardly in the mood for the former."

"What is that? A threat? You're going to come after me, kill me with your mind or whatever it is that thing on your chest gives you? You want to see me ruined, disgraced for something that happened when we were just kids." Tears of outrage welled up in Bartkowski's bulging eyes. Suddenly he erupted, "Just stupid damned kids! Why? Why are you doing this to me? It doesn't make sense. You're going to ruin my life over something that happened twenty years ago?"

Wilkins braced himself for an attack. The light came roaring, rushing out as fear seized him. He sat there, watching Bartkowski shake with fury, then pound the steering wheel. Then the man started sobbing, cursing. For a full minute, Wilkins sat on edge, waiting for the man's outburst to die down.

"Pull yourself together, Tom. Watch the road."

"Why? Why?"

"Stop blubbering, Tom."

Bartkowski wiped the tears off his face, ground his cigarette out in the ashtray with a furious stab, then fired up another smoke. His expression was hard, his eyes cold as he pinned Wilkins in the mirror with his stare. "Okay, okay. I'll do it."

"Really? Tell me, Tom, why? I'm just a little skeptical."

"I said I'd do it, I'll do it."

"All of it?"

"You're asking a lot, damn you! Okay, but let me ... I can start with your brother. Give me a chance, all right? This is all so sudden ... all that's happened. ... You can see how scared I am."

"Surely."

"It'll take time to work my way up to ... my wife."

"And Christine?"

"Oh, God," he cried. "Look, help me with that. You can do it, you have the power."

"What are you asking me to do?"

Bartkowski worked nervously on his cigarette. His mind screamed for a drink, a snort, something. "You say you can see the future, then tell me, please, I'm begging you, for the love of God, tell me what's going to happen. If not for me, then do it for my wife, my kids. Please, Mike, tell me what's going to happen to me."

Wilkins locked the man's feverish stare in the rearview. Finally he shook his head softly. "Nothing will ever satisfy you. Not even that."

Wilkins shut his eyes, turned a deaf ear to the man's cursing, and let himself drift off into sleep.

Sleep came, swift and deep, but even sleep became a new and somewhat frightening experience for Mike Wilkins. He was asleep but he could hear the world around him just as if he were wide awake, right there, though the sound reached his ears as if from a great distance. He still heard the engine's finely tuned purr, but there was a rush striking his senses as the tires rolled over the asphalt. He heard Bartkowksi's mind, again at a distance, raging with fear, searching for alternatives, felt the man's hatred, a wall of fire, trying to reach out for the object of his misery but frozen by his own impotent fury.

Down, down he went. Mike Wilkins tumbled in sleep, deep inside himself, saw some shadowy part of his newly clean-shaven face shrouded in the light. Suddenly, he felt strangely disembodied, on the verge of floating out of the car.

He wanted only to sleep but the power was coming alive, waking up with renewed angry strength. Against his will, Wilkins was filled with righteous fury. Visions of the past, of his brother's face flashed, then held, strong and living in his mind. He had a sudden and uncontrollable urge to hurt his brother, to strangle him with his bare hands. John's crime, his sin, had been that he had done nothing—nothing to help, not even to be there when he had needed someone the most. His brother. Too many of them had been merely critical silent observers, their silence only serving to fan the fires of torment.

Something then felt as if it was taking him away from himself, transporting, carrying him across some vast black gorge of time and space where neither one of those concepts mattered.

He was floating, up and away, his anger lifting him out of the light.

Chapter Eight

John Wilkins wanted to wake up, his desperation mounting the more he wanted to snap out of it, but he couldn't get his body to respond. He couldn't open his eyes, couldn't move his arms, his legs. With an instinctive dread, he knew he wasn't asleep, that he was actually wide awake, his brain active, his sense of the world beyond him working at full capacity—but he was trapped inside his mind, which was shrieking for his body to pull itself out of the darkness.

Good God, if he could just open his eyes! Over and over, he heard the scream of terror echo through his mind, louder and louder, as he realized what was happening to him. He couldn't breathe. He knew with an utter crystal clarity he didn't understand that he wasn't just dreaming—he was suffocating.

It was actually happening.

Oh, God, he heard his mind cry. *Why can't I wake up? I can't breathe! I'm dying!*

He wanted desperately to cry out for Paula. He could feel her, sleeping next to him, heard her soft breathing, felt the warmth of her skin. She was right there, so close. If only he could nudge her. Why didn't she see, sense something was wrong? It was useless; the paralysis only worsened the more he struggled. His wife might as well have been a million miles away.

Icy terror clawed his chest as his throat felt squeezed by a giant hand, the anger in its crushing grip cutting off all air. He felt his lungs fill to bursting, tasted the acid bile squirting up into his throat. His mind shrieked as the air stayed locked in his chest, a relentless fire, eating him with a living, ravaging force. Some rage, not his own, was invading his body. Something—no, someone—was burrowing inside him, a familiar presence, it seemed. Who? Someone he should know, yes, but it was only a shadow in his mind. There. In the distance, down the dark tunnel he found a floating body without a face. The invader.

John Wilkins told himself to move, thrash around, do something, anything to break free of this force coming into his body. What was happening? He felt his mind, his thoughts, his memory being probed by this silent shadow, cold and hard, digging deeper into him. Anger flared in him. He was not going to die without a struggle. And he knew what was happening, wanted to deny it, but he couldn't. This force was raping his mind and his very soul. It was hungry for knowledge, silently demanding something that it believed belonged to it.

Wake me up! Paula, can't you see, I can't breathe, I can't wake up! I can't get out of this!

Then he saw something rolling up in his mind, freezing the scream in his head. At first, the visions seemed ordinary enough in the dreamlike haze of deep sleep; then he wasn't so sure. Sight and sound came boiling up out of the dark, forcing him to remember things he had long since forgotten.

Long since forced himself to forget.

He heard voices from the distant past, angry and frightened voices growling out of the murky shadows, which cleared up quickly as he saw and heard his father storming around the living room of the farmhouse.

"Thank God, we've got at least two normal kids, Norma. Two outta three. I guess they ain't bad odds."

"Don't say that, Dad, you don't mean it. You don't need another whiskey, Dad, you just get mean. All angry and ugly."

From the darkness a chilling cry erupted, piercing the whole house in its hideous wail, shaking the walls with an almost animal plaintive howl for help. It was Mike, screaming awake from a nightmare, gripped by another fever. His brother was crying out that he couldn't see. "Where is everybody? Where are you? Mom? Dad? Mary? John, is that you? Help me! I'm upside down, the room is upside down. I'm falling!"

"Why does he keep crying like that?"

"It's the fever, Big John. He's burning up again."

"Do something, damn it! Doc Milligan says dunk him in the tub with rubbing alcohol. By God, do something, Norma. Anything to keep him from screaming like that!"

The image faded quickly, then burned into another scene. It was a living cinema in his mind. He saw Mike, screaming and thrashing in the bathtub, his face flushed, red as blood, sweat pouring off his chin, eyes wild from fear and fever.

"Be still, boy! You wanna burn up from fever and die? Let your mother help you!"

He saw their mother, pushing Mike into the water. The sharp tang of rubbing alcohol bit with invisible teeth in his nose, piercing so deep into his brain he became nauseous, light-headed. My God, he thought, what was happening, what was he seeing? The memory was so alive, he seemed to be right there.

"A hundred and five. Dear God, Big John, I'm going to lose my boy!"

"No. Hold him under, but not too long, Mom. Damn it, he'll drown. Just long enough get the fever down. Let him breathe."

Another vision.

"What in God's name is this garbage? Is this what you sit up here and do all day? This is pure filth. Is this what's in your mind? Is this what me and your mother raised?"

"No, Dad, don't do that. You don't understand, it isn't him, he doesn't know. He's just a kid. They're only pictures. He heard something the older boys talked about, that's all. There are other drawings, Dad. Look at them, Mike has talent, he's good."

The belt, coming down, lashing naked buttocks. Again and again. Mike screaming, "I didn't mean anything! I didn't mean to do it!"

"The Devil is in you, boy, and this is the only way to get him out of you!"

"No, Dad, it's the oldest Peterson boy. You don't know. He lured Mike in a bush over by the baseball field. I saw it, I walked in on it by accident. Mike doesn't even know I saw. He touched Mike, pulled his zipper down. He was showing Mike how to fool with himself. Mike screamed and ran. I beat Ritchie Peterson senseless, until he cried like a girl for me to stop. It's like you always say, there's a lot of bad things out there, a lot of evil in the world."

Suddenly John Wilkins felt the force of rage soften

inside, diluting itself, smoking out in all of its fury, as if it were appeased. As if it had seen something in him that now made it struggle to show mercy and compassion.

Then he saw something that, indeed, looked like a wisp of smoke curling around the visions, far down the dark tunnel of his mind. His throat felt gradual but blessed relief from the pressure on his windpipe. Then the smoke vanished, the vision evaporated. His swollen brain, his pounding heart, gripped him in another wave of pure terror. But the air slowly burned down his throat, giving him hope that he was being freed.

He felt the weight float off his chest, ease up on his eyes. The harsh rasp of his breathing filled his ears. He was coming back, he was being released, he could feel his body. He didn't want to but he opened his eyes. He stared into the darkness, gasping for air. He looked around the bedroom, feeling the same presence he'd felt inside. It was there in the dark, somewhere. John Wilkins didn't want to know what it was, but he feared he was in the presence of something unholy. He stifled the impulse to shake his wife awake. Who would believe him? He was just having a nightmare, right?

He heard her faint snores, felt her curl up on her side, away from him, so far away. He was so grateful she was there that he felt like weeping.

He heard a sound, like a soft rush of wind. He thought something was moving above him, going toward the window. He stared at the window shades. What was striking the shades? The light seemed unnatural, its rippling sheen unnerving him again. It seemed to be coming through the shade and out the window at the same time.

John Wilkins lay utterly still, afraid to move, feeling, knowing, something was in the room. His breathing slowly returned to normal. Cold sweat was running down his face, a chilly puddle forming on the pillow beneath his head. He rolled his eyes to the window. A shadowy semblance of reality clawed its way to his senses. He was awake, thank God. It was only the moonlight he'd seen striking the window.

Or was it?

John Wilkins listened to his wife's soft snores. Man and wife, alone again. Whatever had been there was now gone. And he knew something had been in the room, as real, as alive, as the visions of the forgotten past he'd just seen.

Rapidly, Mike Wilkins was tumbling back toward the light. From above he caught a glimpse of the Taurus; then he was inside the shadowy interior. Faster and even faster still, the light seemed to be sucking him back into his body. A voice, clearly his voice, called to him from the light as the falling sensation yielded to a slow drift.

Yes, you were right all along, you knew but you had made yourself forget. Yes, yes! You forgot about the fevers, the beatings, the alcohol baths that saved your life. Yes, yes, your enemies are numberless, and they surround you. They scheme and they plot and they seek to do you harm—and just for being alive, for being human, with more humanity inside you than they ever showed you. Oh, yes, they know not what they do. I understand that, now more than ever. But that can no longer be an excuse. Your righteous fury demands their humiliation, if not their blood. They all had their chance to be forgiven.

Wilkins gave praise to the power for sending him

this lightning bolt of startling revelation. Of course, the memory had always been there, but buried so deep beneath the shame and the guilt, beneath his shame and anger, that lying took on a life force of its own. To survive meant to deny—bottom line. Oh, what the human heart will hide from its eyes to justify its wrong. The genesis of his anger, the years of brooding, the isolation and the unshakable negative energy of feeling separate and apart from everyone and everything became clearer. And more, he sensed, was yet to be revealed. *Patience, patience.*

There was no doubt he had been there, had wanted to go there, inside the deep and, dark and, before now, unreachable fathoms of his brother's memory. The power was getting stronger by the minute. And the power, he sensed, now needed him as much as he needed it. They could never be separated from each other.

But something was happening. He opened his eyes, and a world of darkness cleared quickly. Bartkowski screamed but Mike Wilkins already knew he was going to scream before he did. Just like he knew the man's reaction to the sight of— His eyes were on fire, burning without burning. He could see the white glow stretching away in some shimmering halo in front of his face.

Bartkowksi slammed on the brakes. The car careened off the road, sliding wildly down the shoulder of the highway. Tire rubber grabbed asphalt with a deafening screech in Wilkins's ears, his new senses more electrified than ever.

Blubbering, Bartkowski shouldered his way through the door and ran.

Wilkins stayed calm, slid across the seat, curious but afraid. But he had to see, had to know.

And what he saw in the rearview mirror, staring back at him, made him freeze instantly. He was paralyzed with terror, but at the same time he felt a strange, cold arrogance. They shone in the shadows, the darkness shrouding his face giving a life of its own to the two blazing radiant white orbs gazing back.

Wilkins burst out the door. The shadow that was Bartkowski slid into the glare of the headlights. Wilkins searched the highway, found no vehicles in either direction, but he heard, loud and clear, the rumble of a tractor-trailer exactly two and a half miles east.

You have no legs!

Bartkowski cried out, collapsed in a boneless sprawl.

Full of the new arrogance seizing him, Wilkins strode toward the man. Bartkowski kept blubbering. He was like a human worm to Wilkins as he dragged himself off the shoulder of the road on his elbows, his legs dead and heavy baggage, scraping the ground.

"No! Leave me alone! Stay away from me!"

"Calm down, Tom. Stop whimpering now or I'll crush the life out of you. Do you hear?"

The man's whimpering died down, but not by much. He looked up and back at the two brilliant glowing orbs, searing apart the darkness. There was nothing in the dark but those two living balls of white fire.

Wilkins crouched over Bartkowski. The man lay utterly still, petrified.

"What are you, Mike, what in God's name are you?"

"It's time for you to leave, Tom. You're going back to Glendale, right?"

A shaky nod.

"To do as I said? Answer me, Tom. You don't do what I want, I will come and find you. If I have to do that, it won't go well for you. In fact, I'll force you to rip your own testicles off with your bare hand. Are we clear?"

"Okay. Of course. I . . . I'll do it."

"Do I need to find out if you're lying?"

"No, no. Please, just leave. I'll go back. . . . I'll do it."

"You're my messenger, right?"

"Your brother, yes, I'll go see him, right away. I swear I will."

"Right. Messenger before the message. Can you remember to tell him I'll be coming home? And very soon?"

"Yes, yes. Here," he said, digging into his pocket, pulling out a wad of bills. "You said you needed some money. Take it. You can have it all, just go!"

Wilkins didn't need to count the wad to know there was exactly five hundred and sixty-four dollars. He peeled off three hundred-dollar bills, shoved the rest back in Bartkowski's pocket. "I said three hundred, Tom." He showed the man a cold smile. "I've become a man of my word these days."

Wilkins stood and walked off the road. He pulled the sunglasses out of his pocket, slipped them on and gave Bartkowksi back his legs as he melted into the dark depths of the woods. Again without having to know or think about it, he knew he was just inside the Ohio border. He had slept for three hours and six minutes.

Behind him, he heard Bartkowski's labored

123

breathing, so loud, so close he could feel the hot breath in his ears. A thud as the car door slammed shut. A sensation of utter terror reached out to Wilkins, holding, lingering in the light even as the Taurus screeched off and disappeared down the highway.

Mike Wilkins smiled to himself as he vanished deeper into the woods. He was in control of his own destiny.

It was good to be alive, he decided, to have a future. It was such a wonderful thing, such bliss, such freedom to be protected by the light of reason.

Chapter Nine

"Paula . . . was it . . . did it feel cold this morning when you woke up? I . . . I'm not talking about air-conditioning cold. It felt unnaturally cold. Did it seem that way to you?"

She was scrambling eggs, frying bacon, standing with her back turned to him near the stove. Breakfast was their morning ritual before he went to work, man and wife beginning the day together. After last night, though, nothing looked, felt, seemed normal to him. Somehow his world was different, but how? He felt as if he should be drowning, only there was no water to drown in.

John Wilkins sipped his coffee, waiting for food he wasn't hungry for. Gradually, he noticed that his wife was unusually quiet, so still, in fact, that he looked at her to make sure she was even in the kitchen.

Slowly she turned, pinned her husband with a look filled with confusion, worry, and anger. God, he thought, how could he tell her what had happened to him the night before, that something unnatural but so real, so terrifying . . . He couldn't find the words to express what had happened. Instinctively he sensed that the experience had something to do with his brother. After all, things that had happened so long ago and that he had chosen to forget had come boiling out of his memory—alive with fury, calling, it seemed, for vengeance.

How—when—would he tell her about the letter, about his nagging fear that his brother was going to show up on their doorstep, and soon?

"John, I don't know what's troubling you, but I know it doesn't have anything to do with the Sam Watterson situation. I didn't say anything last night, but I smelled the alcohol on you. I suspect you didn't come home yesterday afternoon."

It was true. He had driven around the outskirts of Glendale before going to the restaurant, smoking, thinking near the ballpark.

"Paula . . . I'm going to ask you something. We've known each other for twenty-five years. In all that time if there's been trouble, I've kept it from you and dealt with it on my own."

"The way you keep mentioning past trouble, I get the feeling you're referring to your brother?"

"Yeah."

She grunted. "After all these years, after all the scenes with him . . . you still want to be compassionate."

"He's my brother, Paula."

"I understand that, I always have. But maybe I don't since I was an only child." She sighed. "Don't you remember, John, how it was? I watched from the sidelines, through all of it, but I kept my mouth shut, and I let you handle it. If your mood has something to do with him, I want you to remember how you took money and put him through those treatment centers. After all the money he borrowed from you and never paid back, and one promise after another that he was going to change. How he was so enraged that your parents left you their money, he looked insane enough to kill you with his bare hands. And I'll never forget that look of pure hate in his eyes. You don't think I never heard some of the rumors around this town about him, John? I'd like to think . . . I don't know, that I'm kind enough or whatever to not let gossip cloud my feelings toward someone else before I have all the facts." The eggs sizzling in the pan became a loud, unnerving sound in his ears in the hard silence. Her shoulders sagged. "Good God. Tell me how I already knew this had to do with your brother."

He caught the hint of a frown on her lips. She was wrestling against a sudden impulse to criticize, he knew, but they were both aware of all the pain and humiliation someone who was ill from addiction could create for everyone involved, all the wreckage and hurt that was left behind, most often for others to clean up. It was the most selfish kind of sickness John Wilkins could ever imagine. In his mind, a run-away problem drinker, out of control, beyond the mere foolishness of intoxication to the point where he was recklessly, even wantonly dangerous to himself and everyone around him, was not simply sick—he was a sinner. He caught himself, hearing a voice from the distant past, long since dead but no longer forgotten. *Sinner.* That was his father's voice, not his, or so he desperately wanted to believe.

"Paula, it's been years. It was never that simple a situation. I know you're unhappy, maybe with me for trying to help what you saw as a hopeless situation. I'm not trying to open old wounds."

"John, what's going on? You're holding something back."

"I'm not sure, I'm really not. Listen, I need to think

about something. But I need to ask you, I need to hear you say something right now. I'm asking you to trust me, not to ask questions." He looked her in the eye, held her stare. "Do you believe I'm a good man? Do you believe that I've always been there for you and the children, that I've done everything I can as a husband and a father?"

"John, I don't like this. You're starting to scare me."

"I'm sorry, Paula. Trust me when I tell you there's nothing wrong, at least . . . nothing I can put my finger on right now."

She seemed to think about something for many long moments, her stare locking into a haunted, wounded look. "John, I love you, I always have. Yes, you're a good man. You're kind, you're generous, you're gentle. You have always made me feel loved and appreciated. You are my best friend and my lover. You're a good father; I couldn't ask for a better man. I don't know why you need to hear what you already know, but there, I said it. Whatever it is you're going through . . . yes, I'll trust your judgment."

He smiled. "Thank you. I did need to hear that." He stood, went and kissed his wife, embraced her. He pulled back, smiled with what he hoped was reassurance even though he knew his wife was far from confident. "I need to get to work early."

There was fear in her eyes, a tremor in her voice. "John, don't go . . . not like this. I want to know what's disturbing you so much. Please, don't make me dig it out of you."

He kissed her on the cheek. "I won't do that. Just trust me, please. Look, I'll come to the restaurant for lunch. I just need to sort through this. I'm sorry . . . forgive me."

He could read the question in her eyes, but before she could say, "Forgive you for what?" he turned and left her standing there. The children were still asleep. The house was so quiet, so still . . . he had a sudden impulse to go upstairs and check on his children, make sure they were all right.

He would tell her later in the day, he decided, then show her the letter. He felt slightly ashamed for demanding a little more time to build up the courage to drop the bomb on her. God forgive me, he thought, so much wrong, so much more I should have done.

He was walking out the house, down the drive, head bent, when he heard one of the last two voices he needed to hear right then, call out, "Good morning, John. How are you this morning?"

He looked up, saw her jogging past. The sun was rising with the promise of another scorching day; her voice, sort of crooning, seemed to hang in the hot air. A bead of sweat popped out on his forehead, his heart skipping a beat. He wanted to curse Cassandra Dooley.

There she was again, showing up, in his face, oozing sexual allure. The black spandex hugged her tight body, flaunting the woman's curves, filling his eyes before he was aware of it happening. Lithe, smooth, and graceful as a cat, she seemed to slow her pace for his benefit, her smile insinuating, surely meant to inflame his discomfort. She waved to him. He felt his shoulders tighten with embarrassment and guilt. He knew the kitchen window overlooked the street. Damn her for looking at him that way. He knew his wife was watching him, worried over his mysterious departure, could feel her eyes taking in this scene. She wasn't prone to jealousy, he knew, but she'd mentioned the Dooley woman before, with the wary, guarded tone that preceded jealous anger. How she was single, twice divorced, a ton of money, too much time on her hands, a passing remark that the woman was trouble, she pitied her next victim. Victim. That was the word Paula had used.

"Morning," he mumbled.

She kept smiling that damnable smile, jogging on. She looked smug, like some great cat supremely confident in its ability to hunt down its prey. Wilkins became aware that he was still watching her, feeling her presence, that stab of guilty lust again. More and more, he was not feeling like himself. Something was happening, or about to happen, and he couldn't explain it, couldn't be sure of anything. Some long-sleeping instinct for self-preservation warned him that Cassandra Dooley was only a small part of that something.

Quickly he dropped into the car, fired up the engine. He was afraid to look back, but glanced in the side mirror as he pulled out. His wife's puzzled face was right in the mirror, etched in worry and confusion. The day was not starting well at all.

John Wilkins turned out of the drive, went in the opposite direction Cassandra Dooley had taken, even though the shortest route to work would be the other way.

Mike Wilkins heard the waitress coming, saw her in his mind, scuttling toward the bathroom. His heart grew heavier as something warned him the future would not be good, but he felt more and more unable to stop whatever was going to happen.

Silent Scream

He heard her mind, even though he didn't want to. His waitress was concerned, wondering what was going on with him, if he was sick, could she help, that she felt a certain obligation to fulfill her role for the ten-dollar tip he had left her, thus compelling her to show gratitude, which had not been his intent. She was reading far too much into a simple act of generosity. Perhaps he had just felt pity for her.

He had locked himself in the small bathroom of the diner. For twenty minutes he had stood, hunched over the sink. The power was there, but it was strangely quiet. He suspected many reasons for its distance inside him, but his questions were either met by silence or a vague restlessness in his gut.

After Bartkowski's terrified departure, Wilkins had slept in the woods for four hours and sixteen minutes. By the time he woke, the sun was up. From there, he had legged it to a diner he saw in his mind in the vicinity, just north of the interstate. He needed food, but didn't have the craving to gorge himself that would have seized him had he been the other Mike Wilkins. The gold star took all obsessions, all cravings from him, or at least took enough of the edge off his natural instincts to make him feel whole in his skin. It was a strange freedom.

Walking into the diner, shades on, he had heard right away the maddening swirl of thoughts from the early morning patrons. They all looked sleepy or sullen, sipping coffee, smoking cigarettes, eating food. But he fled from them after ordering his meal, breaking a hundred and paying the waitress. It had hit him with all the force of a devastating body blow. He needed peace from their thoughts, now taking this refuge from their minds, isolating himself from their insanity before it corrupted him.

131

For he was appalled by what he heard out there. Once again, all appeared innocent and quiet enough on the surface, but behind their masks many demons raged.

There was the trucker, sitting at the counter, his mind seething with warped pride and arrogance as he obsessively played over and over the drama of last night in his mind, when he had beaten a man half to death in a barroom brawl over a minor insult, somewhere outside Pittsburgh. He was thinking about the speed in his truck, maybe a few beers later to take off the edge. He had a woman waiting for him in Denver, another man's wife. He took pleasure in tasting what he saw as forbidden fruit.

There was his waitress, sizing up all patrons, weighing her service on her judgment of each customer's ability to tip. She hated her job, but she had two small children to feed. She was angry and resentful toward an alcoholic husband who refused to work. She wanted to leave this man but stayed because of the children, clinging to a fading hope that he would change, life would get better.

There was a young couple. The woman found Wilkins, this stranger she had never laid eyes on, interesting, but Wilkins was repulsed by her lust, sensed in her a need that would never know satisfaction. Thus she stirred up jealousy and anger in her boyfriend, who had viciously cursed Wilkins in his mind for just walking in the place and catching her glance. They were both hiding something from each other, but he found it too much work to discover their secrets. Both of their minds worked furiously with the distorted energy of the pathological liar.

There were others out there, too many others. Money concerns. Anxiety about work. Family resentiments, one mind after another conniving to make the other understand them, accept their way. On and on. All was madness in their relentless desire, their elusive chase of self, each person with an agenda of his or her own will.

And then there was the little redhead, sitting alone. It was she who had inflamed something in him he had not felt in years, had never believed himself capable of knowing. She struck him inside with a longing tenderness that was so alien to his life he became afraid. It was a feeling that bored out of his utter sense of aloneness, a numbness in his soul that had lived with him for so long that he no longer even thought about being with a woman, nor even remotely considered love, giving love or receiving it. It wasn't desire he felt for the redhead—not exactly—but it was a nagging stirring in his belly to know her, simply to talk to her, to have her only acknowledge his existence. A fleeting probe out there and he had caught some of her troubles. *No*, he told himself. *Leave it alone, it's none of your business. Do you feel sorry for her? You think you can help her? Yes, you want to help her, you want to do something good, you have the power, the chance, the responsibility to help the woman.*

After all, he knew she deserved saving. There was something genuine, quiet, decent inside of her, not even a fleeting pang for self. What he vaguely touched in her mind sparked hope inside an ever-suffocating, unfathomable darkness of his own.

Yes, the world was held together by a few good ones.

He had to know more about her. But how would he do it? How could he help her? If he let this opportunity slip away, he knew it would be wrong. Or would it?

Again, he stared into the mirror. At least his eyes had returned to almost normal. Passable, if a little unnerving, he decided. They were now an icy, penetrating blue, searching, weighing with the subdued but hot hunger of a predatory animal. He gazed deep into his own eyes, again trying to find answers that he sensed he would not find. He demanded to see his own future. He called on the power to know the source of the gold star, where it had come from, why he had been chosen, or was it just some freak coincidence he had stumbled over in it in the alley?

No answer. He sensed he wasn't meant to know the beginning and the end. He felt sleighted, toyed with, that the power had its own cruel agenda, and it was using him.

No! Do not be untrue to yourself.

He heard more of the distant and faint whisper, the voice his own, but powered by the other voice, he suspected. He heard that he must have faith or all would be lost before it even began.

A knock on the door, hearing her words before she even spoke them. "Mister? You awright in there?"

He noticed that his face was flushed, his eyes wet with a faint trace of tears. He turned on the water, washed his face. "Yes, ma'am, I'm fine, thank you. I'll be out in a moment. Please, everything is all right."

"Okay. But your food's getting cold. Want I should stick it in the microwave? Want I should get a recook? Be no problem."

He knew she wanted to do something kind for him, that perhaps it wasn't just the money, that maybe his perceptions of her motives were not entirely accurate.

"Yes, ma'am. That would be very kind. Just reheat it, that'll be good enough."

She left, but he felt her reluctance, her worry. He needed to get out of there. He was afraid to go back into the dining room. He already saw it in his mind. Or was it merely a wish? A desire to do something good and decent just for its own sake?

He already knew what he was going to do, saw the mist in his head, cleared by the light. The power had come back. The power commanded him to take charge of the moment, if that was what he wanted.

The opening came suddenly, naturally, or so he wanted to believe. He was settling onto his stool at the counter, his food already back and warmed up, when he glanced at the redhead. She put her coffee down, wouldn't meet his look, and he sensed in her that she only wished to be left alone, to piece her torn life together, to do what was right. He heard the trucker curse, all that simmering violence in the man's mind, not even a glimmer of a redeeming quality. The trucker needed to hate and to hurt just to feel alive. Mike Wilkins knew it was time to go.

Then she did what he already knew she was going to do. She was opening her purse, digging around, her anxiety reaching out to him with something that felt like sizzling electric currents. No, her money was not there. The drive from upstate New York had exhausted her, as had her fear that she might not work out her situation, that it was all beyond hope, repair. The money had fallen out of her purse, was on the floor of her '74 red Mustang, just beneath the seat.

Again, the trucker's hate-torn thoughts invaded his

concentration. *You lookin' at, asshole? You ain't man enough for that. Slap you off that stool for even thinking about her.*

With an effort of will, Wilkins blocked out the man's thoughts. He no longer needed to look someone directly in the eye to hear his mind. He heard without having to hear the redheaded woman's frustration. She was thinking about offering to wait tables for a while, or wash dishes to pay her bill, or maybe leave her driver's license—she had a watch, a gold bracelet she could leave behind. No matter what, she would square her bill. It was only seven dollars and thirty-two cents, not including a three-dollar tip she had planned to leave, but she believed it might bring her good luck to set the matter straight. She could call her sister and ask her to wire her some money. Wilkins didn't find a trace of self-pity or anger in her. She was resolved to do whatever was necessary to make the situation right.

Wilkins got off the stool. It was now or never. If he didn't do this, even though he fought it, he would never know the truth about himself that he was searching for. He found his short, blond waitress with the hatchet face and the sad but proud eyes of the long-suffering by the cashier stand. She watched him approach, smiled ruefully. *Now there's an all-right guy. But I wonder what's eating him?*

Wilkins handed her a ten. "Ma'am," he told her in a quiet voice, his anger rising as he heard the trucker's mind. "I'm paying the lady's check, the red-headed lady over there. Please, don't tell her it was me," he said, even though he already knew she would. It was simply her nature not to let kindness go unnoticed. Was he setting himself up?

He fled the diner. Outside he walked swiftly across

the lot, angling for the road that led to the interstate. There was something he had to do.

He focused on the trucker, pulling forth a mental image of the man's face. He didn't have to be there to see the trucker, to know what was going to happen next. His righteous anger seemed to work on its own, demanding the man's shame to piece itself together. He took the trucker's legs from him, but would release his paralysis in a few minutes.

He heard the cry of alarm from inside the diner, but his mind had put him right there, close enough to stand next to the man in the terrible reality of his mind's eye and smile coldly into his eyes. He felt the trucker's horror as it happened, his eyes rolling everywhere, mind screaming this was a dream, or he wished to God it was. The man was just frozen on his stool, all that evil bursting out of him, helpless in utter terror.

Wilkins let the scene of chaos inside the diner vanish from his mind.

Then his heart started pounding. He was afraid of what was coming, but felt unable to stop what he already knew was going to happen. He felt a fleeting anger toward his power. It seemed a stark contradiction that he could see someone else's future, even catch enough of a glimpse of his own immediate future but that was all. He couldn't see the end. It was as if he saw himself as an actor ignored by the other players, just offstage, there but somehow not there, actors grouping around him, haggling with each other to decide how the odd man out could fit into the play, talking in hushed voices, his fate in their power alone to determine.

Accept! Accept! Have faith!

He calmed his fears, did exactly what he heard in

his mind. He had walked a quarter mile north toward the interstate, when he heard the tires rolling over the asphalt, saw the red Mustang in his mind. He didn't want to turn, wanted to run, but he knew he had to face this, his own fears, accept the course of the only future he could not clearly, absolutely see. His own.

The window was rolled down as she pulled up, stopped beside him. He couldn't look at her. He had seen enough of her life to know he was right to be terrified for her, and for himself. Why was this going to happen?

Her voice was so gentle, her blue eyes so soft, so full of kindness, it flamed a longing in his heart, even though he already knew what he really wanted could never be.

He saw that she had walked out after the waitress had explained her bill had been paid. She had been afraid to inquire who had picked up her tab, worried that it was the trucker who had been ogling her since she came in. The waitress whispered that it was the quiet gentleman in the gray slacks, with the strangest eyes she had ever seen, who just left. "A real decent fella, hon, don't see many like him these days." She had been leaving under the gaze of the trucker just as he was thinking about following her outside and just before he had his problem. Talk about perfect timing, Wilkins thought.

"Mister . . . hello?"

Slowly he turned his head. "Yes, ma'am."

"I . . . uh, I just wanted to thank you. I don't have any money; I seem to have lost it. But I want to pay you back."

"It's okay. I don't want you to do that."

"Please. I insist."

"No."

She eased the car ahead a little, poised to drive off, then stopped. She waited until he pulled even with the window. "Listen . . . can I give you a lift somewhere? It's the least I can do."

He understood her natural reluctance to give a stranger a ride. She was even then weighing it in her mind. He knew she had seen enough bad men to know when she was looking at a good one, or at least one that was harmless enough.

"I'm going west," he told her, knowing she was driving to Chicago. A smile of heartfelt sorrow ghosted his lips. It had started.

Then he felt her relief instantly. She believed that the look she glimpsed told her he was genuinely no threat.

She reached over and opened the door.

Chapter Ten

John Wilkins felt a smoldering fire in his belly. Some ominous chain of events was being set in motion, leaving him angry and afraid every moment. Even worse, there was a swirl of paranoia inside him, pulling him down, deeper and deeper, into himself. Slowly a hardness was building, it seemed, one layer on top of the next, shoving the world back.

In the back of his mind he was beginning to believe he would soon have to defend himself against whatever was going to happen. The problem was that there were no visible enemies, no clear physical threat. Just these rumblings.

Striding into his office, he poured a cup of coffee, dumped enough sugar in it to further agitate the stirrings of subdued anger. What the hell was happening?

First the letter. Followed by a confrontation with Watterson, who was determined to get his way or else. Then the discomfiting encounter with the woman who had helped ruin his brother, inflaming in him a fleeting lust that left him wondering just how solid was his faithfulness to his wife.

Since the letter's arrival these events seemed on the surface to happen naturally, as any day could flow with its ups and downs, conflicts and rivalries, anxieties and joys. But the fear lingered, deepening last night with the perverse experience of the invader in his mind. Was that what had happened? How? What was the thing in his body last night? It seemed so absurd and could be brushed off as a nightmare, but it had happened. And he was still shaken by the experience. He knew it was real.

Then the day got worse.

"You and I need to have that talk now. Sir. A serious talk. No more of your games."

His heart jumping into his throat, John Wilkins looked up, shocked at first at the fiery anger in Sam Watterson's eyes. Silently Wilkins cursed as some of his coffee splashed on his shirt. Then something came over him as Watterson rolled into his office. This, Wilkins decided with a cold resolve he had not before believed himself capable of, was a moment of truth.

Beyond Watterson he saw some of his staff milling around the newsroom. Some of them shot anxious looks his way, the tension out there thick. So there he was, he thought, their leader, on his own, win or lose. In the back of his mind, Wilkins knew this had been coming on for weeks. He had procrastinated giving Watterson his answer, hoping the man would see reason. Because of his silence, the distractions of yesterday, he could be sure now that Watterson had judged him as weak, at best, a coward, at worst.

Squaring his shoulders, sucking in a long, slow breath, Wilkins smelled the booze on Watterson. The big, strapping blond was disheveled, sweating. There was violence simmering in the man. Wilkins knew this could get out of hand in a flash. However, if he didn't confront this situation head-on, he would lose the respect of his staff, and he would lose himself.

"I will not be avoided by you any longer," Watterson growled. "I will not have you run from me again."

Something savage but icy cold took hold of Wilkins. Gently he laid the cup on his desk. For some reason he noticed just how spartan his own office was. Besides the oak desk with its pictures of his wife and children, his computer terminal and fax, the office was bare. No hanging degrees, awards, or accolades. He had all of those at home, tucked away in the attic in a box. It struck him then, staring into Watterson's burning eyes that, indeed, John Wilkins was a man of substance, and not flash.

Wilkins stared straight ahead, knew all eyes were on him, but didn't meet any one stare as he walked past Watterson and quietly closed the door. Teletypes were clacking away in the newsroom. He heard his heartbeat. Then the heavy wall of impenetrable silence seemed to drown any noise out there, and in his office. Suddenly a phone rang in the newsroom, a sound that hit Wilkins's senses from what felt like a million miles away. Through his window he ran his gaze over his people, and they were his people right then, to be damn sure. He gave a fleeting thought to pulling the blinds, but he was going to do this his way, and everyone was going to see it. How it all fell, though, was up to Watterson. Slowly he walked and stood beside his desk. With a stony calm he found briefly amazing, he looked Watterson dead in the eye.

"Sam, I'm going to tell you as kindly as I possibly can to pull yourself together."

Watterson smirked, an ugly glint in his eyes. "What is that, some kind of threat?"

"Okay. It's a threat. Now, this is a warning. I'm

going to give you a chance you don't seem real inclined to give me. I want you to turn around, walk out, and quietly leave the building. I want you to take not only the rest of the day off and sober up, but I want you to take a week's leave of absence. After that, we will sit down and talk like gentlemen."

"Is that with pay?" Watterson snarled, his lips curling back.

"That's without pay."

"You honestly think you've got balls, talking to me that way."

"What I think, Sam, is that I'm using up every last bit of my patience and my self-control at this moment."

"You're unbelievable, Wilkins. Here we are, a chance to put some things to rest, and you want to go on the muscle with me."

"That isn't how I see it, and that's not how it is. Nor would you see it that way, if you gave yourself a chance to calm down. Meaning kindly do what I'm asking you to do."

"You know, you avoid giving me an answer about something that could change my entire career; then you go skirting around me in some chickenshit way—"

"You're about to cross a dangerous line, Sam."

Watterson bulled ahead, clenching a fist. "Kindly kiss my ass with your dangerous line. Before you so rudely interrupted me, I was saying you go and promise some little drunken hack—whose only claim to writing was a few porn novels, born, no doubt, from his own masturbatory fantasies—a position as a freelancer for the paper and you don't even have the decency, much less the courage, to give me a straight answer."

"Not that it would matter to you, now or later, but I made Mickey Tomlin no promises."

Watterson gave a bitter chuckle. "Giving out charity, that it? That's your problem, Wilkins—you're soft, you're weak, you've got a woman's heart in a man's body. Your generosity's a front to cover your lack of spine. You stand there, pretending to be a man, lying to yourself that you're in charge of something. Your life is so sweet, isn't it? But it's all been made for you, Wilkins, handed to you on a silver platter. The proverbial charmed life, and you keep struggling to justify it with charity. Yeah, I'm talking about Tomlin. So you give a handout here and there, thinking you're keeping yourself clean. Just like I heard you did for your fucked-up brother." He laughed. "You see, you don't know what tough times are, that's your whole problem; you don't know what it is to be a man in a man's world."

Wilkins clenched his jaw, felt the blood pressure soar into his eardrums, a relentless pulsing. "And drinking too much, bragging all over town about your sexual conquests and all the ass you've kicked all over the country, I suppose that's what being a man is all about?"

"Being a man is putting yourself through school. It's being whipped to a bloody pulp by an alcoholic, unemployed father whose oldest son had to go out and work two jobs to raise two brothers and two sisters. And, yeah, I've kicked a lot of ass. Far as I'm concerned I've earned my right to be proud. Just like I've earned the right from you to get an answer about what I want, about what I know is rightfully mine."

Wilkins nodded, his heart pounding with hot anger. Somehow he kept his voice level, with not even a hint of a tremor as he told Watterson, "All right, you want an answer, here it is. This is as brutally frank as it gets. You want the truth, hold on. You're a so-so newsman, but you have a long way to go. You're a so-so writer, but you're not that good. This pride you speak of keeps you from taking constructive criticism, which you see as a personal affront. I don't think you'll ever be any better. All you'll do is spew bile and venom in this editorial column you so crave. You hold the world around you in utter contempt. Life is taking for you; you inflict yourself on everyone around you. You want respect but you give none; you want honor but you show none. That I haven't fired you before is because I've taken pity on you, because, yes, I know your background. In short, I've given you every chance, albeit from a cautious distance, to change and make something of yourself. Shorter still, I feel some trace of compassion for you, I see a vague shadow of my 'fucked-up' brother in you. Again, not that it matters, but you don't know a damn thing about Michael Wilkins. For my money, since you crossed the line here, my brother is far more a man than you are right now."

Watterson's shaking went from his head down through his knees. The rage was building in his eyes, making his stare burn with pure hatred.

"I am not saying this to hurt you. I even begged that we do this another time when your head's clear of booze. Okay. Listen very carefully to me, and try to learn something. I've heard the talk, all the angry words you've directed toward me. I've become something of a laughingstock around here, but my pride is secure and I go on. I hear all the time how good you could be, the great American novel is in you, but you need to hone your talents here at the paper, blah, blah, blah. You want to be this great and revered talent, but you'll never be the Steinbeck or Fitzgerald of our time simply because you don't care enough about other people, since their thoughts, their feelings, their lives are insignificant and beneath you. Other people are just there to feed your ego."

"You bastard—"

"My answer, now and tomorrow and beyond that, is no. I cannot and will not let you have what you demand. It would hurt this paper, its reputation, and, I fear, seeing you as you are, it would destroy you."

It came without warning, but Wilkins knew he should have seen it coming. Watterson's fist felt as if it had all the force of a sledgehammer as Wilkins took it on the jaw. Stars exploded in his eyes, and he felt himself falling, legs rubbery. He landed hard on the floor, the wind driven from his lungs. He heard his grunt of pain, felt it, a sharp, lancing din in his ears. The world seemed to freeze, but only for the briefest of moments. He heard the almost animal-like growl of rage from a distance, but the sound cleared away the fog in his eyes. Instinctively he knew Watterson meant not only to beat him senseless, but to murder him.

And John Wilkins felt his own fury erupt, adrenaline sizzling away his fear and shock. He reacted, glimpsed Watterson, rolling for him, looming, lifting his foot to cave his face in. With speed and strength he never knew he had, Wilkins leaped up, seized the foot in his hands. Exploding to his full height, Wilkins flipped Watterson over, sent him reeling on his back.

But the fight was far from being knocked out of the man. Wilkins had a fleeting glimpse of the faces of shock and horror in the newsroom, his employees frozen spectators to this combat.

Watterson sprang to his feet. Again, Wilkins found himself powered by some rage and fear previously alien to him. His life was threatened, and he had to end this, quickly and decisively. Before Watterson could charge him, Wilkins sent an uppercut off the big blond's jaw with every ounce of strength he possessed. There was a sickening crack. Watterson's head snapped up and back, and he careened backward, then crashed through the office glass.

For a long, awful moment, Wilkins stood, paralyzed, appalled and terrified, seeing but not seeing, hearing but not hearing shattered glass breaking all over the floor. A spray of blood trailing Watterson through the window appeared to hang in the air, then spatter like soft falling raindrops to the floor. His first thought was, "God, no, did I kill him?"

The people beyond the window scrambled in his field of vision, rushing toward the office. Slowly Wilkins moved his legs. He was shaking badly, fighting to breathe. They were giving him the strangest looks. What was he seeing in their eyes? Fear?

Wilkins forced himself to look down at Watterson, silently, feverishly praying for the man to get up. Why wouldn't he move?

Wilkins thought for certain he was going to throw up.

Then he saw Watterson twitch, heard the man groan.

Chapter Eleven

As she drove them through the sprawling farm country of middle Ohio, Mike Wilkins told her he was going to Illinois to see his brother. Awkward silence kept lingering, as he heard her searching for several avenues to make conversation to pass time. The usual openings churned in her thoughts. *What kind of work do you do? Where does your brother live?* Yes, polite and simple, quiet and soft, but with too much distance between them in small talk for his liking.

Oh, I kill people with my mind, ma'am. And my brother lives in a paper-and-glass paradise that I'm going to turn into a vision of hell. Indeed, he felt a knifing pang of self-pity, then a flash of boiling anger, already knowing this short journey was going to end badly, that he would never be anything more than a stranger to her. First, though, he would become a demon from her worst nightmare.

Waiting for her to speak, he looked at the countryside, the sunshine blazing off the wheat-and cornfields, brilliant golden rays striking the granaries, glistening off the isolated white farmhouses. It took him back. It all looked too much like his home. He felt haunted, more alone than he had ever felt in all of his life, even though the darkest days and longest nights of walking the streets in rags seemed a thousand years behind him.

Finally, she showed him a tentative smile. "I'm sorry, we've been driving all this time, and I never introduced myself. I'm Mimi."

"Mike. Nice to meet you." He told her he appreciated the ride, but she could feel free to drop him off anytime, that he could find another way to get home.

He heard her decide that she would take him as far as she was going, that she could use the company, before she told him exactly that. He offered to pay his way, even give her some money, but she politely refused. This was a good woman, he thought. She didn't deserve what was going to happen, but she also had to be freed from the past or the future was going to destroy her in a way she would have never conceived. He felt more anger, then shame, already knowing what he was going to do. As the power grew stronger and colder inside, he found himself briefly wondering if he was making decisions entirely of his own will. With each passing hour it became stronger, and the light inside him burned brighter and hotter. He felt he was racing, faster and faster, toward a destiny that would not be of his choosing.

That once the destruction began it would be total and all-consuming.

"I feel like such a fool for losing my money like that. I don't know what I could've done with it. Oh, I guess my mind is on other things."

"No need to explain, Mimi." Then he made the decision on impulse to begin what he had to do for this woman. For what he had seen in her future back at the diner had terrified him. It was time for her to know his power, to make her understand that he could help her. He reached under the seat, picked up the crumpled wad of bills, showed her the money. She looked relieved, then curious.

"It's all there. Two hundred and forty-six dollars. It fell out of your purse back in the parking lot of the diner. No," he said as the thought jumped into her mind, "I didn't see it happen. And, yes, it happened simply because your thoughts are on what's going to happen at the end of this trip. You're afraid of your husband but you want to try to work it out, for the sake of your children."

He felt a ripple of fear in her.

"Who are you?"

"Mimi, it isn't important who I am," he told her. Again, he felt tormented over what he was about to do, felt the intense heat of the light burning hotter inside with each passing moment. She was so fair, so unassuming, so gracious, he wished there were another way. This was just the kind of woman he had been searching for all of his life. Kind and gentle, quiet and selfless. For a fleeting moment he felt heartsick, thought of Christine. Just like way back then, he now found himself faced with something good and decent that was never going to be. He had already seen her future, and he knew that he would never—could never—be a part of it other than what he was going to do to save her.

She was staring at him, confused, and he thought, *Don't be uncertain or afraid. I'm doing this for a reason and you have to trust me, Mimi Sanders. If it will help you, see me as some angel sent to save your life.* The fear reached her eyes as she looked at his mouth.

"What did you say? How did you know my full name?"

I didn't say it; I put it in your mind. No, don't pull over, keep driving. I'm going to help you with your husband; it's why I'm here. You're in a situation that terrifies you. You feel you've failed him somehow, but it isn't your fault, Mimi. You're a good woman; you've had more than your share of suffering to try to save something that can never be saved. He felt the fear rise in her, a cold and clawing tightness in her chest. She started to turn the wheel, but Wilkins made her keep driving.

"What are you doing to me? Why can't I move? Whatever you're doing . . . stop it!"

Her panic was the last reaction he wanted, but he had seen it coming. She didn't understand, but how could she? Again, he saw the flashes of her tomorrow, fragmented images in the mist, but he glimpsed enough to know he must do what was necessary to save her and her children. The power turned colder still, urging him on, relentless in its sudden desperation to seize total control of the moment. He was going to help her whether she wanted it or not. Without him, he knew she would self-destruct.

"Please don't fight it. Listen to me, Mimi, please. I know all about you," he said, feeling his eyeballs heat up, afraid that she would see the change in his eyes even with the dark sunglasses on and start screaming. "You left your husband six months ago. You're living in a small town in upper New York. You and your two children are living with your sister." He burrowed deeper into her memory, saw her husband. He was a big, muscular man with long dark hair and icy blue eyes. In her memory he saw him drunk, livid with rage. The man hit her, staggering around, screaming obscenities. "He lost his business . . . a construction business. He started drinking heavily, beating you, blaming you and the children for his hardship, that you married too young, had children too early. You're going to see him to try to work it out. You'll succeed, at first, you and he and the children reunited, happy, but for only a little while." Another flash, the man having to go find a job, fearing he would never again be an independent contractor, hearing and sensing in the mist that the man believed he was too good, too proud to have to work for someone else. Drinking more heavily, more beatings, far worse. His heart heavy with grief, Wilkins looked at her. He clearly felt her body paralyzed with terror, but sensed, too, that she instinctively knew something beyond her control and understanding was happening and she was powerless to stop it. She was going to go along with whatever he had planned, thinking she would get out of this, whatever it was, and be returned safely to her children.

You will be returned, unharmed, to your children. I swear to you on my own life no harm will come to you.

Then he caught the brilliant split-second flash he'd seen before. It was the gun in her husband's hand. Three shots, smoke and flame seeming to split the vision in his mind apart. Then there were three dead bodies, Mimi and her children, all shot in the head, vacant eyes staring through the mist, directly at him, Wilkins thought, as if the dead of tomorrow were imploring his help. Then he saw the gun slowly going up, into the husband's mouth. Abruptly, though, the image vanished.

Wilkins slumped back on the seat, his face feeling hot. That was the part that infuriated Wilkins; he could only see so far into tomorrow, was given just enough knowledge to act on, to change destiny.

It was enough. He knew he was going to have to kill this man to save her life, the lives of her children.

That he was going to have to change her destiny forever.

It would easy enough to arrange a meeting with the husband, take his phone number from her mind. Find an isolated area where they could meet. Keep her frozen in some catatonic state. Then erase her memory of him, erase his involvement in whatever was going to happen from her mind. But after? She would be grief-stricken, of course, but her life would go on.

But Mike Wilkins knew the experience would somehow scar him forever.

After all, he was planning murder.

Word of the incident had spread through Glendale like wildfire. Wishing he could disappear until the storm died down, John Wilkins had gone in through the back door of the restaurant. He felt blessed relief at being alone with his wife in the back office, but the feeling was fleeting. Anxiety quickly knotted his stomach. His decision was made. It was time to show her the letter.

He sat in a chair in front of her desk as she went to the wet bar, put some ice cubes in a towel. She was quiet in a strange, stony way, glancing at him several times with concern.

He had called her right after Police Chief Paul Keller had arrived at the scene, on the tail of the paramedics who had wheeled Watterson out of the newsroom on a stretcher, the man's head and neck in a brace. After Keller had interviewed him, then took statements from all the witnesses, Wilkins had decided to spend the entire day at the paper. He stayed at the paper with grim resolve to carry on with the day. Damage control. A conference with his employees, apologizing to them for what had happened, something of a quiet pep talk, reassuring them all everything was fine. Cleaning up the wreckage, getting back to work to churn out tomorrow's edition. Waiting then, and calling the hospital to check on Watterson, relieved to find out the man merely had a mild concussion but nothing that a few days' rest wouldn't heal. A call from Paula. He assured her everything was under control, and asked her to wait for him at the restaurant. They needed to talk. After hanging up, he regretted using those four ominous words.

The day was now almost over, but he feared the worst had not even begun. He took the towel from her, put it on his jaw. There was a bruise, a swollen lump on the side of his jaw, but nothing was broken, no teeth even loose. Still, his head pounded, and there was a ringing in his ears that was now only beginning to fade.

"Babe, will you fix me a drink, please?" He watched her go back to the wet bar, pour a stiff whiskey. He was searching for the right words. He wanted desperately to comfort her, reassure her that everything was going to be all right. Her expression seemed grim, distant. She was looking at him, he thought, sort of in the same way the others had at the paper. He was even wondering just who he was right then. Who was this mild-mannered, quiet man who had gone berserk in a flash of violence? Even Keller, a tough, seasoned cop who had been the acting police chief for six years, after retiring as a Chicago homicide detective, had stared at him as if he were looking at another man, one he didn't know at all.

And John Wilkins couldn't deny what he knew. His world had changed.

Taking the whiskey from his wife, he took a long, slow swallow. When the liquor started to calm his nerves, he told Paula exactly what had happened. She listened calmly, then asked, "Are you pressing charges against him?"

"No. I don't want this thing to taint me, or the rest of us, any more than it already has. In time it'll blow over. I just want to forget about it. It'll be enough that I fire the man." He heaved a breath. "I'm just relieved he only has a concussion. Police Chief Keller told me he was amazed that a man Watterson's size, the way he hit me and from the statements he took from everybody there . . . well, he was astounded that neither one of us was seriously injured, or worse. The way Keller told it, I almost got the impression he figured Watterson was long overdue for something like that. Man even looked a little . . . happy." Wilkins grimaced at the memory. That was what he had seen. There was a new respect for him in Keller's eyes, and in the stares of his coworkers. "Anyway, that hardly makes me feel better." He paused, wincing as the pain knifed through his jaw. "It was as if the whole thing . . . I was there, but it was as if it was happening to someone else. I've never done anything like that, Paula. I almost . . . feel ashamed."

"It happened; he attacked *you*, John. You don't have anything to be ashamed of. Listen, we'll have dinner at home tonight, all of us. We'll all talk about it, if you want to."

He wondered how his children would react to the news, worried that they had probably already heard.

"Do the kids know?"

"No, I don't think so. At least they haven't heard about it from me. I have to assume that if they had heard they would've called or come here."

He paused, sipped his drink. "Yeah, what you said, I'd like for all of us to have a quiet dinner at home. We need that now. I . . . can't explain, but I feel we really need to be together as a family."

She came over, gently removed the towel, looked his injury over. "I think you should see a doctor."

"They looked me over at the paper. Nothing too badly damaged. Just some bruising." He dredged up the courage, felt his expression harden with grim resolve. Slowly he took the letter out of his pocket. He noticed his hand was suddenly trembling as he looked deeply into his wife's eyes, handed her the letter. "I want you to read this, Paula."

One hour and three minutes ago and counting, Mike Wilkins had called the man, arranged the meeting. He knew it would take at least twice that long for her husband to arrive, but time alone with Mimi Sanders was what he wanted. After all, he knew it would be the last time he would ever see her. Worse, she would not even remember him; it would be as if he had never existed.

His name was Burt Sanders, and he had sounded every bit as cruel and vicious over the phone as Wilkins had expected, the man barking all kinds of demands to know who he was, where was his wife, what the hell was going on. Wilkins kept it simple, told him exactly where he was, parted with a grim "We need to talk."

They sat in her car on a little dirt side road, just beyond a large rest area off I-57. He watched the sun going down as he withdrew deep into himself. He listened to the swish of traffic racing past them on the interstate, the thunder of a tractor-trailer. He had selected a shadowy pocket, away from the hubbub of the rest area, near a stretch of woods. Travelers were going in and out of the diner, or refueling near the rows of gas pumps before rolling on their way. It all looked normal enough, but Wilkins knew it was going to turn ugly. When it was done, he would have to fade, quickly and quietly, into the woods, walk a good distance down the interstate. Getting a ride wouldn't be a problem. And Glendale was no more than an hour's drive south.

He was almost home.

He turned, stared at Mimi, his heart sick with grief and longing. Gently, softly, he spoke into her mind, told her she was so beautiful, that he would die before he harmed her, let anyone hurt her. To see what he had done to her almost made him weep. She was so still. He had turned her into a frozen but beautiful piece of human porcelain. Beneath her surface he heard her crying. *Please, Mike, whatever you've done to me, please undo it. I don't think you want to hurt me, but I don't see how you can help me with my husband. He sees you with me, he'll fly into a rage. There's no telling what he'll do.*

He found he no longer had to think about using the power to make it do his will. It had become as easy as moving an arm, the light inside of him now an integrated and natural part of the infinite synapses and neurons of his brain. He released the muscles in her face and neck. The husband had to at least believe was she was sitting normally.

He felt overwhelmed by his need to protect this woman. He felt the moisture burn into his eyes, softly told her, "Mimi, I would never hurt you. But the rest of your life will belong to you and to someone else, someone worthy of you."

He could feel that she knew he was sincere, felt the tearing ache in her heart. *Yes, Mike, I believe you, I believe you mean me no harm, but, please, let me go. I don't understand what you've done to me, but I only want to be let go. No one will ever know anything.*

"I will let you go."

He saw her husband coming up the road, in his mind. Slowly he turned, watched as the black Jeep Cherokee slid to a halt several car lengths behind them. He gave Mimi Sanders one last look, choked down the wrenching anguish in his throat, said, "Good-bye, Mimi Sanders," and erased her memory of him.

He got out, all the interstate traffic noise a rushing, swirling din in his mind. He dredged up the final grim resolve to go through with it. He found Burt Sanders just as big and muscular and brutal as he had envisioned. The man slammed the door of his vehicle, squared his shoulders. The whiskey he smelled on Sanders's breath was a pungent odor, like a room full of ammonia in his electrically charged senses.

"I'm gonna ask you just one time, fella. Who the hell are you and what are you doin' with my wife?"

Wilkins stepped to the back of the Mustang as Sanders lurched toward him. "I'm just a friend, a concerned friend with a message for you."

Wilkins already knew what was going to happen, but he decided to let the man commit himself to violence. Self-defense would be his only immediate justification to kill this man.

"And what's this message, pal?"

"You are to leave your wife alone. Leave here and never see or even speak to her again. The life you had with her never existed. If you don't leave, something very terrible will happen to you. However, I already know you."

"That a fact?"

"Yes. Go on and do what you feel is necessary. I can't stop you."

"You're damn straight you can't stop me." Sanders bared his teeth, his blue eyes flashing with menace. "I got a message for *you*. Butt out of my business!"

Wilkins took the blow to the stomach. Normally such a devastating punch would have flattened him as the wind was driven from his lungs. As it was, the power cushioned the force of the blow enough so that it only sent him staggering back. Even so, Wilkins felt his legs buckle. Then he stumbled, pitched on his back, the sunglasses flying off his face, revealing the first layer of white shining around his eyes. He looked up, saw the man loom over him, lifting a foot to stomp his face.

Mike Wilkins allowed pure rage to unleash the power.

Chapter Twelve

"He's coming back here, John."

They were words, delivered matter-of-factly and with some coldness in the voice, that seemed to suck the life right out of John Wilkins. Gently massaging his stiff and aching jaw, he racked his mind, searching for words to comfort her. To deny her statement.

For a long, uncomfortable moment he could only stare at his wife. Instead of relief, he felt guilt. At least now Paula knew what had been disturbing him.

"When did you get this letter?"

"Yesterday morning."

She stood, went to the wet bar, built a tall scotch and soda. "I could have guessed. I sensed something was wrong yesterday when you came in. You were grim. You were a million miles away. I don't think I've ever seen you that way."

He noticed that her hand was trembling, her gaze distant as it wandered around the room. Beyond the door, the talk and laughter in the dining room, the clink of dishes in the kitchen sounded ominously loud to John Wilkins. While she sat behind her desk, eyes riveted on the letter, her expression dark, Wilkins helped himself to another whiskey.

"John . . . I have to ask this. Are we in danger? Is

your brother violent? I don't need to tell you I have every right to know and to be very concerned. That letter . . . it's so raw. All that bitterness and rage . . . God in Heaven, I mean, it seems as if he were right here in front of us."

He understood all too well, but couldn't help but grimace as she spoke about his brother as if he were a thing, a creature of unearthly anger and desperate malevolence. He chose his next words carefully, took time working on his drink before he settled back in his chair. "I haven't seen my brother in more than ten years. A lot can change—hell, everything changes. Just look at this town. Twenty years ago this was farm country, dying quick, a wheezing dinosaur on its last breath. Now it's this gleaming minimetropolis where everyone knows your name and no one worries about a damn thing." He saw her peer at him, and abruptly ended his sudden and strange diatribe. "No, I'm not trying to change the subject. I guess his letter made me take a hard look at some things I've made myself blind to. What I'm saying is, there's a lot of history between my brother and me, our entire family, for that matter. Most of that history's not good. Has he ever threatened me? No. Have I ever seen him strike someone? No. Is he capable of violence? I don't think so, but I don't know for certain. You know about his drug history. You know some dealers made their way down from Chicago and took up residence in the next county. He had about a four-year run with heroin and cocaine that nearly killed him. I was damn glad, to say the least, when these associates of his were finally busted. I did everything I could for my brother at that time, but I guess I was simply trying to make up for all the other times. Times when I did nothing more than stand on the sidelines, silently cheering for him to pull himself together. You know, suck it up, be a man, move on with your life, things are tough all over, take your lumps. Just like good old Dad did, right?

"Then there was our parents' will. I felt terrible when I inherited our small family fortune. So, what did I do? I'd give him money from time to time. Yes, behind your back. I tell you this now to clear my conscience with you. And to show myself that what I did only made the situation worse. Let me ask you, what do you remember of my family?"

"I remember how all of you walked around in this sort of . . . controlled tightness toward each other. On the surface it all appeared cordial enough, but I could feel the simmering. I remember your mother dying from lung cancer, just about six months after your sister was killed. I figured she smoked three packs a day, and I always saw her with a drink in her hand. After she died, I remember how your father took a room with the McNeeleys outside of town. He seemed to fall completely apart. I remember always seeing your father either blind drunk, half drunk, or sort of staggering around town on his way to a drink. He never bothered anyone, never made a scene; in fact, he could be quite charming when he wanted to. I felt deep compassion for your father, John. He was a very lonely man, a very tortured man. I don't think I've ever in my life seen a more troubled and lonely individual. His liver failed but we all knew it would. He died a miserable alcoholic death in the hospital. I remember your brother never came to see him. I remember seeing the tears in your father's eyes right before he died. He never even asked about your brother. You remember what he said, his last words?"

He nodded. "My father said, 'God forgive me.' "

"Yes. 'God forgive me.' " She sighed. "I suppose in some way I'm grateful my own parents died peacefully in their sleep. Forgive me for saying that."

"No need. There are a lot of things you never knew about us, Paula. We had our own secrets, and yes, it was like living in the eye of a hurricane all the time. My brother . . . well, he was a little different, but I always knew he was, in this . . . sort of instinctive way where I wanted to get close to him but couldn't. I guess we were all a little afraid of him, or maybe for him. Sometimes you see certain patterns in children, certain behaviors established that, uh, I suppose sort of point to the future.

"We were a farmer's children, and just for one thing, Mike never liked doing that kind of work. He sort of begrudgingly went along with the chores, helping our father and mother take care of the farm, making sure the crops . . . Well, my brother always suffered from these high-grade fevers as a child. His brain would be burning up, and he was near death more than once. He suffered from nightmares because of the fevers, would wake up screaming, frothing at the mouth, eyes bulging, but he always . . . seemed as if . . . he couldn't see anything when he was like that, as if he were going blind, trapped in darkness and screaming to get out of it. He certainly seemed insane, and it would scare anyone to see it. Sometimes the fevers would last for days. At times he would have to be hospitalized. Sometimes my mother would soak him in tubs full of ice, or rubbing alcohol, or both. It always struck me . . . I don't know, like some sort of voodoo ritual. It made my father angry because I have to believe he felt he had an aberration for a son. He saw Mike using his fevers as an excuse to get out of work. Let me tell you something about Mike. Mike was an artist, a good one. So I figured, at least in my mind, cut him some slack. I never resented him for seeming to be lazy or shiftless. Fact was, I always felt protective of him, even though I never . . . never really showed it. He could draw, he could paint, he could make anything come to life with his hands with a brush or a pencil. It was amazing. The kid had pure talent. But my father came from the old school of hard work with strong hands and an iron back. The pursuit of anything other than physical labor was for city people, 'those people,' as he called them.

"Mike withdrew deeper into himself over the years. But then something changed in him, made it all worse." He told her about the incident with the Peterson kid, the whole truth, including Peterson's thorough ass-whipping of the boy, saw the shock on his wife's face. "Not long after that, he started drawing . . . well, all sorts of obscene pictures. Name it, he drew it: it was as if his mind had become warped by whatever happened to him. I can't say that for certain. What I know . . . well, my father found them one day and nearly beat him to death with a belt; I mean it was a beating that drew blood. We literally had to pull my father away from Mike. A part of me could understand my father's reaction. We were a strong religious family, a good Catholic family, just like everyone else around here. It was about this time, I remember, my father's drinking got heavier, what with the banks closing in and money tight." He flashed a bitter smile. "Of course, we all know we were saved by our Lansing angels. I can see how my father resented them, these same soft city people who were from another planet to a man like him, with their endless supplies of money, their soft hands, and their oily smiles, sweeping in and saving the day. But everyone took the money and ran. Including me."

There was a long pause; then his wife said, "John, listen to yourself. Listen to the words you've been using, myself included. 'Suppose. Guess. Sort of.' What is it you don't want to look at?"

His expression turned grim. "The truth."

"And just what is the truth, John?"

He savored the man's intense agony. One second Burt Sanders was driving his boot down to smash in his face, and in the next eyeblink Mike Wilkins sent a knifing, white-hot pain through his legs and crotch. Next he summoned forth from the light and put into the man's body a thousand unseen but living razors that tore and twisted, digging and slashing through muscle and organs, grating over bone and ripping just beneath the surface of flesh. The man crumpled, slammed to his back as if floored by a giant slab of rock.

Standing, his eyes hot, the faint white light burning away in his field of vision, Mike Wilkins took the man's voice. His mouth moved, all right, open wide and tongue protruding, but only the two of them heard his silent, tortured screams of unrelenting agony. He listened for another few moments to Burt Sanders shrieking, then heard Mimi crying out in her own thoughts to know what was going on. She had seen her husband get out of the truck, but where was he?

As the man writhed on the ground below him,

Mike Wilkins stared at him with utter loathing. He knew this man so well; he judged Burt Sanders deserving of nothing but death. This man was so unworthy of the love of his wife, Mike Wilkins found himself baffled for a moment as to what Mimi had ever seen in him. A fleeting probe into the man's soul told him everything he wanted to know. For all of Sanders's stubborn pride and arrogance, Mike Wilkins found a softness beneath the man's armor of anger and fear. It was an icy sort of worminess that leaped around, slithered in and out and around the man's relentless anger in the dim light of his soul. It was deceit and manipulation he saw in the man.

And so he knew Burt Sanders could be charming and persuasive, had lured Mimi in with smooth talk and easy wit. In short, he had woven a lie around himself, trapped Mimi. But he was essentially a bully, and once he had Mimi married, under his will, he used his anger and muscle to intimidate and dominate her, used the children as pawns to maneuver his wife into his will and lies. She wasn't allowed to work; he selected her friends while he boozed it up with his buddies and caroused with women, actually even flinging his infidelity in her face. He used her own shame to control her, making her believe she had failed him somehow. He was a parasite, a human virus intent only on making her as sick as he was in order to justify his own evil. And it was then that Mike Wilkins knew it would be less than six months before he took the lives of Mimi and her children.

But not if he could help it.

He made the man stand up. He bored his will deeper and harder through all that shrieking. He picked up his sunglasses. Slipping them on, he glimpsed the reflection of his burning white orbs. He felt the man's terror, heard his horrified confusion at the sight of those eyes. Wilkins wanted to end this man's life, quick and ugly, befitting the violence he had inflicted on Mimi.

It was a short walk to the interstate. He made Sanders walk with him, by his side. They moved together, naturally, a couple of buddies just strolling along. Mike Wilkins felt a cold but easy smile tighten his lips. In the distance, in the eye of his power, rolling hard and fast from the north, he saw the tractor-trailer. He gauged the distance, got his timing mentally worked out. Saw the semi thundering along less than two miles away and closing. He looked down the ramp, knew it was going to be close, that Sanders would have to run. So be it.

He spoke into the man's mind. *Okay, Burt, you're going to have to hustle to catch the next train. It's coming fast and I don't want you to miss your ride home. Go on now; it's time to go.*

Sanders's eyes bulged, rolling in all directions. Profound horror and utter confusion would be his death mask—if they ever even found what was left of his face.

Wilkins tuned the man's fear out as easily as snapping off a radio.

Down there they were racing by in their vehicles, so fast and furious, no one paid the two of them even a passing glance. All that angry life on the road. He could feel it in each vehicle, all the running souls oblivious to the reality of oncoming sudden death. How little they knew, or even cared. Ah, well, such was life. He was about to make the world a little bit better place.

And Burt Sanders ran down the off-ramp. The

driver behind the wheel of a pickup truck hit his horn as Sanders sprinted by him.

Wilkins saw the behemoth rig in the distance, less than a half mile away, a great, charging iron and steel mastodon. He released Mimi, then began sliding off toward the edge of the woods. He heard the man silently begging for help, for release, for this nightmare to stop and set him free. He heard Sanders crying in his mind like a bawling child for Mimi to save him, knowing he was going to die in front of that barreling semi, splattered like rotten fruit all over the road.

In his mind, Wilkins saw Mimi burst out of the car. It was the next part he couldn't bear to see. Mimi started screaming for her husband, some dark, instinctive fear welling in her, making her know something terrible was happening.

Shadowing into the woods, Wilkins turned as Mimi skidded to the top of the off-ramp. He didn't have to see it with his eyes, but watched it in his mind.

Burt Sanders raced onto the interstate, stopped directly in front of the onrushing tractor-trailer.

Noooooooooooo! his mind screamed.

The driver's eyes widened in shock, but his foot was frozen by utter disbelief and horror as this insane man flew onto the highway out of nowhere, in front of his rig.

Through Sanders's eyes, Wilkins saw the last living instant of the man's life just before the nose of the tractor-trailer exploded into him. In a momentary blinding flash of light he pulled himself out of the man's mind, but still clearly heard the erupting thud and splat of the body—right there, on top of the impact but beyond and above it—as Burt Sanders was pulped into a spewing sack, hurtled far down the highway.

Mimi saw it and wailed.

Her shriek echoed in his mind, ripped his insides apart with its lingering sound of pure anguish.

Trembling, Mike Wilkins stumbled deeper into the woods. Out there, he heard the din of squealing brake metal and the blare of horns.

And, finally, terribly, the horrified, piercing cry of one utterly alone and lonely woman. He was sweating and felt the fever burn through his head. He kept shaking, choking back the urge to drop to his knees and sob.

If you only knew, Mimi. If you only knew . . .

"The truth is, I can't even blame my brother for what he's done, for whatever he's become. I can't even blame him for wanting to run all of his life. The truth is," John Wilkins told his wife with a mounting passion he had never displayed before, "there's evil in the world and there are too many things in life we choose to turn a blind eye to. Sometimes a man is made wrong by things, by others, by something beyond his control. The truth is, I could have and should have stepped in years ago, and done something for my brother.

"Paula, bottom line, I was the oldest, I was seen as the strongest, the most responsible, but I was scared. Of my father. Of our family falling apart if we lost the farm. Of some insidious thing turning my brother slowly, year by year, into something he didn't want to be: a lonely, suffering, hopelessly addicted wretch who felt trapped and isolated and alone—just like our father."

He stopped suddenly, drained, shaken by his own

words. For a long time, too long, he heard his voice echoing in the silence. He sat staring at his wife, trying to will the shaking from his limbs. Paula swallowed hard, her eyes misting, her lips trembling. There was a pain in her eyes that he had never seen, had never wanted to see in his wife. Beyond that, there was her own fear. A terror, perhaps, that she was losing something, or about to lose something she had cherished and nurtured all of her life.

He killed his drink, seeking to douse the fire in his belly. He wanted a cigarette badly. He wanted another drink, wanted to burst out in weeping in hopes that it would be the only thing, the only act that would cleanse what he felt. That would purify him of his own shame.

"John . . . John . . ."

Slowly she stood, walked around the desk. He looked up, fighting back the tears, his wife's beautiful, stricken face looming in his eyes. Gently she kissed him on the forehead, then wrapped her arms around his neck and held him tight.

John Wilkins clenched his jaw, shut his eyes, and somehow held back the tears.

Chapter Thirteen

Dinner looked destined to be the somber affair John Wilkins had least wanted.

He understood all too well their mood, but the awkward silence was making him self-conscious. Were they afraid the dad they knew and loved had changed into something they didn't understand? That one ugly act of violence, handled in a fashion he had not even believed himself capable of, had revealed a dark side to his nature that had been sleeping all these years? Or was he—God forbid—a hero? A stand-up guy taking charge of a situation not of his choosing, but coming out on top, champion of the meek and mild? Or was his own dark mood reading too much into the silence?

Whatever, he knew they knew, but they were trying to be polite, sympathetic in their silence. Undoubtedly there was tension all around, with no one sure how to broach the subject.

After a few brief exchanges about the kids' day, they went on eating the meal Paula had prepared, again in silence. Sirloin steak, mashed potatoes, corn on the cob, and salad, simple but delicious. Paula sitting at one end of the dining room table, Dad at

171

the other end, with Robert and Timmy on one side, Jenny opposite her brothers.

He could feel them all wanting to talk about the incident, though everyone seemed to wait for someone else to break the ice. He noticed that his oldest son sported a sly grin and was throwing a look his way, so John Wilkins sipped from his glass of burgundy and made the first move. "All right, Bobby, let's have it. What's up?"

Robert ran his laughing eyes over the rest of their faces, shoveled a forkful of steak into his mouth, chewed some, then said, "I heard, Dad. You gotta know we all heard."

There his oldest son sat, proud as a peacock of old Dad, the gunslinger in the white hat, riding into town, ridding it of all the bad guys, then heading off into the sunset. He didn't like one bit where this might be headed.

"What did you hear, Robert?"

"Heard you kicked the sh . . . the stuffing out of that jerk, Sam Watterson."

"Where did you hear that?"

"Does it matter?"

"Yes, it does. I gave explicit instructions for no one at the paper to talk about it. The last thing I want is for this to get around town."

"Too late for that, Dad," Bobby said. He looked set to burst out laughing. "Mickey Tomlin was shooting off his mouth about it all day. Johnny Simpson, he's old enough to drink, you know, so he was over at Miller's Tavern. Guess Tomlin went to see Watterson at the hospital. Johnny, he came to the courts and told us everything. I hear that jerk hit you first, tried to rip your head off, and you hit him so hard you knocked him out of your office, right through your window. On his back and out cold."

Timmy, sullen as usual, glared at Robert. "You think that's funny? Look at the knot on Dad's jaw. He could have been laid up in that hospital instead."

Robert returned the look. "What's your problem? Watterson's a jerk, runs around this town all day, bad-mouthing Dad behind his back. He got what was coming to him."

Jenny's nervous look wandered from her mother, over her brothers, and finally turned into a concerned stare at her father. "I'm just glad you're okay, Dad. I can see you and Mom feel awful about it. Are you going to be in trouble? Are you . . . going to have to go to court?"

"What did I say?" Robert asked, angry, looking around at the family.

John Wilkins held up his hands. "All right, all right, come on. Calm down. All of you. I want everyone to listen to me very carefully. First, I am not proud of what happened, and I would just as soon forget about it. A man attacked me, I reacted, that's all it was." He hoped no one asked if he had been scared. Strangely enough, he recalled not feeling the least bit frightened of Sam. He had just dug in his heels, stood his ground, hard and cold. The fear had come afterward. "Life is not a Charles Bronson movie, and this goes for everyone, not just you, Bobby. In real life, people get hurt and hurt badly by something like this, and the good guys don't always win, and something like this hardly makes me out to be a good guy. I feel some guilt and some shame, to be frank. I look at myself and I have to wonder if I could have handled it better, meaning with no fisticuffs. To talk ill about Sam, Robert, please, let it alone."

"You don't think he got what he deserved?"

"No, son, I don't. I hate violence of any kind. It never solves anything. It only makes for more hard feelings and anger."

"I agree," Timmy said softly.

Robert frowned at his younger brother, the "you would" look, loud and clear.

"Hey, hey, guys," John Wilkins told his children in as firm but gentle a voice as he could find, "let's put this behind us, okay? No more talk about it, no more funny looks. Life's going to go on. And to answer your question, Jen, no one's going to be in any trouble, legal or otherwise, over this. Let's finish our dinner."

He looked at Paula, saw the approving smile dance over her lips, the warmth in her eyes. Since leaving the restaurant they hadn't talked any more about his brother, the past, what might happen if Mike showed up in Glendale. But he knew they would have to discuss the matter at some point.

As they were finishing dinner, John Wilkins said, "Okay, what's everyone got planned for the evening? Jen?"

She hesitated. "I've got a . . . I'm going out with Paul. He's taking me to a movie."

He felt something in his stomach wilt. His daughter was too young, he thought, to be wanting to grow up so fast. She was even dressed a little—what? Provocatively? Obviously she had gotten a perm that day, and he could smell the sweet scent of perfume all over her. Some jewelry, white blouse and blue jeans maybe a bit too tight.

"That's fine," he told his daughter. "I like Paul, Jen; he's a fine young man."

"Summer basketball league," Robert said, wiping his mouth with his napkin, anxious suddenly as he

ooked at the clock. "I'm runnin' late. You don't mind
f I take the Saturn, do you, Dad?"

"You can take it, but before everyone heads out I
want to make clear that I want all of you back in this
house by midnight. Not a minute past, no excuses,
thank you. Are we clear?"

They agreed, a little too quickly, not the usual near
challenge of teenagers toward parental authority.
Things had changed. The father, whether he wanted
t or not, commanded their new respect. He even de-
ected a slight change in his tone. Subtle, but it was
here. It told them he was the boss.

Robert practically ran from the dining room, but
Jenny went to her father, kissed him on the cheek.
I'm glad you're not hurt, Dad. You were right about
what you said. Hey, is the cookout still on?"

"Why not, Jen? This family needs to have a little
fun together. It'll be the best one we've ever had."

"Promise?"

"Promise. Bring any friends you want."

She beamed. Another chance for her to be with
Paul Stallings, he knew, and felt that hollow pit in
his stomach again. "Love you, Dad—and I'll be home
on time."

He grunted softly. Again he found himself wondering why he felt so skeptical these days. Why
wouldn't his anxiety, this nagging dread, go away?

"Timmy?"

"Watch a movie, I guess."

Glum. He wanted to ask his son if he didn't think
he was spending too much time by himself lately, but
didn't want to seem intrusive.

"I don't know, maybe I'll walk down to the mall for
a while. I've gotten pretty good at Pac Man," Timmy
added. A little life there, John detected, and felt hope-

ful. "You excuse me, or you want some help cleanin
up?"

"No, that's okay, hon. Your Dad and I will do it."

When they were alone, he saw his wife smiling a
him. There was a glint in her eyes, a look he suddenl
realized he hadn't seen in a long time.

She sipped her wine and said, "Well, Mr. Wilkins
I think you handled that beautifully. For my money
you will forever be my hero."

He tried a smile, but knew she read his uncer
tainty. Robert's attitude about it all troubled him. H
decided it was just some teenage macho perspectiv
his son was working through and would eventuall
outgrow.

His wife got up, came around, snuggled down int
his lap, and put her slender arms around his neck
She smiled into his eyes.

"You feel good, babe. I tell you today how beautifu
you are?"

"Not yet, but I'm listening. What say we clean u
here then take the rest of the wine upstairs? You u
for that—Daddy?"

He smiled back at his beautiful, redheaded wife. I
was the first genuine and good reaction to anythin
he'd felt in two days. She smelled good. Clean an
fresh, that flower-sweet but slight tangy scent to her
He realized it had been a while since they'd made
love.

"We can clean up later," he said.

Mike Wilkins stepped out of the kid's blue Mazda
He gave the freckled college boy, home from UCL
for the summer, a smile, put *Good luck with your life
son*, in his mind.

After having walked six miles to the next exit, h

had forced Herb Tannenbaum to pick him up. Boy wanted to be a lawyer, was going to see his girlfriend, who lived in a small rural town in southern Illinois. The future looked promising for the kid. He would get his law degree, marry his girl, and they would have three children. Eventually he would land his own practice in Chicago. His road ahead would not be without a dark turn or two. The girl was going to have an affair and Herb was going to be angry with her at first, stew in his betrayal. Eventually, though, he would forgive her, knowing he spent too much time with his law practice. Maybe it was his fault that she felt neglected. Good heart, that one, Wilkins decided. Fair, compassionate, and honest, future clients meaning more than just a hundred twenty-five an hour, completely out of character for a future lawyer. He hoped the world of sharks the kid would soon be swimming in didn't eat him up. Wilkins didn't care to see that far into the boy's tomorrow. Instead he wanted to indulge this momentary hope for the human race.

The blue Mazda vanished into the night. In a little while Herb would be free from his trance, left wondering where he was, of course, how he got there, but he would be fine.

Slowly Wilkins walked through the woods. He had already picked out this strategic spot in his mind. And it came into view, just as he had envisioned. Gradually the infinite lights burned away the darkness, became brighter and brighter with each step. Their beacon of luxury had summoned him home.

Glendale.

He stopped at the edge of the hill. He smiled, felt the power heating up, strong, taking charge.

Home sweet home. At last.

It stretched out before him, a sea of lights, all of it tucked comfortably, all that twinkling surface innocence beneath a velvet sky, the countless stars, and a quarter moon. It was just as he remembered it, only larger, more sprawling, more populated with choice victims. It all looked so grand, he thought, this paradise they had built, clung to, were terrified of losing.

Upon further inspection of this massive suburban mecca, Wilkins felt the hot light of the power turn into a cold swirl inside. He depised these people, what they were, what they had, what they were so scared of losing.

What had they done to him? Over ten years later, how many would even remember?

He would find out soon enough.

Okay, a lot of white split-level homes down there, long, spacious streets winding all through the suburbs. Nice cars, big garages. Massive parks everywhere for the little ones, baseball fields and basketball courts for the older ones. And everyone seemed to have a pool, or a rose garden, grapevines and neatly trimmed hedgerows, spruce trees and azaleas, everything manicured, damn near virginal. To the west rose Center City, uneven chains of low-lying buildings, now bathed in the shadows of neon glare, except for the restaurants and the mall, which were lit up bright as day. Traffic was sparse, but it was there, as they drove at a slow pace to and from Center City or points near the business district.

Then he saw the belfry of Glendale's largest Catholic church, a giant crucifix, looming high into the night.

Suddenly he saw a flash of flames in his mind. There. The church. A cold and overwhelming contempt rolled through him.

Yes, the church. He would burn it all down, fire and ash. In their faces. A final torch song to their hypocrisy, the multitude of sins they had heaped on him.

Later on, though, when he was ready. There was a certain Father O'Shay he needed to see first.

One thing at a time.

He removed his sunglasses, felt the heat in his eyes. He stared down into the valley. Even then he could feel them, all of them, down there, almost to a man, woman, and child. He concentrated on certain homes, absorbing their energy, caught the faintest whispers of their thoughts. Some were concerned with their children. Others were making plans for vacations, some parents wondering about their kids going to whatever college, feeling pangs of loss, worry for the future of their children. Plenty of average, good, hardworking people. The truly good ones might or might not survive, but that depended on how it all fell, how he felt about each and every man or woman. No, it would go down the same way for all, depending on what he saw in their hearts, if they were impure from even the slightest taint of poison.

It wasn't long before the dark and angry energy came to him. Reaching for him, it seemed, pulling him down there, his will swirling out before him as the power searched out certain homes, drawing in certain individuals, for a reason he couldn't quite fathom.

He could hear their lecherous thoughts. They were scattered fragments at best, dispersing and imploding on themselves, but he heard enough as one disembodied voice after another flowed over the next. Indeed, he could feel the heat in their souls, glimpse their acts of adultery. He invaded one mind, then rapidly moved onto the next one. Some were worried about making more money, their minds hatching different scams. Maybe padding some books, working angles against the tax man, expense accounts they needed to justify somehow, wives secreting money from husbands and vice versa.

It was a maddening rush of teeming, endless thoughts, overlapping in angry and demanding self-interest. Everyone rationalizing, justifying, aching for something else, something the other person had. One man was obsessed with his neighbor's daughter, young and tight. Had to be a virgin. Never had a virgin, since his wife was a hard-drinking little trollop he'd met in college. He needed to even the score somehow. Lust for the wife next door. He saw the way she'd been looking at him, bored and lonely, way she bent over, pruning the garden, knew he was watching. Some shady business deal in Chicago. Women suspecting their husbands of cheating. Fear of a sexual-harrassment suit being brought against a . . . lawyer, yes, Glendale's big-shot mouthpiece, sweating it out by himself, thinking he could cover it up, deny it. One brooding guy, married not quite a year, thinking his wife should dress a little more conservatively when they went out to dinner. She didn't pay enough attention to him, made him look bad. Businesses in town too slow, need more, get more, take more. Utter raging madness beneath the placid smiles. Teenage boys wanting girls, a couple of kids masturbating themselves to sleep, a maze of dark images of sexual fantasy and perversion locked but going back and forth in their frenzy for release. Young girls wondering just what a Mr. Right should be. Other voices searching for ways to leave Glendale—life in the Windy City would be more exciting, more opportunities than this stale existence where everyone looked, talked, and acted the same. *Clonedale*, he heard the sarcastic voice of a young girl, laughing to herself, but bitter, contemptuous. Well, a few smart ones saw beneath the surface, after all. Brooding, disillusioned young, honing rebellion toward parents who didn't understand.

Usual stuff, he finally decided, could be Anywhere, USA, but there was more than enough to work with down there. Damn near an overload of darkness.

Best yet, all of their weaknesses would only serve to make him even stronger.

And he knew without having to know exactly where his brother lived, even found John lying in bed next to his fair redheaded wife. They had just had sex, the second time that evening. His brother was feeling pretty damn good about things, content, sated. Full of himself, back in charge, denying himself an after-sex smoke for his wife's sake. Noble stuff. Well, he would fix all that, and in a few short minutes. But wait until Brother John drifted off to sleep.

Likewise he knew the power would direct him to where he could find all the others. A lot to do, an awful lot.

He lifted his sunglasses, looked at the strange white light burning, filling his eyes in the reflection. He felt stronger than ever. He had arrived, after all, and he was ready.

Mike Wilkins laughed out loud, long and hard.

They all wanted more, and he would give all of them all they could handle.

It was good to be home.

It was time to go to work.

Chapter Fourteen

It was happening again. But what was happening? What was it, this slithering, cold, invading force?

"Oh, God, no. No!" John Wilkins snapped open his eyes, stared up into the impenetrable darkness, his cry of fear echoing through his head. He was afraid to move at first, recalling the dream, all too aware of what was going on. One moment his day was being replayed—that living cinema again—in the strange, probing haze of the dream. And in the next moment the vision of him striking Sam Watterson vanished in some boiling, downward spiral of laughter without sound.

The invading force was back. Or was it just a bad dream? Was it just nerves? He couldn't be sure. Once again he could feel it, in the room, stronger than before, angrier, more defiant. But tonight it seemed—felt—different. It wasn't paralyzing him tonight. No, it wanted something. It was calling him, in its silent, pulling force of energy, out of his bed. Or was it simply his own anxiety, he wondered, working on his fear, creating nightmares out of his own paranoia, dredging up doubt and fear about the past, dread of the present, and perhaps working up a mounting terror about tomorrow? What the hell was really happening?

And somehow, he sensed, something other than himself knew how his day had fallen, once again gaining knowledge of him from his subconscious. Or was it his own imagination, fraught with doubt and worry, stirring up problems that didn't really exist?

Still, something was happening. And for some unknown reason that chilled him to the bone, the force had been laughing at him. It knew the fears of his day. Knew the pleasure of the love he had shared with his wife. Knew it all, and chilled him once more with its shuddering, cold contempt. It was all soundless in his mind, but this force was there, back in voiceless words of pure thought.

John Wilkins became angry at this unseen, unknown force, then agitated with himself for doubting that something other than a nightmare was taking place. Then another ball of icy fear lodged in his belly as he heard something rattling downstairs. Instinctively he knew it wasn't the children. Slowly he turned his head. It was just after two o'clock in the morning. Gently he rolled the other way. His wife was sound asleep. The soft glow of moonlight struck her face, making her expression of peace and contentment angelic. For some reason he couldn't comprehend, he became terrified for her, for their children.

Silently he rose out of bed. Someone or something was downstairs.

A primal terror filled him, tightening his chest, his throat. What if it was only the beginning of a nightmare? What if it was only paranoia?

No.

Something downstairs. He heard a rustling noise

as he stepped into the dark of the upstairs hallway. He felt compelled not to wake his family. He felt alone, and in desperate need to search out what he sensed was waiting for him downstairs, in the thick blackness of his home.

He tried the hall light. A click, but no light shone down. Somehow even that made sense in some irrational way he couldn't define. He was being taunted. He could feel something around him, beyond him.

Downstairs. Keeping him, whatever it was, in the dark.

His throat tightened, the fear clawing its way through his chest. With each step down the hall, his bare feet sinking into the plush carpet, the fear grew and he found it harder to breathe. Quietly he opened the hall closet on its well-oiled hinges. He withdrew a flashlight, flicked on the beam. Slow and silent, he opened the door to the boys' room. They were both asleep, tucked beneath their blankets. He let the beam wander around their room. Everything seemed in place, untouched. Next he went to Jenny's room. He found her curled up on her side, her lovely face soft with innocence and peace.

He closed her door, ventured to the top of the steps. No, this thing wasn't interested in his children. At least not yet, he sensed. It wanted him.

He heard a whisper of something as he began moving down the steps. A voice? A low cry? Was it calling him?

He reached the bottom of the stairs, raked the beam around the living room. He looked back up at the hallway. Silence.

He heard that rustling noise again. *There!* In the corner of the living room. He caught something mov-

ng, skirting away from the grandfather clock. The
eam hit the clock but there was nothing there. The
oft sway of the pendulum sounded maddeningly,
earfully loud in the silence.

"Who's there?" he quietly growled, taking a step
oward the sofa.

Everything in the large living room was so still, it
eemed almost unreal in the glare of his flashlight.
The couch. Coffee table. Television. The china cabi-
et and bookcase. He tried the lamp by the sofa.
Nothing.

As he was turning, he saw a shadow whirling from
he hallway leading to the kitchen. A glimpse of
omething dark and hunched over, there then gone
s his light hit the wall. He felt his heart pounding
ike a jackhammer in his chest. The silence became
deafening; then he heard a distant *drip drip drip* from
he kitchen, the faucet leaking ever so slightly, but
rowing louder and louder in the darkness that
hrouded him.

"John?"

The voice reached his ears from a great distance.
No, he told himself. He was dreaming; this was a
nightmare. But he was standing there in his living
oom, in the cold of full wakefulness. It was all too
eal.

The voice spoke his name again. It broke through
he clinging haze of his denial. He recognized the
oice, a woman's voice, low and with a note of plead-
ng in it. He wanted to deny what he heard, told him-
elf it was a cruel memory. The voice came again,
oft, imploring. Oh, God, no.

"John. John."

He felt his eyes widening as he turned toward the
randfather clock, in the direction of the voice. The

beam crawled in a straight, agonizingly slow line to
ward the shadow. Gradually the shadow in front of
the clock came into view. Then the light hit th
shadow, falling directly on the thing that wa
hunched over, naked and mutilated. John Wilkir
became paralyzed in cold terror.

He couldn't believe his eyes. He felt his throat cor
stricting, his scream strangled off by utter disbelie
and horror.

"John. Look at me, brother."

Oh, no, he heard his mind scream. *No, no, no!*

His hand was frozen, the beam of light bathing th
mutilated face in a white glow that seemed absorbe
into the pulped ruins of his sister's face. Mary. H
wanted to call her name but the words were choke
off in his parched throat. It couldn't be! How? Sh
was dead, had been dead for years, but there she wa:
right in front of him. Mutilated almost beyond rec
ognition by the horrible accident. The left side of he
face was smashed in where it had struck the wind
shield, one eye hanging down out of its socket, th
other hidden behind red-black-purple flesh. Ragge
shreds of crimson meat hung in slashed folds dow
her warped face. Another eternal second and he sav
the things that poked and slithered out of her fac
were . . . oh, God, they were maggots! And the res
of her, he couldn't look at it. For years after th
closed-casket funeral he wanted only to recall hov
fair and dainty and beautiful she was . . . but he
whole body was crushed and mangled. Naked, th
hideous, unreal sight of her was even more obscene
The truck had slammed into her, he knew, head-or
The engine block had been driven through the dash
straight into her, nearly severing her at the wais
Now all her wounds, or those he imagined shoul

have been closed by the mortician, were raw and open and oozing. He wanted to turn away, scream, but he couldn't move, couldn't find his voice. Yes, oh, God, he was being forced to look at his dead sister, locked in his own repulsion, immobilized by the invader. She stood, bent over, the gleaming shards of white bones in her arms and legs protruding like ghastly horns. Her chest was caved in, and intestines started slowly leaking out her sides, even as he stood, frozen and watching, wishing, willing this to be a nightmare.

"John." The voice was cold, angry all of a sudden. "Look at me. Look—and see what our father did to me. He used me, a girl, like a woman and drove me to my death."

He felt something release him, heard his voice returning to a low croaking in his ears. Then the light wavered away from Mary. Uncontrollably he was stumbling back, gagging, bile shooting up into his throat. Against his failing will, he couldn't stop the shaking, the light going back to the grandfather clock.

She—it—was gone.

Before he knew it or could stop himself, he pitched backward into the china cabinet. It was a dream, just a hallucination, he heard his mind scream in utter terror and disbelief. He choked down the vomit, his senses returning as glass shattered and plates crashed around his feet.

The din seemed to go on and on. Suddenly he became aware of scrambling noises. Lights flared on, his eyes burning against the sudden brightness as he staggered and slid down the wall, fighting to catch his balance.

"John!"

"Dad!"

They were calling him. His family, their voices rife with panic and fear, clawing across a great distance. His wife, in his face, shaking him, calling him. He felt the flashlight slip from his hands, heard it plunk on the carpet.

Somehow he found his voice as reality dug through his senses. Slowly reality came back, groping, fumbling for long moments to return his vision, his senses to himself, from the clutches of the invader.

Thank God, they were there. Paula. Jenny. Robert.

"I'm okay, I'm all right . . . just a nightmare . . . sleep . . . I don't know . . . walking."

His labored breathing rasped in his ears. He looked at their faces, frozen in concern. A fresh wave of alarm blared in his head.

"Where's Timmy?"

They gave him an odd look. Then, suddenly, he heard the scream from upstairs. He broke free of their grasps, bounded up the steps. The scream went on and on, ripping apart his senses, piercing his ears. It was a sound like an animal in pain, howling out its tortured misery. It sounded so . . . familiar in its eeriness, its fear. Like a cry from the past.

As he raced down the hall, his gaze locked on the darkness of the open doorway, he heard Timmy screaming, "I can't see! I can't see! Mom! Dad, where are you? I can't see."

He burst into the room, threw on the light. John Wilkins hesitated, his heart pounding as he found his son on the bed, his eyes wide, bulging. But Timmy didn't seem to see anything.

He reached Timmy at the same time Paula did. Together they called his name, held him. John Wilkins saw the sweat rolling down his son's face, felt the fever on his forehead, even smelled the sickly taint of sweat.

"Timmy, it's Dad! It's all right, son, it's all right, we're all here. Calm down."

Slowly, ever so slowly, he saw awareness break through the glazed and distant look in Timmy's eyes.

A new terror bulged in Timmy's stare. He screamed, "Dad, everything—it's upside down. I can't stop it . . . the room . . . you're upside down!"

He cried his son's name, shook him as his son screamed. In the back of his mind, he heard his own voice, faint and distant, warning him something beyond his control was seizing control of his life. What in God's name was happening?

Mike Wilkins pulled the power back, retreated from Timmy's room. He was crouched on his haunches, feeling the smile widen his lips. It was beautiful, all that terror, confusion, havoc. He laughed, a low, throaty rumble that filled his ears for long moments. The boy would be all right. He knew they would all play it off as a nightmare.

And what a day his brother had endured. So, his brother had an enemy, this Sam Watterson individual, a cocky, swaggering braggart who had bullied his brother—until that morning.

Mike Wilkins saw the road before him, the power assimilating the plan in the light. As more was revealed in their minds and dreams, he found there was more to do, more angles to work.

He knew his brother's children had been too young to remember him, knew his brother had mentioned his existence only in passing remarks. But how he explained the errant, mysterious Uncle Mike, he didn't know. Not yet. Not that it even mattered.

Now Timmy would be especially vulnerable. They were a lot alike, he determined. Brooding loners, quiet, somber, and withdrawn. Potential artists, too. He found Timmy spent his time reading, writing poetry, drawing pictures, not much caring for normal teenage endeavors, sports, his peers, girls. Interesting. The boy also read a lot about feudal Japan, had a secret interest in the code of *bushido*, the way of the warrior. He had even found Timmy dreaming he was a samurai, wielding a *katana*, doing battle with an evil shogun or the *daimyo*, the feudal dictator landowners. He could reach the boy, he knew. The boy lived in his own world of fantasy. A dreamer, a concern to his father.

And the boy would become his own *katana*, his human samurai sword to wield and slash a little of his brother's life apart, piece by unnerving piece.

It had been a long and exhausting invasion of their minds. But it laid a foundation, as he discovered just how united, disciplined, and honorable his brother's family was. There was Jenny. Sleeping peacefully, dreaming of her boyfriend. Young girl, a virgin, but blossoming quickly, too quickly for Daddy's liking, toward full womanhood. Then there was the oldest son. Young, tough, athletic, full of himself, maybe ready to challenge old Dad.

And the wife? Well, she was some sweet work, a good and loving mother, he had discovered after a quick probe, a devoted and faithful wife. All that was about to change. She would pay for shunning him, damn near spitting in his face when he had needed his brother's help the most. He laughed, envisioned sending Paula off in the shadows of the night, all that sweet cream itching to taste the love and the fire of another man.

Wilkins stood. Yes, the invasion of his brother and family had proven a new revelation of his power. He could now summon up a vision that would seem real, put that vision wherever he wanted it. Of course, he had no idea how the accident had really left his sister, but the power had done the work for him in making her such a hideous sight that he knew his brother would never forget the experience.

"Get ready, brother," he said, staring out over the lights of Glendale. Between short bursts of laughter, he promised, "The best is yet to come. I'll lay your home and your life to waste."

Mike Wilkins laughed, thinking about young Timmy again. The two of them were going to become friends. A couple of samurais in a world that challenged the only real honor around: their own.

Smiling, Mike Wilkins pulled the amulet out from under his shirt. He stared at the black eye in the center of gold piece. The amulet would stay right where it was. His new, charged instincts warned him never to remove the amulet. Chuckling, he gave the gold star a gentle kiss.

Chapter Fifteen

John Wilkins left for work in a haze of confusion and anxiety. All looked peaceful enough on his block, the homes of his neighbors seeming like quiet havens in the early morning of another routine day. Jim Albert scooping up the newspaper on his stoop. Scott Garner pulling out in his BMW to go open his pharmacy in town. Wilkins waved to Scott, gave him a quick hello, the BMW's window down, Garner sitting, staring back. Birds chirping. Sun rising in a cloudless sky with the promise of another blistering hot day. Yes, they were still on for the cookout tomorrow, he told Garner. Bring anything? No, see you tomorrow, Scott, around noon.

It all looked normal enough on the surface, but some dark place in John Wilkins was growing tighter and angrier as he ran last night through his mind again.

He could dismiss what he had seen in the living room as some strange phenomenon of sleepwalking, even not tell his wife what he had seen—that mutilated thing that was his dead sister. Indeed, tell himself it was just some hallucination—only it had happened. Or had it? And what exactly had happened? For a fleeting moment, whatever he had seen in the living room had sure seemed real enough to keep his creeping terror of the future locked in a cold ball of ice in his gut.

She—no, the thing in his hallucination—had said, "See what our father did to me?" What did that mean? "Used me, a girl, like a woman." Had their father been responsible somehow for her death? How? Was there some ugly, dark secret involving his sister and their father . . . no, not that, anything but incest. Still, he racked his mind, trying to recall some distant clue that would give hard and ugly reality to the words he had heard last night.

See what our father did to me.

Surely they would all have known. Surely he would have seen his father leering out of the corner of his eye at his sister, felt his hot lust for Mary, a dark and sinister predatory thing, hidden in the closet. Don't think about it, he told himself. Still, had their sister kept to herself some grotesque and unholy secret that had tormented her right up to her death? He would never know, of course; they were both dead. And no good would come from torturing himself with agonizing questions that couldn't be answered.

Unless, of course, his brother was aware of the possibility of their father having—*Stop it.* Did Mike know something John didn't about their father and Mary? Was that knowledge part of the driving and burning edge to Mike's torment and relentless anger? That even those you think you love and trust can turn up dirty and soiled and unholy? Anything was possible, he had to assume.

Then there was Timmy, waking up, thrashing and screaming, soaked in the sweat of fever. Somehow finally calming down, the fever going away just as suddenly as it had seized him, like a wisp of noxious vapor blown away by a gust of wind. Was there some insidious connection between all the bizarre and terrifying incidents of last night and the night before? But what connection? Or *was* there a connection? If so, why? Was the past boiling into the present, for reasons unknown? But what did everything he'd endured mean? Or was he merely still suffering from guilt? He wanted to dismiss it all as strange coincidence, but instinct wouldn't let him bury what he'd been through under that final layer of total denial he sought so desperately. Something very real but unreal was happening.

So he had eaten breakfast quickly and quietly with his wife, both of them distracted by last night's strange events, saying little, letting the children sleep. Hoping the routine of a normal day would restore order and sanity to their world. But that silent fear of the unknown, a dread of tomorrow, the unanswered questions of what would happen if Mike just showed up in Glendale, lingered on. Their fear had hovered between them, a palpable force in the morning's silence.

He was pulling out of the drive, heading down the street, when a white Cadillac Seville flew up on his bumper. The driver hit the horn, flashed his headlights.

"What the hell?"

He found Tom Bartkowski in his rearview mirror. There was a strange, almost wild look of desperation on the man's face, which seemed to loom, frozen in the glass of the rearview. Frantically, Bartkowski was waving for him to pull over. After another anxious half block, Wilkins found a thinly wooded pocket at the end of the street, near the playground, and parked. Bartkowski braked his Cadillac to a jerky halt, killed the engine.

Wilkins watched, tight and grim, as Bartkowski hopped out of his Cadillac, strode up to the passenger side, opened the Saturn's door, and climbed in.

Wilkins felt his dark mood cling to him, his voice quiet but aggressive as he said, "What's going on, Tom?"

"We have to talk."

Wilkins saw that the man was clearly agitated, ready to start tearing at his own skin, as if he couldn't stand being inside his body. His eyes were red, wide with a frantic glaze that sent a ripple of cold anxiety through Wilkins. Shaking, Bartkowski sat, sweating, looking over his shoulder, then running his wide-eyed, paranoid stare around the block. Wilkins got the grim impression that both of them should brace themselves for some unseen danger. Next Wilkins caught a strong whiff of booze on the man's breath. He wondered how much of Bartkowski's anguish and distress was caused by heavy drinking. Undoubtedly Bartkowski was on edge. He looked like a man running from something awful that was closing in on him fast.

Bartkowski fired up a cigarette, oblivious to Wilkins's frown of disapproval. "We might have a problem."

Suspicious, Wilkins said, "We? Why would we have what problem?"

Bartkowski lifted a trembling hand to draw on his smoke. "It's your brother. I've seen him."

Wilkins felt his heart skip a beat. For a long moment, he couldn't find his voice; then finally he said, "When? Where? Tom, you're acting very strange.

You look like crap, like you've been up all night drinking. Pull yourself together."

Hopped up on his fear and paranoia and whatever else was in his system, Bartkowski began talking in a fragmented, rapid-fire manner. "Hey, believe me, I'm as clearheaded . . . I wish what I had seen, hell, what I'd been through back in Philadelphia was some kind of . . . some kind of paranoid delusion. I don't know how . . . I don't know what the hell happened to your brother. I wouldn't have believed it if I hadn't been there."

When Bartkowksi lapsed into hard silence, gathering himself as he smoked, Wilkins became irritated with the man's mysterious ramblings. "I want you to calm down, Tom. I want you to tell me what it is that has you all unglued. Don't con me, and don't lie to me."

Bartkowski chuckled bitterly. "Yeah, I know you and I were never really pals. I chummed around with your brother a few years ago. . . ."

"Skip the speech, Tom. I know you. You go your own way, then and now. You had a rather strange relationship with my brother, but I suspect there was some ulterior motive, I don't really know. Right now, I want you to say what you have to say and briefly. I need to get to work."

Bartkowski sucked in a deep breath, steeled himself, looked Wilkins dead in the eye. "Okay. Your brother . . . he can read minds."

Wilkins stared hard at Bartkowski, not knowing whether to laugh or throw him out of the car. "What?"

"I said, he can read minds. And, no, I'm not crazy. I was there, I saw him . . . he can do things to people, sort of invade their bodies with . . . his mind, I guess.

He can make you do what he wants just with his will. I don't know how, but I saw this . . . what looked like some gold star, an amulet, I think it was, on his chest. I think that's what gives him this . . . power. I mean to tell you, I swear, to see his eyes . . . they change . . . they burn, inhuman . . . white, or burn like the sun . . . then they're black . . . like coals . . . smoldering . . . crazy, yeah, I can't even believe what I saw . . . been thinking about it . . . it's all I've been thinking about. I've got to get the hell out of this town."

Wilkins decided the man was too scared to be lying, but he stayed cautious and skeptical. "Do you know how that sounds?"

"Insane, I know, without question. I see the guy on a street corner in Philly, a raving goddamn madman, panhandling, saying he knows me. 'I know you, I know you,' he kept saying, screaming it, damn near chasing me into the hotel lobby."

Wilkins scowled. "Didn't exchange any past anecdotes or schmooze a little?"

Bartkowski became angry. "Hell, I was scared, embarrassed, I don't know. You have to understand, I haven't seen, I haven't even thought about your brother in years. Hey, don't judge me. What would you have done?"

"Handled it. Said hello."

"Yeah, well, you're his brother."

"You're holding something back, Tom. What is it you want? I mean, why tell me? We haven't said more than five words to each other in years."

"I don't know. I'm not sure. All I know, something bad, hell, a nightmare, that's what happened to me in Philly. Guy uses his mind to paralyze me, makes me and my girl—"

Abruptly Bartkowski stopped. Something had happened, Wilkins knew, to terrify Bartkowski this much. He wanted to confess more, but a sudden defiance hardened Bartkowski's face. He was only going to reveal so much, Wilkins sensed. But something had happened in Philadelphia that was torturing Bartkowski with not only terror, but shame.

"Other than telling me about your infidelity and this crazy story, what do you want from me?"

"Nothing, not a damned thing, Wilkins. Your brother told me to see you and I did. He's coming back, if he's not already here. He has some serious scores to settle, at least in his own mind, way he sees it."

"He said that? What? He's using you as his messenger boy?"

"I don't know if those were his exact words. Hell, I can't really recall everything. I was scared to death. He blames everyone in this town for whatever he's become, that much I can tell you."

"And that's all you're going to tell me?"

The paranoia came back, stronger than before as Bartkowski started looking over his shoulder. "Look, consider yourself warned. I did my part. Man, I need a drink. I gotta go, I've got some serious thinking to do. You listen to me, Wilkins, you see your brother, you tell him to stay the hell away from me. You understand? He comes near me, I won't be responsible for what I do!" he nearly shouted, then burst out the door and slammed it behind him.

Stunned, more confused and afraid than ever, Wilkins watched as Bartkowski jumped in his own car. If nothing else, he believed Bartkowski had seen his brother. And something unusual—to the point of causing Bartkowski's disbelief and terror—had happened. But he couldn't believe the business about reading minds. Or was it that he didn't want to?

Reads minds. Invades people with his will. Makes them do his will, human puppets? His heart jumped as he heard Bartkowski fire up the Cadillac. Revving the engine, Bartkowski tore past him, not even glancing back.

His brother was coming back to Glendale. Right then, it was the only part of all this insanity he could be certain of.

John Wilkins couldn't stop trembling as he dropped the Saturn into drive.

Already another day, a new morning, began to feel endless.

Mike Wilkins licked his vanilla ice-cream cone. He was sitting near the reflecting pool, observing the surging throngs of shoppers bustling through the sprawling mall. For these people, it was just another day of frivolity, carefree fumbling, making them believe they were really living, he thought. Young mothers with babies, browsing along in search of bargains. Groups of older teenage girls and boys laughing, looking all around, playing chase-me-catch-me mind games. He blocked out their thoughts, not much interested in what he saw as simply the hollow and shallow endeavors of buying and spending and mingling. After all, he was a samurai with a clear-cut duty, not to mention unwavering, unquestionable honor.

At that moment his first target was playing Pac Man in the arcade. Timmy was alone, working himself up into a controlled frenzy as his yellow monster raced around the screen, gobbling up dots, racking up points so fast the boy was mesmerized by his own ability.

Wilkins had his angle of approach worked out. The invasion of the Wilkinses' minds last night had allowed him to discover pretty much their daily routines. Once he glimpsed what they planned to do the next day, the rest was up to him. Attack. Divide and conquer. Watch them eat their own.

He had been watching Timmy from a distance since the boy arrived right after the mall opened its doors at ten. He knew he had to be careful. But in a town the size of Glendale he suspected a stranger could go unnoticed for a good period of time. At least long enough for him to get his plan launched.

Once he started unleashing his will it would all come tumbling into place, fast and furious, crashing down all around Glendale with the rage of a hurricane. At that point, time would be working against him. He didn't intend to stick around longer than necessary.

He knew the boy wanted to shoot pool, was feeling lonely, wanted to go and challenge the older boys to a game of eight ball. There was one empty table out of five in the arcade at the moment. *Work it.*

He stood, tossed his half-eaten ice cream into a trash can. He snugged his sunglasses to his face. He would have to be careful with the boy. At the moment his eyes appeared normal but intense, piercing in their icy blue pools. If the heat built to a fever pitch and he felt his eyes burning, he would have to pull it back. *Work it.*

He walked up on Timmy.

"Yeah, I gotcha!" Timmy said, excited, dots beep-

ng as they were eaten up in a frenzy. When Timmy
glanced over his shoulder, Wilkins showed him an
easy smile.

"How you doing, Timmy?"

Chapter Sixteen

At first, when he probed Timmy, the boy seemed cautious but curious. Timmy flashed him an innocent look with a hint of skepticism. Then Mike Wilkins answered his silent question as it formed in his mind.

"I saw you down at the ballpark the other night. Your teammates were cheering you on. Bases loaded?"

He felt a wall of brooding start to build around Timmy as the boy remembered striking out with the chance to win the game. His Pac Man was gobbled up as he became distracted by the sudden intrusion. But Wilkins found no anger in the boy toward him for causing him to lose his Pac Man, nor was there the least bit of cynicism or fear of a stranger in him. In fact, he discovered Timmy was glad someone might show interest in him.

Looking at the Pac Man screen, Timmy frowned. The game was over, but Wilkins knew the boy had already lost interest in the game.

"Hey, baseball isn't your game. It was never mine either. I sort of played it 'cause it seemed it was what my parents wanted. Let me take a guess. I bet you have a brother, older brother, pretty good athlete?

You look up to him, maybe, kind of want to be like him? But you feel there's maybe some distance between the two of you, that maybe your family thinks you're a little odd. Maybe you spend too much time by yourself? Bet you read a lot of books, hero stuff. You know, lone warriors doing battle against the evil forces of the world. You see yourself as a good guy, because you know you *are* a good guy, one of the few good ones around, a man of honor. I'll bet you treat people a whole lot better than they treat you."

Timmy was staring at him now, the trace of a warm smile on his lips, a puzzled look in his eyes. It was going to be easy reaching him, Wilkins knew. The kid was sullen, lonely to the point of being withdrawn, but he had a good heart. Just a little invasion of his power into the boy's natural warmth and curiosity about life, and Wilkins fed the goodness in the boy with a slow swell of more warmth and curiosity.

"How did you know?"

Wilkins shrugged. All around them kids laughed and bantered with each other, young boys working video games with a frenzy, consumed with beating old scores, a couple of kids even with two-dollar bets going. Beyond the banks of video machines, pool balls clacked away, a few kids trying to sound tough with some cursing, but there was no feeling behind the words, just curse words they'd heard. One kid was even thinking about having his friends over and dipping into the old man's booze, since both his parents were at work. He'd dilute the alcohol with water. He found teenage girls milling around, thinking about which boy they liked, who was cuter, how could they get their attention. He briefly listened in on the thoughts around them, found no one even mildly interested in him, or Timmy. The two of them would be left alone in their own world.

"I've been there, young man. See, I had a brother, older, athlete. I liked to read books, paint, draw pictures. Felt the world didn't understand, made my own world. They still don't understand, but I've learned to deal with it in my own way. Hey, it's what a man does, how a man becomes a man. He finds himself, finds what he's good at, and does it, no matter what. Screw 'em all. Be true to yourself. In the end that's all you have—you."

Who is this guy? How does he know so much?

Wilkins showed him another easy smile, gestured toward the empty pool table. The boy's thoughts were fairly clear, organized, simple; not the chaotic jumble he had discovered in the minds of most people. Wilkins chalked it up to the innocence of youth, a purity of heart.

"You want to play a game? Hey, I'm not much good either, but maybe I can show you a couple of things. I'm Mark, by the way."

"Timmy, I'm Timmy Wilkins. Are you . . . from around here?"

"Well, I'm visiting some family. I'm thinking about moving down here. What I'm doing, well, I'm thinking about opening up a karate studio. You ever hear of Shoto-Kan karate?" he asked, already knowing the boy had all sorts of martial arts magazines squirreled away in his desk.

Timmy's eyes lit up. "Yeah! Geez, you're going to open up a studio in Glendale? You have a black belt?"

Wilkins shrugged. "I'm not one to boast. A braggart or a bully is not welcome in the martial arts, but I think you already know that. I thought I would just mention it, well, I saw you looking at the karate magazines in the bookstore. Hey, I wasn't following you. I'm not some weirdo. I just sort of found you there. I was wandering around myself, looking for a couple of good books on the ninja or feudal Japan. I bet you're interested in *bushido,* the way of the warrior. Honor and duty. Saving face, even if it means committing *seppuku.* Bet you sometimes see yourself as some black-clad supersamurai, huh? Life kind of picks on you, people don't understand. You want power, like to fight back sometimes but you're unsure of your own abilities. You feel alone, trapped sometimes. Want to be somebody, someone who's known by all, respected and admired for his talent." He saw and sensed he had the boy hooked. "Tell you what, when I open my studio, you come see me." He paused, holding the boy's awestruck stare. "You know, Timmy, I look at you, I see a young man on his way to becoming somebody the world will stand up and notice as a man of honor and God-given talent, someone special and unique. Listen carefully to me. I want to tell you this and I want you to remember this and think about it. The world wants you to crawl because the world has no heart, because the world wants what it wants and the world ends up crawling and groveling because of its selfishness and heartlessness. Take heart and fear nothing and no man. Honor. To the end of your life. Honor. Thing about honor and respect is, they're earned. That's how the samurai got it. They earned it. Be a man and not a punk, because I see you're a man on his way. Hold your head high, stay strong. See every day as a test, even a challenge to your honor."

The boy was inflamed with interest, full of new

excitement for life, to learn, to try something new.
"How do you know so much?"

"Time, my young man, and patience. Experience
too. Hey, more than once I struck out with the base
loaded. Thing is, sometimes failing is the best thing
that can happen to a man. I know it sounds strange,
but it can build character if you let it, if you learn
from it. One thing I can teach you right now is never
to fear to fail. All men fail. The winner, he gets up,
shakes off the dust, and keeps going after it. The winner, the man of heart, of honor, dies on his feet."

Timmy was nodding away, eyes wide with keen
interest. "Okay, I . . . Let's shoot a game of pool."

They went to the pool table. Wilkins fed the slot
four quarters, racked it up. Within minutes, using
his power to relax Timmy and feed the necessary
skill into him, Wilkins had the boy dropping all manner of shots. Long shots. Bank shots. Double bank
shots. Combinations. He showed the boy how to
hold the stick to control it better. Get his shots lined
up, make the stick a part of him, concentrate. He had
the eye for Pac Man—find the same eye for the ball
here. Get into a rhythm, a natural groove. "See," he
told him, "everyone has some degree of natural ability; they just have to find a way to harness it, and that
takes practice, a willingness to learn, even to fail."
Work that screw-'em philosophy some more, bore it
a little into the boy's consciousness. Timmy became
ecstatic, mesmerized by his success. Wilkins didn't
have time to work the boy slowly into his plans. He
wanted him to feel good about himself, and quick.
He wanted him locked.

And owned.

It didn't take long before he had Timmy right
where he wanted him. They were friends. A part of

him, though, felt some guilt. He actually liked Timmy. Beyond that, the worst of it was that he knew he would be sorry if the boy got seriously hurt in his scheme. If that happened, he would deal with it as best he could. If he was going to live a samurai philosophy, he had to realize sometimes the good suffer unjustly. That was just the way it went. A man walked on, head high, used all experience as a simple course of learning, growing stronger.

A few more games, and finally Wilkins said, "Listen, Timmy, I've got to go." He felt Timmy's ripple of panic, fear of abandonment. "Hey, I'll see you around, I promise. Chances are you can find me here tomorrow. We can shoot some more pool. Talk karate. Deal?"

Timmy smiled. "You bet, Mark."

"That's what I like to see. Strength. Confidence. You've got it, son. Just keep your head up. Remember, without honor a man is nothing. You're going to be all right. You have the heart of a warrior. Stay strong, be your own man. I'll see you later."

He held the boy's smile for a moment, then left Timmy standing by the table, alone, but smiling with new confidence, and full of wonder and awe and hope for himself. Beautiful stuff, Mike Wilkins thought. The boy belonged to him.

It was dangerous going into their restaurant, but Mike Wilkins was feeling pretty good about himself and his chances of pulling off his master plan. After his success with Timmy, he was full of silent, laughing arrogance. He stifled the urge to shout to the throngs who he was and that he could snuff them all out if he wanted to, human cockroaches to be stepped on. In time, he told himself, all in due time.

He, the power, was getting better, bolder, stronger all the time. He let the light inside show him the way.

A young hostess, slinking along in a short skirt worn to show off her ass and long legs, led him to a corner booth. Her mind was agitated with all the people she had to seat. *Another day, same thing.* She was faking it. Bored and restless, she saw herself as too good to be doing this job, too young, too pretty. She was full of herself, but Wilkins found little inside her other than vanity. Her name was Sandy. A friend of Jenny's. He might get back to Sandy later, bring her down a notch or two. He was feeling a little lecherous right then.

Anger filled him as he briefly looked around at all the hubbub. Their restaurant, little hubbie-and-wife team. Opulence and around-the-clock party time built on his parents' money. Life was sweet for his brother and Paula. Well, life was about to change, turn downright ugly.

Before sitting, he told the hostess he wanted Jenny to wait on him. He ordered a Heineken, caught a silent oath in her mind. Even as the hostess showed him a tight smile he heard her think, *I'm not your waitress, buddy, you can wait. She'll get to you when she gets to you.* She was going to take her sweet time getting to Jenny.

She slinked away and Wilkins decided against putting a sharp little pain in her behind. Sunglasses on, he casually looked around. It was lunchtime, midday cocktail hour for all those who were in charge of their businesses, built, of course, on the generosity of Lansing Development. The place was packed, near capacity. He saw a few faces he recognized from the distant past. Sam Cullman and Mark Steyr, sitting with some cronies, old classmates. He saw the Mulligans, yucking it up with a couple of blue-haired women. Old Man Steinman, one of his teachers in grade school, hunched over a bourbon at the bar, just as somber as he remembered him. No real scores to settle with any of them, but he didn't know what he'd do about them—or to them—yet. It depended on his mood, and the power. No one seemed to pay the least bit of attention to him, everyone engrossed in themselves. Right. Thoughts all around him, an electric swirl of jumbled and distorted thoughts. He would block them out, unless they became too curious about him. Then they'd have a sudden urge to flee to the bathroom. He laughed to himself.

He shut his eyes, left himself to find Paula. He floated outside his body, drifting away from himself in an all-seeing haze, above the lunchtime revelry. There she was, in the office, bent over the safe. Beautiful woman, he thought, still tight and creamy and lean, holding up nicely even after three pregnancies.

And his timing was perfect. She was dialing the combination to the safe. He memorized the numbers. She began counting the last three days' take. With a fleeting probe he found she had decided to wait until after next weekend to make a deposit in the bank. After all, crime was nonexistent in Glendale. That was about to change, too. A deeper probe into her mind, and he discovered that only she and his brother knew the combination to the safe. It looked like four, maybe five thousand dollars in cash was in the safe. Interesting. It struck him then that the power knew more about his destiny and what he had to do to succeed than even he knew or understood. The power, he sensed, knew Paula would be at the safe at that time. Trust in the power, he thought, it would pave the way, help organize his plan.

He pulled himself back. Looking around for Jenny, he found her talking to a man sitting by himself in a booth in the far corner of the restaurant. Right away, Wilkins recognized the man as Jeff Ballanger, an old classmate of his brother's. He remembered Ballanger as a football, basketball, and baseball hero. The man hadn't changed much over the years. Neatly groomed brown hair, brown eyes that glinted with a hint of a lust for life, a touch of arrogance. Broad shouldered and trim around the middle. Ballanger's arms and chest were still well muscled. He was a man who obviously spent time in the gym, keeping up appearances. And Wilkins remembered Ballanger as another self-righteous individual who had snubbed him in the past, treated him like a pariah. Again, it was never so much what Ballanger did or said; it was the way he looked at him. Better still, he recalled that Ballanger and Paula had been high school sweethearts, dating for maybe six months, if he recalled correcty, before Paula began seeing his brother. Beautiful, he thought. The power knew the way.

Wilkins put himself near the booth. What he heard next and what he found in the man's mind set an angle of attack in motion. He heard Ballanger tell Jenny, "When you get a chance, I'd like to speak to your mother. I'm an old friend of hers from high school. My name's Jeff Ballanger."

Jenny said, "Sure," mildly curious, but not giving it much thought, too busy, and left Ballanger to his beer.

Wilkins felt a loneliness, a quiet but tight hunger in the man's belly. He chuckled to himself. Ballanger wasn't there for the food and the ambience.

Suddenly Wilkins felt his eyes heating up, and pulled himself back, settling into his body. Near the bar, he spotted his brother's wife. She spent a few moments laughing with customers, hustling drinks, running food. She would recognize him, but he would be ready to confront her, maybe pour a little smooth charm on her, get her thinking he wasn't such a bad guy. She was a hot number, always had been. He toyed with the idea of putting a little lust in her heart for him. Maybe later. He'd see. At the moment, he would leave her alone, not even probe her mind. Last night he had taken what he needed from her. She knew about the letter, was concerned, nearly terrified the wretched Uncle Mike would just show up on their doorstep. Soft, naive bitch. She never liked him, a lot of cold distance. Even back then she wished he would just disappear, leave her husband, his brother, alone. She saw him still as just some hopeless, unredeemable alcoholic who would always cause trouble and misery wherever he landed. How easily others judged him. Now he could be their judge, since they couldn't hide their true selves from his power. He grinned, thinking of Jeff Ballanger. Misery and anguish and jealous anger were in the future of his brother and his wife.

Moments later, he found Jenny weaving through the tables with his beer and a mug. As she approached him, he probed her gently, found her a little annoyed that she had to wait on a party of one, thinking about her tip, no more than two dollars. She needed money, wanted some new clothes. She was agitated because it was busy and they were having problems getting the food out quickly. All of Glendale's upstanding finest were a little edgy, demanding service with tight politeness and vacillating tolerance. Assholes, all of them, pure and simple, their lives meaningless and hollow and shallow to a man who could crush them in the blink of an eye. And would, eventually.

They sat there, all around him, acting as if they deserved what they had, full of self-importance, talking about money, thinking about money, big vacation plans in exotic places. Well, he would take them places, all right, and he would kindly wish them all a swift and safe journey on their way to hell.

Then he found Jenny looking at him a little oddly, thinking she recognized him. Of course, there was a chance the children might remember him, having seen a picture or two of Uncle Mike in the family album. He had never spent time with them when they were young, but he did bear a faint resemblance to his brother. Still, there was ten years of time for him to have aged, memories of him all but fading to nothingness.

He showed her an easy smile. "No, you don't know me. I'm new in town. I asked for you because I heard you were a good waitress."

She balked, then forced a smile. He sensed her discomfort as she poured his beer. "What are you, psychic or something?"

"Something."

He breathed in her strawberry-blond, tangy-sweet fragrance, felt her unease grow. "Nice perfume. It's something new, isn't it? Called . . . Scent of a woman. Bet it causes your dad to lift an eyebrow?"

She gave a short, nervous laugh, frozen by the table, peering at him. She was of the age where she was aware of her body, all the forces of her sexual nature awaking from their sleeping depths. He could even feel her, on the way to losing her virginity. It would be soon, he knew. She had a boyfriend, Dad was concerned, his little girl growing up too fast, a female longing to be wanted and loved, on the verge of giving in to the kid she wanted, no matter what it took.

"How did you know?"

"Bought my girlfriend the same perfume."

She hesitated again, and he heard her thinking she knew him from somewhere. Thoughts jumbled, fast and furious, scattered and disorganized. It would eat at her the rest of the day, trying to remember but unable to place his face.

"Uh, you want to hear about our special, sir?"

"No, just a Caesar salad."

He felt her wilt inside, agitation back. In a hurry now to get away from the table, go take care of some real customers, the ones running up forty- to sixty-dollar tabs. She was learning. The world ran on money, even when a romantic like her wanted it to run on love.

"Don't worry, I'll leave you a nice tip," he told her, and saw her flush. Sweet kid. Creamy fluff, he decided, feeling a mean stir in his groin. She would make her boyfriend real happy, in every way. She wanted to be a woman, in a rush to get there, but holding back, wanting to make sure it was right. He envied this Paul Stallings.

She was staring at him, thinking about his eyes, that he had the strangest eyes she'd ever seen. Weird, she thought, kind of spooky; even with those sunglasses on, they seemed to glow.

She swallowed hard, trembling. "Oh, I'm not worried about that, sir. Sorry if I'm staring at you." She was self-conscious now, shy. "I'll be right back with your salad."

He killed his beer. It was time to go. He'd made the introduction. She would lay some of the ground-work for him later. At dinner, if he wasn't mistaken. Dinner at the Wilkinses' would be an interesting affair tonight.

Then he watched as Paula went to Ballanger's table. She looked reserved at first, but Wilkins sensed her excitement, found some memories of the two of them, holding hands and kissing many years ago. He put himself near the table, heard their polite but slighty strained exchange.

"Paula."

"Jeff? What are you doing in town?"

He felt the man fighting to hide his lust, thinking it was a shame he'd let her get away. He heard Ballanger say he had been in town for a few days, that he had rented an apartment for the summer, to see what would happen, maybe move back to Glendale. "Nice place," he told Paula, "looks like you've done real well for yourself." With a probe into the man's mind Wilkins discovered that Ballanger was going to ask if Paula would like to have a drink with him sometime, catch up on old times. Concentrating, Wilkins made Paula feel a fleeting heat in her heart for Ballanger, had her recall all the good times, the laughs, the dances, the walks in the park they had taken, the hand-holding, the gentle sweetness of their kissing and necking. Moments later, she was feeling nostalgic, slightly interested in Ballanger, wanting to know but not ready to pry into what he had been doing. Wilkins knew that before long, he would be testing the fidelity of his brother's wife. There would be time enough, but it was now time to walk as he felt his eyes heating up, on the verge of glowing.

Wilkins tucked a fifty-dollar bill under his mug, stood, and quickly left their restaurant. He knew exactly where he could find the oldest son. And he had seen in Jeff Ballanger's mind exactly where he could find the man's apartment.

They had a two-on-two basketball game in full swing. They were sweating, grunting, full of competitive aggression, young boys dying to prove their manhood, as if sports were the ultimate test of courage, masculinity. They believed they were tough, even as they were safe and cloistered and tucked in the security of their parents' money. Food always on the table. College ahead of them. Big plans for the future. Little punks, he decided, never knew a tough day in their lives, what it was to walk in a man's skin. Until now.

Feeling contempt for this shallow and naive display, Mike Wilkins watched from the bleachers. Then he looked around the courts, the baseball diamonds, the big, bleached-white new Glendale High. Kids were scattered all around, baseball and softball games. Volleyball. Little cliques milling around in the distance. It wanted to take him back, but he was a new man and a lot of the past was no longer important. He had outgrown a lot of the foolishness and folly of everyday people. He looked at life now as easily as looking through a pane of glass. So the power had made him cynical and contemptuous. Well, he had earned the right to be that way, to feel contempt toward ordinary humankind.

He watched the four boys passing, driving for the hoop. Robert Wilkins was almost the spitting image of a younger John. Good-looking, dark-haired kid, tanned, blue eyed, well built, lean but muscular. Again, he sensed the aggression in the boys, went to work on that. The tall, lanky redhead was a focal point for his power. He probed Pat Doornan, found the boy using anger and arrogance to over-compensate for his lack of natural ability. He would bump and brush Robert each time Robert whipped past him for a layup. Doornan was slow, clumsy.

He felt Robert growing angry each time they made contact. He heard Robert wanting to tell Doornan to watch the elbows. Wilkins chuckled to himself. He took control of Doornan. As Robert dribbled, faked one way, then started to drive for the basket, he made Doornan spear an elbow in Robert's side. As Robert nearly collapsed, the wind driven from his lungs, Wilkins forced Doornan to curse the Wilkins boy.

"What did you call me?" Robert snarled.

Mike Wilkins bored rage into Robert. Before Doornan knew it, Robert slashed a right cross off his jaw. Doornan staggered back, eyes glazed, a stunned look on his face. Wilkins put the will to fight back into the lanky redhead. He helped clear the cobwebs from Doornan's ringing head, made the kid drive a right that cracked off Robert's mouth. The brawl was on. They grappled, slamming punches off each other's sides, toppled next in a flailing heap as the other two kids tried to jump in, pull them apart.

It had gone far enough. Mike Wilkins put a knifing pain into all four of them. Pain in the knees, the chest, the stomach. They started grabbing them-selves, crying out, forgetting about the fight.

Swiftly, Mike Wilkins strode over to them. He loomed over Robert. With the sun blazing down directly above and behind his head, he knew Robert couldn't clearly see his face. He pulled the power back, eased their pain a little.

Mike Wilkins looked at each of their faces, felt compelled to chuckle quietly at their pain. "Don't you girls know it isn't nice to fight? Look at you, Robert. Hauling off and flattening your buddy here. What the hell is wrong with you? What? Like father like son?"

"Who . . . who are you?"

"You don't know me. And if you ever think you do, you'll wish to God you didn't."

He found some arrogance in Robert, some image the boy had of himself as a know-it-all, tough kid who could do what he wanted. Right then, he didn't like his oldest nephew at all. The kid was in for a hard lesson.

Hearing someone shout, "What's going on?" from a distance, Mike Wilkins turned and walked away.

The day was shaping up nicely.

Chapter Seventeen

It was time to do some righteous work on his brother's wife. If nothing else, he would at least begin to lay the foundation for some ugly marital discord.

As Mike Wilkins walked deeper into the woods, angling toward the apartment complex where Jeff Ballanger had rented a unit, he put the power out there, shutting his eyes and floating toward Paula. The more he thought about trampling her image as the loving and faithful wife and mother, the easier it became to send the power to wherever she was.

It was as if the power demanded that her fidelity be shattered, soiled, and the woman, wife, and mother reduced to some worm slithering in garbage.

Concentrating, feeling his eyes heat up, he found her moments later in her car. She was driving home, alone. And there was a wistful look on her face. Perfect. She was remembering, thinking about Ballanger. *Thy brother's wife may make it all too easy.* Or would she? How strong was her love and commitment to his older brother? Only one way to find out. Beginning now.

He eased the power into her, heard her playing

back her conversation with Ballanger in the restaurant.

"Yes, I married John. We have three children."

"I heard."

She had been curious about how he knew. No, he hadn't been prying or asking questions, laying on some schmooze, old high school sweethearts, going back. Both of them wondering what it could have been like. On the tips of their tongues but not saying it. They were cautious, respectful of each other and their situations, but there was a little sexual tension between them, more so on his part than hers. There. He caught an image. Young teenage love, arms locked around each other's necks. Kissing, tongue action, his hands rubbing and kneading her breasts. She was breathing heavily.

Wilkins decided to turn up the heat, put a little stir of hot tingling between her legs, felt her heart racing. She was trying to force the image out of her mind. He saw her draw back from the embrace and heavy kisses, shy and coy, telling him they'd better stop. He did. She was appreciative. He respected her wishes, but that only made her want him more. The kid was a real gentleman. Her thoughts became chaotic. Their talk in the restaurant flashed back. Ballanger was telling her he'd been divorced for a year, injecting some sadness into his look and tone, but keeping any hint of bitterness toward the ex out of his voice. Just didn't work out, glossing over it, moving on. Next he was telling her he had been a lawyer up in Chicago. His specialty was malpractice suits. He got sick of it, no challenge anymore, was thinking about opening a private practice in Glendale.

"I always thought I would come home again," she was remembering him telling her earlier.

She fought to shut it out, their brief talk, the past, but Wilkins made her tingle again between her legs. Now she was shaking her head, swallowing hard, fighting to focus on the road as she drove away from downtown Glendale.

Enough. Wilkins opened his eyes, the world hazy, bright with intense white light as he concentrated on bringing the power back. As he spiraled out of her, away from the car, he caught one last image of her telling Ballanger, "Don't be a stranger, Jeffrey. Come by sometime and I'll buy you lunch."

Suddenly Wilkins found himself slumped against a tree. He searched the woods, the fading rays of late afternoon knifing through the foliage. He tasted the sweat on his lips, sucked in a deep breath, slowed his breathing with an effort of will. Slowly the power swelled inside him, back and alive and as strong as ever.

Where was Ballanger?

He walked to the edge of the woods, strolled through a park with benches and swing sets and sandboxes. He looked at the white three-story apartment complex that stretched several blocks away from him. Mothers and kids were emerging from vehicles. Laughter, grocery bags, videos. Dinnertime was falling over Glendale, all the good family folk, together again.

Wilkins looked farther down the lot. He already knew Ballanger was on his way home. He waited a few minutes, then spotted the white Mercedes Benz as it swung into the lot, stopped midway down the complex. Ballanger piled out, his hand fumbling for the keys as he pulled out a twelve-pack of beer. Even at a distance, Wilkins sensed the man's heat. Ballanger was making plans to build himself a summer love nest.

It was going to be easy, he decided. Old love rekindled, new flames of lust, burning and yearning out of the past. Only they weren't teenagers anymore, resisting the urge to take it all the way. Oh, this was going to be sweet.

Wilkins chuckled. Turning, he walked back into the woods, pulled out the amulet. He stared into the black eye, lifted the amulet, and kissed it. "You are my one and only. You will show me the way."

John Wilkins couldn't eat after hearing his children talk about their encounters with the stranger with the long black hair, the sunglasses, and the penetrating, almost glowing eyes behind the dark shades. He sat at the head of the dinner table, stunned, read the growing fear in his wife's eyes. Again, he asked each of his children to describe the stranger, what had happened. Intent, he listened, his heart throbbing in his ears.

Three separate incidents, nearly the same description, with the exception of Robert, who hadn't gotten a clear look at the man after his fight with the Doornan boy. But he knew the stranger was of medium height, lean build, almost skinny, dressed in slacks and a sports shirt.

"His back, or his face, it was in the sun," Robert said. "You know what he told me? 'Like father, like son.' If I think I know him I would wish to God I didn't. Like he was threatening me. Spooked me, I know that."

"What about your fistfight, Robert? That's not something I want just to gloss over either."

Robert gingerly rubbed the welt on the side of his

mouth, then looked at his father with remorse. "I don't know what happened, Dad, it was just a fight. I'm sorry about it. Pat and I, we apologized to each other after. All of us were really shaken up by the whole thing. But the thing was . . . I don't know, one minute we were in this fight; the next thing I know, none of us could move. Everyone described the same kind of sudden pain. It was there; then it was gone—after he walked away."

Then there was Timmy. His youngest son was full of excitement about his encounter with the stranger. He listened while Timmy, all smiles and wide eyes, talked about this man, almost in a state of hypnotic euphoria. This man had shown him how to shoot pool at the mall, claiming he was visiting family, thinking about opening up a karate studio. Timmy said he felt some connection with the man, the stranger telling him they were a lot alike. Loners, he guessed sheepishly, liked to read, write. Even down to having an older brother. Wilkins felt a cold ball of ice drop down his chest, lodge in his belly.

Then Jenny, who had waited on the same man Timmy described.

"He had the weirdest eyes," he heard his daughter say, her words seeming to reach him from a great distance. "He never took off his sunglasses, but even through them I could tell they were real strange eyes. I could see them, sort of . . . piercing through me. I can't say if his eyes . . . glittered, or glowed."

"Yeah," Timmy put in, "he did have strange eyes, but I didn't really think about them until now."

"What's even weirder," Jenny went on, "I don't know, it was like he knew me, or things about me he shouldn't have. Almost like he could read my mind, or knew what I was going to say even before I said it. Yeah, it was like you said, Robert, spooky. He had one beer and ordered a Caesar salad, but he had already left when I came back with it. There was a fifty-dollar bill on the table," she added, her eyes bright with fleeting gratitude, as if the obvious overtip made the whole encounter normal but just a little strange. "He was gone, just like that."

Suddenly John Wilkins felt trapped, adrift in his own frightening world. He recalled his bizarre talk with Bartkowski, how the man clearly seemed a raving paranoid, claiming all sorts of unbelievable things about his brother. Now his children, one right after the other, meeting this stranger. Could what Bartkowski had claimed be true? That his brother could read minds? Use his will, some supernatural power he had to make others do what he wanted?

Then he became angry. If it was his brother—and he had little doubt anymore that Mike had returned to Glendale—then Mike was toying with his children, using them as part of some plan that was churning around in his warped mind. John Wilkins felt his instinct to fight back, to protect his family, flare up, stronger, darker than ever. Something had happened to his brother, some unexplainable change, but what?

"What is it, Dad?" Robert asked. "You look like you've seen a ghost."

"What, Dad?" Jenny asked. "Do you know this man?"

"Paula. Can you go find a picture of him in the family album, please?"

Slowly Paula rose, her fear clinging to her face like a dark shroud. But there was something behind the dark look, he thought, watching his wife silently leave the dining room. Paula seemed distracted, clearly concerned about the day's events, but she didn't seem to be quite there.

"Him who?" Robert asked.

"How well do any of you remember your uncle Mike?"

Confused, his children looked at each other. Jenny shrugged and said, "I think we were all too young. You said he left town years ago. That he went east to find work."

"I don't think I ever saw him but one time, Dad," Robert said. "I can't remember him. I was too young."

Timmy was still beaming. "It's Uncle Mike? He told me his name was Mark."

Moments later, Paula came back to the table. She showed each of them a picture. They studied it. Jenny frowned.

"That's an old picture, Mom. I don't know, it sort of looks like him. I mean, the man I saw, he sort of looked like Dad, only he was real lean in the face. Almost . . . it was almost like looking at a skull."

"I don't know, it could be," Robert muttered, shaking his head. "Nah, looks too heavy here, in the face, that is, but the body's thin."

"Paula, let me see that." He took the photo, a black-and-white picture of Mike, sitting in an armchair. It was taken at the old farmhouse. He figured Mike wasn't even quite twenty in the picture. His hair was short, his face full, almost chunky, what bloating he saw in his face most likely due from continued heavy drinking.

"I couldn't find any other pictures of him, John."

"All right, kids, I have a strong feeling your uncle Mike is the man you met today."

"Why would he do that? Just show up?" Timmy

asked, innocently. "Why not just come here? Why be so mysterious? Why lie to me about who he is?"

"I don't know, son. But if you see this man again, you tell him he is to come and see me. I'll know if it's your uncle Mike." He wanted to add, "and tell him he is to leave you alone," but figured that would only alarm them, raise questions he couldn't answer at the moment.

For long, tense moments, he looked at his wife. He knew they would talk about this later, alone. Suddenly he was very much afraid. Worse, he couldn't even be sure of what it was he was supposed to fear.

Wilkins studied his wife for a moment, as she seemed to stare at nothing. Finally she met his gaze, her eyes clouded by some strange distance he couldn't pin down.

"Babe, are you okay?"

She nodded. "I'm fine. It's just . . . I don't want to worry."

Silently he watched his wife as she picked at her food.

Mike Wilkins was a dark shadow in the night, nearly invisible in the thick shroud of blackness cloaking the neighborhood. Slowly he walked up the drive, quietly opened the Cadillac Seville's door, and settled into the backseat. It was almost eleven o'clock. The neighborhood was silent, no one even out walking a dog.

He used the power to take him inside the split-level home.

"Who is she, Tom? Why has she called here three times today? Some little slut you're banging when you claim to be going to Philadelphia on these supposed business trips?"

Dan Schmidt

A misty image of Tom, wringing his hands, panic on his face. "All right, all right, I've been messing around. Can you keep your voice down? The children are sleeping."

"Why is your bag packed, Tom? Running back to her? And no, I won't keep my voice down! Toni, that's what she calls herself. Your little bitch says she wants money from you, that she deserves it, and if you don't give it to her, she's going to the police. Says she knows your drug connections, Tom. Oh, boy, you've just been having a grand old time, haven't you? You bastard!"

"I need to get out of here. When you calm down we'll talk, okay? I don't need this, I've got enough problems."

"Oh, you've got problems, all right! Hey, I'm not finished with you, asshole!"

Wilkins pulled it back, smiled. In a few short minutes, the man's problems would be over. He sank down low behind the driver's seat. He heard the door open, the man's wife still shouting at him, full of her own fury, anguish over his betrayal. The front door of their home slammed shut. Then he felt the closing of Bartkowski's energy. It almost felt like a sizzling heat coming off the man as he opened the door, threw a duffel bag on the passenger seat.

When the door closed and he fired up the engine, Wilkins popped up. Wilkins saw his own face in the rearview, the grin stretching his lips, baring even white teeth. He saw that his eyes were glowing now, white and hot, with a shine that seemed to even turn his dark shades white.

"Hi, Tommy. How you been? Hey, I missed you, old buddy."

Bartkowski's eyes bulged wide with shock and terror as he found the mirrored grinning face. The man started to scream but Wilkins took his voice, made him back out of the drive.

Wilkins heard his own voice turn quiet with controlled savagery. "You had your chance, Tom, to do the right thing. The fact that you didn't doesn't surprise me. I can feel that you have a full tank of gas. Hey, you didn't need to lie to your wife. You don't need a cooling-off period; you were heading back to Philly. Try to smooth the stormy waters with Toni." He listened to the man's terror-stricken thoughts, a half dozen questions racing through Bartkowski's mind. "Just drive, Tom. You and me, we're going to take a little drive out into the countryside. Don't worry, your troubles will all be over soon. Of course, you're going to leave a widow behind." He heard the frantic pleading of the man's thoughts, then fought to block them out. It took some concentration, but Wilkins managed to bring silence into his own mind, ridding himself of Bartkowski's terrified, groveling voice.

"If it'll make you feel any better, Tom, you're only the first of many. Soon, real soon, a whole lot of others, wicked and unredeemable, will be following you straight into hell. Won't have to run anymore, Tom. That's you, isn't it? Things get too tough, you run. Problem is, you create your own hell on earth. Amazing. You're all flash, Tom, all style, no substance; you're that hundred-dollar bill with nothing to back it up, just a piece of dead paper. You wouldn't have lasted one hour in my shoes. Your wife was right, only kindly let me add you're just a pure asshole. Hey, cheer up. You're not alone in your wicked ways. You'll be relieved to know you're not the only one committing adultery around here. Man alive, what

I've heard . . . talk about dressed-up garbage cans."

Mike Wilkins laughed.

When they were just over twenty miles west of Glendale, Mike Wilkins found a suitable place to do it. He made Bartkowski pull over on a dark and lonely stretch of country highway. Out here in farm country, the blackness was impenetrable, seemed like a living thing all around them. Moonlight glazed the wheatfields, sheened the structures of farmhouses, isolated, here and there. In the distance, Wilkins saw the telephone pole. It was just over two hundred yards away, plenty of weight in the sturdy pole to finish Bartkowski. Of course, he would have to leg it back to Glendale, but he had all the time in the world that night.

Bartkowski, though, was on the verge of beginning an eternity in the beyond.

"This is it, Tom. Sorry I don't have time for last requests. It was good of you, though, to return the rental. Hate to damage someone else's property unnecessarily."

He hopped out the car, quietly shut the door. He made Bartkowski gun the engine, floor the pedal. He watched as Bartkowski drove the Cadillac, a white missile, straight for the telephone pole. He heard Bartkowski's mind screaming, invaded the man's mind, sat in his head and watched through his eyes as the telephone pole raced and loomed for the Cadillac. Bartkowski shot the vehicle up to eighty-two miles per hour, his mouth wide in a scream that only he heard, trapped, echoing as he watched his own death rushing at him.

Wilkins penetrated the man's scream with a cold burst of laughter, then pulled out of him, turned, and walked away right before the impact. He didn't have to see it to know Bartkowski was hurled through the windshield, slammed into the telephone pole, and bounced back into the hurricane force of flying wreckage, all but crushed.

Mike Wilkins heard the gas tank blow, a thunderous ball of fire roiling over the highway, lighting the thick blackness of the lonely countryside in a glowing band. Walking on, he laughed even as he felt the fever fire his brain.

Chapter Eighteen

He was going to have to work fast. Already the cook-out was well under way, his brother making the hamburger patties, ready to fire up the large brick barbecue pit. Mike Wilkins saw the revelry in his mind, put himself there long enough to take it all in through the hovering mist of the power that transported him there.

At least two dozen friends and neighbors. Good-sized backyard to allow the merriment to roam at large. Six-foot wooden privacy fence. Pool, but with only the smaller children swimming. Mike Wilkins saw older kids playing volleyball. Women were laying out snacks near the cabana, a lot of shorts and blouses and tank tops, tanned creamy skin, even a couple of young moms with babies in carriages. Most adults had drinks in hand, talking about their jobs, kids, vacations, big plans for the future. Then he heard brief talk about Bartkowski. Naturally, they were shocked, none of them knowing what to make of it. Accident, or suicide?

In short order, the party would be over. Abruptly.

Mike Wilkins paid the cabbie, erased the man's memory of him, then stepped out into the harsh sunlight. He looked around the neighborhood. Probing every household, he felt nearly every other home void of energy. He could hear kids laughing and splashing in backyard pools, but he knew he was otherwise unobserved. One block over, he heard a lawnmower growl to life.

It might prove a problem, walking in then out of the neighborhood, without being seen. But he would deal with whatever came up. After all, mere mortals could not stop him. Indeed, he was feeling more and more aggressive with the power, maybe even reckless in his invincibility. Each time he used the power he found himself needing to use it again and again, to stay strong, grow stronger, take away the fever.

After last night's killing of Bartkowski he had found himself drained, almost lifeless. Feverish and racked with a burning nausea for a good hour, he had wandered along the dark countryside, while the wreckage burned the body beyond recognition. He found that once the fever vanished, a craving arose to use the power again, get it back, act on it. Only using it seemed to satisfy the power anymore. It needed more to feed it, or was it feeding on itself?

For a fleeting moment, he thought about his past addictions. There was some similarity between the two. Get, use, and keep using, no matter what the cost. Briefly he wondered if he should be frightened of this spiraling condition. Then his other voice whispered from the faint depths of the light, *Move on, keep moving, don't question!*

Indeed. And he urged it on, wanting to hear more, to reassure himself.

You are your own god! You are your own creation. Now, go and create. Take heart! Pure and clean justice demands vengeance and the blood of the wicked and the impure.

So be it.

Striding one block down, he spotted Sam Watterson's purple Corvette parked in Cassandra Dooley's driveway. Inside that split-level home, Wilkins sensed the hot energy of pure animal lust. He smiled. They were just about finishing up. She was struggling to reach climax, while he was fighting to keep it going. Just something for him to pass the time, salve his wounded manhood.

It had been something of a stroke of luck when Mike Wilkins had ventured into the tavern, just outside Glendale, less than an hour ago. There, he found Watterson drinking heavily, commiserating with his cronies, Mickey Tomlin and Stan Peterson. All three men had been too busy railing at the injustice of life to be bothered with noticing him as he had taken a seat in a booth in the far corner of the place. After a quick probe of their minds, Wilkins put his plan together while he nursed a Wild Turkey and ginger.

Watterson was on his way to see Cassandra Dooley. It seemed the two of them frequently indulged together. Then there was Tomlin, the town drunk. He knew Tomlin vaguely from years ago, but he had discovered enough darkness inside the man to advance his plan. He found the man had a collection of guns at home, even sat there at the bar, bragging about his proficiency with firearms. Tomorrow would be Tomlin's big day. Sunday. Save the guy for church services.

And Peterson, the kid who had stomped him to a bloody pulp so long ago, then lied about him and Christine? A probe into Peterson found that the man lived alone in a small house just outside of Glendale. He was recently divorced, was now bartending. Found some guilt in the man about dipping into the till at the end of the night, rationalizing his theft since he had to put up with so much crap from everybody. So he was feeling pretty lonely but belligerent, proud but wondering if he had anything to be proud of. Well, in short order Stan Peterson was going to have an unwanted pal from the past to console him and correct his errant ways.

Wilkins focused back on the moment. Watterson was the prize right then. The man was livid at Wilkins's brother. He recalled some more of the angry talk back at the tavern. Watterson let everyone within earshot know just what he thought about John Wilkins, railing out jealous rage and suspicions about some extramarital activity on Wilkins's older brother's part. "What next?" he remembered Watterson snarling. "Son of a bitch takes my job, I'm sitting on my last few hundred bucks. And get this: the other day, Cassandra, she tells me she thinks this asshole is kinda sexy. She sort of shrugs it off, telling me she's always had this thing for married men. Played it off, uh-huh, but I'm starting to read between the lines here. What? Wilkins slipping her the high hard-on behind my back, too? If he is, I tell you what, there'll be hell to pay! That's something I'll talk to her about, you had damn well better believe. Round two may be up and coming."

Beautiful. It was all falling into place.

Another mental sweeping of the street revealed that he was still unnoticed, and Wilkins walked right into her home. He already knew the front door was unlocked. Quietly closing the door, he looked around the spartanly furnished home. Plush white leather couch, glass coffee table, wet bar. Some aerobics equipment, a running machine in the corner of the room. Giant-screen TV and VCR. Lady liked to spend her alimony from two previous marriages on better things than mere furniture. Yup, trips to the Bahamas and Hawaii, fancy clothes and jewelry, especially loved jade, believing, like the Asians, that jade brought good luck. Of course, he knew she had honed her cutthroat trade years ago, when his parents had paid her off for her silence. Another false allegation of sexual molestation by the weird, perverted little Mike Wilkins. Well, he was learning, hard and fast—accumulating and assimilating knowledge and wisdom at light speed—that a lot of things in life that had the same beginning must come to the same end, a sort of cosmic justice. Fact was, there was a strange justice in life, even when most of the human race looked around and wondered why the innocent had to suffer.

Well, the innocent do suffer, he knew, and could damn well attest to that. But he believed it was only to make them better, stronger, more pure and noble. And justice always arrived when the unjust least expected it. Job and Solomon knew and passed that test of courage, he thought, so what could possibly make mere average mortals think they should escape any pain and suffering? The more he looked around, the more he found all the raging and scheming and manipulating in the human heart, the angrier he became, the more he wondered if there were any good men left on earth.

The more he knew he was the only real justice left on the planet.

Either way, it was time to settle up, and there was no time to waste.

He heard them grunting and groaning upstairs, but not a shred of affection for each other could he find. Slowly he walked upstairs, straight into the bedroom. Watterson was just rolling off her. She was the first one to spot the intruder. Shock, then recognition cleared her eyes. She started to scream; then Wilkins took their voices, paralyzed them. Naked, unmoving, eyes bulging in fear, they looked especially ridiculous to him. Animals doing it in the bushes looked more human and loving.

Smiling, he looked at the half-empty wine bottle by the bed, the bottle of Percodan for the guy's pain on the nightstand.

Time to create. He blocked out the jagged chaos of their thoughts, and told them, "It's all right, lovebirds. I'm in control of your bodies and your souls. Give me a second here and I'll explain." He laughed. "Okay, get dressed, Sam, the party's over. Lots to do and there's not much time. Your former boss is getting ready to fire up the barbecue pit."

John Wilkins fought to pull himself out of his somber, distracted mood. Everyone else seemed to be enjoying themselves. His kids and their friends were working up a good sweat around the volleyball net, little ones splashing around in the pool. Paula and her friends were laying out chips and dip and other goodies. Talk was light, strained with politeness, until Jack Hauser, one of his staff reporters, mentioned the violent death of Tom Bartkowski.

"What do you think, John? I mean, I called the medical examiner and the sheriff over in . . ."

He listened, but Hauser's voice seemed to reach his ears from a distance. Lack of skid marks, the explosion, the neighbors saying they heard Bartkowski and his wife arguing violently during the day, the whole thing strange. Body was burned to a crisp, but dental records confirmed it was Tom Bartkowski. It looked as if he *wanted* to drive right into that telephone pole, that his car must have been doing close to ninety, the way the accident scene looked, wreckage and pieces of the man scattered, they figured, a hundred yards in every direction.

"Write it as a standard obit, for now, at least until we get some more facts," he told Hauser. He glimpsed them, his writers from the paper, giving each other strange looks. The boss—the new boss—had spoken, end of discussion. "All right, anybody need a beer? I'm about ready to fire up the pit. Hope everybody's good and hungry. Got steak, filets, burgers, hot dogs. Lobsters are steaming as I speak."

He tried to inject a light air into their sudden dark mood. He knew they wanted to talk about Watterson, Bartkowski, feel him out, understand things. They were looking to their new leader, the man of Glendale, but he didn't feel he deserved—nor did he want—this new respect.

And he couldn't help but feel a pang of guilt, knowing he was holding something back from them. All he really wanted was for his life to return to normal. Could it? Knowing what he knew, or suspected?

It would all sound too insane if he told them about his conversation with Bartkowski. Suddenly he felt very alone. They were his employees, friends, and neighbors, but they seemed like faceless strangers to him just then.

"John, I realize this probably isn't the time or the place to talk about Sam," Hauser said, "but can I say something?"

Wilkins tightened, searched their faces. The dreaded subject had been broached. Ken Foley fiddled with his beer, cleared his throat, and said,

'Thing is, we've been talking about what happened at the office. I mean, we all have."

"And?"

"Well," Hauser said, "Sam's crazy. I mean, he's been known to do some . . . pretty crazy things. I'm sure you've heard the stories, the wife-stealing, the bar fights. For all we know the guy could have a few guns stashed in his home."

Ralph Burrows killed his beer and said, "I think if he shows up at the office, well, you might want to have our good sheriff on standby, at least for the next couple of weeks. Maybe a security guard. It's just a suggestion, John."

Hauser said, "You read about crazy acts of violence all the time, John. Guy walking into McDonald's, blazing away with an M-16. Disgruntled postal worker shooting down fifteen, twenty people. I don't think we're being unduly paranoid."

A tight silence hung among them for long moments. Finally Wilkins told them, "I understand what you're saying. I'll give some thought to hiring a security guard. Last thing I want is to turn the paper into an armed fortress . . . but could be . . . you've made a good point. Okay, enough of that, let's get ready to eat."

Again, he busied himself to distraction, opening up a bag of coals, going to work filling the pit. He looked up, saw his wife smiling at him. He waved to Paula. It looked as if the day might turn out to be a good one, after all. What could possibly go wrong?

He made Watterson dress, blocked out the man's rage. The big blond's heart was pumping with violence, an animal fury, mixed with fear now, and the urge to fight back.

Mike Wilkins recalled the contempt Watterson had viewed him with years ago, had read the man clearly with a look that said Wilkins was a nobody to stay out of his way. Different person, same thing.

Beyond the violence in the man's heart, Wilkins found fear, specifically fear of failure. Anger and arrogance were simply a mask the man wore to keep the world from seeing what he really was: insecure, shallow.

"Don't worry, Sam, you'll get to act on all that aggression soon enough. Man alive," he said, chuckling, checking out the bruise and the lump on Watterson's jaw. "That brother of mine whacked you a beaut. Didn't think he had that in him. All you did, you turned the guy into a hero. Hey, you think he deserves that honor?" Mike Wilkins found a pen and paper. "Okay, listen up, tough guy. I'll tell you what to write. It's a farewell letter. You'll get to spew out all that hate and rage toward my brother. Distraught fired stallion about town finds out not only did the guy can him, but, hey, he's been sleeping with his woman, too. Ugly, I know. Poor Sam, pushed over the edge. Full of booze and pills, guy just went berserk, couldn't take it no more." The man fought it, but Wilkins put the words in his mind, forced Watterson's hand to finish the brief note. It was short, sharp, and to the point. Later the police would read it. Doubt and suspicion would be cast on his brother. Of course, his brother would not be directly linked to the crime, but there would be talk about town, rumors and innuendo.

Wilkins growled, heaved a long breath, tuning out their desperate, pleading thoughts. "Don't ask questions, people. I can read your thoughts, I know your dark and wretched souls, I can control your bodies.

My will is your will. Please stop whining about what's happening. Okay, Sam, leave your wallet and watch on the dresser there." He did a probe of Cassandra Dooley, heard all the usual questions, sensed her terror, her disbelief that this was happening. "I never put a hand on you, at least not where you claimed, Cassandra. Of course, I was the fool back then, thinking a woman as beautiful as you might be interested in me. Oh, well, you live and you learn." He felt his anger growing, knew his eyes were turning white, felt them heating up. He felt a sudden onslaught of fever, then a flash of panic. Their wills were strong, full of defiance, rebellion. "Cassandra, do you have some lighter fluid in the house?" It took extra effort, but he discovered the woman had what he needed in a kitchen cabinet downstairs. He bored into Cassandra's mind. "You always thought you were too good for me, but I can't find anything in you even remotely good, lady, for you even to think you could believe that. Fact is, you're like a lot of women I've seen over the years." For a brief moment he thought about the beautiful little redhead, his heart wrenched by anguish and sorrow, his sense of utter, desperate, and raging aloneness, fully aware, more than ever, that he would never find the connection to something decent and real and genuine he had so longed for over the years. He pulled himself together, clenching his jaw, knew there was no comparison here. "You, like them, look right through me, or not at all. I'm a nobody, a loser, they're too good. Most of the time I'm just ignored. That's the worst thing in life, lady, but you wouldn't understand. To be ignored, well, after a while, man starts to look at himself in the mirror, just to make sure he exists." Rage grew hotter, driving a spreading fire through Cassandra. She started twitching, even as he fought to keep her still. She wanted desperately to flop around, scream, anything to act on the pain she felt consuming, eating up her insides. He put laughter in her head, then shut off the laughter. He heard his voice in her head, growing in a fever pitch, mounting with hot, righteous fury. He told her, "Thing is, you'll never understand because you live on your beauty and you use your ass to conquer men. I have more heart, more soul, more guts, more character, more talent, than you'll ever know, could even dare to conceive of, and I can tell you with no hesitation, beyond a shadow of any doubt, there is no better man around. You used to look at my drawings, yes, I remember. You thought they were good, damn good, but you looked at me like I was a little strange. I saw but denied all the distance in your eyes even as I saw something dark was churning in your heart. Now I can see it clearly. You were afraid to get too close to the fire, so to speak, but you figured you could eat up my soft and good heart and digest my life back then like a tender filet mignon. Lady, you have not a shred of a poet's class, of a real human's fire in the heart, and if I had the time I would teach you a hard lesson, which escapes you. To know life is to suffer and wear your suffering with your head high because you know you're better than the world, and in the end that's all a man needs because that's all he's got. That's your falling-down, that's your evil. No heart, lady. World owes you because you're Cassandra Dooley and they're not. You are the unholy and you are both in the presence of your death."

What is this . . . what-what-what, dear God in Heaven . . . oh, no, please. What are you two doing?

You put something in the wine? Two, you, no, no, stop, let me . . .

She didn't get it, but it was all beyond her anyway. She heard but she didn't listen, wanted salvation but wanted it her way.

No saving grace for this one. Even a quick death was too good for her.

Wilkins said, "No, Cassandra, that's not what's going on here. It's no act, no setup. You're going to die, and Sam's going to do it for me. It's called justice, payback, lady. Look at it like this, and find some little glimmer of gratitude and selflessness. Tough, I know, but try. I'm saving some poor sap from marrying you again and losing his life's savings, not to mention the torment you inflict on your victims. I'm doing all men a great justice here. Hey. You know what the prayer position is, lady? I know you do, I see it in your memory. Well, allow me to allow me." He branded the image in her mind of what the prayer position was, made her see herself on her knees, hungry, slobbering and slurping. He put the same image into Watterson's mind. Watterson's jealous outrage was instant.

"Okay, Sam, let's do it. Now, here we are . . . it has to look like a murder-suicide." Laughing, he bored his will into Watterson, caught the frenzied scattering of thoughts and dark, twisted emotions, tuned them out. There was a strange look of imploring but also anger in Waterson's eyes as he bent over the woman. As Watterson wrapped his big hands around her throat, it looked to Wilkins almost as if he wanted to apologize to her. In fact, he heard Watterson's mind screaming for release, trying to find his voice, wanting this to stop, telling her in the silent shrieking of his thoughts he was sorry, but did she really do that to Wilkins?

Chuckling, Wilkins stood behind him, put his rage into the man's hands. Made him squeeze harder and harder. Gagging sounds tore from her lips, her eyes bulging, face turning red, then blue. He kept her paralyzed, as the life was strangled out of her, her thoughts begging for it to stop.

"No dream, Cassandra. Say good night." He heard Watterson weeping inside. The man was a sniveling coward. Funny what he found out, thanks to the power.

Blackness then slowly clouded Cassandra's mind, shrouding over her on her knees before Mike Wilkins.

He felt Watterson grieving over what he had been forced to do, full of self-pity and fear. "Thought you were a tough guy, Sam. Geez, pull yourself together, man." He made him release her throat. Quickly he made him go downstairs into the kitchen. There, he had Watterson pull out the lighter fluid.

"What am I doing to you, Sam?" He made Watterson douse himself thoroughly, had him soak himself in lighter fluid until the full can was drained. "Why, I'm sending you to a little barbecue party. Grab a good-sized knife while you're here. Yeah, that butcher knife will do just fine. In case someone tries to stop you, you might need to wave it around. Hurry now," he said. He saw his brother lighting the coals, flames leaping to life. "In fact, run, Sam!" Watterson shuddered, moving with wooden steps, then broke into a jog. "Run, Sam, run!" He laughed, then said in Watterson's mind, *Don't worry, Sam, you won't have to worry about fear of failure. In fact, I'm sending you out in a blaze of glory.*

* * *

John Wilkins was heading for the kitchen to check on the lobsters when he heard his name suddenly screamed in a voice of mindless rage. Whirling, he found Sam Watterson bursting into the backyard, waving a butcher knife. For long, terrible, frozen moments, no one moved, no one spoke. Stunned, Wilkins heard the obscenities ripping from the man's mouth, watched as Watterson strode in a strange twitching, jerky motion past the pool, like a human puppet.

Wilkins felt the cold wall of fear all around him. No one knew what to do, what Watterson was going to do.

"You ruined me, Wilkins! All of you are nothing, nobodies, you ruined me! You killed me! You murdered a great man!"

"John!"

Paula called his name, urging him to do something.

Someone shouted, "Call the police!"

"Watterson!" Wilkins yelled, running across the patio. In his narrowed tunnel vision, he glimpsed the frozen faces of shock and disbelief. Watterson wheeled, and Wilkins spotted a distant look in his eyes, a wild, bulging stare of desperation. They were eyes of insanity, Wilkins thought, but there seemed to be something behind the eyes, driving the man— as if Watterson were fighting himself. And the more Watterson bellowed, the more the man's voice didn't sound like his own. What was he seeing in those eyes, rolling all around, seeing but not seeing?

"You, you son of a bitch!" Watterson screamed at Wilkins. "You took it all from me! My job, now you took my woman! You've been fucking Cassandra!

You're a liar and a thief! You took everything I had! You people, this bastard destroyed me!"

Wilkins heard a gasp, felt a hush fall over everyone around him. Horrified, he glimpsed the shattered mask that was Paula's mortified expression.

Someone cried for somebody to get the knife out of his hands. Someone else cried out that Watterson was soaked with lighter fluid.

He glimpsed Mark Attley making a move toward Watterson's blind side. But it was as if Watterson already knew the man was charging him. The right cross Watterson threw cracked Attley on the jaw, launched him airborne in a giant splash into the pool. The children started screaming, thrashing in the water to get out.

"You ruined me, Wilkins! You took everything I had! Now it's my turn! Fuck my woman, will you! Take my job! You bastard!"

And what Watterson did next finally shook everyone out of their numb disbelief.

In a blur of frenzied motion, Sam Watterson snatched up a can of lighter fluid as two more men rushed his back. He squirted the fluid into the barbecue pit, the fire leaping to renewed fury over the grill bars.

John Wilkins couldn't believe his eyes. He was paralyzed in midstride, less than a dozen feet from the man, when Watterson stuck his head into the whooshing flames. The women and children started shrieking, a few men gasping in horror. It was a crescendo of different meshing voices, but their screams and cries were almost drowned out by the hideous wailing that tore from Watterson's mouth as he turned himself into a human fireball. Someone was going to wrest the knife from him before; they stopped short now, skidded, pulled back, recoiled.

Even as he was burning alive, he kept screaming, "You bastard, Wilkins, I'll kill you, I'll take your whole family! I'll rape your wife!"

What was that voice? Wilkins briefly wondered. It didn't sound quite sound like Sam, and the eyes he saw glowing, white with bulging hate and rage inside the sheet of flames, didn't even look human.

Wilkins acted impulsively. He raced down the side of the pool, scooped up a large towel, thrust it in the water. From some great distance he heard Paula cry his name in alarm.

In the next frozen, eternal moment, Wilkins saw Watterson holding the can of lighter fluid. He squeezed the can, hosing forth a tongue of fire that seemed to spring right out of his chest. A fresh wave of terror seized the men near the pit. They dove, stumbled over lawn chairs as the tongue of fire seared over their heads. Then the line of fire caught on itself, raced back into the can. A second later the flames imploded in the can. There was a dull, muffled explosion, but the new burst of fire wrapped Watterson in yet another layer of raging flames.

Wilkins danced up to the human torch that was shrieking, waving the knife, flailing its arms. He started to charge Watterson, the dripping towel held out like a shield, when a flaming leg cracked off his chin. Before he knew it, Wilkins was laid out on his back. He heard the chiming in his ears, saw the white light of flashing stars in his eyes. Then the screaming, the sickeningly sweet stench of roasting flesh pierced his senses, cleared away some of the cobwebs. He heard someone vomiting, saw through the haze in his eyes all the scrambling bodies. Men still tried to charge Watterson, but the knife was flashing, ripping out, just missing flesh, steel in hand glinting as the flames ate the man up from head to foot.

Somehow, John Wilkins stood. Everyone was now recoiling, fleeing from the shrieking, fiery thing that twitched and flailed along the side of the house.

Even though he already knew it was beyond hope, John Wilkins followed the human fireball, those hideous shrieks of a man burning alive echoing in his mind with a bone-chilling clarity he knew he would hear in his dreams at night for a long time.

"Hey! Hey, who are you?"

He was walking swiftly northwest, angling away from the open door of Cassandra Dooley's home. He was concentrating hard, keeping himself there, bouncing his power in and out of Watterson. He felt the fever raging in his brain but couldn't be sure if it was the pure, living heat of the agonizing fire that was consuming Watterson or the power reacting to its use, an overheated machine doing what it could to cool itself down. He had to go in and out of the man to make him do his will, but he couldn't stay more than a few seconds for fear of getting trapped in the man if he died suddenly.

And the man who so hated his brother was burning alive. In the mist, Mike Wilkins saw his skin melting off him like wax, eyes being roasted to blindness, the orbs sizzling goo. He concentrated even harder then, and could clearly see it all. He heard their screams of shock and horror. Children fleeing from the human fireball. Watterson flailing, throwing his knife around, guys leaping back, the fuel catching fire, racing back, igniting in the can, engulfing Watterson yet again in a new wall of fire. It was tough to stay there, to make sure Watterson fought back to keep them from trying to save him. Yes, his brother, trying to play hero. *Throw your leg out!* A leg, engulfed in flames, skin now eaten to the bone, lashed out, slamming his brother on the jaw.

Some voice, gruff and suspicious, penetrated his power. He sensed danger, discovery.

Again, the voice behind distracted him. He pulled the power back, let the events on the next block go over as they would.

The power drifted him back into his body, making him aware of his limbs, the free-floating, boneless sensation gone. Suddenly he became aware of the man behind him. And sensed his suspicion.

Wilkins spun, saw a grim-faced, middle-aged, balding man in shorts and a tank top. Angry at the intrusion, Wilkins shredded the man's memory of him, sent a knifing pain through his chest. As if he'd been poleaxed, the good-intentioned neighbor hit the street, gagging, clutching his chest.

Swiftly Mike Wilkins fled the neighborhood. He was soaked in sweat, fever raging in his brain. His eyes felt as if they were burning up in their sockets. He felt weak, nauseous.

In the distance their screams echoed over the split-level houses. Down the street, he saw his brother's neighbors scrambling from their homes. No one looked his way. He had to get out of the neighborhood quickly. Ahead, there were some woods where he could fade away. He couldn't be discovered now. There was too much left to do.

Chapter Nineteen

"Bottom line, John, way you read it, this was all some bizarre act of revenge against you? It was all lies, how you ruined the man, stole his woman? It was too much for him to take, drove him over the edge? Try to understand how all this looks. You smack a guy through your window at work, justifiable self-defense, I'll grant you; then you fire him; then he comes over to your party, doused with lighter fluid, and sticks his head in the barbecue pit and burns himself to a crisp?"

John Wilkins was sitting on his couch in the living room. He was holding an ice pack to his bruised jaw. Paula was sitting next to him, but she wouldn't look at him. He felt the shock, anger, and shame like an electric current, sparking at him with her lingering fear and humiliation from the nightmare they had endured. And Wilkins still couldn't believe what he'd seen and heard. Why would Watterson lie about him committing adultery? Another twisted act of revenge?

Wilkins clearly caught the skepticism in Chief Keller's voice. He looked up, felt his expression harden, his gaze narrow.

Keller was hunched over in a straight-backed

chair, an antique piece Wilkins had inherited from his parents. Wilkins sensed that twenty years of homicide work on the mean streets of Chicago had flared up all the natural cop's cynicism in Keller. He found Keller scribbling furiously in his notepad. The chief was a big, broad-shouldered man with a bullet head and a crew cut. He had icy blue eyes, razor-thin lips, and a massive jaw. He was dressed in his standard-issue brown uniform, star on his chest, .357 Magnum revolver in his holster on the gun belt.

"If I didn't know better, Chief, I'd almost think you didn't believe that's what happened. I didn't douse the man with lighter fluid and shove him in the fire."

Now Keller met Wilkins's stare. There was no change in the piercing blue eyes, but Keller clenched his jaw. "I know that, John. I'm clear on what happened, but not why."

"Chief," Paula said in a quiet voice of controlled anger, "you and your men have been here for almost two hours. You've questioned everybody, including the children, you've taken their statements, and everyone confirmed the same thing. It's just like my husband told you. I mean, the children, they're scared to death; give us a break here. I'm still shaking; it was something I'll never forget for the rest of my life. Some of our neighbors needed sedatives from the paramedics, they were so terrified. It was suicide. Sam Watterson just came in screaming curses. He was a madman. John went after him and tried to save him with a towel he had soaked in the pool. My husband risked his life to try to save that poor man. But . . . it was so . . . I don't know, Sam, he kept fighting, waving the knife around. It was as if he wanted to . . . just burn himself alive in front of everyone and not have anyone try to save him."

Nodding, Keller looked at his notes. "I don't have a problem with putting it down as suicide. I quote, 'you ruined me, you took everything I had, now it's my turn.'" He looked from husband to wife, paused, a flicker of embarrassment in his eyes as he cleared his throat. "I'll skip the rest of it. Problem I have, John, most men usually stick a gun in their mouth, or hang themselves. This is the first time I ever heard of a suicide where a guy douses himself with lighter fluid and torches himself into a human bonfire. Forgive me if I sound blunt, maybe even a little crude or skeptical. John, you're a newspaperman, you understand. I have to ask hard questions to get the facts. I'm just trying to make some sense of this. I'm sorry, Mrs. Wilkins, but I have to ask this." He asked Wilkins, "Were you having an affair?"

Wilkins clenched his jaw. "No."

Again the chief cleared his throat. Wilkins looked at his wife, read her simmering anger and doubt.

"Only reason I ask that, John, well, there's going to be some ugly rumors all over this town. This whole incident, well, let's just say all of us have a full plate of problems. I'm just trying to help you see what may happen. I mean . . . well, understand, we're still going to need to do some serious talking."

Wilkins nodded. The worst, he knew, was yet to come. A simple denial of his alleged adultery wasn't going to be enough for Paula. Questions were going to be asked of him, by the chief, his wife, friends and neighbors. He didn't have any answers, which would only make it worse, stoke suspicion in others. But he knew the chief was only doing his job. Still, that didn't ease the nightmare reality of what all of them had seen. In fact, Wilkins found himself still so stunned, shaken, that nothing seemed quite real at the moment.

The chief shook his head, his expression mirroring Wilkins's disbelief. "I was a cop for a long time . . . but I've never seen anything like this. I mean, we just zipped up a guy who burned himself to a crisp, down to a skeleton almost—sorry, Mrs. Wilkins. I have to ask your husband some more questions. Mrs. Wilkins, maybe you can go check on your children? Understand they went with some friends of yours?"

"Yes, that's right."

Wilkins met her gaze, a penetrating look that further shook his confidence to restore order and sanity to their lives. They had sent their children with the McMartins. Suddenly he didn't want her to leave, didn't want his family out of his sight. He wanted to hold her, tell her Watterson had lied, make her understand, make it right between them again. Suddenly he felt as if he were losing his wife.

"Maybe I should be with the children right now."

He was going to protest, tell her to call the McMartins and have them bring the kids home, but nodded instead. "Okay, but call me when you get there. And, please, I want all of you home soon."

She stood, not looking at her husband. There was a haunted look in her eyes; her face drained of color. Like some wooden fixture, she rose, excused herself to the chief, and left them alone.

"How much longer do you and your deputies need to be traipsing around my home, Chief? I thought you said you were finished with the questions."

"I'm almost done, John. And we're not traipsing."

"If I didn't know better, and I'm a little familiar with how the police mind works—I did work a crime beat, years ago, in Chicago—well, I sincerely hope you're not thinking maybe I pushed him—unintentionally—into that fire."

"Did I say that, John?" A hard pause. "This is all just routine. This is not an interrogation, you are not under any suspicion, let me make that crystal clear. I'm sure you understand how something this bizarre is going to affect this community. I want all my facts straight. That's all."

Wilkins held the man's stare, decided to drop it. He knew, all right, and he wondered if he'd ever be able to walk the streets of Glendale again. After his friends and neighbors were interviewed, they had all practically fled. Of course, his reporters and staff writers swore to call him ASAP, wanting to know how to write this story, how he wanted it handled, but the paper and getting this story out was the last thing on his mind. He started thinking about Watterson's strange behavior. What caused it? Some . . . state of demonic possession? No, that was too crazy. Maybe an autopsy would find drugs in the man's system that had made him look and act so psychotic.

"Chief."

Wilkins followed Keller's gaze to the kitchen hallway. It was Deputy Reuter. He was one of the six young deputies who worked for the Glendale Police Department. They were all hired by the city council, usually came here from other counties or states, with law-enforcement degrees, fresh out of college. Since there was no crime in Glendale, they didn't need more than a half dozen uniformed cops at any one time.

Keller stood and went to Reuter. The deputy looked grim, and Wilkins saw the man glance his way, a strange expression on his face, as if he were in the presence of something inhuman. Something was indeed wrong, he sensed.

Reuter led Keller a little way down the hall, out of earshot. He heard them speaking in low voices, but couldn't make out the words. Finally Keller returned. The chief's stare was hard, almost angry.

"What?" Wilkins asked as the terrible silence lingered. "What is it?"

"Cassandra Dooley," Keller said. "She's been found dead in her bedroom. It looks like she was murdered." Another pause; then Keller told him, "You and I, we'll talk again."

John Wilkins felt his heart drop. Suddenly the world was turning darker, colder, angrier. He knew his life would never again be the same.

The man lived in a shabby little trailer on the northern outskirts of Glendale, but he already knew that, knew him so well, in fact, that the man might as well have been a pane of glass he could look through.

Less than an hour ago, Mike Wilkins had walked right into the trailer, and turned Mickey Tomlin into his prisoner.

Now Wilkins sat in a leather recliner in front of the television, holding Tomlin hostage on the couch. He took to calling him the Mickster, or Mickster, or the porn hack. Earlier, he had the Mickster make him a tall glass of cheap bourbon and ginger. Now it was time to relax, unwind, let the fever cool. He had created the mayhem he wanted, and now decided to let the confusion and terror of the day's events take hold of Glendale, get its citizens nice and locked up in even more confusion and fear.

One look around the dirty little trailer and Wilkins

had the man's life revealed to him without much probing. Bookshelves were lined with dozens of porn videos, with all manner of porn magazines stashed, almost to overflowing, in a hall closet. He discovered the Mickster's personal darkness but wasn't sure he needed to act on it. It seemed the Mickster lusted for a lot of the young girls around Glendale, especially those in the nine- to twelve-year-old range. The Mickster saw them as ripe and unsoiled, little hot cherries, still young enough to be virgins. Indeed, the man's soul raged with relentless, burning desire to do all manner of wicked things to these little girls. He used alcohol in a futile attempt to kill those twisted passions, but the more he drank, the worse his lust tormented him. Funny how that happened.

"You're a real sick guy, Mickster. People around here knew what was in your head, they'd lock you up and throw away the key—maybe worse. Maybe cut that thing right off you. Thing is, if I let you live, I can see in your future that you'll eventually act on those dark impulses. Stop that, Mickster. Accept what is. I can hear your thoughts; I can control you. My will is yours. I'm getting a little irritated at having to explain that to all you people. I want faith in me, compliance and obedience to my will and my way." He tuned the guy's desperate, whining thoughts out, but he had dug through the man long enough to know his future. Indeed, there would be a rash of ugly sexual molestations in Tomlin's tomorrows. It would be a short reign of terror, involving no more than four girls, but it would bring shame and disgrace and infamy to all of Glendale. In short, Tomlin would put their squeaky-clean little slice of heaven on the map. But it was not going to happen. Not any more.

With his mind, Wilkins flipped through the one hundred and thirty-six cable channels the man had. The bloated little pervert was even behind on his payment to the cable company. That was his nature, though. Squander his money on pleasure, chasing the wind, little trips to Chicago in search of prostitutes. Chuckling, Wilkins watched the TV, one image after another flashing by, a running specter of light and sound. Wilkins could catch each program, know it from beginning to end, in an eyeblink. He was getting stronger and feeling more aggressive, in control, with each passing minute.

So they sat in the murky shadows, the blinds drawn, one lonely light burning down the hall from the bedroom. What interested Wilkins was the man's gun collection. He had Magnums in .357 and .44 calibers, Colt .45s, .22s, two pump shotguns, and hunting rifles. Those guns would be the instruments of fear the man would use on his future victims.

Only Mickey Tomlin was not going to live past tomorrow.

Wilkins put the glass to his forehead. The chilled glass felt good against his hot skin. The fever had cooled some, but he still felt weak and nauseous. He needed to rest. He intended to take refuge here for the night. He knew Tomlin never had visitors, and the few he considered his friends never called or dropped by unannounced, figuring the guy was always blown away on booze, sitting alone and watching porn. Diddling.

"It's unbelievable, Mickster, what I see, what I know about all you people here. Everyone's dissatisfied. Want to be something, do something, create something. Only they grab more, take more, covet more. Too much time on people's hands around here, certainly too much money. Most of them don't even deserve what they have, sort of blindly take it all for granted. Take you, for example. You want to be this hot-shit writer, even groveled before my brother for a chance to be some freelance journalistic word wizard, a student of human nature, way you see yourself. Only all you do is drink and fiddle with yourself here. I don't find a lick of worthwhile, redeemable, forgivable talent in you. You're not good, Mickster, at anything. Not even good enough to kill your own torment with booze, because in order to have the privilege of doing that, a man has to know real suffering, take and give, eat it, get it up and go at it. What I'm saying, Mickster, is that you're better off dead." He sipped his drink. "Okay, I'm going to take a shower. When I come back, you'll wash my clothes, I'll help myself to a little more of your booze; then I need some sleep. I'll put a porn video in for you, give you something to do. Tomorrow, we'll get up, have a little breakfast together. And then . . . we're going to church."

John Wilkins sat on the edge of his bed. He couldn't believe Cassandra Dooley was dead, that it clearly looked as if Watterson had murdered her. Strangled her. Chief Keller had made him wait more than an hour before he returned. And the way Keller had looked at him, suspicious, not knowing what to make of anything, saying in a grim voice that it appeared to be murder-suicide but there would be an ongoing investigation. Keller had also said a suicide note had been left behind and that Watterson had mentioned his former boss in the note. Wilkins asked to see the note, but Keller said it was being logged into evidence. What evidence? Against him?

Was Keller now suspecting him of being involved in this . . . murder-suicide? No, sir. But hold off putting out anything in print. Grim, Keller had again made it a point to tell him they would be talking later.

He looked around the bedroom, then found his gaze fixed on the clock on the nightstand. Two minutes after eleven. Why did time feel as if it were frozen? Thank God, the children were home, safe in their beds. Why was he so afraid to lie down next to Paula, to go to sleep? He knew why, even as he still wanted to deny everything that had happened.

"John?"

He felt his wife's stare boring into the back of his head. Slowly he turned. She wore a look of dread and anger, a hard mask of fear that he feared would never go away.

· "Tell me the truth. I saw the way that woman looked at you the other day. Were you sleeping with Cassandra Dooley?"

Right away, he shook his head. He wanted to be angry with her for even asking the question. Something was happening all around them, and he wasn't sure what it was or why it was happening. It danced through his mind to pack up his family and take a long vacation until the storm died down. Then he shoved down the urge to run. Instinct was warning him that no matter where they went, this trouble, this thing that was happening would dog them, haunt them. No, he had to stay and fight, stand his ground, make his world right again. There was no other way.

"No. I did not ever put a hand on her. I did not sleep with her. Why Watterson said what he said, I can't tell you." She held his stare, her look haunted. "Paula, you believe me, don't you? I would never do that to you. For the love of God, you do believe me?"

Her answer seemed like an eternity in coming. "I . . . I don't know what to believe. I want to believe you. . . . I do believe you."

He wasn't convinced. "Paula, I've always been faithful to you. Please. I don't need to convince you of that. Do I?"

"John, Cassandra Dooley was murdered. Try to understand how all this looks to me. I can't remember the last time there was violence around here, much less a murder. I'm scared, John, for all of us. Something is going on in your head. I feel like you're holding something back from me."

"I'm not holding anything back; I'm telling you the truth. All right." He sucked in a deep breath, his heart racing, throbbing in his ears. "I have a strong feeling that all that's happened . . . it has something to do with my brother. I don't know what or why, but he's here. We both know, or at least strongly suspect, that he's here. Somewhere in or around Glendale. I . . . I know it sounds all too crazy. My brother is behind what's happened."

"How?"

He noted the mounting skepticism in her voice. "I don't know." He turned and fixed her with a grim look. "I'm going to find him, Paula. I have to confront him."

She swallowed hard, her eyes full of fear. "So what do we do, your family? We all just go on like none of this ever happened? John, you're not thinking straight. I don't see how any of this can be connected to your brother."

He didn't either, or at least not in any way he could pin down. It sounded as if he was passing the blame, so he decided to drop the subject of his brother. "Our good chief of police has seen to it that our home is no longer a crime scene, so all we can do is go on as normal. What else can we do? Tomorrow, we get up, have breakfast, and go to church."

She just stared at him, speechless. Finally she stood. Silent and tight with anger, she walked toward the bedroom door.

"Where you going?"

She didn't answer right away. "I need some time alone. I need to think."

He sat alone, fighting down a rising panic.

Chapter Twenty

"We are a community in mourning. No amount of words I could say to you today would express the feelings I know many of you have about the tragedy we have suffered in Glendale. We have lost three members of our community to sudden and unexplained violence. I can only say that none of us can explain why certain things, such as what happened yesterday . . ."

Mike Wilkins laughed to himself, pulled the free-floating sensation of the power out of the church, back into his body. From his passenger seat, he looked at Tomlin as he drove his Chevy Nova toward the heart of Glendale. Tomlin had his .357 Magnum tucked in his waistband, beneath a light windbreaker. There was a frantic, pleading look in Tomlin's eyes, and Wilkins could well understand the man's terror. After all, he had already put into Tomlin's mind what he wanted him to do. And he had shown the man what waited for him at the end of the line.

The power was feeding on Tomlin's fear, so strong now that Wilkins felt light-headed, boneless, beyond his body but still in charge of all his faculties. After its repeated use, Wilkins had come to understand the power maintained its strength, nurturing itself on the darker emotions it evoked from its victims.

Wilkins settled back in his seat, enjoyed the ride, the blazing sunshine shrouding the buildings of Center City in a white sheen. It looked like just another sunny Glendale Sunday morning. Presently there wasn't much traffic, since the good citizens of Glendale were either attending ten o'clock mass or gathered with families for breakfast, either at home or in the restaurants scattered around town.

Wilkins shut his eyes, telepathically told Tomlin, *Just keep driving, Mickster, we're almost there. You know, you should have been going to church all these years. See, if you were at least a believer you could hope to save your immortal soul in a final, groveling moment. You know, Mickster, "spare me, for I know not what I do."*

Wilkins laughed, long, cold bursts of laughter that dredged up even more terror in Tomlin, but strengthened the light inside him with more heat, more brilliant glowing in the eyes. Suddenly the world around him was transparent in the power, radiating, reaching him with all its living energy, fueling the power's invincibility. Then he started to hear countless overlapping thoughts from all around Glendale. For a frightening, almost uncontrollable moment, the din became maddening in his mind in all its distorted, fragmented shrieking. With pure effort of will and angry concentration, Wilkins finally managed to block out the swirling storm of all those thoughts. For a long moment, he sat trying to will his sudden fear away, worried why this onslaught of thoughts had rushed into his mind from all directions, against his command.

It was gone now; that was all he knew, all that mattered.

When he was through here, the home of Stan Peterson would provide him with his next place of refuge.

Then he concentrated, projecting himself back into Saint Paul's Catholic Church. He saw that his brother and his family sitting up front, a few rows from the altar, intently listening to Father O'Shay's sermon. The old priest was saying that they must all trust in God in times of unexplained tragedy, for who could possibly fathom the insanity of evil? Indeed, this should be a time for all men of good faith to pray for the souls of the departed and their families. Through the drifting mist of his hovering, boneless state, he scanned the sea of parishioners. They were decked out in their Sunday best—suit jackets for the men, women in an array of blue and white dresses. He saw a lot of long and solemn faces, even fear in many of their eyes. He could feel the tension, too, of all the good citizens, all God's faithful children. Next he caught the sideways looks of fear and accusation from parishioners around his brother. Yes, there was a whole lot of distress and discomfort toward and about his brother. People who thought they knew John Wilkins were now wondering just what kind of man he was. And Paula was sitting there, a piece of stone, face hard, anger in the eyes. Indeed, she was suspicious, and he even heard her doubting right then her husband's fidelity. Sweet. Soon he would loosen her up but good. Might as well carve a large A for adultery on their foreheads.

Then he saw Christine and felt his throat constrict. She was sitting next to her husband, a handsome man with short brown hair, an aquiline nose, strong features. She was as beautiful as he remembered her. He didn't know the man she had married, but he had a gentle look in his eyes, a softness about his expression that told him Christine had most likely chosen the right man. And they had a small baby, which Christine was holding in her arms. It was a boy. He felt his heart race, a pang of envy, then an ache of longing in his chest. That should have been him sitting next to her, he thought. If only . . .

He pulled himself out of there. The church was just as he remembered it. He spotted the crucifix looming in the distance as Tomlin closed, driving slowly down the main street. It was a large church, built of granite and stone and marble, stained-glass windows depicting a good number of the saints. Best of all, the pews were made of wood. Last night, he had laid out the final touches to his plan in his mind. The power seemed to be urging him to move faster, get it done, that his time was running out. Already he knew that his brother strongly suspected he was in town. He might not even have time to play the children against the father, but he would make the effort just the same. An awful lot of havoc to wreak yet.

He forced Tomlin to roll into the sprawling lot. They found an empty space and Tomlin parked his car, killed the engine. For several minutes, Wilkins sat, staring at the rows of steps leading up to the front doors of Saint Paul's. He felt a sudden and intense hatred for the church, for all it stood for. Hope and forgiveness and reconciliation. Honor and worship of a God he no longer needed, much less believed in. They were fools and hypocrites, all of them.

His other voice, sounding more and more like his own, whispered, *Yes, you're right to feel and believe as you do. It will be here that you will show them all that no one, not even their God, can save them from your righteous judgment. Remember, their weakness is your strength. Their evil is your good.*

With a fleeting probe he saw them all rise to pray. "Our Father, who art in Heaven . . ."

Wilkins felt his eyes heating up, almost sizzling in their sockets. He looked at Tomlin, said, "My brother, it would appear, Mickster, has forgotten all about you. Of course, you haven't done anything to prove you should write for his paper, but he knew you never would. Why don't you go in there and show him you're not a man to be so easily forgotten."

The man fought it, but Wilkins clenched his teeth, bored his angry will into Tomlin, and forced him to get out of the car.

Mike Wilkins laughed. It was going to be another beautiful day.

Unholy but righteously sweet.

After the solemn chorus of "Amen," John Wilkins heard a sudden commotion in the back of the church. He was sitting toward the end of the pew, near the far aisle by the wall, beneath the stained-glass image of Saint Jude. The first warning that something was wrong was the stark look of fear on Father O'Shay's face. When people turned to see what had frightened him, gasps of fear and outrage tore from several mouths.

"Oh, my God," he heard a woman cry, "he's got a gun!"

Turning where he stood next to his wife, John Wilkins froze at the sight of Mickey Tomlin coming straight for him with a very large revolver in his hand.

"Stop! Someone stop that man!" Father O'Shay bellowed, his microphoned voice echoing throughout the large church.

Tomlin was after him and him alone, Wilkins knew. And there was that strange, distant, psychotic stare in the man's eyes, those white orbs, seeing but not seeing. It was the same insane look he'd seen yesterday on Sam Watterson.

A woman screamed. Everyone else seemed paralyzed in the constricted vision of Wilkins's gaze.

"Wilkins! You bastard!" Tomlin screamed.

His only thought to protect his family, Wilkins grabbed his wife and slung her to the pew, then snatched his children down to their seats. He was prepared to throw his body over them as a shield when he saw Tomlin run up to their pew, looming over them, that wild, bulging stare burning with a hate and fury he never thought existed in the man.

"No!" Father O'Shay roared. "Not in the house of the Lord!"

"You betrayed me, Wilkins! You're a liar and a thief!"

The words were shrieked in a voice Wilkins didn't recognize, a voice that sounded almost like the angry growl of a wild beast.

The large revolver was coming up in his hand as Tomlin stopped in the middle aisle. Wilkins sprang to his feet, determined to either get the gun away from him or stand in the line of fire, take the bullet, and hope someone grabbed Tomlin. Behind Tomlin, male parishioners were shoving their way out of the pews in a scuffling frenzy to reach Tomlin.

One man cleared the pew—just as Mickey Tomlin opened his mouth, jammed the long barrel of the revolver past his teeth, and clamped his jaw shut.

Two more steps and Wilkins would reach him. "Don't!" he yelled.

Then Mickey Tomlin squeezed the trigger. There was a muffled sound like rolling thunder, as the back of Tomlin's skull shattered, exploded in a grisly pink mist of bone fragments and blood.

The gore sprayed the man who was charging Tomlin's back.

In utter disbelief, John Wilkins stood watching as the corpse crumpled in a sprawl at his feet. The screaming of women and children erupted, seemed to pierce his skull, chime inside his head for what seemed an eternity.

Mike Wilkins saw it all clearly, the image of the parishioners scrambling or frozen in horror stark and alive in his mind. He kept angling deeper into the woods, in the direction of his next refuge. In the distance, he heard a siren.

Wilkins laughed as he saw his brother crouching over Tomlin, Brother John hung his head in despair. Several women fainted, collapsing in the pews. Already the churchgoing throngs were racing for the nearest exits. Many stood gawking at the blood pooling behind Tomlin's shattered skull.

There were going to be a lot of funerals around town during the next few days. But that wouldn't hinder his plans. In fact, he intended to see the streets of Glendale run red with blood, imagined row after row of body bags lined up on Main Street.

Strangely enough he discovered he wasn't feverish. In fact he couldn't remember feeling better in all his life.

After a short probe of his brother last night, he knew John would not flee his home, pack his bags, and take a vacation, come back when the heat had died down and the carnage was simply a nagging and ugly memory. No, instead his brother was determined now to find him, stand his ground, be a man—for a change. It wouldn't be long before John would get his wish. If his brother believed he could turn his home into a fortress, then he was sadly mistaken. Later, he determined, he might have to go to work on his brother's world from the inside out, show him that his home was far from safe.

POLICE LINE. DO NOT CROSS.

John Wilkins stood by his car, staring at the yellow tape strung across the front doors of the church. It was all an obscenity, a sacrilege. First, a suicide during mass, now Chief Keller and his deputies, the paramedics, the medical examiner inside, treating the church like a crime scene.

Sweating, his suit jacket slung over his shoulder, Wilkins looked at his family. Like everyone else—either milling around in the parking lot or having already gone home—his family wore stony masks of shock. The Saturn's engine was running, the air-conditioning on high. He was waiting for Keller, certain the man would want to take his statement. Or more.

He motioned for Paula to roll the window down. When she did, he told her, "Listen, I have a feeling I'm going to be here a while. Why don't you take the kids home. I'll call you later."

He found anger and uncertainty in her stare. She sounded coldly polite, as if he were some stranger, when she asked, "Are you going to be okay?"

"I'll be fine."

She held his gaze, and he dreaded the future more

267

than ever. She seemed to look right through him, unfeeling, uncaring, distant.

Suddenly Jenny snarled, "I don't want to go home! I hate this! I hate what's happening! It's all your fault, I hate this place. I want to go see Paul. I'll die if I stay with you people! You brought this on your own heads; your own souls are beyond redemption!"

Stunned, Wilkins stared at his daughter. For a frightening moment, he thought he saw the same burning eyes of hate and rage he had seen on Watterson and Tomlin. She didn't seem hysterical; instead her voice sounded controlled with an icy, determined, but savage anger. For another terrifying moment, he wasn't even sure it was his daughter's voice he heard.

"Jenny!" he heard Paula cry in alarm.

Just like that, she seemed to wilt, suddenly, strangely exhausted. Whatever he thought he'd seen in her eyes was gone, leaving a blank stare on her face.

"I'm . . . I'm sorry, Mom, Dad. I . . . I don't know what came over me. I'm sorry, I didn't mean to say those things."

Wilkins read the dire concern in Paula's eyes. His sons, taken aback by their sister's sudden and bizarre outburst, backed up, hugging the doors.

"Should I take her to a doctor? Maybe she's in shock, John."

He thought about it, then shook his head. "No, at least not yet. Wait for me; we might go later. I want everyone home. Please. Go on without me."

His wife's anxious look lingered on Jenny for a long moment; then Paula reversed the Saturn. He watched the car slowly roll toward the mouth of the lot. He stood, feeling a cold wave of fear slithering through him, an unrelenting sense of dread holding him paralyzed.

"Wilkins!"

He spun, jumping a little at Keller's gruff voice. He waited as Keller strode down the steps. Glendale's police chief was scowling behind his mirrored shades. As he closed, Wilkins noted the sweat running down the man's granite-hard face. Keller removed his Stetson, took a handkerchief, and mopped his brow. He was clearly agitated.

"You and I need to have a talk."

"I couldn't agree more, Chief." He resented Keller's aggressive tone. "I suppose you're going to tell me that Mickey Tomlin's blowing his brains out in front of me and my family and several hundred witnesses makes me a suspect in a crime?"

Keller squared his shoulders, slipped his hat back on. "Suspect's not quite the word I'd use, but I'd say everything that's happened is happening around you, and, yeah, for my money, it's damned strange, if not suspicious. In three short days all of a sudden I'm looking at an epidemic of murder and suicide. How would you see it all, if you were in my shoes? And you know that suicide note from Watterson? Seems the man held a double grudge against you. In the note he claims you were having an affair with Miz Dooley, that you stole his job and his woman. What I want is for you and me to have a face-to-face—later, at my office. I've got plenty of questions, and you and me need to get some answers. Time we're through, I want to know you like I've walked in your head for ten years."

Wilkins felt his blood race with anger. "This is crazy, Keller. First off, and I've already told you this, I have never cheated on my wife. I sure hope you're not going to go announcing all over town that I have. Watterson had a grudge against me, that's all, plain and simple. A grudge that obviously ate the man up. Now, his suicide and that preposterous lie he left behind could do serious damage to myself and my family."

"You call it preposterous, Wilkins. I may find another word for it. Give me time. Whatever, maybe you care to try to shed some light on all this. Maybe you've got some theory other than two men committing suicide in front of you as a final act of a grudge that might help me sort all this out."

"It's my brother."

"What? What brother?"

"Well, you wouldn't know, but I have a brother. I can't explain it, but something, I don't know, call it a hunch, my brother is somehow behind all this. I'm sure you've heard of hypnosis."

"Vaguely. It's psychiatric voodoo, as far as I'm concerned. So where's this brother of yours? Maybe I put a few questions to him, what, he's going to turn *me* into a psychotic suicide."

"Chief, please, hear me out."

Wilkins sucked in a deep breath, chose his words carefully, already knowing just how insane he was going to sound. But he had to try. If nothing else he would give Keller a description of his brother.

"I'm listening."

Wilkins glanced around at the departing throngs, glimpsed faces of neighbors and friends. They were suddenly faceless, nameless entities, casting strange looks at him. They looked unsure of him, even afraid of him. He had never felt more alone in all his life. He began, "The other day, a few hours before Tom Bartkowski died, he came and saw me. . . ."

Chapter Twenty-one

John Wilkins felt as if he were being summoned before a medieval inquisition. When he walked into the Glendale police station he had a morbid thought that the only things missing were manacles, a chopping block, and the stretching rack.

It was the events of the past two days, fraying his nerves and carving him up with anxiety, which placed these strange thoughts in his mind. All around him were death and destruction, wrapping him up, a walking mummy with a constant sinking feeling that the worst was yet to come. He was oblivious to the scenery, but he was angrily aware he was under silent scrutiny by the deputies.

Feeling dazed, numb, Wilkins walked toward Chief Keller's cubicle. Keller was hanging up the phone, waving him on as Wilkins walked past the deputies at their desks. He felt their eyes, inquisitive, cynical. Or was he merely imagining it? After all, what did he have to be guilty of? He hadn't pulled the trigger on Tomlin. And he hadn't doused Watterson with lighter fluid and knocked him into that barbecue pit.

As he neared the open door, Keller said, "Come in. Take a seat and close the door."

Keller was grim, and Wilkins felt his cold stare. Slowly, Wilkins closed the door and settled into the straight-backed wooden chair in front of the chief' metal desk. Wilkins noticed that the chief had a cushy black-leather swivel wingback, the chair raised a little too high so that Wilkins and anybody who took that seat had to look up at the chief. I struck Wilkins that the seat he was offered was designed for some degree of discomfort and intimidation. Wilkins was feeling way beyond uncomfortable right then. He was agitated, afraid, paranoid, and anxious.

Keller cleared his throat, torched a cigar with a Zippo. Finally the chief slid a piece of paper across the desk.

"Go on, John, read it."

It was the suicide note, he knew. Wilkins read the letter, noted the jagged scrawl. The penmanship looked forced to him, as if Watterson had gone insane and was struggling to choose the right—or the wrong—words. "Whoever reads this, I want you to know John Wilkins is the cause of what I am about to do. The bastard took away my whole world. I have no job, I have no money, I have no woman. Cassandra, the bitch-whore, told me he was fucking her. I want this whole town to know what a lying, thieving cheating son of a bitch John Wilkins is. He took my whole life."

That was it. Short and ugly, wicked and untrue.

Staring at Keller, Wilkins flipped the note on the desktop as if it were contaminated.

"What, Chief, is this some kind of evidence against me?"

Keller blew smoke, gave a grim chuckle. "John, we've been over this. No, you're not being charged you're not under any suspicion—at least not directly. But let me tell you the flak this created. I just cleaned up the mess at Saint Paul's. I did my interviews, I wrote my report. Tomlin's a suicide, that's it. I just thank God the guy didn't decide to pump a few stray rounds off before he took his life. What I'm saying is, I was down at the Jenkinses' café. They're friends of yours; this whole town knows you or of you. The talk I heard buzzing around there, well, it wasn't pretty."

Now Wilkins sounded a mirthless chuckle. Great, he thought, what next? A boycott of their restaurant? Employees at the paper and restaurant quitting?

"So . . . I'm a leper now."

"I wouldn't go that far. But I might think about watching your step, not let any rumors of affairs and what some around here might see as some sort of sabotage on your part of the lives of two men who committed suicide in full view of witnesses while accusing you of all sort of dirty things and raving to everyone what a dirty SOB you really are—don't let it get to you. Maybe even consider taking your family on a nice long vacation. This thing will blow over; life around here will get back to normal, eventually."

Why don't I believe that? Wilkins thought.

"Have you been looking for my brother?" he asked.

The chief worked on his cigar. "John, understand something here. You're telling me you think your brother is behind all this, that he controls people, how, you don't know. Bartkowski's dead, so I can't very well sit him down for some Q and A. Sure, I could comb the streets, hit all the hotels and motels around the county, but I don't see the point."

Wilkins heaved a breath, glanced at the letter. "Why show me that pack of lies?"

"Just to let you know how this Watterson felt about you, that I believe it was a murder-suicide, guy went berserk. That letter goes no further than this office. In fact, soon as you leave, I file it away. No one sees it. And, for what it's worth, I believe your side of it. It's lies."

"So, bottom line, this is a little sit-down to tell me you're pulling for me, don't believe my brother is behind any of this, keep my nose clean, don't let the rumor mill push me over the edge."

Keller nodded. "Something like that."

"Some friendly advice."

"Something like that."

Wilkins sat in hard silence for several moments. In a way he was almost afraid to walk the streets of Glendale now that the rumor mill was in full spin.

"I'm staying, Chief, just so you know. I've got problems to work out. When my life's back on track, I'll take that vacation, but not until then."

"Suit yourself. Just be careful."

"Is that it?"

"For now. We'll talk again."

"How come I don't like the sound of that?"

"Nothing personal. I'm not going to be shadowing you all over town. Let's just say I'm concerned about you. I'll be checking in, making sure things are under control. Is that a problem for you?"

"I suppose not. If that's all, I'd like to go see my wife."

Silently, Wilkins stood. He heard the chief tell him to take care, but the man's voice struck his back from what seemed like miles away. Wilkins walked swiftly through the station, eager to get away from the silent looks of judgment he saw in the eyes of the deputies.

* * *

Silent Scream

Mike Wilkins sat perched against an oak tree, alone and deep in the woods, just north of Glendale. It was time to expedite some infidelity, or at least get the groundwork laid to stir up some serious heat.

Moments ago, he had found Paula. She was sitting at the bar of the husband-and-wife-owned restaurant, nursing a rum and Coke, looking sullen and forlorn. Better still, he found that her mind was agitated by all the bizarre events, the murder and suicides, the hints of her husband's adultery, her thoughts like a buzzing hornets' nest of questions and doubts, everything in her mind chaotic and jumbled. Wilkins had to concentrate hard to pin down a single revealing thought. Finally he caught one. She was wondering if her marriage was as strong, as solid as she had always believed—before now. And she was thinking about Jeff Ballanger, wondering if maybe she didn't need someone outside her situation to talk to, to trust in.

Mike Wilkins went to work. He called on the power to send him out there. He felt his eyes heat up. Within seconds, he found Ballanger driving into town in his Mercedes. Ballanger looked troubled, but Wilkins found a restless hunger in the man. He was thinking about Paula, knew everything that had happened, had caught wind of the rumor of her husband's alleged adultery. Beautiful. He was hopeful, thinking he had a way in. The guy didn't want to be lonely the whole summer. He was even thinking of asking her out for a drink, giving Paula his phone number. Wilkins inflamed his heart with lust for Paula, put a fleeting but pulsing twinge in his crotch. He discovered that when the pursuit of passion was a clear-cut objective, thoughts were clearer and more straightforward, stronger and more absolute. Ballanger was making it all too easy. Or so he hoped. Paula might prove the one who needed a gentle shove.

So he worked on Paula. She didn't understand why she did it, but he made her kill her drink, pour a double rum and Coke. It was well into the afternoon and their restaurant was nearly deserted. It seemed the good citizens of Glendale, onetime close friends and neighbors and big-spending patrons, were leery of the Wilkins clan. Paula was annoyed that there was very little business on a Sunday afternoon when usually the place was packed to capacity. He forced a moment of hot anger in her heart toward her husband. What were they suddenly, pariahs?

Okay. There he was. Ballanger slid his Mercedes into a parking slot beside the restaurant. Wilkins drifted in over him, hovered, and followed him inside the restaurant. Right away, Ballanger and the Mrs. made eye contact.

"Jeff." Paula sounded surprised but happy.

"Paula, hi. How you doing?" Cautious but with a note of concern in his voice.

"Look around. I get the feeling with all that's happened there's some kind of silent boycott going on."

With a short probe Wilkins discovered she resented her husband, but was fighting not to blame him for all that had happened.

"You mind if I join you?"

"Not at all. I could use the company." A pause; then she said, "I feel . . . well, we were close once. I need someone to talk to. I'm glad you stopped by. What are you drinking?"

"Scotch and water," Ballanger said, sliding onto a stool next to her. She ordered the drink, and a waitress went behind the bar, built the scotch and water.

Ballanger was glancing at her out of the corner of his eye. Wilkins caught his heated thinking, heard, *Man-oh-man, how did I ever let her get away? What a beauty* . . . Then his thoughts scattered, lapsing into other areas, some self-pity that he just stopped dating her back in high school, moving on because he didn't think he was going to score.

They sat in awkward silence, sipping their drinks.

"I've heard about some of the problems," Ballanger said in a halting voice.

Wilkins made her scoff, made her wonder if her husband really had been cheating on her, making her recall that morning when Cassandra came bouncing past the drive, the look she had thrown her husband.

"It's insane, Jeff. I . . . I feel like my whole life's been turned upside down."

There was a long pause as Wilkins caught her wondering how to proceed, maybe broach the subject of her husband's possible adultery.

Ballanger cleared his throat, finished his drink, and Paula ordered him another. When the waitress brought it, Paula suggested they go sit in a booth, implying they needed some privacy. When they were alone in a corner booth, Ballanger looked her dead in the eye. In their silence, Wilkins caught them thinking about the past. Even Paula was beginning to feel a stab of regret, a chaotic buzz that Wilkins barely latched on to as she thought how handsome he still was, that she had really felt something for him back in school, deep and real and caring. What had happened?

"Why did you ever just stop dating me, Jeff?"

He showed her a sad smile. "I don't know," he lied. "I suppose we were just kids. . . . I didn't know how to go about keeping our relationship . . . well, John came along. I was never friends with him, but he seemed like a good guy. I just let it slip away. Sort of bowed out to the better man."

Another lie. Wilkins knew Ballanger had seethed with jealousy those many years ago, secretly hated Wilkins, but had believed himself above a display of anger. Oh, this guy was pretty good, he thought. He could really lay it on.

"Yeah," she said, buying it. "We were just kids. Things change."

"It sure seems like things have changed around here. I come back and all hell's broken loose. I've . . . heard some rumors. . . . I don't mean to pry, but Paula, you know, I never stopped thinking about . . . I know you're a married woman . . . and I'm not here as anything other than a friend, maybe a shoulder to lean on. But . . . I was down at Miller's Tavern, and there was some talk about John maybe having an affair."

She hesitated.

"It's none of my business," he said. "Let's drop it."

"No, it's okay. Things have changed, Jeff. I don't know how or why, but I feel this great distance between John and me. I don't even know what to believe anymore. Worse, I suppose anything is possible. He said . . . he wasn't having an affair. . . ."

"And you're not sure whether or not to believe him?"

"I want to believe him."

"But you're having your doubts."

"I don't know, I really don't know."

They sipped their drinks in silence.

Then Wilkins saw his brother pulling up outside the restaurant. *Uh-oh.*

"Listen, Paula, tell you what. Would you mind if I gave you my phone number? Maybe we can have a drink sometime, you know, if you need someone to talk to."

She smiled. "Sure, that would be nice."

"There wouldn't be any problem with that?"

"Of course not. I don't see any reason why I can't have a male friend." And she thought, My husband trusts me or he better trust me. Then she had a flicker of doubt about her own intentions.

He wrote the number down on a napkin and she took it, just as he saw John Wilkins stroll in. When John spotted his old high school rival, sitting alone with his wife, he got a slightly disturbed look in his eyes.

Mike Wilkins pulled himself back. His eyes had grown too hot, the fever starting to rage. He had to cool down before going back, then decided to let events in the next few hours take their own course. It looked like there was going to be some real ugliness in what was once marital paradise.

Even as he sweated and shivered with fever, he chuckled long and hard.

John Wilkins balked near the bar. When he discovered who Paula was talking to, alone, with a wistful look of remembrance, a longing, Wilkins felt his heart skip a beat. Already he felt alone, walking around town, a few grumbled hellos, the strange stares he was treated to by people he thought he knew and could trust. Now this. Jeff Ballanger. The man hadn't changed a lick since their high school days. Handsome and well built, trim and neatly groomed.

Wilkins couldn't believe his eyes, didn't know how

to proceed. They were so engrossed in whatever they were talking about they didn't even notice him.

Slowly, dumbfounded, Wilkins walked toward their booth. Paula spotted him. Was she tensing up? He felt as if he were intruding.

"John?"

He felt silly. And very much alone.

"Yeah, hi," he said, hoping he didn't look as awkward as he felt.

"Uh, you remember Jeff Ballanger?"

"I do. He was our school sports star. How you been, Jeff?"

Wilkins believed he spotted some flash of resentment in the man's eyes. But Ballanger was quick to stand and offer his hand. Wilkins hesitated but shook Ballanger's hand, feeling the tension between them.

"It's been a long time, John."

"Indeed. I haven't seen you around Glendale in years. I heard you had a practice up in Chicago," he said, hating his own forced politeness.

"Gave it up. Got tired of the big city, the hustle."

After a tight silence Paula seemed obligated to interject. "Uh, Jeff's staying in town for the summer."

"Yeah, I thought I'd give my hometown another shot, maybe set up a private practice."

"Well, I'm sure you'll do well."

Another awkward pause; then Ballanger said, "Well, I was just dropping by, exchanging pleasantries with old friends. Can't stay, I've got some things to catch up on back at home. Listen, it was good seeing the both of you again. Let's not be strangers."

"Our restaurant's open seven days a week," Wilkins said. "Feel free to drop by anytime."

"Will do. Listen, got to run. I'll be seeing you around," he told them.

"Bye-bye, Jeff," Paula said.

"See ya," Wilkins said as he caught what he believed was a forced, false smile thrown his way. When Ballanger was gone, Wilkins looked at his wife. A strange silence hung between them. Wilkins felt a growing distance between them. He suspected the two of them, onetime sweethearts, had been exchanging more than polite pleasantries about old times. Then he had a strange and disturbing thought, wondering just how far the two of them had gone back in school. He remembered that Paula was still a virgin when he had married her. But that didn't mean they hadn't done other things.

"John, are you all right?"

"Yeah, I'm fine."

"Where have you been?"

Why did she sound so aloof, almost cold? "Chief Keller wanted to see me. A friendly face-to-face. Seems I'm off the hook."

"Were you ever worried that you might be implicated?"

"Paula, there was sarcasm in my voice."

"Oh."

Why did he feel so far away from her? Why did he suddenly feel so threatened by what he had seen? Or was it merely something as innocent as two people catching up on old times?

"Mind if I get something to eat?"

Aloof again, she said, "Sure. What do you want?"

It would prove an endless Sunday night for the Wilkins household. Already Mike Wilkins had spotted the children, in his mind, from a safe distance.

Timmy was the only child in the house. Briefly he invaded the boy's mind while he slept. Timmy was dreaming he was a national pool champion, winning trophies and big money, basking in the endless adulation from wildly cheering throngs. The image retreated, fading in the mist. Next he was a lone samurai, wielding his *katana*. Wilkins decided to add some bloody violence to the boy's dream, as Timmy battled the evil shogun's warriors. Laughing, Wilkins filled the boy's mind with living cinema images, graphic and so real the boy would wake up and remember it all as if he had been right there. Timmy dreamed on, lopping heads, slicing off arms, disemboweling other samurai, forcing a *daimyo* to commit *seppuku* to save his honor. Finally, Timmy was a ninja, shadowing into the shogun's castle. Sword in hand, he crept up behind the shogun as the shogun stared at his pebbled garden. And Timmy lopped off his head with one swift flash of steel. Then Wilkins planted a strong urge for Timmy to sneak out of the house the next evening after dinner and meet him at the mall.

It seemed his brother had already told the children who he might be, that they were to call their father immediately if they saw him again. Very well. It was time to speed things along. After Tomlin's suicide, it seemed brother John had a long talk with the town cop. This Keller was former Chicago homicide, a tough, streetwise cop. Seemed John had told him what Bartkowski had said about the possible return of brother Mike and his strange powers, crazy as it sounded, before he spread himself all over a lonely country road. The cop was skeptical. For the moment the police were shrugging it off as maybe hypnosis, maybe some kind of drug, but Keller had a description of this errant brother and would be looking for him to pull him in for questioning. All Keller could really do was write his reports, clean up the messes, talk to the coroner. Either way, he would stay in close contact with brother John, who had a busy day at the paper tomorrow, his mind agitated and tormented with how these bizarre stories of murder and suicide were going to be written by his staff.

Wilkins moved on in his roving search, smiling, mesmerized by this ability to play God.

No, to be God, he reminded himself.

Next he found Jenny with her boyfriend. They were in his car, holding each other. She was seeking comfort, some connection to humanity after two days of unexplained terror. He intended for her to find what she wanted, so secretly desired, and for his brother to realize one of his worst fears.

Finally he found the oldest son down at the basketball court. Through the mist, he discovered Robert and his friends had all chipped in for a case of beer. A mental push, and Wilkins had Robert chugging one beer after another. Somewhere nearby a cop was sitting in his jeep. Why not add some more shame and embarrassment to brother John's life?

Wilkins pulled himself back into his body. He had a plan for the evening, but it would require perfect timing.

At the moment, though, he had another sweet victim to work on.

And for Stan Peterson it would be a night of undying agony. For this man who had helped beat him to a bloody pulp so long ago, it was simply the tortured beginning of his agonizing end.

Wilkins sat in a wooden chair he had pulled out of

Peterson's living room. The one-story wooden farm-house was tucked off the beaten path, down a long, narrow dirt driveway from the main highway that led to Glendale. Like the man, Wilkins had found the home dark and brooding. But there was plenty of privacy. Better still, the man's Jeep Cherokee and the three ten-gallon gasoline cans in the woodshed would provide Wilkins with what he needed to bring a personal Armageddon to Glendale.

Wilkins smiled down at Peterson. Waves of steam wafted from the hot water Peterson was submerged in, the man's bloated, naked body red as a beet, a few blisters already popping up on his skin. To keep the man from passing out, Wilkins alternated the boiling water with cold. He didn't need the man dying of a heart attack or lapsing into shock.

"Just think of this as a day at the beach," he told the man, and laughed. "You do look like a beached whale. All blubbery and frozen up. Call you my beached whale, old buddy."

He chuckled. Wilkins had already gleaned enough of the man's thoughts to know his life, and there really wasn't much there that was noteworthy. The man was a bully, a thief, and a lecher. Funny how not much changed in a man's basic character over the years, he decided. A convenience-store robbery somewhere in Oklahoma was in his future. There, Peterson would gun down an elderly couple, steal from their cash register, and for just a little over a hundred dollars. Shallow, self-centered, nothing but a prick, Wilkins judged. The world was a better place without the guy. It seemed Peterson was long since fed up with his small, nowhere life as a bartender in Glendale. He saw no hope for his future.

How right he was, Wilkins thought.

Wilkins kept him paralyzed, then let him raise his head just above the water's steaming surface. Wilkins sipped from a can of beer, playing with the man's Zippo. The lighter was made of ivory, with an engraving of a male lion that looked poised to spring on unsuspecting prey. Peterson saw himself as king of the lions, always hungry, always on the hunt. It was an image he kept secreted in his mind, not wanting to risk some drinking flunky's sarcasm.

Wilkins clicked the lid open, then clacked it shut. He liked the noise. Click. Clack. The sound irritated Peterson. He heard the man's mind snarling for him to stop fooling with the Zippo. Wilkins became amused by the man's pain and terror, laughed out loud, then drove the laughter through the man's mind.

"Hey, king of the lions, my beached whaleboy. You always thought I was a little strange, but what you really were was scared I might be smarter, better in some way than you and everyone else. Well, King, all I'm doing is just proving you right. I am better, I am stronger, I am smarter. Good thing for the others they've moved away from here. I can hear your wretched, ugly thoughts. I see your soul. I am the Lord your God, I am who's in complete control of your television set. There is nothing wrong." He worked the Zippo, then fired it up. He stared into the big dancing flame, saw his eyes in the fire, bright and burning with the heated white light. Clack. Click. "Okay, here we go. Not to mention your brother, Richard. So, he got himself killed in a bar fight, couple years ago. Man shot him dead, put one right between his eyes. Not too shabby. You know, he tried to molest me when we . . . never mind. Another dark secret around here that only a few people knew.

Now, now, there's no need for that kind of language, and, no, old buddy, I can't explain how I can do what I can. Man alive, can't any of you people just accept things on faith? I know, I know, I can hear all that hate and rage inside your head. No wonder your wife left you, Stan. Hey, this next round is for her. Remember that time you slapped her around out there in the living room and forced yourself on her? If she went to the cops, you'd kill her. Don't ask how I know, Stan. Please. Have faith. Show some courage for a change. Where are your balls? Oh, yeah, I see them, I think. King of the lions, huh?"

Laughing, he stood and went into the kitchen, where three large pots were bubbling over on the stove, near one pitcher of cold water. He took two of the pots, went back into the bathroom.

He laughed at the fresh look of terror in Peterson's eyes as he stood over the bathtub. "I purify you and cleanse you of all your evil, in the name of me, myself, and I, Mike Wilkins." Laughing, he dumped the searing water over the man's head, listened to his silent screams for a moment. He stood, looming, feeling stronger, more aggressive, reckless and enraged as the power fed on Peterson's hate and fury and craving for vengeance.

Curious then about himself, wondering about his own tomorrow again, he went to the mirror. He stood frozen before his image. His eyes were now a blazing white, with only his pupils showing, two tiny pinpoints of black, almost hidden by the white burning light. He searched the light inside, demanding to know his own tomorrow. Nothing but silence. Not even a flickering of an image. He thought he heard something whisper from the light. He listened hard.

Now . . . where is your faith? Where is your courage?

He nodded. Good enough. He took out the amulet and kissed it.

"You always lusted for Christine, Stan. But you knew you were never good enough. I see in your mind a hatred for the man she married. I believe his name is Bob . . . Stanton. Yes. He's a doctor, a general practioner, has his own office in town. You seethe every time you see this man. You've even thought about doing to Christine what your pal Bartkowski did to her."

With utter loathing, he stared at Peterson's reddened face. The man was a grotesque sight, overweight from food and drink, a fat white slug.

Sitting by the tub, Wilkins pulled all the man's venom out of his wretched soul, using all that raging negative energy to feed the power. He shut his eyes, let himself drift to his brother's home. He hovered out front. It was getting easier to work the power, back and forth, control as many minds as he wanted.

Jenny was pulling up in the drive with her boyfriend. Earlier, though John was reluctant, she had convinced her mother to let her go see Paul Stallings, promising Mom and Dad she would be home early.

Wilkins felt the smile stretch his lips, his eyes glowing with heat. He heard the terror and the cursing in Peterson's mind, fed the power with the man's fear and hatred. Then he bored a fiery animal lust into the teenagers. Right away, they reacted, kissing slowly at first, even tenderly, sliding some tongue in, gentle in the heart, but burning inside. Young love, he thought, laughing. Beautiful stuff. Of course, both of them were confused by their sudden raging hunger for each other, but he made them lose control, hands going down to the groin, tongues of fire probing deep in their mouths. And she was a sweet little work of ivory cream, cherry still intact. Working the boy, he made Paul Stallings fondle her breasts, unbutton her blouse. Then he saw his brother staring out the window. Shock, then outrage, seized John.

Yes, run downstairs, brother. You know what's going on. Damn kid, that's my daughter. John, already suspicious, had heard the car pull up, and thought they had been out front a little too long.

Wilkins laughed. Click-clack. He worked the Zippo furiously—click-clack—so fast in his hand, the lid was a blur. As John raced up to the car, he saw his daughter, half-naked and sitting on Paul Stallings. She was moaning in passion, laughing.

Wilkins roared with laughter.

Click-clack.

Wilkins picked up the pot and dumped boiling water over Peterson's head. After he had enjoyed the man's long, silent shrieking, he cooled him off with a pitcher of cold water.

"What the hell?" he heard John bellow.

John kept thinking, *They're only kids, just kissing. Keep control, that's my daughter, take charge, I'm her father.*

Next Mike Wilkins saw Robert, driving drunk, in Dad's car. He was weaving all over the road, speeding.

Then it happened, just the way he had planned it.

Flashing lights raced up on the Saturn, and Keller barreled out of his jeep.

It was going to be a long and ugly night for big brother.

Click-clack, clack-click.

*   *   *

"I'm sorry, Mr. Wilkins. We weren't doing anything."

John Wilkins pulled his daughter out of the car. He was stunned, desperately trying to keep himself under control.

"Go home, Paul," he told the boy, taking charge of the moment. "You and me, we'll talk later."

He stared at his daughter, found her eyes brimming with tears. Her blouse was unbuttoned. She looked on the verge of hysteria. Suddenly he had an urge to pack up and flee Glendale. Life had spiraled out of control, plunging toward rock bottom.

"Dad, please, we didn't do anything."

He marched Jenny into the house. Paula was standing in the living room, her eyes wide with confusion.

"John, what's going on?"

"Just go to your room, Jen. We'll talk in the morning."

Then he heard a scream from the boys' room. *Now what?* His heart racing, his mind swirling with questions, he bounded up the steps. From somewhere in the house, he heard the phone ringing.

He barged into the room. "Dear God, no, not again!"

Timmy was sweating, his eyes wide, his mouth open. Strange gagging sounds sputtered from Timmy's mouth.

"Timmy? Timmy?" He shook Timmy by the shoulders. Just as before, the distant, unseeing look in his son's eyes faded, and reality cleared away the glazed, almost frantic stare . . . of what?

"He said you betrayed him," Timmy said in a low growl.

For long moments John Wilkins stared at his son,

terrified. That was not Timmy speaking, or was it?

"I need to sleep, Dad," Timmy said, in the soft and familiar voice John Wilkins knew.

Suddenly he heard his wife's voice lashing him from behind, a stinging verbal whip.

"John. Chief Keller is on the phone."

Turning, he saw Paula standing in the doorway. There was a desperate look of confusion in her eyes. A fresh wave of fear rippled through Wilkins. Robert. His oldest son wasn't home.

He took the portable phone from his wife. "Yes." His heart throbbing in his ears, he listened to Keller's voice. The police chief's words seemed to reach him from another planet. "You might want to get down to the station, John. I just picked up your son for drunk driving."

John Wilkins stared at the phone as if it were some obscene object.

"Hey, you there?"

He struggled to find his voice. "Yeah. I'm on the way."

Mike Wilkins was burning up with fever. Sweat was rolling down his face, streaming off his chin. He was shaking uncontrollably, his stomach knotted and churning with nausea. The pain felt as if it would go on forever, his eyes like two searing, smoking coals in his head.

Why was it happening like this? He had done all he wanted to do, controlled everything.

But the fever was worse than ever, his brain feeling as if it were on fire. He growled, bored his own pain into Peterson, filled the man's head with burning heat, images of leaping flames, eating him alive.

Silent Scream

While Peterson's scream tore through his mind, Wilkins turned on the bathroom sink. He stuck his head under the cold water.

Slowly, the fever began to cool.

Chapter Twenty-two

At five o'clock on Monday afternoon, Mike Wilkins sat in the confessional at Saint Paul's. Other than Peterson, who was kneeling in the pew of the front row—the man's face red and blistered beneath his baseball cap—the church was empty. From a distant and fleeting probe of Father O'Shay's mind, Wilkins knew the church would remain vacant, unless a distraught sinner wandered in to say a few prayers or implore the good father to hear his confession. If that happened, he would deal with it. In fact, he was going to deal with everything and everyone by tomorrow night. His three days and three nights, he thought, were nearly over. It was time to let all of Glendale know he was about to rise from the dead.

Monday—the beginning and the end of their new week. His judgment would be total and final. But he wanted one more day to work on big brother.

Besides, he couldn't get the fever to die completely. Time, he feared, was working against him, angrily urging him on, driving him ahead in an ever-speeding rush of insatiable and reckless frenzy, deeper and deeper into some swirling abyss. Even so, he managed a gray area between borderline agony and irritating discomfort, fighting with desperate fury to ward off the onslaught of fire in his head. But his will to cool the fever altogether was weakening, it seemed, something inside him feeling as if it were collapsing on itself. Worse, he began clinging to a nagging, icy fear that the power planned to betray him. He even thought he spotted some looming shadow in the outer limits of the light inside him, some laughing specter of himself, compelling him to act against his will.

No, have faith, he told himself, gritting his teeth against the wave of fire boiling up in the center of his brain. *Stay strong.*

He was almost finished with these people. One more day.

Tomorrow. Tuesday, terrible Tuesday.

It was something of a stroke of luck that Peterson wasn't scheduled for another bartending shift until Wednesday. So Wilkins kept the man his hostage, knowing the loner wouldn't be missed about town. People who associated with the guy would think he was off on a bender. Now, the priest would be a different, perhaps even difficult, situation. It might prove a strain on the power, but Wilkins intended to keep the good father isolated in the rectory, control him from a distance. His secretary could handle all calls; Father O'Shay was in mourning, fasting and praying. Wilkins figured the priest's forced wish to be left alone would be respected. But if it all went to hell suddenly, Wilkins would handle the situation, even kill the priest from a safe distance. Either way, the good father would be doing a lot of sleeping during the next day.

So Wilkins sweated in the tight confines of the booth, his eyes glowing and burning hot behind the sunglasses. And the fever and the roiling sickness in

293

his stomach began merely feeding his mounting anger—like maggots on dead flesh.

It was maddening and he began to fear for himself more and more. Fire and death were all he could now envision beyond the light, saw but couldn't will away those sudden flickering images of masses of writhing worms and maggots. So, while he waited for the priest, his desperation kept growing to finish what he started. He was in dire agony but his senses felt electric, his body, mind, and soul not his own, above and beyond himself, reaching out, drawing in. And despite his pain and a gnawing anxiety of discovery by his brother or a confrontation with the local police, he was feeling bolder and more powerful than ever. If he had to, he would destroy the entire town. He could create a mass suicide and murder epidemic, behold the carnage, sweeping the town and turning Glendale into a sprawling abattoir, with only a few survivors left to report the wailing and gnashing of teeth. After all, his rage was his righteousness, his vengeance his armor.

He probed the church. Sunlight lanced through the stained-glass windows of the saints. Light spilled from the vestry as the old priest ventured in through the back entrance of the sacristy. He gave Father O'Shay a strange compulsion to inspect his church. The priest, wondering why he was being drawn there, moved woodenly, tugged along from the rectory.

Father O'Shay looked just as Wilkins remembered him. His white hair thinning up top, the man was short and lean, face chiseled but sagging some in the jowls. Still he had those penetrating blue eyes, gentle but firm with a strength and conviction of faith that seemed to lend him added stature. At the moment, he was wearing his collar. It was good to know that Father O'Shay had just concluded his day's business. The phone calls, the morning mass, visiting the widow and children of Tom Bartkowski, saying a few prayers down at Johnson's Funeral Home. The day was done. Now the priest could read his Bible, pray, plan a dinner. Then Wilkins chuckled to himself as he invaded the deeper corners of the priest's mind. The good father was still tormented by the suicide in his church. He was planning a memorial later in the week, a community gathering for prayer and reflection, a time for healing.

He couldn't possibly know yet that tomorrow night Saint Paul's would no longer be standing.

Indeed, it would be a pile of smoldering ash.

As the priest walked toward the altar, peering curiously at Peterson, Wilkins telepathically told him, *Fear not, Father. Come to me. Fear not.* He rolled a burst of cold laughter through the priest's mind, and Father O'Shay thought he recognized the voice, searching the church for its source.

"Who's there?"

Fear not, I tell you, for I am your lord and your master. You know, Father, that phrase or a variation of that phrase is written three hundred and sixty-five times in the Bible. Three sixty-five. Coincidence?

He took the priest's voice. Father O'Shay's mouth locked, his jaw dropping. With sudden fear, he wondered why he couldn't hear his own voice.

What is this? Who's here?

"I control you, Father. Fear not. Do not question my power. I know your mind, I see your soul. I control your body, Father. Please don't question me."

The priest believed he was being marched into the presence of evil, his heart racing with fear. As the priest opened the door to his confessional booth and settled in, Wilkins said out loud, "Father, do not forgive me, for I have not sinned. It has been a blessed eternity since my last confession." Wilkins laughed and basked in the rolling boom of his laughter as it exploded into the priest's confessional, echoed through the church. He could feel Peterson in the pew, trembling with fear, his mind screaming for release.

Wilkins put a knifing pain down the priest's spine. He heard the man's cry of pain, imprisoned in his head, and felt the priest stiffen.

"I'll get right to it, Father. My brother is John Wilkins and I have the power to hear thoughts, to see the past, to know the future, to see the darkest secrets in men's souls. I can control others with my mind and make them do my will. I have created myself and my own way. I have used my will to cleanse the wicked from this town. Having problems believing me, perhaps? Okay. For instance, I know Father Manning has gone away on a sabbatical. Just two nights ago, I know the two of you prayed for your God to take the good young priest's homosexual urges from him. The man actually wept in your arms for forgiveness, just like a baby—though he has yet to act on those impulses, but I'm here to tell you that in the future he will. There will be a suicide in his future. Actually he will buy a gun, a .44 Magnum, to be exact—hey, the guy likes Eastwood—he'll sit in his car on a lonely country road and blow his brains out. Tragic stuff. Oh well, we both know a man's sins are a great burden on his shoulders."

The priest was shaking with terror, his mind frozen with horror.

"Now," Wilkins went on, "at the time all this was

happening, well, you felt . . . some repulsion, I think, but you forced yourself to dredge up a degree of compassion and understanding, hoping to give the fine young priest some hope, maybe solidify his faith and resolve to pray and ask for relief from that peculiar and abhorrent sickness. I mean, picture two men doing that . . . oh, it's too ugly. Here, I quote you—'Father Manning, remember, God hates the sin and not the sinner. It is only the act itself that is an abomination in His eyes. As long as you do not act on this urge, the Lord will forgive you.' Am I touched by that, or what? You need more? Here it is. I know that when you give sermons, you stare out at the solemn masses, fully aware and angry they sin, that they steal, they lie, they covet, they curse each other in their hearts, they commit adultery, and now, well, now here's the truly messed up thing—they do all this, then they come to you and ask for forgiveness, get it, maybe even feel it; then they walk right out and do the same damn thing again. Not good enough, not enough insight to what I am? Okay. There you are, tormented by your lust, I mean it is a burning you feel right in your balls for some of your faithful women, especially those young mothers, you know. Fact is, not long ago, you almost caved into your lust for a woman who came to you to confess her adultery—and while she was pregnant, and by a man other than her husband. More? Yes, I do see more; fact is, I see it all. There you are again, Father. After no more than three drinks at night, well, on Saturday night you'll have five scotches with a splash of soda—Dewars, you drink—you sometimes plead to your God to forgive you, to understand that you are only human, demanding forgiveness for this weakness of yours. I mean, you actually leap up, full of shame and disgrace, wishing your God was blind to your sin."

He heard the priest say in his mind, "Our Father, who art in Heaven . . ."

Rage exploded in Wilkins. He drove a wrenching pain down the priest's spine, made Father O'Shay twist and writhe, eyes bulging out of his skull, made the man feel as if he were being snapped in half by the powerful jaws of some giant machine. "Stop that!"

"Hallowed be Thy name . . ."

"Stop that now, or I'll crush the life out of you. Stop that, and I'll stop the pain. Do what I command! Obey me, Father, or die now!"

The priest stopped praying, thinking he was powerless in the face of this evil, but his thoughts came together, clear and strong, but grim.

The priest said in his mind, *This power of yours, yes, I know who you are; you are Michael Wilkins*. The priest was growing frantic, believing he was in the presence of a man possessed by demons. *My son, this power you have, I believe it's real, but it's an unholy thing. It's evil. . . .*

Wilkins chuckled. "Is that so? I may have been that way before, but I no longer want or need anyone or anything. I made myself my own God. You remember, Father, how I came to you so long ago in a desperate plea for you to help me rid myself of my addiction to drugs and alcohol. Back then, I was in desperate search of some answer, any answer, so I turned to the church. I prayed, I needed confession, I needed to be set free of what you called the demon of addiction." The priest was thinking back now, seeing the two of them, alone in his study in the rectory.

"Remember your final words to me. What did you tell me?"

I told you . . . oh, yes, my son, my tortured son, yes, I told you that all these years you had the power to say yes, that you also had the power to say no.

"Right. So simple, so easy for you to let those words roll off your lips. I knew then that you didn't understand, that you couldn't help me, that there was no power on earth that could save me. I left feeling utter contempt for you. I felt alone and more betrayed and adrift than ever. And now, Father, I quote Solomon in Ecclesiastes: 'Next I observed all the oppression and sadness throughout the earth—the tears of the oppressed, and no one helping them, while on the side of their oppressors were powerful allies. So I felt that the dead were better off than the living.' " He laughed out loud, even as he tasted the acid bile of the sweat on his lips. "Yes, wise old Solomon, seeing the mad scramble of men, chasing the wind as he wrote. Don't say it in your mind, Father, yes, we both know that even Satan can quote scripture, and, no, I do not pervert the word of God. And, no, I am not in the power of Satan, I am not evil. I have been the oppressed. I have been the downtrodden. Everywhere I turn, seeing all with the eyes of Solomon, with this star of Lazarus on my chest to guide me, do you hear—and, no, do not say this is blasphemy, Father—I see those who have wealth and privilege and stature and status, who are undeserving and unworthy and completely without heart, not to mention without honor, who spit on me if they even acknowledge me. They live their lives, full and fat and content, cocooned, going on eating, drinking, and making merry, while the good and the innocent and the truly honorable and worthy suffer and die, and perish from this world as if they never existed. Even your Jesus walked among the desperate and the angry and the lonely and the tormented and the criminal. Surely you know what the twelve apostles were. They were thieves and liars and murderers and fornicators and drunkards."

My son, they found God through Christ. They found salvation and confessed their wrong and repented of their ways.

Softly, Wilkins chuckled in contempt. "Is that right? You were there? What man among us can judge another man—other than I, who have seen, known, tasted, and been made to devour the human heart? Again, Solomon: 'For I have seen foolish men given great authority, and rich men not given their rightful place of dignity.'" His wrath burned hotter still in his heart, a fire in his eyes, but at the same time he felt strangely uplifted and relieved. "By rich men, I have to assume Solomon meant those rich in wisdom, but even he concluded that wisdom is futile, that it only adds more grief and sorrow to a man's heart—the good man, the wise man, his day becomes endless. Knowledge is not good, Father, it's overrated, it kills. It drives a man to self-destruction because he knows death is the end to his torture. To his unfulfillment, his unwantedness, his wretchedness, the futility of his life. Days full of sorrow, man chased by the ghosts of his sin, heaped on me, at least, by the callousness and the brutality and the dishonor of other men. And women."

He felt the priest's heart breaking, an imploring and beseeching cry in his mind. *My son, oh, my son, what you really feel is envy and bitterness and betrayal. Oh, don't you know, God will forgive you this thing, only forsake this evil power before it is too late. Don't you know? In your search and your struggle and your suffering, all men suffer, even the good and the faithful, and we cannot explain the will of God, nor is man meant to.*

For a fleeting moment, Wilkins felt stunned and ashamed. He slumped back against the wall of the booth, drained. He started to think about what the priest had just said; then he told himself that it wasn't true. Not all of it anyway. For some reason, his heart softened, against his will, it seemed. Or was his will even his own any longer? The fever began to subside as he sat, silent and still, exhausted and burning up with fever. Then he decided the priest was a fool, that just like so long ago, Father O'Shay was searching for a truth that was eluding him. That, yes, this priest was a mere mortal with his own torment, his own darkness.

Show mercy to those who never showed you mercy, the priest told him. *Show heart to the heartless, forgive the unforgiving. God will forgive, God will have mercy on your soul. Please, my son, it's the only way for you. It's your only hope to be free of this evil.*

Wilkins felt a lump in his throat, a mist of tears burning into the corners of his eyes. "Love thy enemy."

Yes.

"That got your Christ killed, Father."

Oh, my son, forsake this evil—

Wilkins became angry, cold again. "Shut your filthy mouth! Listen to me. For now, I'm through with you, Father. You'll wait in the rectory for me to return. Someone should enter the church or the rectory to come looking for you, I'll control you, I'll tell you how to handle it." He put laughter into the priest's head. "Fear not. I shall return. We have much work left to do."

Mike Wilkins stood, suddenly hating this man, but wondering about his words. Envy? Bitterness? Betrayal? If that were true, then he had earned the right to feel that way.

He walked out of the confessional. He looked around the church, remembering how he used to come here every Sunday morning with his family. For a fleeting moment, he thought that might have been the only time, the only place where he had felt some peace.

Then his other voice, stronger, angrier than ever, snarled, *That is not true! You know what must be done! Do it! Just do it! Do not fail yourself!*

And then he heard his mind tell him that his time was short.

He made Peterson stand, come to him.

At that moment, strangely, Mike Wilkins felt utterly hopeless, beyond redemption, beyond saving.

After all, the human race was surely doomed, he judged.

He had seen the hearts of men with his own eyes. Surely, he believed, all men were destined to burn in hell.

Two hours later, he found Timmy at the mall arcade, playing Pac Man.

The boy knew about him, but that was fine with Mike Wilkins. Already he was controlling his brother, the wife, and the other two children from a distance. He was sending subtle impulses for the rest of the family to finish the day's affairs, gather at the home.

Paula was at the restaurant with Jenny, but only

one of them found they had an inexplicable urge to go home. Paula was on her way to have that drink with Ballanger. It looked like tonight was the night for her.

And brother John was working late at the paper, more worried than ever, dreading he was losing control of his world. Robert was down at the basketball court with his friends, feeling confused and ashamed about last night. A probe of his brother had found that John had bailed his son out at the police station. Keller was still chomping at the bit about all the strange events surrounding him, and now he had kids riding around in their parents' cars, drunk. The whole town seemed on the verge of insanity. Still nothing from toxicology about the victims. Brother John was holding up a pretense of stumbling through the day, diving into work, calling Paula, checking up on his family. He had kept himself isolated in his office all day, ordering out for lunch. He was annoyed with the tension he sensed in his employees, wondered if maybe he should have a talk with all of them, but putting it off.

Wilkins had to move quickly. He was sweating profusely, trying to avoid eye contact as he walked among the throngs. He needed a diversion. He found an elderly man near the fountain. He knifed a pain through the man's chest. The scream and the man's collapse created the fear and confusion he needed in order to walk right out of there with Timmy. People were scurrying to the stricken man, while a security guard called for an ambulance on his handheld.

Wilkins kept Timmy in his semicatatonic state, walked right up to the boy, took his hand. Peterson was waiting out front in the Jeep Cherokee.

It would be dark soon.

"Are you Uncle Mike?"

He found some fear in the boy, but Timmy couldn't possibly understand what was happening to him. Still, the boy's innocence and purity of heart made him a believer in Uncle Mike.

"Yes, I'm your Uncle Mike." He felt his heart soften, a profound sorrow welling in his chest. He looked at the frantic, scrambling mobs surrounding the man who was having an obvious heart attack. He told Timmy, "Don't ask how I know, son, but I saw you in your dreams last night. Yeah. You were a pool champion; then you were a samurai. You know, I helped you kill all those samurai, helped you cut off the evil shogun's head. But that was just a dream, Timmy. Tonight you and me, we're going to do the real thing. Just think of us as a couple of warriors who have to save our honor."

Head bent, desperately trying to block out the boy's anxious thoughts, Mike Wilkins led his brother's youngest child out into the parking lot.

A part of him began burning inside as he hoped he didn't have to harm this boy. They were so much alike, he found he was fighting back a dammed-up wall of tears.

"Timmy," he told the boy. "Can we keep a little secret, just you and me?"

The boy hesitated, but nodded. "Sure. What is it?"

"Well, I want to surprise my brother. I want to see him but I'm not ready yet. Tomorrow evening, same time, you meet me here and we'll go see your father together. Will you promise me not to tell anybody?"

The boy's eyes lit up. "You bet."

"On your honor?"

"On my honor."

A short probe of the boy's mind found Timmy was eager to keep their secret, and would.

"Go on home, Timmy. I'll see you tomorrow."

Quickly Wilkins walked to Peterson's truck and hopped in. Turning back, he found Timmy standing alone on the sidewalk, waving good-bye.

Terrible Tuesday, he thought, and felt an intense hurt for his brother's youngest.

Tomorrow.

But first tonight.

Chapter Twenty-three

Mike Wilkins sat beside Peterson in a truck parked on a lonely and isolated dirt stretch of country road. They were a mile north of Ballanger's apartment complex. Night was fast falling over the farmland that reached away from Ballanger's home.

Darkness was beautiful, Wilkins thought. His cloak, his armor.

He probed the town, sent himself out there. Father O'Shay was sound asleep in his room, having just sent his secretary home for the night and killing a stiff drink to ease his fears. And his brother was wrapping up his day's work, shutting down the terminal in his office. He was the last one at the paper. Brother John intended to go their restaurant to eat, but his real motive was to check up on Paula.

Only Paula had other plans.

Wilkins drifted into the restaurant, which was nearly vacant. He found Jenny slouched at the end of the bar. She looked especially disturbed behind her mask of brooding silence. Now Paula was coming out of the office. She was nervous, her mind spinning with lies and half truths. She had just called Ballanger to tell him she'd like to see him but not in public. She didn't want to stir up any more rumors, even though she knew she was playing a dangerous game. But she told herself she needed a friend at that moment in the worst way. He had told her he was preparing dinner, prime rib and scallops, to come on over, they'd have a drink and talk. Right. The guy was hot for another man's wife, excited by the prospect of stealing something that didn't belong to him. What did he expect of Ballanger anyway? Wilkins thought. The guy was a lawyer.

"Mom," Jenny said in a soft but whining voice, "can I go home? There's no business. What's happened here? It's like nobody wants to come in anymore."

"I don't know, hon." Paula looked around, recognized a few of the regulars. The place struck her more like a funeral home than a bustling, happy-times eatery.

Wilkins concentrated, found her struggling with her desire to be with Ballanger and her need to stay loyal and faithful to her husband. He made her a little moist, thinking about Ballanger, the old days, the good times, the innocence of youth, how she had denied herself to him, denied him. *But, oh, yes, things change. Marriages fail, people cheat.*

"Mom? Are you listening to me?"

"Hon, tell you what, finish up your tables; Mark will close up tonight." She was thinking she needed to count two weeks' worth of receipts, the cash, annoyed that she hadn't made a trip to the bank. She would do it tomorrow. So much had happened, she'd been too distracted.

Outstanding, Wilkins thought. Tomorrow she would discover that there wouldn't be much left to deposit.

"Mom, are you angry with me?"

"About what?"

"Last night. We didn't do anything. Dad was so angry. It scared me."

"I know. Hon, you have to understand. With everything that's been happening, your father's under a lot of pressure. I'm sure he didn't mean to upset you. He knows you and Paul weren't doing anything."

But she had her own doubts as to how far her daughter had gone with the Stallings boy.

"Listen, I'll talk your dad later. Cheer up, okay? Everything's going to be all right."

She was hot, her heart racing. She suddenly wondered why she felt so out of control. Wilkins helped her feel lust, kept her throat dry, her heart racing.

She picked up her purse from behind the bar. Jenny gave her a curious look.

"Where are you going, Mom?"

She wanted to lie, but Wilkins forced her next words out.

"I . . . I, uh . . . I have to go see someone."

"Who? Mom, you're acting real strange."

"A friend, just a friend. I'll be home later."

Wilkins chuckled, pulled himself back as Paula looked as if she were fleeing the restaurant.

John Wilkins strolled into the restaurant and found the place almost empty. He searched the dining room. A few regulars were at the bar. Then he saw the Thompsons, a young couple with a small child. There was an elderly couple, the Johnsons, married for forty years, seemed like they'd lived in Glendale forever. Then he found Jane Summers, one of his staff reporters, eating dinner with a date, a man Wilkins didn't recognize. Beyond that, there were two scattered parties. He met their gazes in turn, Ben Thompson throwing him a curt nod and wave. The Johnsons stared at him for a moment, then returned to eating. Damn it, Wilkins thought; they were all looking at him as if they shared some dark secret about his life. His anger mounting, he found Jenny coming out of the kitchen. Swiftly he reached her at the end of the bar. He glanced at Paul Mitchelson, the computer hack nursing a beer, and said, "Hey, Paul."

"How you doing, John?"

"Been better," Wilkins said, cold.

What was that look in Mitchelson's eyes? Cynicism? Laughter?

"Jenny, where's your mother?"

Now she was looking at him strangely. It seemed like it took an hour for her to answer.

"She's not here, Dad."

"I'm beginning to gather that much. Where is she?" he asked, feeling his heart sink, knowing something was going on and Jenny was holding back. "Jenny, answer me. Where is your mother?"

"She was acting kind of weird. Is she okay, Dad?"

"She's fine," he said, biting down his impatience. "Jenny?"

"Mom, well, she said she had to go see someone."

"Who?"

"She . . . she didn't say who. She said . . . said it was just a friend."

Wilkins fought to keep the pain and anguish out of his expression as he squeezed the bridge of his nose, shut his eyes. He knew. Ballanger. Suddenly his world was gone forever. He felt like screaming, his heart pounding with jealous fury. When he opened his eyes, the world seemed to spin.

"Pour me a drink, Jenny. Whiskey. Rocks. Now—please!" he snapped.

She looked afraid of him, but they all looked scared of him. Right then, John Wilkins didn't give a damn about anything or anyone. He squared his shoulders. It was time to deal with these people. He met their nervous looks. They were faceless entities to him in his mist of anger. They could kiss his ass. What did they know anyway? Or was he taking out his jealousy on any available targets? Whatever, he decided. He was sick and tired of their cold treatment, silent judgment.

"Everybody having a good time?" he growled. He felt the tension burn from their bodies, forks frozen midway to mouths. "How's the food?"

"It's . . . everything's fine," the young kid with his young wife said. "Food's always great here."

"That the only reason you people came here? The food? Surprised there's not a picket line out front. Surprised I haven't been stoned to death yet. You know, the male Mary Magdalene."

"John, what's wrong with you?" Mitchelson said. Then Jenny cried out, "Dad! Stop it!"

"Watch your mouth, Wilkins!" Johnson warned.

"What's wrong with me? I'll tell you what's wrong with me. It isn't me that's wrong; it's you people. Sitting in judgment of me, with your cynical stares and critical eyes. Okay," he snarled, running his furious stare over them, not caring, knowing his world was most likely lost. "First, I did not cheat on my wife. Yeah, I've heard the rumors. Our good chief of police told me everybody's whispering behind my back. Uh-huh, I see the way people look at me when I walk the streets, some sort of pariah. Second, I didn't have a damn thing to do with anyone's murder or suicide. I am not to blame, people, for the perverted and twisted acts of sick men."

Old Man Johnson slapped his napkin on the table and stood up. He was a big, rawboned man who had farmed all of his life.

"Wilkins, get yourself under control. Only reason I came in here was for the food, and I was hoping to speak to you alone. But since you're making this little scene, I'm going to say something to you. This is a clean, God-fearing town. What you did or didn't do to your wife ain't none of our business. But I'm getting sick of the talk, you being the center of some real ugly controversy. You got people, good people in a good town, scared, people dying all around you, claiming all sorts of nasty things about you. What's anyone around here supposed to believe?"

Wilkins sounded a mean laugh, his blood boiling. He searched their faces, knew they all felt the same way as Johnson.

"Come on, Martha, we're leaving."

"That's what I want, old man. In fact, all of you get out of here. Get out of my restaurant and don't come back. I don't need your judgment, I don't need your criticism, your sneering, sneaky ways, your spineless contempt."

"Dad!" Jenny screamed from a great distance.

No one moved except the Johnsons, the old man brushing against Wilkins as if daring him to take a swing at him.

"You people hear me?" he bellowed. "Get the fuck out of my restaurant. You fucking bastards! Get the fuck out of my place!"

They were leaping to their feet now, scared to death.

"Don't bother paying, it's on the fucking house! All

of you, fuck you and kiss my ass but get the fuck out of my restaurant!" he roared over and over, until he was completely alone.

Then he saw Jenny running for the door, tears streaming down her face. Some of the kitchen help were standing at the end of the bar, blank stares in their eyes.

Mark Warren, the nighttime manager, looked around the empty dining room. He swallowed hard and asked, "Are we closing down, Mr. Wilkins?"

"No. Stay open."

When Warren disappeared into the kitchen, Wilkins stood there in the middle of the empty dining room, shaking uncontrollably, feeling utterly and completely lost. Somehow he made his way to the bar, went straight for a bottle of Wild Turkey. He sucked down a long, burning swig. For a moment he stared at his reflection, still shaking, shocked by what he had just done.

Mike Wilkins laughed. Oh, that was sweet, he thought, seeing his brother sitting at the bar, all alone, desperately trying to rationalize his behavior, but knowing life would never again be the same.

Now big brother knew how it felt. Sitting there, getting drunk, isolated, trapped, beyond hope and help.

Then he found Paula running up the steps to Ballanger's apartment. He was urging her along, giving her a mental shove, feeding her heat. No foreplay, just go for the good stuff.

He hovered in, watching from above, as she knocked on the door. She was anxious, looking around, hoping nobody saw her.

She was ready to cheat, even as she fought her desire, worrying about getting caught.

He concentrated but suddenly found her hard to reach. She didn't want to do what she really wanted to do. She believed, in fact, that John had been faithful to her, that she was reacting out of revenge, that her humiliation had driven her to do this. Maybe she should just walk away, apologize to Jeff. *No*, Wilkins urged her. *Go on, do it*.

The door opened. Wilkins fought against her stubborn refusal to give in to this man, then made her fall into his arms.

"You okay?" Ballanger asked.

"No, I'm not."

Man alive, she was hot for this guy, but fighting it hard. She bulled past him, into a living room of love seat, big white leather couch, giant screen TV, wet bar, and aroma of prime rib.

"What's wrong, Paula?"

"Everything's wrong," she cried as he closed the door. "My marriage, my life, my children. Everything's just suddenly a total disaster. I don't deserve this!"

Wilkins fed her doubt and fear with lust. She grew weak in the knees.

Do it, bitch! he urged her, making her throw her arms around him.

Then something he didn't understand began to happen. Just like that, there was a disjointed, disconnected image, the power fading, fighting even to stay in control. He grew angry as he caught a flash of the priest waking up, alone, crying to God: "My Lord, save us! Oh, Jesus, my Lord and my savior, save us from this evil thing that walks among us."

Distracted, the light inside dimming, he heard Ballanger say, "Paula, are you sure you want to do this?"

She kissed him hungrily on the mouth.

"Yes. Yes!" she cried breathlessly.

Ballanger was stunned for a moment by her sudden and raging hunger.

Wilkins drove a fire into her heart, but she shuddered, pulled back, her eyes misting with tears.

Then Ballanger started to grow a conscience, believing it was all happening too fast. In the past, he had cheated on his wife and was almost proud of his womanizing. Wilkins caught a flash of the woman as Ballanger remembered. She was dark haired, olive skinned, perhaps Spanish or Asian, but Wilkins wasn't getting a clear picture of the woman.

Father O'Shay's prayers carved into the power.

"Dear Jesus, forgive him his evil, for he truly knows not what he does. The man is Paul, the man is Peter, he is Jude. . . . He is a terrible sinner in dire and anguished need of forgiveness and your grace and redemption. . . ."

"Noooooooooo!" Wilkins screamed, fighting to keep Peterson, the priest, and Paula and Ballanger in his power. "Fuck Paul! Fuck Peter! They were unclean!"

He was losing them. He had to focus on the priest; he needed the priest.

"I want you."

"Paula, think about this."

"I have. We were kids. We should have been . . . lovers . . . lovers, naked and in the woods. . . ."

Wilkins screamed, "Say it, bitch, do it. Go down, you goddamned bitch!"

She dropped to her knees, her mind screaming that this was wrong, that she believed in her husband, that he had not wronged her. She pulled his zipper down. Ballanger was getting hard.

"Paula, oh, Paula, I always wanted you."

The whole situation was getting out of control. No, it was beyond his control. The power was demanding something bigger, something more, more vengeance, hungry for justice but in blood and death.

The priest was crying in his bed, begging for his God's mercy and forgiveness.

Wilkins couldn't control himself. The past flashed through his mind.

So long ago, he remembered, there was a girl. Tammi.

She loved him, no questions asked, no pressure, sweet and gentle and kind, feminine. He had believed he had found the closest thing to love, so he took her virginity in a strong moment of pure male aggression. Pure and sweet and beautiful. But she had denied him. He had to force her.

He lost Tammi, and now he was losing control of Paula. *Oh, you, yeah, yeah, you, like then, like now. Losing. Losing her, losing life. Gone. Forever. Kiss it good-bye.* Death was the only answer.

Denied!

Still, Paula was hungry, kneading Ballanger's buttocks, slipping his pants down, her mouth wet and hot.

But her mind was screaming.

"Bitch!" Wilkins yelled, then saw the past with Tammi, his first, his only real love, his woman, a fire of something real and right between them—dying.

Oh, the redhead! Back in Ohio, oh, my little redhead. Then a flash from so long ago. Denial. But it was there. He was coming out of a convenience store, six-pack in hand. The booze gave him courage to do it. He needed it. He needed her love so badly.

Paula stood, shoved Ballanger away.

Ballanger became angry. "What are you doing?"

"I can't, I'm sorry, I love my husband!"

"Noooooooooooo!" Wilkins screamed.

And there was Tammi, staring him dead in the eye, with the most painful, lost, and angry look he had ever seen. As he got in the car, her car, popped a beer, he recalled her shrieking, "I hate you! You're so *lonely*! You are the loneliest son of a bitch I've ever seen! I can never be any good to you! I can never change you! You are so lonely!"

"Paula!" Ballanger hollered through the mist.

Wilkins sweated, shook, growled. He had lost the moment. Paula would keep the faith.

Saw some light breaking through her, hauling her away.

"You are so lonely!"

Why was this memory flashing like that, when he had not thought of Tammi in all those years? He had wiped her out of his mind. Now this torment. Left her. So brokenhearted. His life without meaning, empty, with only torment.

And Wilkins slammed his foot, over and over, against the dashboard, crushing the radio and cassette. At the same instant he recalled how Tammi had kicked out the window of her own car as he forced himself on top of her. She kept shrieking, "You are so lonely! You will die alone!"

Then he remembered quietly driving away, shocked, dropping her off at her home. Stunned, drunk.

"I can never see you again," he had told her. "I'm sorry."

"So am I!" she wept. "Go!"

And he went.

He walked on.

Paula was running from Ballanger, hurling open the door.

She would not do it. She had kept the faith. She walked.

And the priest was howling for his God.

Wilkins concentrated, burning up with fever. Keep the priest under control.

"No!" he screamed. "I am *not* Paul. I am *not* Peter! I am not *Jude*! I am *Judas*!"

Mike Wilkins fell out of the truck, hit his knees, and vomited.

Chapter Twenty-four

His head swimming with booze, John Wilkins stumbled a little up the sidewalk. He glanced at his wife's car, parked in the drive, saw the living room light shining through the curtains. She was home. Big deal, he thought, who cares? She had not returned to the restaurant and it was now almost ten o'clock. The night surrounding him looked and felt especially dark, and eerily quiet. Hope she had a good time, he thought.

The restaurant was still open, about to close, and only a few guests had ventured in after his outburst. He had stubbornly refused to close the restaurant or send anyone home, despite the fact that business had been almost nonexistent.

For long moments, feeling as if he were being marched to his execution, Wilkins stood at the door to their home. He didn't know what he would say, much less do, when he faced Paula. He had a lot of questions. He didn't even care if he came across like the spurned and cuckolded husband. Screw it. He was angry, hurt. Everything was going to hell. If things got any worse, he was thinking about leaving Glendale for good. But he needed to deal with his wife, his children, the townspeople. God, he thought, how many apologies would he need to issue in the next few days? Or would he even bother? Did any of them even deserve an apology?

Screw it. He keyed open the door, ventured into his home. The living room was empty. Then he heard sniffling from upstairs. It was Jenny, crying to her mother.

Slowly he walked up the steps, then stood in the doorway of his daughter's room. Paula was cradling his daughter in her arms. Jenny was crying, eyes shut. When Paula spotted him in the doorway, she jumped a little, tightened her embrace of Jenny. He couldn't read her expression at first. Then he saw anger and disgust in her eyes.

Jenny opened her eyes, tears pouring off her cheeks.

"What is wrong with you, John? Have you lost your mind?"

Jenny shuddered, shut her eyes again.

"Jen, honey," he said, finding his voice. "Listen, baby, I'm terribly sorry about the way I acted tonight. Please . . . forgive me. We can talk in the morning."

"We need to talk now."

"Exactly what I was about to say."

Mother caressed daughter. He stood there, frozen in the doorway.

What the hell was going on?

"Try to get some sleep, Jenny," he heard Paula say, as he turned and walked toward their bedroom.

Mike Wilkins found every key player in his master plan through a short probe. Brother John was home, looking every bit the wounded husband and father, poor guy, looking and feeling abused and misjudged and misunderstood. Father O'Shay was sound asleep. And the chief and his deputies had either gone home for the night or were sipping coffee in the station, trying to stay awake for their shift.

Wilkins had Peterson park his vehicle behind their restaurant. The lot was empty. One kid, Mark Warren, was inside, he found, closing up for the night, locking up the cash drawer in the front, at the end of the bar. He looked like a soft, apple-cheeked blond, now tired and nerve-racked by everything he had seen earlier, glad to be going home.

Wilkins had to work quickly.

He slid out of the vehicle, slipped through the night, having already summoned this Mark Warren to the back door. He kept the night manager in a trance. The kid thought he was letting in Mr. Wilkins, or at least that was what he would believe tomorrow.

Quickly Wilkins went in through the back door, the kitchen entrance, everything aluminum and steel, dishes cleaned and racked, pots and utensils hung up. He made Warren go out and sit in the main dining room. The office door was rarely locked, since Paula trusted her employees completely. That would soon change.

He dialed the combination, clicked in the tumblers from memory, opened the safe. The wad of cash was substantial. He counted a little over five thousand in cash, took it all. Shutting the safe, pocketing the cash, he swiftly made his way back outside.

Settling into the Jeep Cherokee, he looked at Peterson, showed him the wad, and laughed. "You be a good bully, now, and I might cut you in for a sweet slice."

As he made Peterson pull away, Wilkins chuckled,

pulled out the amulet, and stared it for a moment.

"You know, Stan, I wonder if this thing would work on anybody else. You think you're man enough to take it off me?" He put it back under his shirt, heard the cursing in the man's mind. "I didn't think so."

John Wilkins stood at the end of the bed, a bourbon and ginger in hand. He drew hard on his cigarette, watched Paula sitting on her side of the bed, sipping her vodka. She wouldn't look at him. She acted as if she were the one who had been betrayed, he thought, growing angry at her cold silence.

"You know," she began, "Jenny wasn't going to come home. She was over at the Stallingses'. I had to practically beg her. She's scared to death of you, John. And I've already gotten a dozen phone calls from friends all over town about your ugly little scene. They said you either issue an apology to all of them, or they'll never come into our restaurant again."

Screw them, he thought. "Where were you tonight?" he asked, and saw her stiffen in the shoulders. She folded her arms defensively.

"I went somewhere. To see a friend."

"This friend, does it happen to be one Jeff Ballanger?"

She gave him a look he read as contempt, then looked away, sipped her drink.

"Well?"

"Is that what your tirade was all about? Some mindless fit of jealousy?"

"Hey, I asked you a simple and straightforward question. Answer me," he said. He heard the aggression in his voice, loud and clear.

"Okay." She paused. "I went to see Jeff. But before you have another outburst and alarm the children again, I'll tell you nothing happened."

"And that's supposed to make me feel better? My wife goes traipsing off to see an old flame, see if the fire is still there. The guy was practically drooling over you when I saw him."

"You want the truth, I'm telling you. Whether or not you believe me is up to you. Nothing happened."

"Just like you didn't believe me about Cassandra Dooley?"

"John, I thought about that, long and hard. I believe nothing happened between you and that woman."

"So you and Ballanger just had a little chat; you needed a shoulder to cry on. 'My husband doesn't understand me,' that kind of thing?"

"Don't get ugly. It wasn't like that. What do you need? A lie-detector test? Or for me to go see a doctor now and have a—"

"That's enough."

"You're right. It's enough. My word is enough."

"And mine hasn't been."

"I didn't say that. You know, it's very unattractive to see you act this way."

"What way would that be? Like a concerned husband and father, trying to keep his family together?"

"No, like an insanely jealous man who's being unduly hard on himself and taking his anger out on everybody else."

"I get the feeling you're about to issue me a bottom line here."

Another long pause. "If things don't get any better between us, John, I'm going to have to think about the children."

He felt panic rise in his throat. "Before you make any rash decisions I want you to think about our children."

"Believe me, I will."

He stood there, searching her face. She was cold and distant, not looking at him.

"Anybody see you with him? Did you go to his place?"

"Is that what you're worried about? How it looked if somebody saw me? I won't answer that."

"I get the feeling you want me to sleep on the couch tonight."

"No," she said. "You can sleep in the guest room."

"Don't do me any favors."

"Don't make a scene."

"Don't worry, I'll leave the house before the kids wake up so they won't have to wonder why Daddy didn't sleep with Mommy."

She looked at him with contempt again.

He was moving to the door, ashamed of his behavior, his suspicion and distrust, when he stopped to look back at his wife.

"Paula. I need to know something. Have I lost you?"

She took a few moments before answering, "I don't know, John. It's up to you. I hope not."

He took little comfort in that, decided to go make himself another drink. It would take a good deal more booze to make himself sleep that night.

When he walked into the newsroom the next morning, John Wilkins instantly felt the tension, caught the sideways looks. Then he stopped cold in his tracks. He searched the empty bays, counted six of his staff missing. Something felt terribly wrong.

He checked his watch. It was almost nine-thirty. He had been running late, stopped for a cup of coffee at a convenience store, then sat alone in his car, gathering his thoughts, hoping it was going to be a different day. If not better, at least not worse.

He knew who was missing.

"What's going on here?" he asked Hauser. "Why's everybody running late?"

"Uh, John?" Hauser seemed to fumble for the right words. Then he rattled off the names of his staff who had called in sick or were going ahead and taking their vacation time. Then he said, "Jane called about an hour ago. She said she's quitting."

Wilkins felt his shoulders sag, a wave of anger, then depression, settling over him. He would call Jane later, apologize, try to change her mind. She was too good a reporter and writer, and she certainly had not deserved his ugly treatment at the restaurant.

At the moment he needed to address the fears of whoever was left.

"Okay, everyone, please listen." He met their gazes in turn, sucked in a deep breath, sounding every bit as conciliatory and sorry as he felt. "I deeply apologize for my behavior. I'm sure everyone's heard what happened at the restaurant yesterday. I'm not making excuses for my abhorrent behavior. I have been accused of things I did not do. Rumors are flying all around me. All I want is for you to accept my apology, and let us all have life get back to normal. There are many people I will be seeing in the next few days. I will do my damnedest to try to smooth the waters. Believe me when I tell you there will be no further problems, no more wild outbursts. I hope everyone here understands."

A few nods, a couple of "Sures."

So why wasn't he convinced life would go blissfully marching on? Why did they still look nervous and afraid? Why was he still so very afraid?

"Let's go to work," he said, and went into his office.

He was sitting at his terminal, going over the day's stories for tomorrow's edition, when he glanced up, saw Paula storm into the newsroom. There was a wild look of pure rage in her eyes as she swept past his skeleton crew, her stare drilling fire into him. John Wilkins tensed for the worst as she barged into his office. And he got it.

"What's the problem?" he asked.

"Where is it, John?"

"Where's what?"

He looked past his wife, caught the nervous and tense expressions out in the newsroom.

"The money."

"What money?"

"Don't play stupid, John!" she yelled.

"Paula, get yourself under control. I have no idea what you're talking about."

"You don't, huh?"

"Would you mind closing the door and lowering your voice?"

She slammed the door, rattling the windows. Wilkins felt his blood running hot when he saw some of his people flinch. His office was hardly soundproof. And since it seemed that Paula was hell-bent on shouting, their conversation would be crystal clear to his staff.

"What's wrong with you, Paula?"

"I guess you didn't trust me, huh, John? I guess you really didn't believe me when I said I didn't have sex with him. So what did you do, pilfer the safe at the restaurant? Get a little nest egg together? Maybe I should check our bank accounts and see if you've plundered those, too. I hope you leave me and the children with a few hundred at least. What's your plan? Leave me before I leave you? Maybe you have some little honey lined up on the side?"

"Paula, slow down and tell me what the hell you're talking about."

"Okay, you want to play it like that?"

He stood, held his arms out. "I'm not playing like anything!" he said, and realized he was now shouting.

"The money from two weeks' worth of business. The safe in the office, John. Five thousand dollars in cash is gone. Only you and I have the combination."

He was stunned, speechless. "And you think I took it? Come on, be sensible. If only you and I have the combination, would I be stupid enough to do something like that?"

"Not stupid, no, but desperate!"

"Now I'm a liar as well as a thief? Maybe you should talk to Mark Warren, since he closed up last night."

"I did. He said you came in late last night."

Wilkins felt his jaw drop. "That's impossible. Why would he say that? He's lying."

"Is he?"

"I'll talk to him, you can damn well believe that."

"Don't bother. I gave him the day off. I told him not to answer the phone, not to talk to you."

"Paula, this is insane."

"You bet it is. That's it, John. I have to get away from you."

He nearly panicked. "What?"

"You heard me. Tonight, I'm leaving tonight. I'm

packing some things. I'm going to make some calls today. I'll be leaving tonight."

"What about the children?"

"They're going with me."

"No, no, no."

"Yes! Don't force my hand. Don't make me go to Chief Keller and tell him what I suspect."

"Paula . . . Paula, don't do this. There has to be some mistake, there has to be some explanation."

"When you have it, maybe, *maybe* we'll talk."

She threw open the door and stormed out.

Shocked, Wilkins staggered out into the newsroom. "Paula! Paula!"

She nearly ran out the door. In disbelief, Wilkins searched the faces of his staff, his jaw hanging. Finally, he told them all, "It isn't true, none of it." He paused, looking at each of them with silent imploring. They looked doubtful, fearful. It danced through his mind that he was going to lose a few more employees by tomorrow. He had a vision of himself sitting in an empty newsroom by week's end.

"Everybody, please, go back to work."

Numb he staggered back into his office. Quietly he shut the door, collapsed into his chair. The whole world, it seemed, had gone mad.

He had Timmy meet them out front. As Peterson pulled up into the parking lot of the mall, Mike Wilkins said, "You can speak now, if you want. Try to yell and I'll choke the air out of you. I want to hear if you have anything intelligent to say."

Struggling to find his voice, Peterson growled, "I don't know what you've done to me, but if I get my hands on you, you little—"

Wilkins strangled the air off. "That's enough. I

knew it was a mistake to let you speak. You have nothing worthwhile or intelligent to say. Thing is, I don't want anybody to speak; it's why I take their voices. I like silence, I demand only silence, and, of course, obedience and compliance."

He saw Timmy walking out the mall doors, made Peterson pull over into an empty slot. It had been a long but good day. It seemed brother John's wife was leaving him, but she needed to make arrangements, wanted all the children gathered. Timmy had slipped out of the house, just as the both of them had planned. The final straw was the missing money. Brother John had buried himself in work all day, full of fear and worry. Three calls to Paula, each one ending up in an argument. He couldn't change her mind. She was leaving, needed space, time. When he chose to come clean with her, they would talk. He insisted he'd done nothing wrong. He knew the rumor mill was spinning wildly, so he was afraid to venture out of the paper.

Soon there would be no place for anyone to hide.

Mike Wilkins was ready. Glendale was about to burn. He had spent the day with Peterson, resting, eating well, preparing himself. He had let the power rest, using it only to keep Father O'Shay subdued, give the man's secretary the day off, the good father forced to make feeble explanations.

Wilkins hopped out of the vehicle, held the door open for Timmy, pulled up the seat. He smiled at Timmy, who returned his smile.

"Hi, Uncle Mike."

"Hi, Timmy. Keep our secret?"

"Yup. Why wouldn't I?"

"There was never any doubt. Ready to go see your Dad?"

"Sure am. This is going to be a real surprise, isn't it?"

"The biggest surprise of his life, Timmy."

He waited until Timmy was settled in the backseat, then looked around to make sure they were unobserved.

Night was falling fast on Terrible Tuesday.

Chapter Twenty-five

John Wilkins turned onto Alden Street, spotted his wife's Honda parked in the drive. He had called her three times in the past hour, his fear growing colder and tighter in his belly like a mass of writhing serpents. Each time he had heard the distress and anger in Paula's voice. She had sounded odd, as if she were struggling to talk, coherent one moment, then cold and distant, as if she were drifting away, or somehow withdrawing into herself. It almost didn't quite sound like her voice at all—it was as if some other voice was choosing her words for her.

Something was terribly wrong. Something was happening beyond his control. At the moment, he even felt tugged by some force outside his body, toward his home.

And the real crisis was that Timmy was missing.

Of course, Paula had blamed him for that, calling it a ploy on his part, accusing him of holding the boy hostage. He denied it, angry his wife would even think that, and in no uncertain terms.

"Maybe he's home now, Dad."

He glanced at Robert, having just picked his son up at the Glendale High playground. He wanted to tell him, "Maybe you're right," but he suspected he would be lying to his son, and to himself.

Alone, he had already searched the mall, but with no luck. Then he had called the few friends Timmy had, but no one had seen or heard from him. If Timmy wasn't home when he went inside, he would call Keller and demand all available resources be marshaled to find Timmy. He didn't want to sound an unnecessary alarm yet, but he had a strong, nagging, and ugly suspicion what had happened to Timmy.

"Damn it!" Growing frantic, thinking about his conversations with Paula, he recalled that both of them had specifically told Timmy to stay home, not to go out of the house.

Now it was nightfall. Despite the lights that glowed in most of the homes, the surrounding darkness looked and felt total, and alive with something sinister.

He parked, killed the engine, hopped out, slammed the door. With his son on his heels, Wilkins nearly burst through the front door.

And froze in the foyer.

He found his wife and daughter sitting side by side on the couch. Right away, he feared the worst but couldn't explain or fathom what he found. There was a wild look of desperate terror in their eyes. They didn't move, seemed paralyzed, didn't even look his way, at first; then they rolled their eyes toward him.

"Paula? Jenny?"

He was moving toward them, his heart pounding, watching their mouths open a little, a strange sputtering rolling past their lips, when he caught the sound of an engine outside. It was a faint and distant noise in the pulsing he felt in his ears. Then it gradually struck him that someone was outside, walking up the steps. He was about to grab his wife and shake her, when he became aware of a presence in the doorway. He was turning, hearing the cold laughter already recognizing the voice and knowing who was standing in the doorway, when a sharp, knifing pain tore through his groin. He cried out, slumping to his knees. Next he saw his son fall beside him, Robert's eyes bulging with pain.

Somehow he managed to look up—slowly, ever so slowly, toward the doorway, knowing but hoping it wasn't true, feeling the cold presence of living evil fill the entire home, then swarm through his body.

And John Wilkins felt his heart skip a beat at the vision of the white and glowing eyes that stared back at him.

John Wilkins struggled to find his voice, his senses shattered, his insides seeming to collapse in his utter terror. Then the pain tore through his crotch again, but he suddenly had no voice, his own cry of torment trapped in his mind. In the next eternal second, even as the question formed in his mind, he knew that Bartkowski was right.

His brother's cold voice didn't even sound like the voice John remembered, as Mike growled, "What have I become? That's what you're thinking. Well, I've become something more than merely human, that's about all I can tell you. Fact is, I do believe I have become, if not God, then the next best thing. So, what I'm going to do is, I'm going to demand your worship and your glory. And, yes, my errand boy, the Bartster was right, John. You should have seen the look in his eyes right before he slammed himself into that telephone pole. It was beautiful. I got a good chuckle out of that one. Hey, believe me when I tell you, the guy deserved what he got."

Those eyes! He couldn't stop staring at those brilliant eyes, which burned and pierced him with that radiating glow.

Mike Wilkins softly closed the front door. "Now that we're all here, I think we need to have a long talk. I will allow you people to speak, but try to scream and you'll feel more exquisite pain. Have faith, believe, do not ask questions. I am who I am, and I stand before you, able and ready to crush your lives. I am in complete control of all of you."

He laughed.

A hazy veil of tears burned his eyes, as John Wilkins doubled up, then crumpled into a fetal position as the white-hot pain kept ripping apart his insides with what felt like countless razors and knives.

He listened to their terrified and angry questions, their voices choked with fear and pain. Amused, smiling, smoothing back his sweat-soaked hair, Mike Wilkins took a seat in the leather recliner.

The wife was cursing him. "You bastard, what have you done to Timmy?"

Next John. "Where's Timmy, Mike? Why? Why are you doing this? If it's me you feel you have a score to settle with, then just hurt me, but let my family go. I beg you, please, let them go."

Mike Wilkins stared down at Robert. "What was that, Bobby? You just used the f-word on dear old Uncle Mike. Where did you learn to talk like that, son? You know, kid, I've been meaning to tell you, you should have been kinder to your younger brother. Timmy's a dreamer, a romantic. He has talent, a good and big heart. Maybe later I'll let him slap you around a little, maybe put one right in your nuts. Think you're tough, do you, Bobby? You don't know what tough is, kid, little fucking punk. Couldn't survive two minutes in the places I've walked."

Then the daughter, as he heard her frantic cries, and began mimicking her words with cold contempt. " 'What's wrong with me, Daddy? Why can't I move? Oh, please, help me, help me, Daddy.' Daddy isn't strong enough, honey, he's not man enough to take me on. You know, your mouth looks pretty damn sweet, yes, I know, you want to use it on your boyfriend, go down on him, but, hey, I'm here." He put an image in his brother's mind of Jenny naked and on her knees before him. He heard John curse him, his brother squeezing his eyes shut, fighting to will the obscene image out of his mind, telling himself it wasn't real, it wasn't happening.

"But it could happen like that, John. Here. Allow me to show you both the little cream puff and the Mrs., kneeling naked and hungry before the sports hero, one Mr. Jeff Ballanger. Damn near slobbering, aren't they? I can even put the same image into Paula's head." And he did, felt their outrage and filled their minds with his laughter.

"You vile, sick bastard!" Paula snarled. "Stop it! Stop it now! That never happened!"

Mike Wilkins laughed again, bounced a few other obscene and living cinema images through their minds, making his brother watch his women pleasure Ballanger.

"Okay, that's enough. I think you've got the picture, brother."

Then he made a probe to get a fix on his pawns. The good father was now frozen in his confessional, the church still empty. Outside, parked by the curb, Peterson was fighting to will his arms to move, desperately wishing he could just drive away. And

'immy was lying on the backseat, wanting to cry.
'or a brief moment, Wilkins almost allowed the boy
he escape of at least shedding some tears. It was
oing to be a shame to have to do what he was going
o do to the boy, but he saw no other way. His de-
ision was made. After all, he had not created this
ituation; others had brought this shame and
uffering upon themselves.

He saw his brother looking at his chest. "You're
hinking that if you could just get to me, right, John?"
Ie showed his brother the gold star with the black
ye. "This what you want to tear off me? That if you
ould, you'd be able to fight back. Tell you what,
ince I'm such a good sport, I can at least give you
ack your voice, but be careful what you say. I've
arned your respect and honor."

"Where's Timmy?" John Wilkins said through grit-
ed teeth.

"Sit up, John. You look silly, curled up like a baby
ike that. It's very undignified for a man like you. At
east those are tears of pain in your eyes. And it does
urt, doesn't it? Feels like you have knives tearing
hrough your crotch, slicing up your balls."

Slowly John Wilkins sat up, braced his back
gainst the couch, next to his wife.

"All right, all right, I'll humor you people. This is
ne time where I actually enjoy hearing others
peak. Okay, Timmy's fine, John, he's with me. Now
don't want to have to answer a bunch of trivial
uestions, so please spare us both some torment. I
now you think I'm a fearsome, evil sight. Covered
n sweat, eyes like white fire, my flesh reeking of fe-
er. Whatever happened to the younger brother you
emembered? You're thinking back. Even when I
eemed disturbed or brooding, you thought there

was a gentleness, a kindness inside me, even to my aloneness. I lived and let live. Could laugh, my eyes showed that I actually kind of liked people, despite everything." He laughed. "Well, things change. Let's just say I've grown up and I've certainly outgrown the human race. You know what Dad did to Mary when we were children?" He branded an image of their father fondling and undressing their sister in his brother's head.

"You think I'm making that up, John?"

"Yes. You are. We don't know that ever happened."

He shrugged. "Perhaps you're right. Let the dead rest in peace, huh?"

"What do you want, Mike? I asked you why you're doing this. Revenge?"

"Revenge is just part of it. I want you to suffer, I want you to see your family suffer, as I suffered since I was a child. You know the beatings I took, the disgrace and humiliation I suffered and endured. Hey, I know, life's tough, but it was always a little tougher for me." He felt his eyes burning hotter and hotter, the sweat pouring off his chin. He twitched, his head cocking to one side. He was puzzled by, then afraid of his sudden loss of control. Even the amulet felt hot on his chest, glowing. "What? Is that pity I feel in you, John?" For some reason, his brother started to stand. In a flash of panic, Mike Wilkins thought he was losing control of his brother. Dredging up his rage, he concentrated, boring his will into John. Still his brother rose, trembling violently.

"Why, Mike? Why are you doing this? Do you hate me that much? Or do you hate yourself? You hate your own life that much to cause innocent people suffering like this? To destroy my life with lies and rumors? To make my wife want to leave me and take my children? That's it, isn't it, you hate yourself!"

"You . . . I . . . I . . . Don't judge me! Sit down! I command you to sit down!" He forced a knifing pain through his brother's knees and watched John collapse, fold up in front of the couch. For a moment, he saw the light inside dim. He was shaken by his fear that the power might abandon him, but the light burned back inside, and he felt his eyes heat up. He fought for breath, then composed himself as his lungs slowly filled with air.

"This town of yours, John, it makes me ill. To know what I know is in their hearts, well, you'd judge them harshly, too."

"There are a lot of good people in Glendale, Mike. Hardworking and honest people who have families they love and care about."

"Again, you could be right. But there's enough bad ones here for all of you to earn my final judgment. You know all the years I've suffered because of lies about my maybe molesting Cassandra, the rumors and whispers of rumors, the talk that maybe I was the kind of guy who might jack off on some woman's bedroom window. I was even accused of stealing when I bartended around here. Branded a thief and a pervert, when I always knew I was neither. Father always treating me like some hopeless, bizarre animal that needed to be put to sleep. How's it feel to be a pariah, John? Not pretty, is it?"

"Mike, I believe in your innocence, I always did."

"But you wondered. Maybe it was true."

"Of course, that's only natural."

"Never came to my defense."

"You know that's a lie. You've picked apart my memory and you know I did my best, everything I could do for you."

"Took Mom and Dad's money and ran like hell. Built yourself a sweet little kingdom, a real slice of paradise."

"That money helped put you through two drug rehabs."

"Most kind of you. Most generous. But I'm through talking about the past. What I demand now is your homage." He looked at the women, smiled, took his brother's voice as John began to say, "No, don't do it, Mike!" Those snarling words of alarm and anger bounced back into his mind.

"Whatever you are, you're sick and evil," Paula snarled.

"Really, Paula. Okay, you feel that way, allow me to indulge you. Tell you what, you and the cream puff, you two, come to me, crawl to me on your knees. Don't resist. I demand your unconditional love for John's old rival. Let's drum up a sweet picture of you and loverboy Ballanger. A mother-and-daughter team."

He forced them on their hands and knees. He heard Paula cursing him, Jenny begging for this to stop.

"Damn you, Mike, leave them alone! Take me, kill me, if you have to. . . ."

Mike drove the knifing pain through his brother's whole body, trapped the scream in his head.

He laughed, made his brother watch even as John wanted to close his eyes. What his brother saw was his wife and daughter, naked and crawling across the living room. He seared an image into John's head of Jenny and Paula, turning their heads and smiling back at him. Together, his brother's wife and daughter told him in the forced hallucination, "We love a new man, Daddy—John—we want Jeff Ballanger, we can't help ourselves. We love him much more than you. We have always belonged to him."

Mike Wilkins roared with laughter.

Chapter Twenty-six

It stopped.

First, John Wilkins saw a blinding flash of white light; then he found that his wife and daughter were allowed to return to the couch. They were walking now, and—thank God—fully clothed, as he knew they always had been. Outrage and fury burned in his wife's eyes, but there was pure terror and confusion on Jenny's face.

Nothing sick and obscene had happened to them, but something was happening to his brother. And John Wilkins was beginning to believe he understood how to handle this nightmare evil he was faced with.

He had to keep his mind clear of all negative thoughts, his heart still and quiet. No anger, no hatred, no fear. Whatever was inside his brother, perhaps even controlling him now, seemed to feed on the worst in the human heart and mind.

It was a stretch, he knew, but it was the only chance he had.

When he had believed Mike was going to further vent his insane wrath and either conjure up more obscene hallucinations or commit the real act, forcing his wife and daughter to do his will, John Wilkins accepted the fact that he was powerless. A numb ache swelled in his heart, a feeling of intense pity for his younger brother shrouding over him. Then he let a silent faith fill him that he would somehow prevail. After all, the belief that he would, *could*, overcome this evil was his only hope. And hope was his and his family's only chance for salvation.

Now he watched his brother twitching and sweating in the leather recliner. His pity turned to compassion. He understood far more about Mike and his suffering than his brother would ever give him credit for understanding. In many ways, he shared the same torment. But he had always managed to leave the past, his own failings and shortcomings of yesterday, where they belonged—as yesterday. And to keep his failings in perspective—lesson learned, history to make himself a better man.

Whereas Mike clung to his past suffering and any personal and real injustice done to him, a living "other-force" getting him through, day to day, as if it were his only reason to live. Perhaps it was.

For a moment he wondered if he could move his arms, even stand, but didn't want to risk his brother's rage and insatiable hunger for revenge, thus unleashing a new round of mental and physical torture. John Wilkins kept the warmth he felt for his brother in his heart, but out of his mind. It gave him confidence, some courage to know that all the unholy and bizarre events of the past several days had been orchestrated by his brother's evil power. He knew, and now Paula knew, that his brother had manipulated their lives. There was hope in that knowledge. But would hope be enough?

What are you thinking, John? Go on, speak to me.

He listened to the angry words, rolling telepathi-

cally through his mind. The brilliant white glow
burning like pure living fire in Mike's eyes, appeared
to fade, but would come blazing back in all its arrogance and rage in the next few moments. Then the
eyes would flicker behind the veil of fire, the blinding
glow fading once more, as Mike spasmed. Then the
terrible brilliance of the fire in the eyes would return
again as his brother seemed to fight with desperation
and fear to regain control of whatever it was that
gave him this evil power.

"I understand, Mike, and I'm sorry. I'm sorry if I
ever let you down, if I ever hurt you. I truly am. I
know you were wronged. Our father was a sick and
angry man, but he loved you in his own way, and
despite a lot of things he was a good, loving, and
hardworking man."

"He was."

Not a question, but maybe a fleeting acceptance of
the truth in Mike, spoken softly, levelly. "Yes. Perhaps instinctively, I don't know, he feared for you,
he feared you might be headed for a long and troubled life. He wanted to spare you that, but he didn't
know how to reach you. I can't say for sure. You
know, as far as the money goes, I put a chunk of it
into a trust fund for you years ago, not long after our
parents died, as a matter of fact. You never knew. I
never even thought about it until now, hoping maybe
someday we could work it out. But you know now."
The burning intensity in the fiery eyes faded. "Yes,
Mike, you know I'm telling you the truth."

"Five hundred a month, that's what I'm allotted—
if I'm reading you right, which, of course, you know
I am."

"Look, all of what I'm saying now, it's what you
always wanted to hear—about our father, the

money, a lot of other things, but never got to know or hear. You want acceptance, some respect, some real companionship, the love of a good woman, something to have, someone to hold and call your own. You want to be a part of life, you want to live, you want to be something. I know you've lived in shame and hurt all these years, tortured by your own addictions and anger. A lot of these things have been beyond your control, but it no longer has to be that way." He saw the glow fading. "It's okay. We're family. We can work this out. I can even forgive and forget what has happened here tonight."

He saw his brother grit his teeth. The eyes had almost returned to normal, and he would have sworn he saw remorse in his younger brother's eyes. But something was happening to Mike, instantly changing him back to the arrogant, judgmental, seething monster who wished only to destroy life, all life. Yes, some force he had clung to up to that point would now not let him go, would not free him. John Wilkins feared the worst for his brother. Whatever controlled him now kept him gripped completely in wretched and furious pride.

"I don't need you, John. All I need is what I am and what I have become."

He saw Mike stand. "That's not true, Mike; it's this thing, whatever it is you've become, that's telling you that. Forsake this evil and you will be free. Please!"

Mike Wilkins laughed. "Funny. That's what the good Father O'Shay told me."

"Mike, bring Timmy back to us. Don't hurt him. I know you like him, you care about him, you see a lot of yourself in Timmy. You're right about Timmy, and you know I know that's true, that I believe in all I've said. But you'd feel even more shame and self-hate if you hurt him. Where will this all end, Mike? I don't even think you know."

Was he reaching Mike? His expression looked so torn, it reached his eyes right away, and they burned with the brilliant white glow again. Whatever John Wilkins believed he could have reached and saved had vanished.

Mike Wilkins stared at his brother. He felt intense disgust and self-loathing over what he had done here in his brother's home. He wanted to strip the amulet off, but it was only a fleeting urge as his other voice snarled and raged from the light.

What? Are you going to stop now? Are you going to deny yourself your just due? He's lying to you; he only wants to be left alone so he can keep his clean, quiet little world. Your suffering means nothing to him other than keeping his family safe. Stay strong!

So be it. He wasn't even sure he was in control of himself any longer. Nor did he think it mattered. Anger burned in his chest, faded as cold despair shrouded his heart.

"In a little while, you will go to Saint Paul's. You will find Timmy there."

He felt the intense warmth in his brother's heart, wanting to despise the compassion he found in his brother, the honesty he discovered in John. Then the power seemed to grow angry that he couldn't hurt his brother right then even as it urged him to destroy them all, burn down the house. Even as he heard the words begin to form in John's mind, he told his brother, "Perhaps . . . John . . . you may be . . . After what I have done these past days, after what I have done here tonight, how can I ever possibly be forgiven?"

Mike Wilkins practically fled from his brother's watching eyes.

He kept Timmy stretched out in the backseat of the Jeep Cherokee, while forcing Peterson to lug the ten-gallon can of gasoline up to the back door of Lansing Development.

Dispersing the power to control all of his pawns had brought the fever to a raging, unbearable, agonizing fire in his brain. He was soaked to the bone in cold sweat, shivering as if he were naked in an icy arctic wind, the nausea like rolling acid in his stomach. It was all Mike Wilkins could do to watch Father O'Shay spread the twenty gallons of gasoline around his church, stay standing, and use the power to make the priest prepare his shrine for the power.

He now knew he was no longer in control of the power. Indeed, he sensed he had reached some critical point of whatever destiny the gold star had already set for him.

His worst fear was about to become reality.

Abandonment. And total betrayal.

Gritting his teeth, he injected fire into Father O'Shay's chest and stomach as the priest frantically prayed in his mind, *Hail Mary, full of grace . . .*

Stop that, Father!

The priest splashed a stream of gasoline down the center aisle, toward the altar. Like an electric current, Mike sensed the old priest's mind alive with fear and cries of pain, heard him calling on God to save him, save all of them from this monstrous evil.

Then he had to fight to block out Timmy's cries of fear and confusion.

He felt the boy's terror and the fiery dam of tears welling up behind his eyes. Mike Wilkins felt utter, wretched self-hate, wanting to stop what he was doing, wanting to spare the boy what he had planned. Then the light would burn through him, fill him with a craving to kill, destroy, firing him to the marrow of his bones with a feeling of pride and pure, terrible invincibility. Still he remained torn, becoming more and more frightened with each passing second that either the power was betraying him or that he was about to betray the power. He couldn't stop now.

He believed he was beyond hope, redemption. Salvation was meant for other men.

Don't kill me, for the love of—

"Shut up!" he snarled at Peterson as they slipped through the darkness of the nearly empty back lot, and tuned out his terrified begging. So the man had been reduced to a sniveling coward. Wilkins laughed out loud. He would shortly silence those frantic pleas.

Beyond the one-story white building that housed the financial geniuses—no, sorcerers, he knew—of Lansing Development, Main Street was bustling with many of its fine citizens. They were specters in the mist, going to and from the restaurants and bars, with late-night shopkeepers still grabbing up the last bit of the day's business.

His plan was in motion, no turning back now. He took in the layout around him, through his mind. The real-estate building was at the edge of town, one block away from the police station. The church was in the opposite direction. He probed the street, found a squad car pulling out of the station lot. It was a deputy—*Reuter*, he saw on the man's badge. The cop was suspicious of something. In fact, he had seen the Jeep Cherokee as he walked from a deli, called in

Keller . . . yes, confirmed the description of Mike Wilkins.

Wilkins had to work fast. He was pulling Andy Cullman to the back door, had Lansing's special-interest lawyer unlock the door. Of course, the dark-haired, handsome, forty-year-old financier in his thousand-dollar suit didn't understand what was happening. Cullman's jaw was gaping, his heart pounding as he twitched and shuddered under the power. Wilkins laughed at the man's terror.

He found the squad car rolling toward the back lot.

Wilkins knifed a terrible pain through Cullman's chest, sent the man backpedaling for his large oak desk. He did a quick probe of Cullman, lancing telepathic laughter through the man's head as Cullman collapsed in his big, brown leather swivel chair. "I see all you people who brought your front company down here. All of you are dirty. You used dirty money . . . laundered organized-crime money down here . . . that's how everyone got wealthy. You built and used Glendale . . . ah, why is it I think of Solomon right now? The unworthy and the undeserving, the mediocre given great authority and privilege. Corruption and crime all over the earth. My friend, for you there is only death." He saw that the man was planning a divorce, was even then working on a new deal to expand Glendale, wondering how much he could reap in the bargain. Seemed the man had dreams of beachfront property in Hawaii, visions of brown-skinned island girls dancing through his mind even then. Cullman was screaming in his mind, begging for release, the usual terror and confusion.

Wilkins put Peterson to work. File cabinets were thrown open, papers strewn all around the office. Finally, Peterson emptied out the dozen cabinets, a sea of papers and folders stretching around the man.

Laughing, Wilkins pulled out the ivory Zippo. Click-clack. He laughed harder and more angrily, working the Zippo's lid in a blurring fury.

There was a marble statue of a frontiersman on Cullman's desk, rifle with bayonet, pointed up. Wilkins looked at the statue, chuckled.

"That's how you people who work for Old Man Lansing see yourselves, huh? The new frontier, new frontiersmen. Too bad the old man and the rest of them aren't here. But you'll do. Tell you what, why don't you eat that statue, Andy?" The man shuddered, his mouth forced wide open. Slowly, Cullman reached out, drew the statue toward him with a trembling hand.

Wilkins made the man drive the statue deep into his mouth.

"Having problems swallowing, Andy? Here, here. Allow me." In a sudden, savage explosion, he grabbed Cullman by the back of the head, then drove the man's face toward the desktop, the statue now filling his mouth. Bone and cartilage and flesh were ripped as the bayonet speared out the base of Cullman's skull. The man convulsed in death spasms, his lifeless eyes bulging up at Wilkins.

Wilkins wadded up some papers on the desk, flicked the Zippo. As Peterson begged for his life to be spared, the pungent stench of gasoline in Wilkins's nose, burning his senses, he put the flame to the papers, then tossed the flaming wad in the gas-soaked pile of paperwork and folders around Peterson's feet. A whoosh, and a wall of fire screamed to life, consuming Peterson instantly.

Wilkins gave the man his voice as he was turned

into a human torch. Swiftly, as fire raced through the office, Wilkins moved outside, the banshee wailing of Peterson being burned alive lashing his back.

He already knew the cop, Keller, and his six deputies were just then emerging from their vehicles. The mist was now a blazing light in his own eyes, everything glowing in his sight.

Wilkins released his brother and his family from their paralysis but jerked them along, out of their house, into the Saturn.

When he saw the big cop and his deputies converging on Peterson's vehicle, heard Keller, confused and angry as he recognized Timmy, Wilkins called out, "Gentlemen? How may I help you?"

They looked from the fire and smoke, blazing and boiling out the open back door, to the brilliant, glowing eyes of Mike Wilkins.

Chapter Twenty-seven

The big cop was drawing his .357 Magnum when
Mike Wilkins froze them.

Flames were now leaping against the windows of
Lansing Development, a tongue of fire shooting out
the doorway to Wilkins's side. An umbrella of flickering light washed over the back lot; the fear and
confusion and anger was a living and glowing force
in the eyes of the cops.

And Peterson shrieked on.

Wilkins laughed, was backing them up, jerking
them toward a narrow alleyway off Main Street,
when the human fireball crashed through the window.

"What the . . ."

"What's wrong with his eyes?"

"What is he?"

Listened to their terror, probed their minds as they
were torn between confronting him and wanting to
race to Peterson, wondering why they couldn't move,
couldn't draw their weapons.

"Because I won't allow you to, gentlemen!" he told
them, laughing.

But the fire was now eating up his brain, and it
took every bit of furious and desperate will to hold

them in place. And for a moment he was confused, wondered why everything in his vision was now brilliant light, with pockets of darkness, here and there. In his eyes, the cops looked like shining glass figures. He believed what he actually saw were their souls. Some light appeared stronger than others, but the power, now roaring inside him with an uncontrollable rage, told him that only made sense.

Some good, some not so good. But none of them are worthy of anything except to die in your presence.

Keller had the strongest light, he found. The big cop had nearly lined up his weapon on him, but Wilkins knifed a pain through his chest and stomach. He roared at Keller, "Don't fight me, cop."

They watched in shock and horror as Peterson hit the pavement, flopping and screaming, slapping at his face and head.

The laughter that ripped from Wilkins's mouth seemed to stretch throughout all of Glendale, a peal of thunder in his own ears, it sounded.

Finally Peterson lay utterly still, a smoking, blackened mummy.

Stepping past the burning corpse, Wilkins opened the door of the Jeep Cherokee. He took Timmy by the hand. Beyond the boy's fear, he felt the strong warmth, the tender innocence of youth, the boy's basic humanity holding strong. For a moment, Wilkins was stunned at how blinding and pure the light was that was laid out on the backseat.

"Uncle Mike, is that you? What's going on?"

"It's okay, Timmy. Come on, son, it's time to go."

"Why can't I move? What's going on?"

Gently pulling Timmy out of the vehicle, he told him, "Don't look, Timmy. You're too good to see what I am about to do. I can't allow you to speak for a few minutes. Fear not, son."

He made the boy look away as he backed the cops out into the middle of the street.

Now countless figures of light were scurrying everywhere, a siren piercing the night from the distance. Wilkins shuddered, growled as a din of voices and thoughts swirled in a penetrating, jagged, and distorted maze that seemed to swell his brain with excruciating agony.

Do it!

Only one way to relieve the pain, he believed.

"On your knees, cop!"

"What the hell are you?" Keller roared.

Wilkins forced Keller to his knees. Suddenly, out of nowhere, he felt the power explode from inside, reaching out to everything around him. Then a chorus of deafening shrieking rang out through the town. All around him, Wilkins saw the light figures collapse, writhing.

Fuck them all! he thought, and put it into Keller's mind. *They're less than dogshit!*

Then he focused on the cops. The deputies toted 9mm Glocks, seventeen rounds, he knew. To a deputy, he bored the vision in their minds of what they were going to do.

Uncle Mike, are you doing this? Why are you hurting people? Why?

Blocking out Timmy's thoughts, Wilkins showed the deputies their final moment. They cried out in fear and raving confusion. Laughing, his voice striking him, flung back in his face—it seemed as not even his own voice any longer—he showed the deputies all the birthday parties, the graduations of their children, the Christmas mornings and other joyous family moments they were never going to know.

You'll never see your families again. If it makes you feel better, you will be buried with honors. If it makes you feel even better, I've never even known a second of what you've had. Hey, call me envious. But my envy is my righteous wrath and you have brought this horror upon yourselves.

They were nameless, lighted shapes. He didn't even care who or what any of these people were, if he had known them, where they had come from.

All that mattered was what he could take and destroy, what he could deny them in a future that would never happen.

"Nooooo!" two of the deputies screamed.

Keller was on his knees, cursing, fighting to point his weapon at Wilkins.

Two of the deputies shot each other in the head. From the light that cloaked them, Wilkins saw the darkness of their blood spurt in arcing fingers.

"Show these people who is in charge, gentlemen!" Wilkins bellowed into the piercing symphony of shouting, crying, and shrieking voices.

The four deputies began shooting at the citizens.

Wilkins laughed, on and on, as countless light figures darted in a pell-mell scramble, several of them skidding, toppling to their faces under the dark showering of their own blood.

A crash of glass.

The sirens.

He focused on the flashing lights, toward the north end of the street. Light figures, sitting up high, but nothing that was solid in shape seemed to fill his sight. He made the drivers of the ambulance and the fire engine throw the steering wheels to the side. A horrendous rending of metal tore the night apart as the light figures riding high bounced over bodies, barreled through parked vehicles. Then the relentless crack of gunshots echoed all around Wilkins, the screaming and chaos reaching a feverish crescendo.

Wilkins looked at the remaining deputies, the light figure of Keller prostrate before him. He jerked the deputies in front of Keller, heard the jagged din of their terrified confusion but found he could no longer focus on any one thought.

To a deputy it sounded to Wilkins as if they all shouted, "Nooooo!"

And he forced them to shoot each other in the face and head, squeezing the triggers over and over, screaming in shock, terror, and pain even as they took bullets through the brain, died on their feet. Then the light shrouding them wavered as they crumpled; then the light faded.

Vanished.

And Wilkins could see their dead bodies clearly, heaped around Keller.

"I'm going to spare you, Keller. Only because I want you to remember this night the rest of your life."

"You bastard . . . you're . . . not even human."

"More than human. Take the gun and shoot yourself in the leg."

It took a dredging up of iron will, but Wilkins made the cop place the barrel of the revolver against his thigh. Keller squeezed the trigger. The peal of the Magnum and the man's sharp cry of pain and outrage lanced Wilkins's ears, but the power laughed inside, his voice churning somewhere in the light, drawing in, it seemed, the crackling of the inferno that consumed Lansing Development.

Wilkins took Timmy by the hand.

Why, Uncle Mike, why are you doing this?

As he led the boy toward the church, Mike Wilkins found that he wanted to be overwhelmed with grief and self-hate, but something inside him, far beyond his power to control or stop it, wouldn't let him.

Indeed, it wanted to deny him any last clinging shred of humanity and sorrow.

The spire of the church loomed in his sight as the world turned even darker, but looked once again to have shape and substance. He heard the priest praying.

Our Father, who art in Heaven . . .

Wilkins let the priest pray on. It wouldn't do Father O'Shay any good. God could not save any of them.

But for some reason, Wilkins felt drawn to enter that church, as if he belonged there, knew it was there he would find his final destruction or everlasting peace.

Again, he heard Timmy cry in his mind. *Why?*

Wilkins swallowed hard, let the boy do what he wanted to do so desperately.

He let the boy cry, glimpsed the stream of tears rolling down Timmy's face, felt his own heart wrenching with a burning anguish and grief.

He was closing on the front doors of Saint Paul's. His heart felt shredded with torment as the cries of suffering lashed his backside.

After all I have done, how can I ever possibly be forgiven? How? My own . . . pride . . . wrong . . . my own self . . . hatred . . . How can I ever possibly be forgiven?

Who cares about your forgiveness? the light roared.

It was all beyond hope, salvation, or redemption. Or so the raging light inside told him.

He squeezed Timmy's hand, told the boy, "Fear not. Fear not, Timmy. Trust in me. I am your only hope and your only salvation."

John Wilkins felt he was regaining some control of his body as he bounded up the steps to the front doors of the church. His wife, daughter, and oldest son were right behind him, tugged along in that awful mind control his brother gripped them in, like human puppets. He didn't want them there as he confronted Mike, but he knew he had no choice.

His brother controlled the night.

Something terrible had happened in Glendale, but John Wilkins's only concern and fear was for Timmy. If his brother hurt his youngest . . .

What had happened in town? he couldn't help but wonder for a brief moment. The klaxon wail of sirens and alarms was merciless, ceaseless, seemed to shred the night.

Then he caught the whiff of gasoline as he entered the church. And he knew what his brother was prepared to do.

"Deliver us from evil. . . ."

"Stop that, Father. I allow you your voice only because I want to hear your terror and you blaspheme me!"

He felt the force, a living wall that seemed to slam him in the chest.

John Wilkins saw his youngest son lying in the middle aisle, felt the sharp bite of gasoline in his nose, and heard his mind scream, *Nooooo!*

They were coming. He saw them in his mind but couldn't get a clear mental image. Dozens of flashing lights. State police, he believed.

Do it, do it! Mike Wilkins heard his other voice raging in his mind, the fever burning up his brain, an undying fire. Then he felt the gold star, hot, scalding on his chest. What was happening?

Abandonment.

Betrayal, he knew, and when he needed the power most.

His heart swelled with a storm of torn emotions. Anger. Hatred. Self-hate. Outrage.

Despair.

There was Timmy, laid out in the stream of gas that stretched away from the altar, down the aisle. The boy must be spared.

"Hallowed be thy name . . ."

Mike Wilkins roared in pain and rage. Why wouldn't the priest stop praying like that? Why couldn't he kill his brother and his family? Or could he?

And there was John, held frozen at the end of the aisle.

"Thy kingdom come, Thy will be done . . ."

Flicked the lid on the Zippo.

"On earth as it is in Heaven . . ."

He made the priest scream in agony as he filled his chest with a knifing pain, glimpsed the blinding light figure topple in the front pew.

He fired the Zippo.

He lost control of the boy, heard Timmy cry out, "Uncle Mike, why are you doing this?"

They were charging up the steps now, guns drawn. It was all beyond him; the power he had so cherished had used him, betrayed him. And now he was on his own.

"Nooooo!" his brother shouted.

"Almighty God in Heaven, deliver us from this evil. . . ."

He heard the priest grunting in pain as he repeated the same thing, over and over, until it seemed to pierce his brain.

The words were almost on his lips as Mike Wilkins saw the lighted figures barrel into the church.

"Don't move!"

He knew what he must do, where it would end, where it would have to stop. He released his brother, heard the words tumble from his mouth as the first shot thundered. "Dear Jesus, forgive me. . . ."

He felt the impact of the bullet tear into his chest, but something else, something far more painful, was exploding from inside the light. He cried out, his voice a distant and fleeting sound in his ears as he felt the Zippo fall from his hands.

As he toppled, an animal in agony, he bellowed, "John, you were right!"

John Wilkins raced for Timmy as the line of fire whooshed to life.

Behind him gunshots were exploding, his wife and daughter crying in fear.

From somewhere in the church the tortured voice of Father O'Shay kept imploring, "Almighty God, deliver us from this evil! Spare us Your fury and Your wrath! Forgive this man his evil!"

The fire blazed toward Timmy, a living tongue that streaked for his youngest son's paralyzed form.

Then, beyond the wall of leaping fire, John Wilkins saw his brother burst into flames. Screams of agony shrilled through the church.

"You were right!"

Timmy! Two more feet, his legs pumping, his heart

pounding so hard it felt as if it might explode out of his chest.

Three feet, the fire racing to beat him to his son.

"Nooooooo!"

The flames closed, nearly on top of Timmy.

Almost there!

Almost!

Dear God, he heard his mind scream, give me strength, give me the speed.

"Almighty God, deliver us from evil!"

And he snatched up Timmy, dove into the pew, his boy locked and cradled in his arms. He slammed to the hard wood of the pew, felt the searing heat of the fire as it whooshed past him.

He looked at Timmy, the tears bursting from his own eyes. His son was unharmed.

"It's okay, son, it's okay!"

John Wilkins held his son to his chest, felt Timmy shaking uncontrollably. He looked up, realizing then that his brother was burning alive.

Up there, around the altar, the human torch was shrieking, flailing. Then, for some reason, the piercing wail ended but his brother stood, straight and tall, his arms outstretched as he was burned alive.

"You have abandoned me! Why?"

Voices of fear, sounds of gasping and retching sounded from behind John Wilkins. He found his wife racing up the far aisle, into the pew. He handed Timmy to Paula, then leaped over the pew, surging out into the aisle, opposite the wall of fire.

He watched as the human torch slumped to his knees. What was happening to Mike? What was he doing? Why was he allowing himself just to burn alive?

Stunned, a sickly sweet stench of roasted flesh

piercing his senses and swelling his head and stomach with nausea, John Wilkins closed on the burning thing—his brother.

And watched as Mike slowly toppled onto his back.

He ignored the state police as he stood over the flaming mass of sizzling and smoking flesh. He saw that his brother's eyes had been burned to two hideous red orbs.

"John . . . you're there. . . ."

The words croaked from the blackened hole.

"God forgive me . . . you were right. . . . Timmy . . . is he . . . alive?"

John Wilkins almost reached down, put his hand on the charred face, the eyes burned out, the face nothing but red and green and white slime, but his brother was still shrouded in fire. He nearly vomited as he told his younger brother, "Timmy's . . . alive. You spared his life. I know you did."

"Forgive me . . . you were right . . . my own . . . I hated myself . . . I was wrong. . . . I was so wrong. . . . I can't explain. . . . I can't explain. . . ."

John Wilkins heard the frantic voices all around him, felt hands on his shoulders, a voice urging him to get out of the church.

Someone was throwing a jacket over his brother, slapping the flames until they died. He looked at his brother's chest, bent, and shrugged off the hand on his shoulder.

It was gone.

There was no sign of the amulet.

"We need to get out of here, sir!"

The crackling of flames filled his ears.

"He's dead, sir! Please, outside!"

*   *   *

They were all safe, huddled in the lot. They were crying, holding each other in a tight, clinging embrace.

John Wilkins turned, saw the firemen charging into the church, hoses already unleashing streams of water.

He felt lifeless. His heart throbbed with a merciless ache he thought would never stop.

His wife and children called his name. He fell into their arms, felt the fire of tears well up in his eyes. Paula held him tight, pulled back and stared into his eyes, a tear breaking and rolling down her cheek. She was back, he knew.

Tonight, he would weep.

Tomorrow, he would pray.

WHEN SHADOWS FALL

BRIAN SCOTT SMITH

Martin doesn't believe his aunt's death is an accident, and he and a couple of buddies are determined to find the truth. But when he starts sneaking around the house of his aunt's new "friends," he never expects to witness a blood-drenched satanic ritual. But he does see it, and more important, the witches see him!

Suddenly Martin is in a horrifying race for his life. He has to stop the witches before they stop him for good. And he has to do it before Halloween night, the night of the final sacrifice, the night when the demons of hell will be unleashed on the Earth, the night when shadows fall.

___4313-0 $4.99 US/$5.99 CAN

SHADOWS

Kimberly Rangel

WHERE TERROR RULES...

In the distant past, in a far-off land, the spell is cast, damning the family to an eternity of blood hunger. Over countless centuries, in the dark of night, they are doomed to assume the shape of savage beasts, deadly black panthers driven by a maddening fever to quench their unspeakable thirst. Then Selene DeMarco finds herself the last female of her line, and she has to mate with a descendent of the man who has plunged her family into the endless agony.

_4054-9 $4.99 US/$5.99 CAN

DRAWN TO THE GRAVE — MARY ANN MITCHELL

"A tight, taut dark fantasy with surprising plot twists and a lot of spooky atmosphere."
—Ed Gorman

Beverly thinks that she has found something special with Carl, until she realizes that he has stolen from her. But he doesn't just steal her money and her property—he steals her very life. Suddenly she is helpless and alone, able only to watch in growing despair as her flesh begins to decay and each day transforms her more and more into a corpse—a corpse without the release of death.

But Beverly is not truly alone, for Carl is always nearby, watching her and waiting. He knows that soon he will need another unknowing victim, another beautiful woman he can seduce...and destroy. And when lovely young Megan walks into his web, he knows he has found his next lover. For what can possibly go wrong with his plan, a plan he has practiced to perfection so many times before?

___4290-8 $4.99 US/$5.99 CAN

ROUGH BEAST
GARY GOSHGARIAN

"[Treads] territory staked out by John Saul and Dean Koontz...a solid and suspenseful cautionary tale."

—Publishers Weekly

A genocidal experiment conducted by the government goes horribly wrong, with tragic and terrifying results for the Hazzards, a normal, unsuspecting family in a small Massachusetts town. Every day, their son gradually becomes more of a feral, uncontrollable, and very dangerous...thing. The government is determined to do whatever is necessary to eliminate the evidence of their dark secret and protect the town...but it is already too late. The beast is loose!

_4152-9 $4.99 US/$5.99 CAN

Max Allan Collins

"Chilling!"—Lawrence Block, author of *Eight Million Ways to Die*

Meet Mommy. She's pretty, she's perfect. She's June Cleaver with a cleaver. And you don't want to deny her—or her daughter—anything. Because she only wants what's best for her little girl...and she's not about to let anyone get in her way. And if that means killing a few people, well isn't that what mommies are for?

"Mr Collins has an outwardly artless style that conceals a great deal of art."
—*The New York Times Book Review*

___4322-X $4.99 US/$5.99 CAN

Dorchester Publishing Co., Inc.
P.O. Box 6640
Wayne, PA 19087-8640

Please add $1.75 for shipping and handling for the first book and $.50 for each book thereafter. NY, NYC, and PA residents, please add appropriate sales tax. No cash, stamps, or C.O.D.s. All orders shipped within 6 weeks via postal service book rate. Canadian orders require $2.00 extra postage and must be paid in U.S. dollars through a U.S. banking facility.

Name_____
Address_____
City_____State_____Zip_____
I have enclosed $_____ in payment for the checked book(s).
Payment <u>must</u> accompany all orders. ❏ Please send a free catalog.

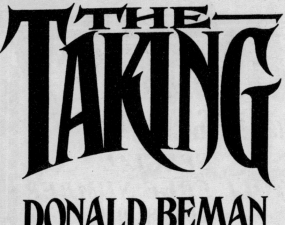

DONALD BEMAN

What could Sean McDonald possibly have done to deserve what is happening to him? He was a happy man with a beautiful family, a fine job, good friends and dreams of becoming a writer. Now bit by bit, his life is crumbling. Everything and everyone he values is disappearing. Or is it being taken from him? Someone or something is determined to break Sean, to crush his mind and spirit. A malicious, evil force is driving him to the very brink of insanity. But why him?

_4202-9 $4.99 US/$5.99 CAN

ATTENTION ROMANCE CUSTOMERS!

SPECIAL TOLL-FREE NUMBER
1-800-481-9191

Call Monday through Friday
12 noon to 10 p.m.
Eastern Time
Get a free catalogue,
join the Romance Book Club,
and order books using your
Visa, MasterCard,
or Discover®

Leisure
Books